NORTH TYNESIDE LIBRARIES

LOVE2READ

With our new Love2Read library card
you can borrow 20 books at a time and make unlimited free
reservations all for a £5 annual fee.

Ask for further details on your next visit.

Please return to any North Tyneside Library by the
last date stamped above or renew online at

www.northtyneside.gov.uk/libraries

follow our story @
www.facebook.com/northtynesidelibraries
http://twitter.com/NorthTyneLibs

ARB
UTH
NOT

This edition published by Arbuthnot Books 2017
ISBN 978-0-9927467-8-0

Cover illustration and design by Marina Esmeraldo.

Out Of Shot

A. C. Koning

ARBUTHNOT BOOKS

In memory of my grandmother, Annie Sheila Thompson (1888—1972)

O what is that sound which so thrills the ear
Down in the valley drumming, drumming?
Only the scarlet soldiers, dear,
The soldiers coming.

W.H. Auden, *O what is that sound?*

CONTENTS

MISE-EN-SCÈNE

1

THE TRAM WHICH HAD brought them from Zoo Station stopped at Potsdamerplatz; as they got off, there came a roar, which seemed to split the night. To Frederick Rowlands, who had just set foot in the city, it seemed to come from all sides at once. It made him think of a football match he'd attended before the War: Arsenal versus Tottenham Hotspur. Three minutes before the end, Arsenal had scored the winning goal, and the sound its supporters made was like the one he'd just heard. A hoarse yell of triumph. 'You couldn't have picked a worse time to arrive,' muttered his companion. 'They're out in force tonight. Well, nothing for it...' Rowlands felt his arm firmly grasped. 'Stick close to me. If anyone speaks to you, just shake your head. You're deaf and dumb, all right? They don't like foreigners.'

'All right. But...'

'I said, can it!' hissed the other. 'Trust me. I know what I'm talking about.' With which Rowlands had to be content. What, after all, was he going to do? Alone in the middle of a strange city, with a fair—but sadly rusty—knowledge of the language, and none of the familiar clues of smell, sound and visual memory to assist him, he was more at sea than he'd been in fifteen years. Because it had been a little over fifteen years ago that a burst of shrapnel had taken away all but a fraction of his sight. Since that day in 1917, he'd had to make his way through the world relying on his wits, and his other senses. It wasn't true that blind men had better hearing—they made better use of it, that's all...

Just now, it was being tested to the limit, with sounds coming from all directions: shouts, screams, whistles, and over it all, the relentless beating of drums, like the pulsing of a monstrous heartbeat. 'Quick!' said the youth, who had introduced himself a bare half-hour before as Joachim Metzner. 'This way. If we're lucky, we might just make it before they get here...'

Still holding Rowlands by the arm, he began to push his way through the crowd which filled the square, and which seemed to be moving very slowly in the direction in which they themselves were going. It was bitterly cold; a few flakes of snow drifted on the icy wind, which seemed to penetrate to Rowlands's very bones. His progress was made slower still, because he was encumbered with a suitcase; he silently blessed Edith for having made him wear his heaviest coat. 'And don't forget your hat,' she'd added, knowing his preference for going bare-headed. 'It's Germany, in winter. You can be sure it'll be colder than it is here...' Well, she was certainly right about *that*, thought Rowlands, as, guided by his impatient young friend, he shouldered his way through the press of bodies. They reached the edge of the square at last. 'We'll go this way,' said Metzner. 'If we can get across Wilhelmstrasse, we can pick up a tram to the Alex. That is, *if* we can get across...'

From up ahead, the sound of drumming grew louder.

'Who are all these people?' Rowlands ventured to ask, since the crowd had thinned out a little. 'SA,' was the curt reply. 'Celebrating their great victory.' It was said with such withering sarcasm that Rowlands refrained from asking for further explication, in case the young German's temper got the better of him. In any case he—Rowlands—now knew all he needed to know. Hadn't the London papers been full of speculation as to what the outcome of these elections could mean for Germany, and for the rest of Europe? They emerged into what Rowlands guessed, from the sheer volume of noise arising from it, must be a major thoroughfare. Here, the crowd was even thicker; it seemed to have come to a halt. '*Scheisse*!' muttered the lad. 'We're too late...'

Moments later, there came the sound of marching feet—a sound forever associated, in Rowlands's mind with his army days—and the mass of people surged forward. Hemmed in, as he was, by solid bodies, he had little alternative but to do the same. From somewhere near at hand, a woman cried out, in a

12

shrill, excited voice—her cry taken up and repeated by others, as the parade went past. Drums. Marching feet. Shouted orders. And, over it all, a sulphurous smell, emanating from the burning torches carried by those at the front of the parade. These cast their smoke into the bitter air, stinging the eyes and filling the nostrils with the stink of the Inferno. Other smells, of body odour, and the meaty breath of a man standing next to Rowlands, mingled with this smoky vapour, to claustrophobic effect. He was uncomfortably aware, as he stood there, of the proximity of others, and of the impossibility of escaping from that proximity.

At the head of the procession, someone began to sing, in a clear tenor voice. Others took up the refrain, which sounded like a marching tune, although not one with which Rowlands was familiar. Soon it was being roared out by a hundred voices: more.

Die Fahne hoch! Die Reihen fest geschlossen!
SA marschiert mit ruhig festem Schritt.

It seemed an age until the parade had gone past, but it was probably no more than ten minutes, Rowlands guessed. The new regime had lost no time, it seemed, in proclaiming its victory. 'They'll go on like this all night,' muttered Metzner in his ear. 'Let's get out of here while we can...' Once again, Rowlands found himself being half-dragged through a gap in the crowd, his progress arrested by occasional collisions with the over-coated forms of various members of the local populace, and by one not wearing a coat, but shirtsleeves and a Sam Browne belt. The man growled something at him, to which—mindful of Metzner's warning—he did not respond. '*Taub und dumm,*' shouted his companion, by way of explanation, to which the S.A. man responded with a coarse laugh, and a word whose vulgarity was evident from the guffaws of those around.

Fortunately, this exercise of wit seemed to satisfy him—or perhaps he was impatient to join his comrades at the tail-end of the procession—for, after giving vent to another oath, he strode off. '*Schwein!*' said Metzner, under his breath. 'Come, we must go this way. Give me that...' It was Rowlands's suitcase he meant; for a moment, the two of them engaged in a friendly tussle, which the younger man won. 'I do not want you to think that all Germans lack manners,' he said, in English

'Of course not,' smiled Rowlands. 'Your English is very good,' he added. 'I studied English two years in school,' was the reply. 'Ah, that explains it!' said Rowlands politely; then, as it seemed that the embargo on conversation was at an end: 'Tell me—is there any news?' Before the other could reply, there came the sound of running feet, and a gang of youths—four or five of them, at a guess—came tearing around the corner of the next street. A stifled exclamation came from Rowlands's companion as, dropping the suitcase with a thump, he half-pulled, half-shoved the older man towards the shelter of a shop doorway.

But it was too late: the gang was upon them. One of them yelled a filthy name, eliciting hoots of derisive laughter from the rest. Metzner's reply was evidently no less abusive, for the other—the gang leader, Rowlands guessed—flew at him, raining blows. As if waiting for just this signal, the others moved in. Kicks and punches were traded, with Metzner initially getting the worst of it. With only the sound of the conflict to guide him, Rowlands's own contribution to the fracas was necessarily limited. He managed to bang two heads together, and dragged one of the assailants off his intended victim by the scruff of the neck. They were little more than children, he realised—an impression confirmed by Metzner afterwards. 'H.J.,' he said. 'Just kids, you know. But there were more of them. If they had been S.A., we would be in a much worse state...'

Perhaps realising that, despite their superior numbers, they had underestimated the resilience of the foe, the juvenile thugs soon tired of their sport, and ran off, cat-calling. 'Are you all right?' said Rowlands, dusting himself down. Beyond a bruised shin, where a kick had caught him, he'd sustained no injury; he had a feeling that the same could not be said of Joachim Metzner. 'I'm fine,' said the latter. 'Do you have a handkerchief, perhaps? My nose bleeds a little...' Rowlands duly supplied the article. 'Thanks.' The young man attended briefly to his injuries. 'No, if I am sorry for what happened just now, it is because it will have given you such a poor impression of our city.' With a little grunt of effort, betraying bruised ribs, he bent to pick something up from the ground. 'Here,' he said. 'Your hat, I think.'

'Thanks.' Rowlands put it back on. 'It is I who must thank you,' said the other, with a shaky laugh. 'Don't mention it,' said Rowlands.

They reached the tram-stop without further incident, and joined a straggling queue of people heading for the eastern part of the city: those who'd finished work, and were in no hurry to join the public festivities, it seemed. By contrast with the noisily ebullient crowd they'd encountered in Wilhelmstrasse, these were a silent crew. Only a pair of drunks, weaving past on their way to or from the celebrations, disrupted an otherwise sombre mood. At last, with a wild clattering of the bell, the tram appeared. The queue surged forward; Rowlands, caught up in its momentum, felt himself shoved from all sides. 'This way!' hissed Metzner, propelling him unceremoniously up the steps of the first car. A fierce altercation then arose with the driver of the tram, which was only resolved after much shouting on both sides.

'He refused at first to take me because he said I had been fighting,' said Metzner, as they barged their way towards the back of the tram, from whose passengers a warm communal smell of beer, tobacco, and sweat arose. 'There is blood on my face, you understand. I said to him that I have fallen in the street, celebrating his party's great victory—he wears a NSDAP badge, you know. He could not argue with that.'

Rowlands nodded, guessing that this was neither the time not the place to pursue the discussion. As the tram lurched and swayed along what seemed—from the speed with which they were travelling, and the frequency of the stops—to be another of the city's great boulevards, he let his thoughts drift, reviewing the events of the past forty-eight hours, since the telephone call had come. It had been late on Saturday night—he had just been locking up, before going up to bed. 'Hello?' He was already apprehensive: they never got calls this late. 'Fred? Is that you? Oh, thank God...' He'd known at once from Dorothy's

15

tone of voice that something was wrong. Not even on the occasion, some years before, when she had been in peril of her life, had she sounded so frightened. 'What's the matter?'

'It's Billy. He's...' Rowlands held his breath. 'He's disappeared.' He let himself breathe again. 'How long is it since you missed him?'

'They've been gone since yesterday afternoon. I was expecting him back from school, and...' Here she broke down. 'Oh, Fred, what am I going to do?'

But he'd picked up something in what she'd just said. 'You say "they've" been gone since yesterday? Is there someone else with him?'

'Yes, he's with Walter, his cousin. Oh, Fred...'

'Try and keep calm, old thing. It *has* only been a day. They're probably camping out somewhere. You know what boys are...'

'In January?' His sister gave a tremulous laugh. 'Billy's not that daft. And Fred... there's something else...'

'Three minutes, caller.'

'Yes, we haven't quite finished.' It was a remarkably good line, he thought, with the part of his mind that wasn't occupied with what Dorothy was saying. '... it seems there's a man about.' She gave a sob. 'Oh, Fred, it's too horrible! He catches little boys and... and kills them. There've been at least twenty so far.'

'Now, don't upset yourself,' he said. 'I'm sure Billy'll turn up safe and sound. His cousin, too. How old is the cousin, by the way?'

'Twelve. A year older than Billy.'

'Is he a sensible sort of lad?'

'I don't know. I suppose so.'

'Well, then. I'm sure he'll look after Billy. He'll know his way home at least.'

'Yes, that's what Jack says. He thinks the same as you—that they're just having an adventure. But Fred...' Here she lowered her voice, as if she were afraid of being overheard. 'You don't know what it's like here. It isn't the same as it is at home...'

Well, he was certainly finding that out for himself, thought Rowlands, as the tram lurched to a halt with a screeching of brakes, and the driver bellowed, 'Alexanderplatz!' Evidently

16

this was the last stop on the route, for the passengers now began shuffling towards the doors, carrying Rowlands and his
young guide along with them. The square—he assumed it must
be a square of some kind—was loud with traffic: the rumble
of motor-buses and the rattle of horse-drawn carts over the
cobblestones competing with the sound of trams arriving and
departing. 'Piccadilly Circus,' thought Rowlands, as Metzner,
muttering something about their being just in time to catch the
Number One, grabbed him by the arm once more. 'You needn't
hold me quite so tightly,' Rowlands protested, as the younger
man dived off in the direction of the tram-stop. 'It'll be enough
if you touch my sleeve when you want me to follow...'

The other apologised. 'I was told I must not lose you,' he said
in an undertone. 'And you see how it is... At least, you do *not*
see, but...'

'I'm familiar with the expression,' said Rowlands drily. 'And I
do see. But even if I did get lost, I have the address, you know...'

Metzner made no response to this, unless it was a shrug, for
the tram was now in front of them, and it was a matter of once
more jostling for a place on the already crowded vehicle. This
time, for a wonder, they managed to get a seat—vacated, at that
moment, by a burly man in rough tweeds and his no-less sub-
stantial wife. Subsiding with a grateful sigh onto the wooden
bench, Rowlands realised how tired he was. Hungry, too—he
had eaten nothing since the last of the ham sandwiches Edith
had made, to see him through the journey.

At the thought of his wife, he felt a warm glow of affection.
Dear Edie! What a brick she had been about the whole affair. It
wasn't every woman who'd have put up with this—admittedly harebrained—plan, but—'Of course you must go,' she'd said.
'Will Jack be going with you?'—his sister's husband having already expressed his intention of so doing. 'I've told him to stay
put for the time being,' he replied. 'There isn't a lot of point in
our both going. Not unless...' He left the sentence unfinished.
Unless the news turned out to be worse than they expected,
was what he meant. 'At any rate,' he went on, averting his mind
from this grim prospect, 'I'm not sure what earthly use it'll be
having *one* blind man joining the search—let alone two.'

17

'Oh, you're good at that sort of thing,' was Edith's reply. He wasn't so sure of that, but he'd do what he could—pull what strings he could, too, if it increased the chances of finding the boy. The day before he'd set out on his quest—which was only yesterday, he reminded himself—he'd telephoned Alasdair Douglas at home, apologising for troubling him on a Sunday, but explaining the circumstances. The two men had been friends for years, having met under conditions which might have precluded that friendship. Now the Chief Inspector waited until Rowlands had had his say, before replying gruffly, 'Well, I don't see as there's much I can do, given that it's a foreign country—but as it happens, I *do* know a man there who might be able to help...' This, it transpired, was a certain Inspector Gentz, whose offices were to be found in that very square through which they had just passed: Alexanderplatz. 'Not a bad sort—for a German,' was Douglas's laconic assessment. 'He and I worked together on the Streicher smuggling case, ye ken. Rounded up the gang quite nicely, between us.'

So it was armed with a letter—thoughtfully left for him at Waterloo Station, and addressed to this useful official—that Rowlands now arrived in this strange city. A city made all the stranger, he reflected, as the tram rattled its way along the unfamiliar streets, by the fact that most of its inhabitants seemed, at least temporarily, to have taken leave of their senses. He felt a touch on his arm. 'We get out here,' said Metzner. Once they had turned off the main street—Prenzlauerbergstrasse—the snow, which had been reduced to icy slush in the main streets, lay thickly on the pavements, muffling their footsteps, until it seemed to Rowlands, light-headed with fatigue, as if they might be alone in a vast wilderness, instead of in the heart of a great city. For a few minutes, they tramped along in silence, then the youth said: 'You asked me if there had been any news?'

'Yes.'

'There has been no news.'

'I see.' It was what Rowlands had supposed. He tried for a lighter tone. 'We have a saying: "No news is good news."'

'You mean that, as far as we know, they are not dead.'

'I suppose that *is* what I mean,' said Rowlands, a little taken

18

aback at this bald statement of fact. It appeared that Metzner realised that he had gone too far, for he said, after a pause, 'I apologise. I am behaving very badly. But you see, I am enraged... Is that how you say it?'

'Perhaps you mean "upset"?' suggested Rowlands gently. 'I am angry at what is happening in my country,' replied the young man. 'I think "enraged" is the correct word, is it not? Perhaps I am a little bit upset, too, that my stupid little brother has run away. But what I feel most of all is angry.' They had reached the corner of the street; another led off from it. 'We go down here,' said Metzner. 'It is not far.' Here, the snow was still thicker underfoot, the silence more absolute. When the young man spoke again, it was in a subdued tone. 'Was it because of the War? That you are blind, I mean?'

'Yes,' said Rowlands 'It was because of the War.'

'Then you must hate us...'

'No.' Rowlands was unable to suppress a smile at the other's bluntness. Was there nothing he wouldn't say, this irascible youth? 'I don't see the use of that.'

'You are not like most of my countrymen,' said the youth. '*They* see the use of hating—very much! In here,' he added, directing the other, by a touch on the shoulder, through an archway and then through a heavy street-door. A flight of stairs lay before them. '*Verdammt!*' muttered Metzner. 'The light's gone again. I don't suppose it makes much difference to you, does it? Come on. We're on the third floor.' They had just reached the second floor landing when, on the floor above, a door opened and someone came out. A familiar voice called, 'Is that you, Fred?' and Dorothy came running down the stairs to meet them. 'I wondered what had happened... You've been so long,' she said, as they carried on up the stairs together. 'We got a bit held up,' said Rowlands. They reached the third floor landing, where someone else was waiting. 'Here they are, *Gott sei Dank*,' said a woman's voice; then: 'But what has happened to your face?'

'It's nothing, *Mutti*,' said the young man, now speaking German; Frau Metzner was evidently not an English speaker, thought Rowlands, determining that any further exchanges

19

should be intelligible to her. 'A scuffle with some H.J. kids, that's all. Herr Rowlands saw them off for me...'

'I think you were doing quite well without my help,' said Rowlands, with a smile, as the four of them went inside. A savoury smell of cooking—some kind of stew, he guessed, his mouth watering—mingled with the smell of smoke from a wood-burning stove. After the icy blast into which they had been walking for the past quarter of an hour, it was a welcome relief. 'Even so, I must thank you,' said the woman Rowlands supposed must be Viktor's sister, Sara Metzner. 'You are welcome to my home.' He bowed, by way of acknowledging what she had said. 'Since no one has seen fit to introduce *me*, I had better introduce myself,' said another, no less attractive voice: a young woman's, this time. 'I'm Clara. Do let me take your coat.'

'Thank you,' said Rowlands, gratefully surrendering this. A few minutes later, he found himself seated at a large oilcloth-covered table, with a steaming plate of beef stew in front of him. Joachim Metzner sat opposite him, wolfing down a plate of the same, while the women hovered nearby, ready to fill glasses and plates as needed. There seemed a tacit agreement not to mention the subject that was uppermost in all their minds, until the men had finished eating. So it was Rowlands who broke the silence. 'I gather you've heard nothing?' he said. 'No.' It was Dorothy who spoke. 'Not a word.'

'What do the police think?' At which his sister gave a scornful laugh. 'What do they think? I don't get the impression they *think* very much at all. If they do, they haven't said anything to *us*...'

He nodded, then pushed his plate away. 'Is it all right if I smoke?' he asked, turning his face towards where he guessed Frau Metzner to be standing. 'Please,' she said. He took the pack of Churchman's from his pocket, extracted one, and lit up; then: 'You'd better begin at the beginning,' he said.

They hadn't realised anything was amiss until dinner time, Dorothy said. 'I'd been out that afternoon, trying to find some winter boots for Victor—he's outgrown last year's. When I got back to the flat, it was already dark. I just assumed the boys

20

must be in their room...'

'We, too, were thinking this,' put in Clara, who had been following the conversation.

'...so it wasn't until I went to call them for supper, that I found they hadn't come back.'

'What time was this?'

'About six. We thought at first that they might have met up with some other boys from school... But when Sara went round to ask, none of Walter's classmates knew anything about it—did they, Sara?'

'No. All they said was that Walter and Wilhelm had left school at four o'clock, when class was dismissed. They did not know where they went after that. It is not like my Walter to behave thoughtlessly.' Frau Metzner gave a tremulous little laugh. 'I wish I could say the same for Billy,' said his mother. 'But he'd never be deliberately cruel.' Her voice, too, betrayed signs of agitation. 'Of course not,' said Rowlands. He hesitated a moment before putting his next question. 'Was there... well, any *reason* why Billy might not have wanted to come home?'

'Had he and I had a falling-out, you mean?' said his sister. 'The answer's no. Although he wasn't awfully keen on the prospect of going back to England next week.'

'Ah,' said Rowlands. Now we're getting somewhere, he thought. It seemed to him that his nephew was quite headstrong enough to pull a stunt like this, if it meant getting his own way in the matter. And I know where he gets *that* from, he said to himself. 'So he'd made himself quite at home here, then?

'Yes,' said Dorothy, not without pride. 'He speaks quite good German—doesn't he, Sara?' she added, reverting to that language. 'That was Viktor's doing, of course' Dorothy's voice softened at the mention of her late husband. 'And he's got even better at it since he got permission to attend school with Walter.'

'Yes, I wondered about that,' said Rowlands.

'I thought it'd be good for him to see the inside of a German classroom. The school was very good about it. And then, he and Walter have really hit it off, these past few weeks.'

'It is good for Walter to have a friend, because he has not so many friends at school now,' said Frau Metzner. 'They have their groups and societies, you know, and...'

'What Mutti means is that he's not allowed to join the Deutsches Jungvolk,' put in Joachim, from the far side of the room, where he had taken himself with the newspaper, after supper. 'Because we are Jews,' he added, in case Rowlands had missed the inference.

'Do you think Billy might have persuaded Walter to help him run away?' said Rowlands to his sister. 'So as not to have to return with the rest of you to England?' It seemed to him an all-too likely scenario. In the two years since Dorothy had re-married, relations between Billy and his stepfather had not always been of the most cordial. 'I do my best with him,' Jack Ashenhurst had confessed to his friend, in an unguarded moment. 'But he's not the easiest of customers. Vic's a sweet boy,'— this was Dorothy's younger child—'but I can't seem to get Billy to listen to a thing I say...'

'It's his age,' Rowlands had said consolingly; thinking privately that, regardless what age he was, his young nephew had always been something of a mystery. Now here was the proof.

Dorothy considered the question. 'It's possible,' she said. 'But... to leave it so long, without a word to let us know they're all right...' She broke down at last. 'It's been three days!'

'Now then, old thing. No need to take on...'

'I'm sorry.' She blew her nose sharply. 'It's hard for you, too.' This was to her sister-in-law. 'But I can't shake off the feeling that something terrible must have happened...'

'Put that thought right out of your mind,' said Rowlands, with more conviction than he felt. 'There's nothing more to be done tonight. First thing tomorrow, I'll go to police headquarters. I gather there's an Inspector Gentz who works there. He might be able to help us.'

'Gentz?' came the voice from the far side of the room. 'I have heard the name, I think. Let us hope he is not one of the new intake, that's all. Party members, all of them. They don't have time for *us*. In fact, they would very much like us to disappear. We are not true Germans, you understand...'

'From what I know of this man,' said Rowlands, fervently hoping that this would prove to be the case. 'He isn't that sort at all.'

22

2

ROWLANDS WAS WIDE AWAKE the moment he opened his eyes. He groped for his watch; it was just on six. Careful to make as little noise as possible, he got up and, having folded his bedding neatly at the end of the put-you-up on which he had spent the night, made his way to the bathroom on the landing, which was shared with the downstairs flat. He was relieved to find it unoccupied at this hour—although, as he'd anticipated, the water was stone-cold, since the geyser had not yet been lit. He wondered, as he performed his necessarily swift ablutions, whether he could get away without having a shave; then decided that, today of all days, he needed to make a good impression.

As he deliberated, there came a rattling of the door-handle. '*Besetzt*,' he called out. 'Herr Rowlands? It's me—Joachim,' said a voice through the door. Rowlands opened it. 'You're up early,' he remarked. 'I must be at work by half-past seven,' was the reply; then: 'If you want to shave, there is a pan of hot water on the stove for this purpose. I usually do this at the kitchen sink,' said the youth. 'It is much warmer, I find.'

'Thanks,' said Rowlands. A few minutes later, washed and shaved, both men sat at the kitchen table, nursing cups of black coffee—or what passed for coffee, Rowlands thought. 'Where is it that you work?' he asked, more out of politeness than because he really wanted to know. Metzner's response took him aback, its defensiveness seeming out of proportion to the casualness of the enquiry. 'Where do I work? I... I work at UFA. The... the film studios,' he added, in a voice that trembled with some suppressed emotion. 'That must be an interesting job.' Rowlands was puzzled at the young man's seeming agitation. What an excitable fellow he was—and how strangely he'd

23

reacted to what was, after all, quite a straightforward question! Perhaps it was another feature of life in this foreign city—that one didn't ask questions.

Suddenly, without a word of explanation, Metzler pushed back his chair. 'I am sorry,' he said. 'I... I must go.' To his astonishment, Rowlands realised that the young man was on the verge of tears. 'Of course,' he said. 'But...' Before he could discover what it was that had so upset Metzner, the latter grabbed his coat, and with a muttered 'Goodbye', rushed out of the flat—as if, Rowlands thought, the devil were at his heels. A strange young fellow, he reflected, gingerly sipping the watery ersatz coffee. I wonder what it was I said?

He was still puzzling over this, when he heard his sister come into the room. 'You're up early,' she said. 'I might say the same to you,' he replied. 'I couldn't sleep.' She poured herself a cup of coffee from the jug on the table, took a sip and gave an exclamation of disgust. 'Horrible, isn't it?'

'I've had better.'

'I keep thinking about him,' she said, as she sat down in the place just vacated by young Metzner. 'About Billy. Wondering where he is at this moment, and if he's frightened...'

'At least he's not on his own,' he said, unable to think of any better way of comforting her. 'No.' She sipped her coffee. 'There is that. But they're children, Fred!' she burst out, in a tone of such anguish that it made his heart ache for her. 'Children can be very resourceful,' he said. 'I mean, think of that time with Anne...' The event to which he was referring had taken place two years before, but its horror still had the power to rouse him, sweating and trembling, from sleep. 'I was forgetting that you'd been through something of this kind,' said his sister. 'Although at least...' She let the sentence tail off. 'At least I got her back safely,' he finished for her.

After a moment, Dorothy said: 'What are you going to do?' *That* question, at any rate, he could answer. 'I thought I'd pay a visit to the police station. I've a letter of introduction from...' He broke off, but she'd already guessed who it was he meant. 'From your copper friend, the Chief Inspector, you were going to say.' Rowlands didn't deny it. 'Oh, don't think I'm not grateful.

24

He saved my neck once before, as I'm sure you remember. But this...' She seemed unable to speak for a moment. 'This is a thousand times more important. Oh, Fred! What if we *don't* find them...'

'We will.' He reached across the table, and gave her hand a squeeze. 'And it might make all the difference, having someone in authority on our side...'

'If he turns out to be on our side,' she said morosely. 'It's hard to tell whose side anybody's on, the way things are here...'

'If Chief Inspector Douglas recommended him, then he'll be a good sort,' said Rowlands. 'Have you got the photographs there?' This had been his idea since—for obvious reasons—he was unable to give more than a cursory description of the boys. A class photograph of Walter Metzner had accordingly been found; the only available image of Billy was a snapshot, taken the previous summer, of the boy with his step-father. 'I brought it so that Sara could get an idea of Jack,' said Dorothy. 'I never thought it would end up being used in a police investigation.'

'Of course not.' Again, he patted her hand. 'How *is* he, by the way?' he said, meaning his old friend. 'Jack? He's fine—at least, he was when I last saw him.' This was a month ago—Dorothy having been invited by her late husband's sister to spend Silvester with them. 'He's very worried by all this, of course...'

'Yes, I had the devil's own job to persuade him to stay at home,' said Rowlands. 'But I pointed out that he'd be at the same disadvantage as I am, when it came to getting results. Speaking of which,' he went on, 'I was hoping young Metzner might have been able to accompany me to Alexanderplatz. But it appears not...'

'I'll come with you,' said Dorothy. 'Although it'll mean bringing Vicky...' Just at that moment, her six year-old son ran into the kitchen, and clambered onto his uncle's lap. 'Where's Joanie?' he demanded—this being his favourite cousin. 'Tucked up in bed, I should think,' said Rowlands, ruffling the child's hair. 'I'm assuming, from what Douglas said, that this man Gentz speaks English,' he said to his sister. 'Although my German isn't too bad—I've Viktor to thank for that...'

'You will allow me to accompany you, please.' Clara Metzner

25

must have slipped into the room while they were talking. Evidently, they were early risers in the Metzner household, Rowlands thought—either that, or they'd all slept as badly as he had. Now the girl busied herself setting out plates and knives around the table. 'You will need someone with you to...' She broke off, perhaps afraid that she might have embarrassed him. 'To show me the way,' Rowlands finished for her. 'That's kind of you. But don't you have classes to go to?' He'd gathered from last night's conversation that Fräulein Metzner was in her last year at high school. 'Not so many, now,' she said, setting down a basket containing slices of bread in the middle of the table. 'Two of my teachers have left. One has gone to America. It is better there for Jews, you know.' Unlike her brother, she gave no particular weight to this statement. It was as if she had re- marked on the weather.

They were at the police station by nine, although it wasn't un- til after they'd sat for a good hour on one of the hard wooden benches in the waiting room that the police officer to whom Rowlands had stated his business on arrival, tapped him on the shoulder and barked an order. At which the girl also rose to her feet, only to be told to sit down again by the same official. 'Just you,' he said curtly to Rowlands. 'Don't worry,' the blind man told his young companion. 'I'm used to finding my way about.'

He touched his breast-pocket, to check that the photographs of Billy and Walter were still there. Then, at a further impatient command from the policeman, he followed the latter along a corridor, through a set of double-doors, and along another cor- ridor. Their footsteps echoed hollowly on the tiled floor. From somewhere else in the building, came the sound of voices raised in anger, followed by the sound of a crash, as of a fist against a table; then silence. At length, the two of them came to another door. The officer knocked: a smart double rap. '*Komm herein!*' called a voice.

The man who rose from behind the desk as Rowlands en- tered was big and burly, to judge from the deep, guttural tones of his voice, and from the vigour with which he shook hands. 'Ah! Herr Rowlands! My apologies for keeping you waiting all this time, but you see how it is, just now. There is so much for us to do, with the new administration having taken over only yesterday, you know.'

'I'm sure there must be,' said Rowlands, relieved to find that the man spoke excellent English. 'Comings and goings, with this one in and that one out, you understand...' The big man laughed. 'I assure you it makes one's head spin! And then there is all the fun of clearing up after last night's celebrations,' he went on, still in the same tone of—was it forced?—joviality. 'So many broken heads and bloody noses! You know what young people are... Always in such high spirits, are they not?'

Rowlands smiled thinly, recalling the high-spirited young people he and Joachim Metzner had encountered the night before. 'But enough of such matters,' said Inspector Gentz. 'I have read the letter you brought from my good friend Chief Inspector Douglas. He tells me you are in need of my help, to find a missing person.'

'That's right.'

'Do sit down, Herr Rowlands. There is a chair two paces in front of you. So. Let us begin. According to the Chief Inspector's letter, it is your sister's son who is missing, with another boy...'

'Yes.'

The policeman grunted. 'Boys go missing,' he said. 'In this town more than most. I suppose you have heard of our "Ghoul", as we call him? He has so far succeeded in making away with twenty-four boys between the ages of seven and thirteen—most of them fished out of the Landwehr Canal, although a few have been found in the woods, and one on the railway tracks... It is to be hoped that your nephew has not been added to their number.' There seemed nothing to say to this, and so Rowlands merely nodded. He took the photographs from his pocket and held them out towards the Inspector. 'Perhaps these will be of some use,' he said. The other took them, and studied them for a moment. 'Nice-looking lad,' he said. 'Is that his father with him?'

'His father's dead. That's his step-father.'

'And the other lad's one of ours, I gather? Funny little chap. Those glasses don't do him any favours, do they?'

'I really couldn't say,' said Rowlands. 'No, I suppose not,' said Gentz, evidently unperturbed by the cool reception his remark had received. 'How did you become blind, by the way? Got a face-full of mustard gas, did you?'

'Shrapnel,' said Rowlands.

'Bad luck. Where was this?'

'Passchendaele.'

'Ah, yes, A "bad show", as you English say. I myself was at Verdun, with the Fifth Army. It is funny to think,' said the policeman in the same phlegmatic tone with which he had described the activities of the child-murderer, 'that we were on different sides during the War. I remember once saying to the Chief Inspector, "Alasdair, old man"—we were on quite friendly terms, you understand—"Only think that, a little more than a dozen years ago, you and I were doing our best to kill one another..." How we laughed at that, he and I!'

'I suppose it does have its funny side,' said Rowlands. He was beginning to wonder if they would ever get to the heart of the matter. But just then the Inspector, dropping his affable manner for one of businesslike acerbity, said, 'Well, I will see what I can do. But I cannot promise anything. You will leave these with me, of course?' He tapped the photographs on the desk. 'Of course,' said Rowlands. 'But don't you need to take a few more details?'

'I believe my colleague, Inspector Schneider, made a note of the same when he called at Frau Metzner's flat two nights ago,' said Gentz, turning over some papers on his desk. 'Yes, here it is: "Walter Leopold Metzner, aged twelve years and four months; height: four foot eleven inches; black hair, brown eyes, glasses; resides at Flat 3, 139, Marienbergerstrasse; missing since the night of 27th January, 1933; last seen leaving school—the Heinrich Heine Oberschule, on Driesenerstrasse—at around 4pm, with his cousin, William Frederick Ashenhurst, aged eleven years and six months; height: five foot one inch, brown hair, green eyes, no distinguishing marks—also missing." Is that good enough for you, Herr Rowlands?'

'Yes,' said Rowlands. 'Thank you.'

'As a matter of fact, it is rather irregular for me to concern

28

myself with a case already assigned to a colleague,' said the Inspector. 'But I am willing to do it, as a favour to an old friend.'

'I'm very grateful.'

'But you must understand that there is very little I can do unless one of two things happens,' the policeman went on. 'Either we receive information that the boys have been seen alive, and are then able to use that information to discover their whereabouts, or...' He paused for a moment. 'We do not. Do I make myself clear, Herr Rowlands?'

'Oh yes,' said Rowlands. 'Perfectly clear.'

The two men shook hands—again, Rowlands was made aware of the forcefulness of the other man's grip—and then Gentz went to the door, and gave an order to the man waiting outside it. 'Officer Schultz will see you out,' he said. 'Good day, Herr Rowlands.'

'*Auf Wiedersehen*, Herr Gentz,' said Rowlands, feeling that he should make at least this minimal effort to return the courtesy the other had shown him. The Inspector seemed to appreciate the attempt. 'Very good!' he cried, his booming laugh echoing along the corridor after Rowlands. 'We will make a German of you yet!'

By the time they left the police station, it was getting on for midday, and Clara said she had a class to attend. 'But first I will have my lunch,' she said, as they boarded the Number One tram. This would take Rowlands to the end of Marienburgerstrasse, and the Metzners' flat; the school was two stops further. 'Is this the school your brother attends?' asked Rowlands. 'Yes. That is... he is at the Gymnasium,' she said. 'It is the building next door, you know.'

'Good,' said Rowlands. 'Then perhaps you could point it out to me?' After his somewhat inconclusive interview with Inspector Gentz, he thought it could do no harm to carry out a little sleuthing on his own account. Because whether the police were dealing with the matter or not, the fact remained that the last time the two boys had been seen was at school, and the last to have seen them were Walter's classmates. But when he explained what he had in mind to Clara, she seemed dubious.

29

'I do not think that they will want to talk to you, these boys. They have already said to my mother that they know nothing of Walter's disappearance.'

'Who are they, in particular?' said Rowlands, undeterred by this. 'I mean, what are their names? They *do* have names, I take it?'

'Of course.' She sounded almost offended, as if perhaps he were accusing her of making things up. 'Their names are Dieter Geisler and Kurt Bauer. They are Walter's friends. At least,' she corrected herself, 'they *were*.'

'Then,' he said, 'I should like to talk to them. They might perhaps have remembered something. Do you think,' he added, with an innocent air, 'that their English will be as good as yours?' Clara Metzner laughed. At once, the stiffness of manner which made her seem older than her years was dispelled. 'I am sure it will not be,' she said. 'They will only just have begun to study this subject. And besides, they are very lazy boys.'

They arrived at Heinrich Heine Oberschule as classes were being dismissed; a torrent of girls and boys poured out of the school's main entrance—on their way home for lunch, Clara explained. 'It is only those who live near enough to get there and back in an hour who may go,' she added. 'It is too far for me... and Walter.' As she pronounced her younger brother's name, her voice trembled. It struck Rowlands that, beneath her reserved manner, Clara was as upset about what had happened as the more volatile Joachim. 'Don't worry,' he said. 'We'll find them—I promise.'

'I hope so,' she said. 'Come. We must go in here...' This was the entrance to the Middle School, which was next to that of the main building. A shallow flight of steps led to a heavy oak door—now standing open, as pupils released from class came hurrying out, talking at the tops of their voices. It was, thought Rowlands, like walking into the Parrot House at the Zoo. Much the same thought must have occurred to someone else, for a voice cried, with what seemed to Rowlands a certain desperation, *'Ruhe! Kein Laufen in den Gängen!'* No running in the corridors—the age-old cry of the schoolmaster, thought

30

Rowlands. 'That is Herr Hinck—Walter's teacher,' said Clara, confirming this guess. 'Then he's just the man I want to see,' said Rowlands. He stepped into the man's path. 'Herr Hinck? *Einen Moment… Ich heiße…*'

'But you are English, are you not?' said the teacher—adding, with some complacency: 'I of course speak English.'

'Oh, jolly good. The name's Rowlands. I wondered if I might have a word with you? It's about the two boys who went missing last Friday.'

The other seemed taken aback; then he recovered himself. 'Ah, yes. Poor Walter and his English cousin. You are the boy's father, perhaps?'

'His uncle.'

'Of course. But let us not stand in the corridor.' He opened a door into what Rowlands guessed, from the smell of ink and chalk-dust, must be one of the classrooms—empty at this time of day. 'We will not be disturbed in here. Come in, come in. You too, Miss Metzner. Although I do not see how I can help you. I have already told everything I know to the police.'

What he had told them, which he now repeated for Rowlands's benefit, was, on the face of it, unremarkable enough. Yes, he had taken the last class of the day—it was History; that was Herr Hinck's subject. They had been discussing the Prussian victory over the French, which had led to the setting up of the German Reich. Walter and Wilhelm had both been in class. He could not remember whether either had said anything of note; he rather thought not—although both boys were generally quick to put their hands up when a question was asked… yes, indeed, Wilhelm, too. His German was surprisingly good, with almost no accent at all. It had improved a good deal since he had been attending a German school, of course… So there it was. Class had been dismissed at the usual time, and the boys went home—at least, so he had supposed. It was only later, when the police called…

'Was there nothing at all that struck you as unusual?' interrupted Rowlands. Throughout the teacher's recitation, he had become increasingly convinced that the man was holding something back. Maybe it was no more than that his tentative manner of speaking seemed constantly to be undermining what it was he had just said. Rowlands pictured a typical middle-aged schoolmaster, with thinning hair and a wispy moustache, his shabby tweed jacket and grey flannel trousers the uniform of his kind everywhere; his nervous mannerisms betraying a lifetime spent in the atmosphere of the classroom, with all its petty rivalries and repressions.

'I... I am not sure what you mean.' There it was again! That note of hesitation. The man knew something, thought Rowlands. 'I mean was anything said or done by any of your pupils which seemed to you out-of-the-ordinary?' he persisted. 'Anything at all?'

'Well...' Herr Hinck appeared to consider the question. 'There was a trivial matter... hardly worth mentioning. I am sure I would have forgotten it if you had not reminded me, Herr Rowlands.' The schoolmaster gave an awkward laugh. 'We teachers must deal with incidents of this kind every day...'

'What happened?' said Rowlands softly.

'Oh, nothing of any significance, I assure you! I was merely obliged to confiscate a certain publication from our young man... Walter, I mean.' Again came the embarrassed laugh—it was more of a snuffle, thought Rowlands. It struck him that it would be an easy sound to mimic, and he felt a stab of pity for the man. 'You know how it is, with boys of that age... Or perhaps you do not?'

'Go on,' said Rowlands.

'I hardly think,' said Herr Hinck, 'that, in front of the young lady...'

'I have two brothers, Herr Hinck,' said Clara. 'I am not easily shocked.'

'Very well. It was a magazine with... with pictures of actresses, and the like. Women... I am sorry to say... without their clothes. There! You cannot say I did not warn you.'

'No, indeed,' said Rowlands gravely. 'And do you still have it— this magazine?'

'Certainly not. I threw it in the stove, at once. It is of course possible, Herr Rowlands,' went on the other, 'that young Walter did not realise what kind of publication this was. He might have

32

picked it up unwittingly. The older boys—though they are forbidden to do so—sometimes bring this kind of thing to school.
So you see, he might be completely innocent...' Having unbur-
dened himself of his distasteful secret, Herr Hinck was evidently anxious to justify the fact of his having said nothing about it
to the police. 'It seemed completely unimportant to me, you
see? A foolish prank. I did not think it could have anything to
do with what happened after...'

'And what was that?'

It seemed to Rowlands that the schoolmaster hesitated before replying, 'Why, the boys' disappearance, of course. A most
distressing occurrence. And now, Herr Rowlands,' he went on,
his manner suddenly brisk, 'I am afraid I must bring our interview to an end. I have enjoyed this opportunity of practising my
English, and of re-awakening memories of that country. I spent
many happy days there, in my youth. Do you know Dorking?
A very pleasant town. And such delightful countryside! Our
German mountains are magnificent, of course, but I confess to
having a "soft spot" for your gentle Surrey hills...'

Since there was evidently nothing more to be got out of
Herr Hinck, Rowlands and his young companion took their
leave of him. 'This way,' said Clara, once they were in the corridor. Unlike her brother, she did not drag him by the arm, but
touched Rowlands lightly upon the elbow to indicate the direction in which they should be going. Although in this instance
the mob through which they were having to make their way
was composed, not of Storm Troopers, but only of schoolchil-
dren. 'I hope you will not think me a prude,' said the girl, 'when
I say that what Herr Hinck told us about Walter surprised me
very much. My younger brother is a serious boy. I do not think
he is interested in looking at pictures of unclothed women.'

'No, of course not,' murmured Rowlands. 'Perhaps, as Herr
Hinck suggested, Walter merely picked up the magazine, without realising what it was...'

'Perhaps.' But she did not sound as if she believed it.

At the end of a corridor, they came to a set of double doors.
'We must go in here,' said the girl. 'I think we will find those for
whom we are looking within.' This was a dining-hall, of what

Rowlands guessed to be lofty dimensions; the muted chatter of the assembled pupils—perhaps fifty, all told—was lost in its vaulted roof-space. Taking Rowlands by the arm, Clara drew him across the room, threading between rows of trestle-tables until they reached the furthest one. Here, she sat down, and directed Rowlands to the place next to her. To judge by the muttered remarks and stifled laughter which arose at the appearance of the strangers, there were three or four others occupying the table. Fräulein Metzner issued a command, and several of the boys got to their feet and sloped off. 'They will sit elsewhere,' said the girl to Rowlands. 'These two are the boys you want.' At once, one of the two got up as if to leave. 'Sit down,' said Clara sternly. 'This is Herr Rowlands, who wishes to ask some questions about Walter.'

'*Ich weiß nichts!*' cried the boy who had leapt to his feet. 'Speak English,' said Clara. 'Or if you cannot manage *that*, then at least answer Herr Rowlands's questions with civility.'

'We have already said everything to the police,' said the boy who had remained seated, in a sullen voice. He had not taken up her invitation to practise his English. 'Well, you can say it again, Dieter Geisler,' replied Clara; then, when he began to protest: 'We know about the dirty magazine.'

'What do you mean?' spluttered the youth. 'I don't know about any dirty magazine...'

'Oh, don't pretend to be an innocent!' said Clara scornfully. 'You know what I'm talking about—the magazine confiscated by Herr Hinck. In fact, I wouldn't be surprised if it was *you* who gave it to Walter...'

'You've got it all wrong.' It was the turn of the other boy, Kurt Bauer, to protest his innocence. 'It was Metzner's magazine, all right. He said his brother gave it to him...'

'*What!*'

'That's right,' put in Geisler. '*Film-Welt*. It had a picture of that actress he's so mad about. The one with the...'

'Shut up, Geisler!'

'... blonde ringlets, I was going to say,' said Geisler, with the same butter-wouldn't-melt-in-his-mouth air he had assumed earlier. 'So it was a film magazine that Walter was passing around?'

34

said Rowlands, thinking it was high time he took charge of this interrogation. 'Yes, sir.' Again the oleaginous Geisler took it upon himself to answer. 'Metzner was mad about films. Because of his brother working at UFA, you know...'

'Yes,' said Rowlands. 'I do know. And what happened afterwards?'

'Afterwards?' A wariness had crept into the boy's manner, now. 'I don't understand...'

'Don't you? Then let me spell it out for you. I want to know what happened after the magazine was confiscated, and after class was dismissed for the day. I know that *something* happened, and I want you to tell me exactly what it was.'

Before Geisler could reply, the other boy, Bauer, pushed back the bench on which he was sitting, with a scraping sound. 'We have to go now,' he said. 'We must be in class soon.'

'Sit down, Mr Bauer,' said Rowlands quietly. 'I want an answer to my question before you go. What happened after school? Did you wait for Walter and Wilhelm outside, with some of your other friends? Was there a bit of rough-house, perhaps?' When the two boys remained silent, he went on, keeping his tone light and amused, 'Oh, come *on*! I know how it is, when what starts as no more than a bit of fun gets out of hand. A snowball gets thrown a little bit harder than intended. Somebody's lip gets cut. Somebody else's jacket gets torn...'

'Since you seem to know all about it, why are you asking us?' said Dieter Geisler.

'Shut up, Geisler!'

'Perhaps,' said Rowlands pleasantly, 'I'd prefer to hear it from you.'

'We didn't start it,' said the boy sullenly. 'In fact, we tried to stop it—didn't we, Bauer?'

'That's right. It was von Richter and his crowd who started laying into them... I mean...' The boy broke off. 'It's all right,' said Rowlands. 'I know you don't want to land your classmates in it. But you must see that I have to know what happened.'

'Nothing much happened,' said Bauer. 'It was just a bit of pushing and shoving. Name-calling, you know...'

'Oh yes,' said Rowlands. 'I know.'

'It was because of that stupid film magazine,' put in Dieter Geisler. 'Metzner was always bragging about all the actresses his brother had met—and how easy it was for him to meet them, too. In fact, he was going to meet one of them that very night, he said. The most beautiful of them all...'

'Sybille Schönig,' put in Bauer. 'It was all rot, of course. And so we... that is, von Richter... decided to teach him a lesson. There was a bit of rough-house, like you said. But it wouldn't have come to anything if the English boy hadn't started fighting back. He's a dirty fighter,' he added, with what seemed a grudging admiration. So then we... von Richter and his friends, I mean... had to carry on. It was a good fight,' he said. 'Metzner's nose started bleeding. It was then that Herr Hinck came out...'

'Ah,' said Rowlands. He had guessed the man had known more than he'd let on. 'So we had to stop,' Walter's former friend was saying. 'Fighting is forbidden, you see.'

'Indeed,' said Rowlands. 'And was that the last time you saw them—Walter and Wilhelm, I mean?'

'Yes, it was. Can we go now?' said Dieter Geisler. But his friend hadn't quite finished. 'It was funny what Metzner said, as we were leaving,' said Kurt Bauer. 'I have to admit he was plucky. He was standing there, with blood running out of his nose, and he shouted out, "You wait until Monday! You'll be eating humble pie *then*!"'

'Do you know what he meant?' said Rowlands.

'I haven't the least idea,' said the boy.

3

ROM ANHALTER BAHNHOF, IT was a half-hour train journey to the Babelsberg Studios outside Potsdam. Clara had insisted on accompanying Rowlands—even though, as he pointed out, he'd have been perfectly all right making the journey alone. 'I do it all the time at home,' he said—to which she replied, 'But this *isn't* home,' adding under her breath, 'not even for some of us that live here…' When he'd reminded her that she'd be missing her class, she'd seemed unperturbed. 'It's only French conversation. I can make it up next week. If there *is* a next week,' she'd added, with the droll humour he was starting to see as characteristic.

So, having first sent a message to Dorothy via the superintendent (owner of the apartment block's only telephone), Rowlands and his young guide set out on the next stage of their quest—one which, he fervently hoped, would bring them closer to the heart of the mystery. Because even though it wasn't much to go on—the confiscated film magazine, with its picture of a beautiful starlet, and young Walter Metzner's boast that he'd be meeting her that very night—it was more than they'd had before.

When he'd asked Clara if she'd heard of the actress in question, she'd seemed amazed that anyone could be so out of touch. 'But surely you know Sybille Schönig?' she'd cried. 'She is famous, in Berlin. She has made several films here, at the UFA studios. It is where my brother Joachim works, you know,' she added, with pardonable pride. 'He will be there now, I am sure.'

'Then that's where we should go, too,' said Rowlands. 'How late does he work, as a rule?'

'It depends on whether they are shooting a film, or not,' she said. 'Sometimes he has to work very late, you know. But if they

37

have finished shooting for the day, then he is usually home by six or seven. He has to start at half-past seven, so it is a long day for him.'

'Yes,' said Rowlands, thinking of his early morning encounter with the young man. What had made him so agitated?, he wondered. Perhaps he was having problems at work... or in his love-life. If so, would he have confided in his sister? It didn't seem right to fish... 'What is his job exactly?' he asked instead. Clara laughed. 'A bit of everything, I think. He must run here with this piece of film and run there with that so-important message. To hear him speak, you would suppose that, without him, the studio would collapse altogether.'

'I see. A sort of Jack-of-all-trades, then?' They were on the train by this time; Rowlands could not help but be distracted from what his companion was saying by all that was going on around: the rattle of the carriages over the tracks, and the slowing down of the same as the train pulled into a station. Teltow Stadt, Yorkstrasse, Priesterweg, Südende—this would be the fourth stop they'd made; theirs would be the sixth. The stuffiness of the compartment in which he and Clara were sitting was another thing; if it had not been for the presence of an elderly lady in the seat opposite (the violet *cachous* she was sucking lending their sickly perfume to the air) he would have pulled down the window. 'Exactly. But what he really wants to be is a cameraman.'

'Well, we all have to start somewhere.' It was hard to form more than the most cursory impression of the city, he thought, as the train passed through what he supposed must be a suburban district. Berlin was surrounded by forest, wasn't it? He remembered something from one of Dorothy's letters... If they hadn't been so preoccupied with the matter in hand, he might have asked Clara to describe what she could see from the window. But for the moment, he'd have to contain his curiosity... 'What I can't understand,' his companion was saying, 'is why he said nothing of this to the rest of us... that he'd invited the boys to the studio, I mean.'

'Yes,' said Rowlands. 'It does seem a bit odd. But I'm sure there's perfectly good explanation.' The train came to a halt once more, with a grinding of wheels. From the platform, the guard shouted, 'Lankwitz!' Then the door of their compartment opened and someone got on. '*Heil Hitler*,' said the newcomer, throwing himself into a corner seat. A middle-aged man, Rowlands guessed, from the gruffness of his voice. His breath smelt of beer. When his greeting was not returned, he said aggressively: 'What's the matter? Are you deaf? I said…'

'I heard you,' said Rowlands. 'And I'm not deaf.'

The man seemed taken aback for a moment; then he laughed. '*Aha! Du bist ein Engländer?*' he said, reaching across to tap Rowlands on the knee. 'I said—you are Englishman, *nicht wahr?*'

'Yes,' said Rowlands coldly.

'You like our great country?'

'Very much.'

The man gave a self-satisfied chuckle. He took a pack of cigarettes for his pocket. '*Zigarette?*'

'*Nein, Danke.*'

Another chuckle. He lit up, and puffed a cloud of foul-smelling smoke into Rowlands's face. 'And what do you think of our great Leader?'

Before Rowlands could reply, there came an interruption. 'Young man!' said the old lady, in a freezing tone. 'I did not give my permission for you to smoke. Kindly extinguish your cigarette when a lady asks you to.'

'It was so funny, the look on his face!' said Clara, when she and Rowlands had reached their stop and were safely on the platform. 'I think to myself I will die laughing…'

'Well, I was certainly glad of the distraction,' said Rowlands. Because in the irritable exchange that followed—made more so by the fact that one of the speakers was slightly deaf—the question was forgotten, and so he never had to say what he thought of the new German Chancellor.

From Babelsberg station, a brisk ten-minute walk along pavements still thick with snow brought them to the gates of the UFA studios. Here, they were detained for a few minutes, while the gatekeeper rang through to Studio One, where it appeared

Joachim Metzner was working that day. As they waited, in the one-storey gate-house beside the main entrance, Rowlands took stock of his situation. Despite his earlier boast to Clara about his being accustomed to getting around by himself, he knew he couldn't have managed without her. In such unfamiliar territory, he'd need every scrap of concentration he possessed not to go hopelessly wrong. 'I'll need you to describe things a bit,' he said to Clara. 'I don't think I've much idea what a film studio looks like...'

'It's a big place,' she said, with the note of pride he had heard in her voice when she'd first mentioned the studios. 'The largest in Europe, I think. Even I have not been all over it, although Joachim has promised to show me around, when he is not so busy... But here is Joachim now! He can explain it better than I.'

It soon became apparent that her brother was in no mood for explanations—in fact he seemed to be in a towering rage. 'What are you doing here, Clar?' he demanded of his sister, ignoring Rowlands. 'You know I'm not supposed to have visitors when I'm at work. Do you want to lose me my job?'

'We had to see you,' she began, in a faltering voice, 'It's important.'

Metzner gave a disbelieving snort. 'What's so important that it couldn't wait?'

Rowlands decided he'd had enough of the young man's irascible moods. 'I'm afraid it was my idea to come,' he said. 'And it really *can't* wait. Is there somewhere else we can talk?' he added, conscious of the presence of the gatekeeper. Metzner sighed. 'You'd better come this way. But I can only spare you a few minutes. I'm supposed to be at the Sound Stage until six.'

'They don't allow members of the public onto the lot as a rule,' whispered Clara to Rowlands, perhaps to excuse her brother's graceless behaviour. 'It upsets the actors, Joachim says. And of course, there is always the risk that someone might turn out to be a spy...'

'I don't understand,' he said, as the three of them crossed a wide expanse of cobblestones from which much of the previous day's snow had been swept; it was still icy underfoot, though, and Rowlands was conscious of having to tread carefully. 'Are

40

there secrets worth stealing here?' He couldn't help laughing at the absurdity of it. As if this were a factory making munitions or aeroplanes, instead of what it was—a glorified theatre. 'Oh, yes,' said Clara. 'Making a film is a very complex business. There are all kinds of technical processes a rival might want to steal. Joachim knows more about it than I, but...'

'In here,' said the latter curtly. He opened a door. This led into a vast, cavernous space, in which the sound of their footsteps echoed hollowly. Rowlands was reminded of the aircraft hangar in which he had once had the misfortune to stumble across a corpse... He brushed away the thought. They crossed to the far side—'Take care! There are cables on the floor,' said Metzner—and went through another door, that led into a corridor. Off this led other rooms—offices, or dressing-rooms, Rowlands guessed—into one of which Metzner led them. 'Five minutes,' he said, as he closed the glass-panelled door behind them. 'They'll have my head if they find I've left the set...'

'This won't take long,' said Rowlands. 'I just want the answer to a question. Why didn't you say anything about having invited Walter and Billy to the studio the night they disappeared?'

For a moment Metzner seemed dumbfounded. 'I... I... What are you talking about?' he said at last. 'I did no such thing. What! Invite my little brother and his cousin to my place of work? I tell you, it would be more than my life is worth.'

'Nevertheless,' said Rowlands. 'We've reason to believe they *did* come here that night—whether you'd invited them or not.' Briefly, he summarised what they'd learnt from Walter's classmates. 'So you see,' he concluded, 'there's a strong possibility that they were here—or on their way here, at least—when... well, whatever happened to them, happened,' he finished lamely. 'But... that's ridiculous,' said Metzner. 'The idea that two kids could've smuggled their way in, without anybody being the wiser...'

'Children are resourceful,' said Rowlands. 'It doesn't surprise me in the least that they found a way in. *If* they found a way in. We still don't know for certain that they achieved their goal...'

'I am afraid I do not follow,' said Metzner stiffly. 'Why,' said Rowlands. 'To see the young lady they were so keen on, of

41

course. Sybille Schönig. I gather from your sister that she's quite a rising star?' The deafening silence which followed his remark surprised him a little. But then Metzner spoke, his tone so subdued that it was an effort to hear him. 'Of course,' he said. 'You do not know... But then, how could you?'

'What is it, Joe?' cried Clara, having evidently seen something in her brother's expression that frightened her. But all he said, in a broken voice, was, 'No, no. You could not know...'

'I assure you, I've no intention of troubling Fräulein Schönig any longer than absolutely necessary,' said Rowlands. 'I just want to ask her if she happened to see the boys that night...'

'And I tell you, it is impossible for you to see Sybille Schönig!' Metzner's voice had risen to a shout. He was once more on the verge of tears, Rowlands realised. 'I say, what's up?' he said sharply. But before the young man could speak, the door opened, and someone put his head in. Then, to Rowlands's surprise, he heard himself addressed in English. 'Herr Rowlands, is it not? I did not expect to see you here.'

'I'm a little surprised to see you, too, Inspector Gentz.'

The other laughed. 'Why, there is no mystery about *my* presence here,' he said. 'Nor that of my assistant, Officer Schultz, whom you have met also,' he added, as the latter appeared behind him in the doorway. 'We are merely doing our jobs. Which in this instance, means investigating the circumstances surrounding an untimely death.'

'Whose death?' It seemed to Rowlands, as he asked the question, that he already knew the answer. 'Her name,' said the Inspector, 'is Sybille Schönig. An actress. But I think you already know this?' he added slyly. 'Otherwise why did I hear her name mentioned as I was passing the door? Yes, she is dead. Shot through the head with a .22 calibre revolver. Apparently she did this herself...'

'Apparently?'

The Inspector ignored the question. 'We are treating it as suicide, for the present,' he said.

'When was this?'

'I suppose there is no harm in telling you. The newspapers will have it soon enough,' said Gentz. 'She died on Friday evening, sometime between six o'clock and eight. Why? Is it of any significance?'

'It might be,' said Rowlands guardedly. 'You see, there's a possibility that my nephew and his cousin were on their way to see Fräulein Schönig, the evening they disappeared. So you see that...'

'Why wasn't I told of this before?' said the policeman sharply. 'You're saying that these boys were with her that night?'

'Well, it's only a supposition,' said Rowlands. 'But it would help enormously if you'd allow me to find out for certain.'

'And how do you propose to do that, Herr Rowlands?' There was an edge of amusement in the Inspector's voice. 'You would like to question my witnesses, perhaps?'

'Oh, I wouldn't expect to do that,' said Rowlands quickly. 'Only... if I could have your permission to ask around... just to see if anyone here remembers seeing the boys...'

'You are not satisfied, then, with the way my esteemed colleague Inspector Schneider is conducting the investigation?'

'It's not that,' said Rowlands. 'I'm sure the Inspector is doing a very good job. But, as you said yourself, your department is very busy at present. At the very least, it might save Inspector Schneider's officers the trouble of coming all the way out here, if I were to ascertain whether or not the boys were at the studio last Friday...' Inspector Gentz laughed. 'You are very persuasive, Herr Rowlands! But what you ask is out of the question. Even if it were not certain to offend Inspector Schneider, it is still a contravention of procedure for a member of the public to interfere in a police investigation...'

'But...'

'And in any case,' went on the Inspector, paying no attention to this interruption, 'what you propose is not so easy. Suppose I were to allow you to ask your questions—have you any idea how many people you would have to interrogate? UFA has several hundred employees. At least fifty were working here that night.'

'I'd only want to talk to those who could give me an idea of Sybille Schönig's movements that evening,' said Rowlands. 'Since it was she the boys were intending to visit. I'd hoped to talk to the lady herself, but…'

'But she is dead,' the policeman said drily. 'An unfortunate coincidence.'

'If it *is* a coincidence,' said Rowlands.

'You think, then, that there may be some connection between this young woman's death and the boys' disappearance?' The Inspector's casual tone did not altogether conceal his interest. A shrewd old fox, thought Rowlands. 'Come, come, Herr Rowlands! That is unlikely, you must agree.'

'On the contrary,' said Rowlands. 'I think it highly likely.'

'Well, I will pass on what you have said to Inspector Schneider,' said Gentz. 'That is the best I can offer. Now I must leave you. Officer Schultz and I are on our way to interview one of Fräulein Schönig's colleagues—the actor, Helmut Hartmann. Another of our big stars,' he added. 'We were told his dressing-room was along here…'

'It is.' Since his earlier outburst, Joachim Metzner had remained silent, so that Rowlands had almost forgotten he was there. His subdued tone indicated that he would have preferred to have remained unnoticed. 'Then perhaps you will show us the way?' said Gentz. 'I do not think,' he went on, 'that I have seen you before. Your name?'

Metzner supplied it. 'Ah, yes. The brother. So you work here, do you?'

'Yes,' muttered the youth; adding—not before time—'Inspector.'

Gentz turned to his subordinate. 'Have we questioned this man?'

'Not yet, sir. There are a lot of them to get through.'

'Yes, yes,' said the other impatiently. 'Well, you might as well take his statement now. He can take us to Hartmann first.'

'But…' Metzner's protest died in his throat. 'Yes?' came the steely reply. 'I… I must get back to work,' stammered the unhappy youth, evidently fixed by Gentz's gimlet eye. 'That will have to wait,' snapped the Inspector. 'When it is matter of a police enquiry, everything must wait. Goodbye, Herr Rowlands,' he said, switching briefly to English. 'It has been an unexpected pleasure.'

'Goodbye, Inspector.' The two shook hands. Then Gentz, followed by his Sergeant and Metzner, left the room. Their footsteps could be heard retreating along the corridor. Only when the sound had faded away, did Rowlands speak. 'I wonder, Fräulein Metzner...'

'Clara.'

'Clara, then. Would you mind very much continuing to act as my guide? Only I think, if I am to ask questions...'

'I will be your guide,' she said.

They didn't have much time, if they were to do what Rowlands intended to do, and get away before the Inspector knew what they'd been up to. 'And of course, we were only trying to find our way out of the building,' said Rowlands to his companion, as they walked cautiously along the corridor down which, a few minutes before, Gentz and his assistant had followed the reluctant Metzner. 'It's hardly our fault if we got a bit lost in doing so...'

'No,' she agreed. 'This is a large place. It is very possible to take a wrong turning. We might find it necessary,' she added drily, 'to ask some people for directions.' Passing the door of what the blind man guessed must be Helmut Hartmann's dressing-room, they heard voices from within. One—the Inspector's—said something Rowlands didn't catch, to which another—presumably the actor's—replied with some heat: 'But that is ridiculous! I do not believe it...'

'That was Herr Hartmann, I take it?'

'Yes.'

'What do you think he meant?'

'I don't know.'

'Perhaps,' said Rowlands, 'it was the suggestion that Fräulein Schönig had committed suicide that he found hard to believe.'

'Then you think she was murdered?' said Clara. '

'I couldn't say. It's what the Inspector seemed to be suggesting. And it would explain why the police are still interested in the case—if, as it appears, the young lady died three days ago. Presumably, the studio wanted to keep it dark as long as possible—the fact that she'd killed herself, I mean. It can't be very good for business, to lose your leading lady in such circumstances…'

They had reached the end of the corridor; another ran at right angles to it. Rowlands knew this because, as they'd been walking, he'd been trailing the fingers of his nearside hand along the wall, the better to get a sense of his surroundings. With the part of his mind that took notice of such things, he'd counted three doors down from the office where Metzner had taken them, to Hartmann's dressing-room; then another four doors down from that, to where they now stood.

'Oh-oh,' he heard Clara say under her breath; then: 'Police.'

Of course, he thought—if the police suspected foul play, then Sybille Schönig's dressing-room must now be regarded as a crime scene, and as such would be out-of-bounds to the public. 'How many?' he said softly.

'Just one.' She thought for a moment. 'Give me two minutes,' she whispered. 'Then you may follow. It is the fourth door down, on the right-hand side…'

'What are you going to do?'

'I will tell you afterwards.' Then before he could protest, she had walked off down the corridor that led to the late starlet's dressing-room. A moment later, from his hiding-place around the corner, he heard her address the policeman. A brief conversation ensued, of which the only words intelligible to Rowlands were the names 'Gentz' and 'Schultz'. 'What's she up to?' he wondered, hoping that his young friend knew what she was doing. But whatever it was that Clara had said to the man guarding the door, it seemed to have done the trick, for within a minute, by Rowlands's watch, there came the sound of boots tramping off down the corridor, with the lighter footsteps of the girl scurrying in their wake.

Rowlands didn't hesitate. A few strides brought him to the dressing-room door, which proved to be unlocked. In another moment, he was inside. If he'd had any doubt about its being the right place, the smell that greeted him would have reassured him. Greasepaint and face-powder predominated, but a lingering trace of some floral scent confirmed that this was—or had been—a woman's domain. As he took a cautious step inside, he fervently hoped that the room had already been dusted for fingerprints. The thick gloves in his coat pocket would prevent his leaving traces, it was true, but would also make it harder for him to learn anything from the room's contents; he decided at once not to bother with them.

Another step brought him into contact with a chair—one of the flimsy bentwood kind—and the dressing-table against which it was pushed, and which took up almost the whole of one wall. Taking care to disturb things as little as possible, he ran his fingers lightly over the surface of this, encountering the objects with which it was covered. These were arranged with some precision: a row of scent bottles lined up to one side of the mirror, with sticks of greasepaint, boxes of rouge, powder-puffs, and other tools of the makeup artist's trade arranged in front of them. Something about this arrangement struck him as peculiar—he couldn't have said what, exactly.

The dressing-room was not large—three paces brought him to the far side of it, and a door which, once opened, disclosed a minute bathroom with a sink and lavatory. But although his search yielded a good many clues as to the character of its former occupant—from the keepsakes to the right of the mirror (a toy dog; a china basket of roses), to the silk underwear draped carelessly over the back of the chair—he found nothing that pointed to the presence of anyone else—least of all that of two schoolboys. Perhaps, he thought, it had all been a mistake, and Walter Metzner's boast about meeting his idol that night had been an empty one?

Beside the dressing-table was a rail, on which hung a large number of dresses, coats, and petticoats; all costumes of some sort, he supposed. These garments were of various materials: taffeta, satin, velvet, lace; some heavy with sequins, others light as gauze. His fingers skimmed the surface of the fabrics, as if through touch alone, he might gain a better sense of the identity of the wearer. A sweet, artificial scent—the one he had identified earlier—rose from the silken layers, as he disturbed them. 'No,' he thought. 'There's nothing to be found here...'

Beyond the rack of clothes was a screen—one of the kind decorated with pasted paper cut-outs of flowers, cherubs, society beauties and the like, which had been popular when he was a boy. As he brushed against it, he dislodged a dangling fox-fur. He was restoring it to its place—because it wouldn't do to leave signs that anything had been disturbed—when his foot kicked something metallic that had rolled against the base of the screen, and which had, presumably, been concealed by it until now. He bent to pick it up. It was a propelling-pencil, of the cheap kind that all schoolboys have... He put it in his pocket.

As he did so, he heard a slight sound behind him. *'Was macht du hier?'* said a woman's voice. She must have slipped into the dressing-room so quietly that he'd been unaware of it. 'I'm sorry,' he said, with an apologetic smile. 'But I simply couldn't resist it... The door was open, and...'

'You are English.' Her voice had a gruffness to it that was disconcerting, but not unpleasant. 'Yes.' Evidently his German accent wasn't as good as he'd thought. 'You see, I'm such a great admirer of Fräulein Schönig's, that...'

'You have seen her films?'

'Oh, yes,' he said, hoping she wouldn't ask him which ones he'd seen. He knew his blindness was apparent to the more observant, and hoped his new acquaintance didn't fall into this category. But she seemed satisfied with his reply; perhaps she assumed, as Clara had, that everyone must have seen Sybille Schönig's films. Or maybe she had other things on her mind. 'You are not police?' she said sharply. Rowlands shook his head. 'Oh no,' he said. 'Nothing like that.'

'She is dead, you know.' The gruffness in her voice seemed expressive of some deep emotion. It was hard to guess her age. Perhaps fifty, Rowlands thought. 'Yes, I'd heard,' he replied. 'I'm sorry. It's a terrible thing...'

'Terrible,' she echoed, in that harsh, strangely beguiling voice. 'They are saying she killed herself. But this I do not believe. Why would she have chosen this manner of killing herself—she was shot through the head, you know. She, who was so beautiful, and who cared so much for her beauty? It makes no sense. Nor would she have used her right hand to shoot herself...'

'So she was left-handed?' said Rowlands. That explained the

48

arrangement of the cosmetics on the dressing-table, he thought.

'Yes. As you say, she was left-handed. Which means that whoever killed her did not know this. But in any case she would not have done such a thing. She had too much to live for...'

The voice broke off, then continued: 'The night before it happened, she was in fine spirits. "Gretchen," she said—that was her name for me—"Gretchen, I'm so happy." She was like that, you know. Always her feelings on show. "Gretchen," she said to me that night, "I have made my decision. I am going to America—and when I get there, my Gretchen, I will send for you. I could not do without my faithful Gretchen..." I was her dresser for six years,' the voice went on. 'Ever since she started at UFA as a skinny little scrap of eighteen, doing walk-ons and bit parts. I knew everything that went on in her head—when she was sad, when she was sick, when there was a man around... and I tell you, she would not have done this...'

Again she broke off. When she spoke again, it was in a voice devoid of expression. 'I found her,' she said. 'Not two paces from where you are standing. It was the last day of shooting her scenes in *Gefallener Engel*, and so I did not arrive at the studio until a quarter to seven. I knew they would go on later than usual, with re-takes, and the like... Sybille had said she did not want me before seven. "I can manage quite well without you, my dear old Gretchen," she said. I was to wait for her in the dressing-room until she returned... Except that she had already returned. Her body was on the floor. She was still wearing the dress she wears in the final act. Silver-gilt satin, cut on the bias. Such a beautiful dress,' murmured the dresser. 'Of course it was ruined. Her face, too...'

'It must have been very hard for you,' said Rowlands gently. 'She was my life,' was the reply, delivered in the same brusque tone as before. 'Now she is dead. It makes no sense.'

'The police seem to think much the same,' said Rowlands. 'I mean, that Fräulein Schönig did not kill herself...'

'You said you were not police.'

'I'm not. But... I heard something to that effect,' he said. 'If Sybille did not kill herself, then somebody else must have killed her,' said the woman called Gretchen flatly. 'Yes, it would seem

49

so,' said Rowlands. 'And there's something else. It appears that there may have been a witness to the killing... or rather, two.'

'Explain, please.'

He did so, conscious, as he did so, that he didn't have much time. He wondered what had happened to Clara, and what subterfuge she had employed to get rid of the police guard. He hoped she hadn't landed herself in trouble, because of this. Well, he would know soon enough... 'So you think your nephew and his cousin have seen who killed my Sybille?' said the dresser, when Rowlands had finished speaking. 'I don't know,' he said. 'It's a possibility, that's all. But until we find them—or someone who saw them—there's no way of knowing either way...'

'I did not see them, if that is what you are asking,' she said. 'But I can find out if anyone else did.'

'Thank you.' It was better than nothing, he thought. Then he remembered the pencil. 'Do you recognise this?' He held it out to her. 'It did not belong to Sybille, I can tell you that,' said the woman, after she had given it a glance. 'She used a gold pen, with her initials engraved on the barrel. A present from one of her men,' she added, with a certain pride. At least that eliminates one possibility, thought Rowlands. 'If you think of anything...' he began. But before he could finish, the door of the dressing-room was flung open. 'Quick!' cried Clara breathlessly. 'He will be back any minute. I've only just given him the slip...'

'And who are you?' demanded the dresser.

'I...'

'This is Fräulein Metzner,' said Rowlands. 'She is helping me look for the boys. Now I think we must go, Fräulein...'

'Pabst,' was the reply. 'And your name?'

'Frederick Rowlands.'

'Goodbye, Herr Rowlands. I hope you find what you are looking for,' she said. 'Goodbye, Fräulein Pabst.' It was frustrating to have to cut their conversation short, thought Rowlands. He had the feeling that she knew a good deal more about what had happened than she let on. But there was no help for it; to stay even a moment longer, would have proved fatal. Because

50

as they stepped out into the corridor, there came a shout from the far end of it. 'Halt!'

'Run,' said Clara, seizing Rowlands by the arm. He didn't need telling twice.

FOCUS

4

WITH THAT FURIOUS COMMAND ringing in their ears, they hurled themselves in the opposite direction, not stopping until they reached the relative safety of the echoing, hangar-like chamber though which Metzner had led them, not an hour before. 'We must hide,' whispered Clara. Still holding Rowlands by the arm, she steered him towards what appeared to be a room-within-a-room, composed of stage flats. This walled-off space was furnished, he discovered by stumbling into the said items, with a sofa, a low table and a potted palm. A folding screen similar to the one he had lately encountered in Sybille Schönig's dressing-room completed the set—for that, he guessed, was what it was. 'In here,' hissed Clara, pulling him behind the screen. It was not a moment too soon, for just then the door of the studio burst open, and the sound of heavy boots announced the arrival of their pursuer.

As they stood, hardly daring to breathe, they could hear him crashing around, muttering under his breath. One of the trailing wires about which Metzner had warned Rowlands earlier must have tripped the man up, for there came a thud, as of someone falling, followed by a stream of invective. Fortunately for the miscreants, the risk of being found to have left his post must have outweighed the desire for revenge in the police officer's mind, for he abandoned the search after a few minutes, and the studio reverberated to the slamming of a door, followed by the sound of retreating footsteps. Only when these had died away, did Clara venture to speak. 'We must go now. It is not safe for us here at present.'

'No,' said Rowlands. It had been a stroke of luck to encounter Fräulein Pabst; it would be pushing his luck to try and talk to anyone else, while Gentz and his men were still about.

He resolved to return the next day, with photographs of the missing boys. Perhaps somebody would remember something. Already four days had passed, each day diminishing the likelihood of finding the children by a considerable factor. This was not a thought he had shared with his sister, but he was sure it must have occurred to her. But then there was the pencil... 'I don't suppose you've seen this before, have you?' he said to Clara. He took the little steel object from his pocket and handed it to her. She paused for a moment to examine it. 'I do not think so,' she said, handing it back. 'Where did you find it?' He told her. 'It's probably of no consequence,' he said. 'All I know is that it didn't belong to Sybille Schönig.'

They had reached the outer doors by way of a short vestibule that lay between it and the studio, and which provided some degree of sound-proofing, Rowlands guessed. Weather-proofing too, he thought, as—Clara having lifted the latch which kept the heavy metal doors from falling open—they stepped out into the icy blast. In the hour that they had been inside it had got much colder; a few flakes of snow announced the imminent arrival of a heavier fall. 'Dark already,' said Clara, although it made not the slightest bit of difference to Rowlands. 'You still haven't told me how you managed to persuade our policeman friend to leave his post,' he said. The girl laughed. 'I told him his boss—Inspector Gentz—was waiting for him in the Studio Manager's office and that he had sent me to conduct him there. This is a big place, as I told you, with more than ten Sound Stages, so he had little choice but to follow, if he didn't want to get himself lost. The only difficulty was in getting away from him again. Fortunately, I know my way around here a bit. I just had to choose my moment. But it wasn't easy...'

'I don't imagine it was. You've been very resourceful. I...'

'I couldn't have managed without you,' he'd been about to say, when Clara gave a muffled exclamation. 'It's them!' she said. 'The police!' Once more, Rowlands found himself bundled into a doorway. She pushed the door open, and the two of them tumbled inside. They were in another vestibule, leading to another of the sound stages, Rowlands guessed. But if Studio 4 had been silent and deserted, this building—as cavernous as the first—was full of noise and bustle. A voice which seemed, from its note of command, to belong to someone in authority, was shouting orders, while from all sides came sounds of activity: of equipment being shifted, and (he supposed) of sets being subjected to last-minute alterations.

'What's going on?' he said in an undertone to Clara—but before she could reply, there came another voice—a woman's, this time—sounding very far from pleased. 'You're late,' she said. 'You know very well the call was for three. It's a quarter-past now...'

'I... I'm sorry,' stammered Clara. 'But...'

'Well, don't just stand there gaping. Come along!'

'We'd better do as she says,' muttered Clara.

'Now, look here—what's all this about?' Rowlands's protest died in his throat. Because from across the vast echoing space came a voice he recognised: the Inspector's. He was talking to someone—Rowlands thought he recognised the other's voice as belonging to Helmut Hartmann. 'They are coming this way,' muttered Clara. 'Quick! We will go in here...'

This turned out to be a dressing-room of sorts, in which a dozen or so people were already gathered. It was hard for Rowlands to make out exactly what was being said, given that there were several conversations going on at the same time: '...so I said, "I never play tarts. French maids, yes—but never tarts..."'

'This corset's killing me...'

'If they think I'm wearing this beard,' said a man standing next to Rowlands. 'They can think again. It won't be *my* fault if I sneeze in the middle of the big scene...'

Rowlands was still more mystified when, a moment later, he found himself addressed by yet another woman—this one sounded young, but no less harassed than the first. 'No, no, no, that hat won't do at all,' she said. It was the Homburg, that Edith had insisted on his wearing. Now he found it snatched from his head, and replaced with a soft hat—a Fedora. 'That's *much* better,' said the girl, in a satisfied tone. 'All you need is this, and you'll do fine...' It was a silk scarf. Before he could protest, she had slung it deftly around his neck. 'There!' she said, and

57

walked off.

'Clara, I wish you'd tell me what all this is about...'

'Just do exactly what I do,' said Clara, who had been subjected to the same treatment as Rowlands, it transpired—except that instead of a hat, she'd been given a shawl to wear, and a dab of lip-rouge. 'Not that I ever wear the stuff,' she muttered. 'Come, we must go with the others...' And indeed, the people who'd been standing around complaining of beards and corsets were now filing out of the dressing-room into the studio—the sound stage, rather, thought Rowlands, pleased that he'd remembered this. Here, he found himself part of a crowd almost as dense as the one which had assembled the previous day to greet the new Chancellor.

An order was shouted by the man who'd been issuing orders when they'd first come in. The crowd, with Rowlands and Clara in the rear of it, shuffled forward a few paces, then came to a halt. A moment later, everything became clear, because it was then that the man, whoever he was, shouted something else. This was an order, too, and its meaning was unmistakable: '*Kamera läuft! Und, Action!*'

'Oh,' said Rowlands softly, to which Clara replied in a whisper: 'Yes. We are to be actors in this film, you and I...'

Their rôle, such as it was, seemed at first sight to be straightforward enough: they were to walk a few paces, then stand still. It was a street scene, Clara explained to Rowlands in a whisper. 'It looks like one of the streets around Nollendorfplatz,' she added, although this conveyed little to him. The crowd of which they were a part had gathered outside a theatre, said his informant. 'The name of the play is written up in lights. It is *Gefallener Engel*, which means...'

'The fallen angel,' said Rowlands.

'*Ruhe!*' At once the murmur of voices died, and absolute silence reigned, as they prepared for the next take. Given the relative simplicity of what was required, it was extraordinary how much time it took to get it right, thought Rowlands. Time and time again the director—he of the authoritative voice—sent them all back to the beginning, to do it again. Forward! Now

58

stop. Go back. Now forward again. After a few minutes of this, Rowlands began to feel a healthy respect for actors in general, and for those of the theatre especially, who had only a single chance in any given performance, to get things right. Forward. Back. Forward. Back. At last, the director pronounced himself satisfied—or so it seemed, from the general air of relief.

Now might be the time make their escape, thought Rowlands.

Because Gentz was now in conversation with him—the man Rowlands had supposed must be the director. 'I am sorry, but I cannot keep the crew waiting any longer. You will understand that, in spite of the unfortunate circumstances, this is still a working day. It is so for me, at least. And indeed for others— Herr Hartmann, in particular. It is he whom I require for the next scene...'

'I have finished with Herr Hartmann,' was the curt reply. 'You may carry on. Come, Sergeant.' Was there the faintest touch of irony in the Inspector's tone? 'We will let this gentleman get on with his work.'

No one spoke until the two policemen had left.

Then came another voice. 'I will not do it.' It was Helmut Hartmann who spoke this time. 'It is disrespectful to Miss Schönig's memory, to carry on as if nothing had happened...' The voice—a beautiful voice, rich and full, with the warm notes of a finely-tuned instrument—rose to a shout. 'I tell you, I will not do it!'

'Come, come, my dear Helmut! You know we all feel as you do. But life—and work—must go on...'

'And I say there are considerations more important than work...'

'Now, now, my dear fellow. You are naturally upset...'

A few more exchanges of the same kind followed, at the end of which it seemed as if the actor had allowed himself to be per-suaded. Now, at the command 'Aktion!' he gave an indication of what the voice could do. It was not much—just a couple of lines of dialogue—but it sent a shiver up Rowlands's spine. He was reminded of the time, years ago, at the Wigmore Hall, when he'd heard a virtuoso play Bach's Cello Suite in G...

'*Nein! Sie ist nicht hier!*' It was the crowd he was addressing,

Rowlands realised, as the voice, powerful but full of heartfelt emotion, rang out. *She is not here.* Hartmann allowed a beat of silence. Then: '*Sie ist weggegangen,*' he added, in a quieter register, as if speaking not to the crowd, but to himself. *She has gone away...* The dreadful significance of the line was all-too apparent, and the silence, when the actor had finished speaking, was profound. For a long moment, no one, in all that crowd of extras, scene-shifters, cameramen, make-up artists and technicians, moved a muscle. Then the director called 'Cut!' and there was a general relaxation of tension. 'That was remarkable,' said Rowlands softly. 'Yes. He is a great actor. One of our best,' said Clara.

It struck Rowlands that, since they had reached a lull in the proceedings, it might be a good time to leave; although there was a part of him that would have liked to stay a bit longer. It was a fascinating world into which he had accidentally strayed—a world of secrets and make-believe. Blind as he was, he was already half-beguiled by its ingenious trickery. But it was getting on for six o'clock, and Dorothy would be wondering what had become of them. If only he had a little more in the way of progress to report to her! But with that confounded policeman making himself so awkward...

'We should go,' he said. 'I'll just fetch my hat.' But as the two of them were making their way back across the studio floor towards the communal dressing-room, Clara suddenly stopped dead. '*Hilfe!*' she muttered under her breath. A moment later, Rowlands realised why. 'And what, please tell me, are *you* doing here?' demanded an irate Joachim Metzner. 'I do not remember inviting you onto the set...'

'You didn't,' said Clara. 'We... Oh, it's too complicated to explain.'

'I don't doubt it,' he said sarcastically. 'Well, you can explain it to me on the way home. I have just been told that I may go. Whether they will want me to return is something I have yet to find out,' he added. 'Come, Herr Rowlands, if you have seen enough of my place of work—or perhaps I should say, my *former* place of work—we will go and catch our train.'

'I'd be glad to,' said Rowlands, who had by now retrieved his

Homburg. 'Although it's been an interesting experience.' But as he made to follow the Metzner siblings, somebody stood in his way. 'Wait!' It was the woman who had scolded them for being late. Now, it seemed, they were to face another scolding. He turned to face her, his expression apologetic. 'Look,' he said. 'It was all my fault. You see...'

'This man is a guest of mine, Fräulein Dunst,' intervened Metzner—to his credit, Rowlands thought. 'It was I who invited him...'

'That is of no consequence. It is Herr Direktor who wishes to speak to him...'

And indeed they were joined at that moment by the great man. 'Ah, that is good, Fräulein Dunst! You have managed to track down our elusive extra...'

'I was just explaining to the lady,' said Rowlands, before he could go any further. 'That I alone am to blame for what happened...'

'Blame?' The other seemed surprised. 'Who is talking about blame? I am offering you a job. My name is Klein, by the way. You may have heard of me,' he added, with a certain complacency. 'I am directing this picture.'

'I'm afraid I don't understand. I'm here by accident... of a kind. I'm from England, you see, visiting family in Berlin, and it just so happened that...'

'You are an Englishman?' said the director, in perfect, almost accent-less, English. 'But that is delightful! It is a pity I cannot offer you a speaking rôle. However, you are exactly what I need for the final scene. It is a small, but important, part. You will allow me to test you?'

'I've never done any acting,' Rowlands confessed. 'Apart from this afternoon, of course...'

'So much the better,' was the reply. 'It will seem more natural, so. You can read a newspaper, I take it?'

'Well...' Rowlands explained that this, too, was somewhat out of his range, given that he could no longer see to read. 'But this is better and better!' cried the irrepressible Klein. 'You know what it *is* to read a newspaper, I suppose—even though you are blind?'

Rowlands agreed that this was so.

'Then you will please look when you are reading the news-paper as if you could in fact read it,' said the director. 'That is called acting, you know. I will tell you what the headlines in this newspaper say. They announce the death by suicide of a beautiful young woman... Ah! I see from your face that you know of our terrible affair already. It is a case,' said Klein, 'of Life imitating Art. Or is it the other way around, I wonder? Tomorrow morning at nine,' he added, suddenly brusque. 'This young man'—it was Metzner he meant, Rowlands guessed—'will show you where to go. Until tomorrow, then.'

'Until tomorrow,' echoed Rowlands, with the feeling that he had walked into a strange, and not altogether pleasant, dream. Nor was he the only one whose sense of reality had been put to the test, it seemed. 'I don't believe this!' said Metzner, when the great director was out of earshot. 'That Herr Klein should ask you to do a screen-test... I mean, there are people who would *kill* for this chance,' he said. 'And you are not even an actor...'

'Joe!' said his sister, in a warning tone. 'You are impolite.'

'I did not intend to be.'

Conversations was momentarily suspended as the three of them stepped out into the icy wind, in which large flakes of snow were now drifting. When Rowlands had got his breath back, after the first shock of it, he picked up the thread again: 'Why do you think,' he said, 'that your Mr Klein chose me, out of all the other extras? There must have been thirty or forty of us, and yet...'

'It was your face he liked,' said Clara. 'I heard him say so to the wardrobe mistress...'

'Fräulein Dunst,' said Metzner; adding gloomily: 'She's never liked me.'

'Well, whatever Herr Klein's reason for choosing me, it'll be a good excuse to return to the studio tomorrow,' said Rowlands, as they reached the gate. An idea struck him. 'Perhaps,' he said to the young man, 'you could enquire whether our friend here remembers seeing Billy and Walter that evening?' But the por-ter had been off work the previous Friday, he said—and in any case, he did not suppose that his colleague, old Krüger, would have let a pair of boys slip past him. Why, it'd be more than his life was worth… Which was pretty much the answer Metzner had expected, he said, as they trudged back through the snow—thicker here, than in the studio compound. 'Why are you so convinced that they were at the studio?' he said. 'Oh, I know what that young idiot Bauer said, but that was probably all rot. Boys make things up, you know…'

'Yes.' But Rowlands wasn't convinced. Young Bauer hadn't struck him as imaginative enough to make up a story like that. 'Then there's this,' he said, taking the propelling-pencil from his pocket and handing it to Metzner. Briefly, he explained how he had come by it. 'I've never seen this before in my life,' said the young man, returning it after a cursory examination. 'You say you found it in Fräulein Schönig's dressing-room? Surely that's forbidden to the public? I mean,' he stammered. 'She… she never likes to be disturbed when she's preparing…' He broke off, as if aware that he had said too much.

'You knew this morning, didn't you?' asked Rowlands gently. 'That she was dead, I mean?'

'Yes,' said Metzner. 'I knew. Everybody at the studio knew. They told us to say nothing.' He gave a bitter little laugh. 'It would be bad for business, if the news got out, they said.'

'I see.' It was as Rowlands had thought. 'And do *you* believe she killed herself?'

'I don't know. I…' Metzner swallowed convulsively, as if trying to dislodge something that was stuck in his throat. 'I didn't know her that well. How could I possibly know what was in her mind?' he burst out passionately.

'Herr Rowlands didn't mean anything by it, Joe,' said Clara. 'He only asked what you thought.'

'I know.' The youth seemed to make an effort to pull himself together. 'I'd rather not talk about it,' he said.

They had now arrived at the station. A train was just pulling in. At this hour of the day, it would be crowded with people heading back into the city after work. Conversation on anything but the most banal subjects would be impossible. One thing was increasingly clear, thought Rowlands, hanging onto the leather strap for dear life, as the train swayed and rattled its way through the suburbs—which was that Joachim Metzner had been in love with Sybille Schönig. Once you took that into account, then everything—the youth's irascible moods, his secretiveness—made sense. Even the fact, Rowlands thought, that he was hiding something. Because of that he was in no doubt at all.

Three quarters of an hour later, they arrived back at the flat in Marienburgerstrasse. 'When *will* they fix the light?' Metzner said irritably, as the three of them began the long climb up the stairs in darkness. Rowlands, who was not in the least affected by this circumstance, said nothing, preoccupied by his own thoughts—chiefly, how he was going to explain to Dorothy and Frau Metzner that he had so far failed to track down their missing children. But Clara replied: 'Why don't you say something to Herr Schmidt? This was the janitor, Rowlands gathered. 'It is his job after all...'

'It would do no good,' replied her brother wearily. 'He already hates my guts, after I complained about the stairs not being washed. I'm just a troublesome Jew, as far as he's concerned.'

'You don't know it's that.'

'Oh, but I do, dear sister. He wears the badge on his lapel, like all the rest...' Perhaps drawn by the sound of their voices, Frau Metzner now appeared on the landing above. 'Clara? Joachim?' Her voice sounded anxious. 'Yes, Mutti. I know. We're late,' said the girl, as they reached the third floor, and went inside. In the kitchen they found Dorothy, with little Victor. 'Any news?' she said. Then, seeing the look on Rowlands's face, she added dully: 'Thought not. That policeman was here again,' she went on. 'Schneider. He returned the photographs.'

'Good,' said Rowlands. 'I'll need them tomorrow.' As Frau Metzner bustled about, setting out plates and soup bowls for their supper, Rowlands explained about his unexpected move into films. 'It'll give me a good reason to go back,' he said. 'And with the photographs, it'll be easier to prompt people's memories...'

'But how do you know that they were ever there?' said his sister listlessly. She'd taken no more than a few mouthfuls of the watery vegetable soup her hostess had placed in front of her, before pushing the bowl away. 'You're only going on what those other boys said... and the fact that some actress has killed herself, or been killed, or whatever it was that happened. I don't think it adds up to anything,' she added. 'Why, they could be anywhere in the city. Anywhere at all...'

'You're right,' said Rowlands. 'It isn't much. What did Inspector Schneider have to say?' He crumbled a piece of bread and ate it, absent-mindedly. It tasted of sawdust. 'Nothing much. They're searching the canals and waste ground,' said Dorothy. 'And putting up posters with the boys' pictures on...'

'Well, that's something. Somebody might remember seeing them.'

'Perhaps.' She pushed back her chair, and stood up. 'Time for bed, Vicky,' she said to her younger son. But as the two of them moved towards the door, Rowlands remembered something. He took the little steel pencil from his pocket and held it out to her. 'Does *this* mean anything to you?'

She almost snatched it from his hand. 'Where did you get this?'

'You recognise it, do you?'

'Of course I do! It's Billy's. Look, it's got his initials scratched on it. W.F.A.—for William Frederick Ashenhurst...' Suddenly, she burst into tears. 'Oh, Billy, where are you?' she wept. 'Shh...' Rowlands gathered her into his arms. 'You're upsetting Victor,' he said. 'Don't worry, old thing, we'll find him. Because this proves he must have been at Babelsberg that night.'

5

WHEN THEY ARRIVED AT the studio next morning, a little after eight thirty, Bruno Klein was not to be found; although his office betrayed signs of recent occupancy: the smell of Havana cigars hung in the air. 'He's about somewhere,' said a languid young man, who introduced himself as the Lighting Director. On hearing that Rowlands was English, he'd obligingly switched to that language: 'I was in England two years ago, in fact,' he said. 'My aunt is married to an Englishman. She lives in Haslemere. Perhaps you know it?'

'I'm afraid not,' said Rowlands. 'But I've heard it's very...'

'We should go,' interrupted Metzner. He had, in the interim, been questioning another of the studio crew. 'Herr Klein is in the Screening Room. I will take you there.'

'No need,' said the Lighting Director cheerfully. 'I'm going that way myself, as it happens...'

'In which case, I will leave you, Herr Rowlands,' said Metzner stiffly. 'I have lost too much time today already.' With the briefest of farewells, he was gone. As far as Rowlands was concerned, it was something of a relief to have a respite from the morose young *cinéaste's* company. His new companion—Günther Herz—was altogether more approachable. 'Oh! I *adore* London,' he said as they made their way through a warren of corridors. 'In fact, if I were not about to go to New York, London would be my preferred destination...'

'You're off to New York?' said Rowlands, more out of politeness than genuine curiosity, but the young man burst suddenly into nervous laughter. 'Yes—but don't *tell* anybody, will you? It's supposed to be a secret. As soon as this picture's finished... that is, if it ever *is* finished, what with the leading lady deciding to end it all... I'll be on my way.'

Rowlands assured him that he would say nothing of Herr Herz's plan. 'Of course, I'm far from being the only one,' went on the indiscreet fellow. 'Just about everyone who works at the studio is waiting to see which way the cat jumps before deciding whether or not they have a future here. Especially the Jews,' he added casually. 'Not that I have anything to worry about in that respect,' he added.

'Fortunate for you,' murmured Rowlands.

They had by now reached the Screening Room—entrance to which was through a set of heavy doors—edged with rubber, to muffle sound. 'Be careful—it's dark,' whispered Herz, obviously unaware that this hardly mattered to Rowlands. Once inside, they stood still for a moment, while the Lighting Director located his employer—presumably with the aid of the light cast by the screen, for he gave a grunt of recognition, and touched Rowlands on the shoulder, by way of getting him to follow.

But at that moment there came a voice—a woman's voice—clear, but with a slight huskiness which softened its crystalline quality. '*Musst du gehen?*'

'*Ich muss gehen.*' The voice of a man about to depart: bored, and impatient. Helmut Hartmann. Then came the woman's voice again: '*Wann kommst du zurück?*' It was a disembodied voice, Rowlands realised, in the same moment. It hung like an auditory ghost upon the air.

'The last scene she ever played,' murmured Günther Herz.

'*Wer ist da?*' barked a voice Rowlands recognised as Bruno Klein's; then: 'Oh, it's you, Herr Rowlands. I shall be with you in a few minutes. 'And what do *you* want?' This, reverting to German, was addressed to Herz. 'Didn't I say I wasn't to be disturbed for the next hour?'

'My apologies, Herr *Direktor*,' said Herz. 'The fact is, a small technical problem has arisen with the lighting rig for the crowd scene. They have rigged blue gels instead of yellow, and it is a daylight scene...'

'Then you must see that it is changed before we shoot,' said Klein. 'But never mind about that now. What I want is for you to set up the lighting for Herr Rowlands's screen-test.'

'Yes, Herr Klein. But you see...'

'Well, don't just stand there!' commanded the director. 'Studio 3 is free at the moment, is it not?'

'Yes, Herr *Direktor*.'

'Then get to it,' said Klein. 'We will be along in a few minutes. That fellow is an idiot,' he added, in English, to Rowlands, as the unhappy Herz went off to do his bidding. 'But he is also good at his job, which is why I keep him. Why don't you come and sit down?' he went on, in a more genial tone. 'I will be finished here very soon.' Rowlands accordingly felt his way along the backs of the seats until he reached the middle of the row, where Klein was sitting. 'I realise that this will not mean very much to you,' the director continued, as the other sat down. 'But I wanted to take look at the rushes, as we call them, before I start the day's filming.'

'I'm not really in a position to appreciate Fräulein Schönig's talents fully,' said Rowlands. 'But I can appreciate her voice—and Herr Hartmann's too, if it comes to that.' The director laughed. 'I knew you were an extraordinary chap the minute I set eyes on you,' he said. 'It's all there in your face. Such an interesting face,' he added. 'Ah! This is the part I wanted to see,' he went on, signalling to the projectionist in his booth to run the scene once more. 'It was filmed the day of Sybille's death—so you see it is really the last footage we have of her...'

'I wish I could see it,' said Rowlands. 'Yes, it's a pity you can't,' was the reply, as the reel began to whirr, and a series of clicks, stops, and starts announced that the film was about to begin. 'She really had something, our Sybille. It wasn't her acting ability, as such—I've worked with far better—but something to do with her screen presence. A luminosity. All I had to do was point the camera at her, and she did the rest... There!' he said softly, as—Rowlands surmised—the actress's face appeared on the screen. 'Such expressive eyes she had! You'd almost have thought there was a soul behind them...'

'You didn't like her?'

Again, Klein laughed. 'She was like all the rest of her kind,' he said. 'Interested in one person only: herself. A hard little thing. But,' he went on, as the woman on the screen began to speak, 'to look at her, you'd have thought an angel had come down

69

from Heaven to walk about on Earth...'

'To listen to her, too,' said Rowlands. 'A great loss to the studio, too, I imagine?'

'Indeed. It is not easy, in these times, to make films... or at least, not the kind of films I want to make,' said Klein. 'So, yes, Sybille's death will make a great difference to the studio. Perhaps, in fact, it will be the end,' he added in a meditative tone. 'Yes, I think it is over, all of this.'

Both were silent a while, as the film played on, Rowlands making what he could of it. The scene that he was listening to concerned a quarrel between lovers. A man's voice—Hartmann's—angry and accusing, was followed by a woman's—Schönig's—first placating, then seducing. The scene had reached the moment Rowlands recognised as the one where he'd come in. *'Müssen Sie gehen?'* Must you go? Then Hartmann: *'Ich muss gehen.'* I must. And the woman's heartfelt reply: *'Wann kommst du zurück?'* When will you return? Although it was she who would not return, thought Rowlands.

Klein must have signalled again to the projectionist, for the reel whirred to an abrupt end. 'I've seen enough,' he said to Rowlands. He got to his feet. 'Fortunately, Sybille was not only a competent actress, but a very professional one. She didn't often make mistakes. Which is just as well,' he said, as the two of them began to walk back along the aisle that led between the rows of seats. 'Since there can be no re-takes...'

'Will you be able to finish the film without her?' asked Rowlands, whose knowledge of the process of film-making was far from extensive. 'It would have been better, certainly, if what happened had not happened,' was the dry response. 'But we have enough footage in the can to make something—with a little editing—that will pass. That is why I must shoot the final scene that will explain what has happened to my "Angel"... Since we cannot *see* her final hour, we must learn of it some other way. That is where you come in.'

'The newspaper headline.'

'Precisely. That, and a close-up of your face...'

'What about Herr Hartmann?' said Rowlands. 'Shouldn't *he* appear in the closing scene?'

70

'Allow me to direct my film in my own way,' replied the director. 'Helmut's is not the face with which I wish to close my picture. Yours is. Now let us see what that imbecile Herz has set up for us in the way of lighting...'

Emerging from the screening room, they began walking in the direction of Studio 3. A thought occurred to Rowlands. He drew the photographs from his pocket. 'I wonder,' he said, 'if with your eye for faces, you remember having seen either of these?'

Klein slowed his pace a moment, as he looked at the snaps. 'A handsome young man, this one,' he remarked. 'He knows it, too. The other, not so good-looking, but full of feeling. And no, I have not seen either of these boys. What is it that they have done?'

'I think,' said Rowlands, 'that they might have witnessed a murder.'

'You are talking of Sybille's murder, I presume? Oh yes, I am sure it *was* murder,' he added softly. 'Women like Sybille do not kill themselves for no reason at all. Nor do they employ such a method. Pills, perhaps. Or they turn on the gas... But a gun to the head? No.'

Before Rowlands could get the director to expand on this interesting topic, there came an interruption. The smart click of boot-heels sounded along the corridor. It didn't take very great deductive skills to guess that those approaching were soldiers. The marching feet came to a halt. *'Heil Hitler!'* said a voice; then: *'Herr Klein. Genau der Mann den ich sehen wollte!'* Just the man I wanted to see. Klein murmured a reply—omitting, Rowlands could not fail to notice, the prescribed greeting. Then he said in English: 'Let me present Herr Rowlands. He is visiting our studios. Herr Rowlands, this is Obersturmführer von Fritsch.'

'So,' said the SS officer, when salutations had been exchanged. 'What brings you to our fine city?'

'Well...' began Rowlands; but Klein answered for him: 'Herr Rowlands has kindly offered to lend his services as an actor for the last scene of *Fallen Angel*. We are on our way to the studio now,' he added pointedly. But von Fritsch seemed oblivious to the hint. 'Then you will allow me to accompany you,' he said. 'You know the Minister takes a special interest in your work.'

'As you wish,' said Klein, and the three of them, with the Obersturmführer's two subordinates following behind, began to walk back along the corridor, von Fritsch talking all the time. 'How is the film progressing? he said, reverting to German. 'You have not been too much held up by recent events, I hope?'

'Sybille Schönig's death, you mean?' replied the director drily. 'Thank you, we are managing to carry on.'

'Excellent. I know the Minister will want an early screening.'

'Of course, there is still quite a bit to do,' said Klein hastily. 'The film is only at rough-cut stage. It will not be ready for weeks...'

'That is no matter. The Minister, as you know, understands the artistic process. He will be happy to see what you have done so far.' They had reached the door of Studio 3. 'We go in here,' said Klein. 'I am afraid I am pressed for time, or I would ask you to stay longer.'

'Very well,' said von Fritsch. 'But remember what I have said. The Minister is in a hurry to see how your film is going. He hopes it will be everything he could wish it to be.'

Klein gave an uneasy laugh. 'I can only do my best, Obersturmführer...'

'I am sure of it. And you would want your film to express the very best of our German culture. This is something which concerns the Minister a great deal,' he added silkily. 'He would not wish the world to see anything less.' When Klein said nothing, the SS man turned to Rowlands. 'I hope you will enjoy the rest of your stay in Berlin,' he said. 'Also that you will convey good things about us to your friends at home. Our Führer is a great admirer of your country.'

There was nothing to say to this, and so Rowlands merely nodded. It was an effort to smile, and he gave up the attempt.

'One more thing, Herr Klein...' The Obersturmführer's tone, by contrast with his previous affability, was cold. 'I must remind you that you are first and foremost an employee of UFA, and that the studio itself is the property of the Reichsfilmkammer. You are therefore obliged to make films of which the Reich Minister would approve. I tell you this for your own good.'

'That sounded remarkably like a threat,' said Rowlands, when at last von Fritsch had gone, taking his brace of Stormtroopers with him.

'Believe me, Herr Rowlands, that is not the worst of it,' said Bruno Klein. 'If these people confined themselves to empty threats, then...' He broke off. 'But I have already said more than I should. If you will please take a seat... There is chair in front of you. Then we can begin.'

Given that all Rowlands had to do was sit at a table—'it will be a café table, when we come to shoot,' said Klein—unfold a newspaper, read (or make a pretence of reading) the newspaper, and having read it, gaze off into space, as if reflecting on what he had read, it took almost two hours to achieve what the director had in mind. Rowlands was reminded of the time, some years before, when he had sat for his portrait, and there had been the same meticulous attention to detail on the part of the artist—only on that occasion, all he'd had to do was sit as still as possible. As on that earlier foray into the world of art, he had discovered that being filmed was an exacting process, requiring the utmost concentration. It wasn't enough just to sit, and let one's thoughts drift.

'You look worried, Herr Rowlands,' Klein had said at one point. 'Please try not to think of anything which makes you look worried...' He had, indeed, been thinking about Billy. Where was the child at that moment? Was it conceivable, after all this time, that he and Walter Metzner were still alive? He composed his features into a bland mask. 'Is that better?'

'Much better. Now, if you will pick up the newspaper once more...' He did so. 'Good. Now unfold it.' The fact that no bodies had yet been found was a good sign, thought Rowlands, keeping his face expressionless. 'Now look towards the light...' This he could do with ease; the little vision he had left allowing him to distinguish between dark and light. A strong light, such as the one currently trained on his face, was still easier to perceive. 'Just so. Hold it like that. You are thinking about this woman you have never met, except through the medium of the cinema screen. She is Everywoman to you... A beautiful, unattainable vision. Now she is dead. You think of this, and of life's impermanence...'

A long moment passed. 'Cut!' said the director. 'We will stop there, I think. You have worked hard today, Herr Rowlands,' the director went on; although it seemed to Rowlands that he had done nothing at all. 'If the screen-test proves satisfactory, I will want you to start tomorrow morning—if that will not be inconvenient for you?'

'Well,' began Rowlands, for whom it certainly was inconvenient. 'I'm not sure...' But at that moment, the door to the studio was flung open and someone came rushing in. 'Ah, Bruno! I've been looking for you everywhere... I have to talk to you.' He broke off, evidently having realised they were not alone. 'Helmut, this is Herr Rowlands,' said Bruno Klein, in English. 'He will be Man at Table in the final scene.' The actor paid no attention to what might have been intended as a warning to curb his indiscretion, but went on, in the same agitated tone as before: 'I tell you, what you're asking is impossible.' *Unmöglich.* 'To expect me to give a good performance when she... when Sybille...' At the mention of the dead actress's name, Klein's affable manner underwent a change. 'We can't talk now. Come to my office later...'

It occurred to Rowlands that it was his presence which was creating the awkwardness between the two men—a situation he was in no hurry to resolve. 'Herr Hartmann, isn't it?' he said innocently. 'I was lucky enough to be present during yesterday's shooting. The scene outside the theatre,' he prompted, when there was no reply. 'I thought you were very good.'

'Thank you,' said Hartmann stiffly. His accent, when speaking English, was more pronounced than Klein's, which had an American twang. 'So you were there yesterday, were you?'

'Well, only as an extra,' said Rowlands modestly. 'My first experience of being in a film. But I found it a fascinating one.'

'You thought my acting good, you say?'

'Rath*er.*'

'I was terrible,' said Hartmann flatly. 'The whole scene was terrible.'

'Helmut...'

'You know it is true! It is impossible, what you are trying to do. Without Sybille...'

'I said we would discuss this later,' said Klein in a warning voice. A brief, strained, pause ensued. 'I must be getting along,' said Rowlands. He held out his hand. 'Goodbye, Herr Klein.'

They shook hands. 'Until tomorrow,' said Klein.

'It was a privilege to meet you, Herr Hartmann,' said Rowlands to the actor. 'And I *did* enjoy your performance yesterday...'

'You are too kind,' said Hartmann indifferently. It was obvious that his mind was otherwise engaged. 'Oh, by the way,' said Rowlands, as if he had just thought of it, 'I don't suppose you've seen either of these boys before?' He took the photographs from his pocket and held them out towards Hartmann. There was a startled pause. Then Hartmann said: 'No, I am afraid I have not.' Rowlands couldn't have said what it was in his tone of voice that convinced him the man was lying.

Having refused Klein's suggestion of summoning a runner to guide him, Rowlands made his way back to the main gate. Passing Sybille Schönig's dressing-room, he heard voices. One of them was Greta Pabst's; he'd have known her throaty growl anywhere. '*Dummkopf!*' It sounded as if she was taking somebody to task. '*Ich hab dir schon hundertmal gesagt...*' I've told you a hundred times.

The reply was said in such a low voice that Rowlands could hardly make it out. '*Ich... Ich...*' He knocked, then opened the door. 'Fraulein Pabst? I wonder if I might have a word?'

'Herr Rowlands!' She sounded taken aback; then quickly recovered her *sang-froid*. 'Of course. Come in.'

'But you've got company,' said Rowlands, as if he had just realised this. 'Perhaps you'd rather I came back some other time?'

'*Nein, nein.* That will not be necessary. There is only Fritzi, and he does not count for anything, do you, *mein Schatz?*' The other occupant of the dressing-room giggled nervously, at being thus addressed. 'Fritzi is our *Handlanger...* I don't know how you say this in English...'

'Handyman,' said Rowlands.

'Exactly!' Fräulein Pabst gave a little bark of laughter. 'You know, Herr Rowlands, I believe your German is quite good...'

'I learned most of my German during the War.'

'Ah, yes. The War,' said Greta Pabst. 'Fritzi fought in the War, too—did you not, *Schatz*? He was at the Messines Ridge when they set off the mines, the British. He was blown clean out of his clothes by the first explosion. They found him next morning, crawling around stark naked in the hole that was left by the blast. He was deaf in one ear and and all his hair was burnt off. Eighteen years old, he was—a child. He is a child still, you might say... They never found the rest of your platoon, did they, *Schatz*?' she added, addressing the handyman. 'Or only pieces of them. A hand. A foot. Fritzi doesn't remember anything about it, he says. Only waking up in the field hospital, in new pyjamas. He remembers *that*, don't you?'

The man remained mute. 'He doesn't understand English,' she said to Rowlands. 'So you can speak freely...'

'When we last met,' said Rowlands, 'you were kind enough to say that you would ask around and see if anyone at the studio had seen the boys—that is, my nephew and his cousin—before they went missing last Friday.' Once again, he produced the photographs. 'I thought these might be of some help. Somebody might remember,' he added, trying not to sound as hopeless as he felt. Greta Pabst took the photographs from him. 'I know this boy,' she said, after a moment. 'The little Jew.' Then, as Rowlands felt his hopes begin to rise, she added: 'But I did not see him on Friday. He has been to the studios before, I think. With one of the runners. A thin, dark young man, with a scowling face...'

'His brother,' said Rowlands.

'*Ja*, you can see the likeness.'

'Can you remember when it was that you saw him last?' Rowlands wondered why Metzner had made no mention of this earlier visit. 'I couldn't say, exactly,' was the reply. 'Six weeks ago, perhaps? My Sybille had many visitors, you understand. I can't recall the particulars of every one... *Hallo! Was machst du?*' This was to Fritzi, who—unbeknown to Rowlands—had crept closer, in order to see what Fräulein Pabst was looking at

76

with such interest.

Now he snatched the photographs out of her hand, and flung them violently away—or so Rowlands gathered from the ensuing fracas. '*Fritzi! Was machst du?*' cried Greta Pabst again; then, apologetically, to Rowlands: 'He has these fits, you understand... He doesn't know what he is doing, do you, *mein Schatz?*'

But it seemed to Rowlands that, on the contrary, the handyman knew exactly what he was doing. '*Ich habe sie nicht gesehen!*' he shouted. He sounded terrified, Rowlands thought. 'He says he has not seen them...'

'Yes,' said Rowlands. 'I gathered that.'

'*Ich habe sie nicht gesehen!*' cried the man again. 'Nobody says you did, you poor fool,' said the dresser, bending, with a little grunt of effort, to pick up the fallen photographs. 'I wonder what has upset him so?'

What was obvious to Rowlands was that—despite his anguished denial—Fritzi *had* seen the boys, at some time on that fateful Friday night. He felt a quickening of excitement. This was progress at last! But what he needed was confirmation that his suspicion was correct. 'Could you ask him what he was doing on Friday evening?' he said to the woman.

'I can try. But you see for yourself how it is.' She addressed a gruff enquiry to the handyman: '*Fritzi, Schatz. Wo warst du am letzten Freitag?*'

But his response was merely to repeat what he had said before: '*Ich habe sie nicht gesehen...*' Nothing more could be got out of him, and a moment later, he scuttled away, dragging his mop and bucket with him. Which was frustrating, thought Rowlands, because this was the closest to a sighting of the boys they'd had so far.

'Can *you* give me an idea of where he might have been that night?' he said to Fräulein Pabst. 'Fritzi? He'd have been sweeping up in the studio—or washing the floor in one of the corridors, perhaps. It's hard to say. Why? Do you really think he saw them?'

'I'd bet my life on it.'

'I hope it will not come to that,' she said sharply.

6

HE'D ARRANGED TO MEET Dorothy at Anhalter Bahnhof at noon; from there they were to go the the police station at the Alexanderplatz. He checked the braille face of his watch. He was already late, he realised. But at the station, there was another hold-up. He'd got off the train with his usual caution, and was making his way towards the exit with as much despatch as possible, in the wake of a slowly moving crowd of his fellow passengers, when a voice barked: *'Papiere!'* A hand was thrust in front of him; when he did not at once respond, a face brought itself close to his. He got a whiff of beer and garlic sausage. *'Papiere!'* the man said again. Not the stationmaster, Rowlands guessed, but some other kind of official... He fumbled for his passport. *'Schnell! Schnell!'*

Suddenly, Rowlands was overcome with fury. *'Ich bin Engländer,'* he said coldly, handing the document to the man. But if he had hoped to quell the other's aggressive self-importance by this announcement, he was disappointed. 'Komm!' snapped the official. He must have gestured to Rowlands to follow, because a moment later he repeated the injunction, his tone ever more impatient. *'Schnell! Schnell!'*

Since he was still in possession of Rowlands's passport, the latter had little choice but to do as he was told. The platform was crowded with arriving and departing passengers, and it was hard to keep from blundering into people. Once, he walked into a protruding barrier, and struck himself a painful blow on the hip. Having lost all sense of his direction, he was unable to suppress a feeling of rising panic. Where was the man taking him, for God's sake? But just then he heard a familiar voice: 'Fred? *There* you are, at last! I was beginning to worry...'

'Hello, Dottie.' He'd never been more relieved to see her.

'Sorry you've had to wait. I got a bit held up…' Before he could explain further, he felt a sharp tap on his shoulder. The petty official was evidently losing patience. *'Komm!'* the man said again. 'What's all this about?' said Dorothy. 'You haven't got yourself arrested, surely?'

'I've no idea. He hasn't explained. Just demanded my papers, and rushed off…'

'Let me talk to him. *Was ist das Problem?'* she said to the official, in an emollient tone that was new to Rowlands. His sister was usually the first to take up arms, when officialdom overstepped the mark. The man's reply was grudging—but he did at least give some explanation: *'Ich muss alle Papiere von Ausländern überprüfen…'*

'He says he needs to check all papers…'

'…belonging to foreigners. I got that.'

'It's a new directive, apparently,' said Dorothy, after another exchange with the official. 'From the new administration,' she added grimly. 'All foreigners' passports to be checked, in case of forgeries…'

'You mean there are people who'd actually go to such lengths to come here?'

'Don't joke,' she muttered. 'They don't like jokes—especially not against the new lot.' She turned again to the S.A. man—if that was what he was. *'Wir können nicht warten,'* she said sweetly. We cannot wait. 'We have to be at the police station very soon. We have an interview with Inspector Schneider, concerning the latest child kidnappings. I am sure,' she added, in her most cajoling tone, 'that you would not want to be responsible for holding up an important police investigation.'

'You did well,' said Rowlands, when both were safely on board the tram to Alexanderplatz. 'I don't think I've ever heard you be so conciliatory.'

'You have to know how to handle these people,' said Dorothy. 'Now tell me—what have you found out? I know you've found out *something*. I can see it in your face. Is it about the boys?'

'I think they've been seen,' said Rowlands. 'By at least one witness—perhaps two. But I'm going to have the devil's own job to prove it…' As the tram rattled through the cobbled streets, he told her what he had learned thus far. 'It isn't much,' he concluded apologetically. 'But...'

'It's a lot more than those pigheaded policemen have managed,' she said. 'Keep your voice down,' said her brother in an undertone. 'Some of them understand English, you know...'

'I don't give a damn,' said Dorothy, but she lowered her voice nonetheless. They were now passing along Königstrasse, and the Berlin City Hall—or so Rowlands learned from his sister's angry commentary. 'It's absolutely *covered* in their horrible flags,' she muttered. 'Great blood-red things, the size of a bedsheet, with a black *Hakenkreuz* on a white circle. The whole city's festooned with them. You're lucky you can't see them, Fred...'

'Very lucky,' he said drily.

At the police station, they were made to wait while the desk-sergeant went slowly through a register, presumably to check whether the names they had given him tallied with those recorded there. Satisfied at last, he gave an order, and they were conducted by another officer to Schneider's office. He, too, kept them waiting a few minutes, while he finished leafing through some papers. 'Ah, Frau Ashenhurst... and Herr Rowlands, is it not?' the Inspector said at last. 'Sit down, please. I have not much time to spare. So many things demand my attention.'

'Of course,' said Rowlands, sensing an imminent outburst from his sister. 'But Inspector Gentz suggested...'

'Inspector Gentz,' interrupted the other man, 'is... how do you say this? *Altmodisch...*'

'Old-fashioned.'

'Thank you. Yes, he is *old-fashioned* in his methods.' Schneider gave a condescending laugh. 'We like to think we are a little more up-to-date...'

'"We"?' said Rowlands. ('That wiped the smile off his face,' said Dorothy afterwards.) 'You will be aware, Herr Rowlands,' said Schneider coldly, 'that, as of last Monday, we have a new government. Our Führer will not tolerate inefficiency. Nor the outmoded methods of the past. That is what I meant.' Now it was Dorothy's turn to be placatory. 'All my brother wanted to ask,' she put in quickly, 'was what progress there had been on

81

the case.'

'Progress. Yes, there has been progress. Another body has been found in the canal.' Then, evidently gratified by their shocked response, the police inspector went on: 'But not, I think, that of either your son, Frau Ashenhurst, nor that of the Metzner boy. *This* boy was older. His throat had been cut,' he added, with what seemed to Rowlands an unnecessary relish. 'Not the method employed with all the others. So you see, we are making some progress, as you say—if only in eliminating the unlikely. Now, you see, I have much to do, and so...'

'I think the boys were last seen at the Babelsberg studios,' said Rowlands. The only sign that Schneider had heard him was that he stopped shuffling the papers on his desk. 'I've spoken to a witness.'

'Indeed? And who might that be?'

'A man called Fritzi. I don't know his other name. He's the studio's handyman. He denies seeing the boys, but I'm certain...'

'He *denies* seeing them, you say?' There was a sarcastic edge to the other man's voice. 'That, surely, would suggest that he did *not* see them...'

'He's lying,' said Rowlands. 'I think he's afraid...'

'You appear to *think* a great deal, Herr Rowlands,' said Schneider. 'Unfortunately, it does not seem to me that your thoughts bear any relation to the facts of this case. We have a murderer in Berlin. That is one fact. He kills boys and young men. That is another. The fact that your nephew and his little Jewish friend have not yet been found does not, alas, mean that they have escaped this fate. No amount of *thinking* that they have been seen by some employee of the studio can change that fact, I am afraid...'

'I believe,' said Rowlands deliberately, 'that they witnessed Sybille Schönig's murder.'

'It was suicide,' said Schneider, too quickly.

'Perhaps. But regardless of whether it was murder or suicide, I believe the boys were there.'

'And what evidence do you have to support this theory?'

'This.' Rowlands took out the propelling-pencil from his jacket pocket, and held it out towards the policeman. 'It belonged

82

to my nephew. His initials are scratched on it. And it was found in Fräulein Schönig's dressing-room.'

'All this proves nothing.' But for the first time, Schneider sounded uncertain. 'It might have been dropped there at any time.'

'But it was not. My nephew had never set foot in the studio before. You must agree,' said Rowlands, adopting his most emollient tone, 'that it's worth investigating if there's a connection with the Schönig case?'

'I am not in charge of the Schönig case,' snapped the other. 'It is your friend, Inspector Gentz, who is looking into that.' He seemed lost in thought a moment. 'I might, as you suggest, investigate this a little further,' he said grudgingly. 'It can do no harm, I suppose.'

'Thank you,' said Rowlands. He touched Dorothy on the arm. 'We should go. I am sure we have taken up enough of Inspector Schneider's time already.'

'Well, that was a fat lot of good!' said Dorothy, as they left the building, and crossed the cobbled yard that lay between it and the street. 'I don't think we did too badly,' said her brother mildly. 'He really sat up when I mentioned the Babelsberg case...'

'Only because he thinks the death of some actress is of more importance than finding the boys...'

'Exactly. If he thinks there's a connection, it might make him take the whole thing more seriously...'

'Perhaps.' She did not sound convinced. 'I'm not going back to the flat just yet,' she went on, as they emerged onto the bustling city square.

'You must feel like a change of air.'

'It's not that. Well,' she amended, 'it *is* partly that. I feel as if I haven't been outside the place since last Friday. But quite apart from that, I want to *do* something. I can't just sit there, and wait for Billy to turn up. If he ever *does* turn up,' she added in a small voice. 'Now, there's no need to talk like that...' he began, but she cut across him. 'I keep thinking that he might be hurt,' she said. 'Or frightened. And I'm not there to comfort him...'

'There's no sense in tormenting yourself.'

'I know. Which is why I have to do something to stop myself

from thinking. Last time the police called at the the flat, they left one of their flyers—with Billy and Walter's photographs on it. I've had some more printed for distributing around the neighbourhood. I thought that as I'd done the streets nearest the apartment...'

'You'd widen the circle,' he finished for her. 'Yes. I thought I'd start with the "Alex", because all the trams go through here, and then move to the city centre...'

'I'll go with you,' said Rowlands. 'It'll be a chance for me to get to know the place a bit better. So far I've seen more of the film studios than I have of Berlin.' He was glad of his sister's arm as they crossed the busy street which made up one side of the square. Trams, buses, motorcars and goods lorries roared past, at what seemed to him a reckless speed, and with little regard for the traffic hurtling in the opposite direction. But that, he told himself, was doubtless because he was a stranger here. Above the pervasive stink of motor-oil and petrol fumes, there wafted from the nearby restaurants other, more agreeable, smells—of *sauerkraut*, *kartoffelsalat*, and the ubiquitous garlic sausage. Rowlands's mouth began to water. It was long past lunchtime.

At once he reproached himself for thinking of such quotidian matters when he should have had his mind on the task in hand. But then Dorothy said: 'Let's go in here. I could do with something to eat, and they might agree to put up a poster.'

It was a rough kind of place, to judge from the clientele; the harsh Berlin accent was much in evidence, as was the acrid smell of cheap tobacco—but the food was plain and plentiful, and both were glad of the warming properties of the meatballs in caper sauce which was the day's 'special'. 'I'm afraid the coffee's not very good,' said Dorothy, when they'd eaten their fill. 'It never is here—unless you can afford the real thing.'

'At least it's hot.'

Having persuaded the manageress of the Konzert Café to put a poster in her shop-window, they put up another on the 'Litfuß column' in the middle of the square. 'What does it actually say?' asked Rowlands, meaning the poster, not the column, although this—a tall pillar on which news items and advertisements could be displayed for the edification of the public, and of which examples were to be found all over Berlin—seemed to him a good idea, and one he would like to see adopted in his native city. 'It says: "Have You Seen These Boys?"—in German, of course, and with the photographs of Billy and Walter underneath. Then: "Information to Box No. 7578, Berlin Alexanderplatz, and the police station telephone number.'

'Does it mention a reward?'

'No. I hadn't thought of that. Do you think it should?'

'It's one way of getting people to pick up the telephone.'

'What do you think we should offer?'

'How much can we scrape together between us? A hundred marks?'

'Yes. But the police...'

'Forget the police,' he said. 'This is our show, now. Have you got a pencil handy?'

'No. But you have.'

'So I have.' He took the little propelling-pencil from his pocket and gave it to her. 'Go on, he said. 'Write "100 RM BELOHNUNG" as large as you can, and see what that brings.'

From Alexanderplatz they walked back down Königstrasse, passing the Red Town Hall, so called because of the colour of its bricks, but now the opposite of 'Red' with regard to its political affiliation. 'Unless you count the fact that their banners are red,' said Dorothy acidly. He'd asked her to describe things as they went along, since this was the only way he'd get to 'see' the city. What he could *hear* of it seemed lively enough, with the usual racket of goods vans—some of them horse-drawn—mingling with the shouts of street traders, the roar of motor engines, and the screeching of brakes from passing trams. It was still very cold.

Outside the Town Hall, there was another Litfuß column; they stopped to put up a poster, but before they could do so, a man came out of the building, and shouted that it was forbidden to post bills on government property. A spirited exchange of views between Dorothy and this official followed, during which Dorothy pointed out that the government didn't yet control advertising and that members of the public were free

85

to put up what posters they liked, and the irate man replied that posters with a political message were prohibited under the new rules... 'If you can see anything "political" about *that*,' said Dorothy, brandishing the poster under his nose. 'You're welcome to tear it down...'

At which the man went off, muttering under his breath.

'I'm afraid your poster probably *will* be torn down,' said Rowlands.

'Perhaps,' said his sister. 'But a few people might see it before then. They're not all bad, the Berliners, you know.'

'I never supposed they were.'

'Although what Viktor would have made of *this* crowd, I can't imagine,' she went on, as they crossed the bridge over the river. 'He was very active during the Revolution, you know. It's the reason he had to leave Berlin.'

'I thought it must have been something of the kind,' said Rowlands. He had been fond of Dorothy's late husband. Even the fact that he was a German hadn't got in the way of their friendship for very long. 'I was against the War from the beginning,' Viktor Lehmann had said. 'All we Communists were. We saw it as a capitalist war, to enrich the profiteers at the expense of the working man...'

'I miss him, you know,' said Dorothy. 'Although Jack's been very good to me...'

'Viktor was a fine man.'

'It's because of him that I wanted to bring the boys to Berlin,' she said. 'I thought they ought to see what it was like for him when he was their age. Growing up in a cramped workers' tenement, with barely enough money for food and clothes, while less than a mile away, the rich were living off the fat of the land...' Her voice had risen, as always when she was carried away by her feelings, and he laid a cautionary hand on her arm. 'All right,' he said. 'No need to get on your soapbox. It wasn't so easy for us, either.'

'At least Dad was in work,' she said. But she seemed content to let it go. There was a time, Rowlands thought, when she'd have taken him to task for what she saw as his acquiescence to a corrupt system. 'The trouble with you, Fred, is you accept things the way they are,' she'd railed at him, on one such occasion. '*I want to change things...*' Perhaps Jack had had a steadying influence, he thought.

They passed in front of the Royal Palace—'where the Kaiser lived, until he did a bunk,' said Dorothy—and came out into a wide street, lined with trees, and with a double row of trees lining a central pavement. 'Unter den Linden. It means "under the lime-trees." It's supposed to be beautiful in the summer.'

'I imagine it must smell of lime-blossom.' It didn't smell of much at that moment except petrol fumes and horse-dung. But at least the wind had dropped. They strolled on. 'Just imagine it full of workers with their red flags,' said Dorothy. 'All cheering for Liebknecht and Rosa Luxemburg...'

'It must have been quite a sight,' said Rowlands, hearing the catch in his sister's voice as she spoke of her murdered heroine. He remembered her coming in from work that day—it must have been January 1919—brandishing the *Mirror* in his face, although she must have known he wouldn't be able to read what was written there. 'They've killed her,' she'd said, her voice trembling with fury. 'The filthy swine. They've killed her.'

They turned down Friedrichstrasse. This, to judge from the volume of traffic which hurtled along it, was another broad boulevard, with shops and restaurants on either side. From up ahead came the shrill blast of a steam engine's whistle. There must be a station nearby, thought Rowlands—a supposition confirmed a moment later by his sister. 'I thought we'd go this way,' she said. 'We can put up some posters at Friedrichstrasse Bahnhof.'

Like most of the city's principal stations, this one was elevated above the street, its arriving and departing trains adding their noise and smoke to the general confusion. Pushing their way through the crowd, the two of them climbed the stairs which led to the platforms, under the great glass canopy—which, built only a few years before, was considered the height of modernity, Dorothy said. Here, after some discussion (since bill-sticking was strictly forbidden, he told them) they persuaded the station master to put up a poster on each of the platforms. 'Which will mean everyone coming or going from the city centre will see it,' said Dorothy, with some satisfaction.

After this small triumph, they continued along the street, reaching the junction with Liepzigerstrasse after a few minutes. Here, the crowd was denser—this being one of the city's main shopping streets. Expensively-scented women in fur coats dived in and out of its emporia, in search of gloves, hats, high-heeled shoes, and other essentials of the fashionable life. Whatever the privations currently being endured by the city's less affluent citizens, here, at least, prosperity reigned. 'What a hideous hat!' was Dorothy's only comment, as they trudged past the enormous plate-glass windows of Tietz's department store. 'Just as well I can't afford these prices...'

A few yards further on, she came to a halt, outside what was obviously a cake-shop, to judge from the enticing smells of *Pfannkuchen* and coffee that drifted from within. 'Wait for me here,' she said. 'I'll just be a moment.' After a minute or so, she emerged once more. 'I asked then to put up a poster in the window. The woman behind the counter had a kind face,' she said. 'And it's a popular place. Lots of women go there, after their shopping. Some of them will be mothers too,' she said sadly. 'I keep seeing him, you know. Everywhere I look. I'll see a boy of the right sort of age, with dark hair, and I'll think it's him. Only it never is...'

He gave her hand a squeeze. 'Never fear,' he said. 'We'll find him.'

'Will we?'

'Of course.' He smiled, although he didn't feel much like smiling. 'Edith says I'm awfully good at finding things—for a blind man.'

'How *is* Edith?'

'She's well,' he said. 'At least, she was when I left her...'

'It was good of her to let you come,' said Dorothy. 'Oh, it was she who suggested it...' he began, when his sister laid a warning hand on his arm. 'Let's cross over,' she said. 'They're touchy about people walking too close to their precious Chancellery.'

Because they had by now reached the intersection with Wilhelmstrasse, along which he and Joachim had come, the night of Rowlands's arrival in the city. It was quieter now, although there were still crowds of people—more even than in the busy shopping streets. And indeed, there seemed to be a good deal of jostling and shouting going on outside the building where the newly-elected Reich Chancellor was in residence. An opportunistic street trader, who had set up his stall selling postcards of the Führer, was being moved on. 'They like any excuse for a row, these people,' muttered Dorothy. 'Let's just keep walking, shall we? Don't hurry.'

'I wasn't going to.' Rowlands wondered a little at her reasons for choosing this particular street, since it consisted mainly of government buildings, from what he could gather, with no shops or restaurants in sight; but then she said: 'I thought as you'd come all this way, you might like to visit the Brandenburg Gate. It's really quite impressive. A sort of gigantic version of Marble Arch.' Leaving the mob of vociferous Brownshirts behind, they emerged once more onto Unter den Linden. A few more steps brought them within sight of the monument. 'I don't believe it!' said Dorothy in a disgusted tone. 'They've hung their rotten flags between all the pillars...'

'I suppose one might have expected it.'

'Yes, they're certainly rubbing it in. Look at it! Draped in scarlet bedsheets, like all the rest of the city. One thing's certain,' she said. 'The manufacturers of flags won't be going out of business, any time soon.'

'Well, at least somebody's making a profit,' he said, relieved that, for the time being, she seemed to have shaken off her melancholy mood. 'And to think this town was on the brink of declaring itself a Communist Republic!' said Dorothy. 'Never mind about that now,' he said. 'You've brought me here to show me the city. So describe it to me.'

'All right. This is Pariser Platz. It's an enormous square, surrounded by grand buildings, in the classical style. The Brandenburg Gate takes up almost the whole of one side of the square. Through its pillars, you can see the trees of the Tiergarten—that's their main park, you know. I took Billy and Vicky for a walk there, only the Sunday before last...'

She was silent a moment; then resumed: 'Over there is the Adlon Hotel—Number One, Unter den Linden—where all the toffs hang out. Viktor always said he'd take me there one day,' she added, with a laugh that sounded as if she might be on the verge of tears. '"You'll wear your fur coat, *Liebchen*," he'd say to me. "And I'll have a diamond pin in my tie. Then we'll march up to the bar, with all the other swells, and hold up a banner saying Long Live the Revolution…"'

'That sounds like Viktor.'

'Yes. Not that I ever… Oh!' She stopped dead, so that, since he was holding her arm, he was forced to do the same. 'I think we'll give the Adlon Hotel a miss today,' she said. It didn't take Rowlands long to work out why. Because at that moment, a car drew up in front of the hotel, and a group of men got out. Car doors slammed and boot-heels clicked smartly across the pavement. 'Don't look now,' whispered Dorothy. 'But I think the Reichsminister and his boys are dropping in for tea.'

'Oh?' said Rowlands, for whom the Minister had loomed large in the past twenty-four hours. 'What does he look like?'

'He's an ugly little blighter—although I gather he fancies himself as a ladies' man,' was the scornful reply. 'Walks with a limp—a club-foot, so they say. Why? Do you want to meet him?'

'It's just possible I might, if I keep on going to the studios.' He gave her a brief account of his meeting that morning with Obersturmführer von Fritsch. 'So Goebbels is interested in films, is he? Film actresses, more like,' said Dorothy. 'I'd stay clear of him if I were you. I've heard that nasty things happen to people who get in his way…'

TRACKING SHOT

7

AT THE FLAT IN Marienburgerstrasse, they found Joachim, just returned from work. With him was a young woman, whom he introduced as 'Miss Blumenfeldt—a family friend.' At this perhaps disingenuous account of their relationship, the girl laughed. 'Call me Hettie,' she said, as she shook Rowlands's hand. '"Miss" is so formal, isn't it?'

'It is, rather.' Rowlands took an instant liking to Hettie Blumenfeldt. 'Do you work at the studios, too?' he asked—eliciting another peal of laughter from the 'family friend'. 'What, me? I'm hardly the actress type! I work in a factory...'

'Hettie designs wonderful clothes,' said Clara, coming into the room at that moment. 'By rights she should have her own *atelier*, like Coco Chanel.'

More laughter. 'I'd like to see that! "House of Hettie" sounds rather fine,' said the girl. 'What do you think, Joe? Would your Sybille Schönig wear my creations, do you think?'

There was a dead silence. Then: 'Sybille Schönig is dead,' said Joachim coldly. 'Haven't you seen the papers?'

'No. I...' The girl seemed momentarily lost for words. Rowlands came to her rescue. 'I don't think there can have been much about it in the newspapers up until now,' he said quickly. Just then, Frau Metzner called from the next room that dinner was on the table. There was a brief interlude while they all sat down—Hettie having been persuaded to eat with them, although she protested that she really wasn't hungry. 'Fred thinks the boys might have seen something,' said Dorothy, when the homely meal of *Bockwurst* and mashed potato had been served out. 'Of Sybille Schönig's murder, I mean...'

'If it *was* murder,' put in Rowlands. 'We don't know that for certain...'

93

'Of course it was murder!' Joachim seemed about to develop this theme, when his mother intervened. 'I do not like this talk,' she said. It struck Rowlands at that moment how like her late brother she sounded. Viktor Lehmann had hated violence, too. He had believed that hanging was wrong—even for murderers. 'It is murder by the state,' he had said. 'You cannot erase one crime with another...' Dear Viktor! Rowlands could imagine what he would have said about the present administration. 'I agree,' he said. 'It's not a subject for the dinner table.' For the next few minutes, the scraping of knives and forks against plates was the only sound. Then several of them began talking at once. 'But Fred thinks...'

'So you think that Walter and Billy...'

'Let's talk about this later,' said Rowlands. But then Frau Metzner spoke again: 'I was wrong,' she said. 'If there has been news of the children, then you must tell us, please...'

'All right. But it isn't much...'

'It's more than we had before,' put in Dorothy. 'Fred spoke to someone at the studio earlier today who might have seen them—didn't you, Fred?'

'In point of fact, he was quite insistent that he *hadn't* seen them,' said Rowlands. 'But I couldn't help feeling that he was protesting too much, as we say...'

'"The lady doth protest too much, methinks..."' said Clara. 'That is *Hamlet*, is it not? You see, we are familiar with your Shakespeare, here in Germany...'

Ich habe sie nicht gesehen! cried Joachim suddenly, catching the pitch and intonation of the terrified handyman so accurately that it made the hairs on the back of Rowlands's neck stand on end. 'So *that's* why he kept saying it! We couldn't get any sense out of him, poor devil...'

'I take it you're referring to Fritzi... I didn't get his last name,' said Rowlands. 'Fritzi Henkel,' said the other. 'Yes, you seem to have upset him all right!'

'I think he saw them.'

'Maybe. He's a bit strange, our Fritzi. Once he gets an idea into his head, it's very difficult to get it out again. *Ich habe sie nicht gesehen!* He kept muttering it to himself over and over,

94

as he pushed that broom of his up and down the corridors. In the end, we had to chuck him out, because he was disturbing the actors...'

'But this man—this Fritzi Henkel—works at the studio, does he not?' interrupted Frau Metzner eagerly. 'Then it is there we should be looking...'

'Herr Rowlands has been doing so, Mutti.'

'But perhaps it is already too late,' she murmured. She got to her feet, and began, mechanically, to stack the dishes. 'Clara, you will help me, please?' she said. But then Dorothy intervened: 'Leave that to me, Sara. You've done enough. Why don't you go and sit down, and I'll clear the table? The girls'll help me—won't you, girls?'

In the brief confusion of chairs being scraped back and plates collected, Rowlands leant across the table to Joachim. 'I spoke to Fräulein Pabst again today,' he said in an undertone. 'She told me she remembered seeing you and Walter in Sybille Schönig's dressing-room about six weeks ago...'

The young man said nothing for a moment. It was at times like these that Rowlands felt most at a disadvantage. Invisible to him were the minute shifts in facial expression, the changes of colour, that betokened another's thoughts—or the attempt to conceal them. But that moment of hesitation was enough. 'Yes, I took him to the studio once,' said Joachim. He sounded flustered. 'What of it?'

'You might have mentioned it, that's all,' said Rowlands quietly. 'Mentioned what?' It was Clara who spoke; he hadn't noticed her return. 'Oh, only that I took Walter to the studio one day a few weeks ago,' replied her brother off-handedly. 'He wanted to meet Fräulein Schönig, and so...'

'*You* wanted an excuse to meet her, you mean!'

'Don't be stupid...' replied the young man, in a furious tone; but then both siblings fell silent. Rowlands guessed that Hettie Blumenfeldt had come back into the room. 'Would anyone like some coffee?'

'No, thanks.' Joachim got to his feet, muttering something about having some work to do. 'But you'll be at the meeting later, won't you?' said Hettie. 'I don't know. Maybe.' Then he was gone, his footsteps clattering away down the uncarpeted passage that led to his room.

'Did I say something?' Hettie's tone was light. 'Of course not. You know my brother's moods,' said Clara. 'Well, *I'd* like some coffee. How about you, Herr Rowlands?'

Rowlands smiled. 'I think I'll have one of these, instead,' he replied, taking out his cigarettes. 'Will you join me, ladies?'

'No thank you,' laughed Clara. 'Mutti would have a fit if she saw me smoking!'

'I'll have one.' Hettie accepted a cigarette from the proffered packet. 'It isn't often I get to smoke decent tobacco. These are an English brand, aren't they?'

'Churchman's,' said Rowlands. 'I think you'll find they're quite mild.' Both lit up, and then Hettie said: 'Bother! I was to make the coffee...'

'I'll do it.'

When Clara had gone out, the other girl said: 'I was sorry to hear about Sybille Schönig—but I was not surprised. A woman like that...' She let out a mouthful of smoke. '...has many enemies.'

'Oh?' said Rowlands. 'What kind of enemies?'

She laughed. 'I do not refer to other actresses! Even though I am sure there are many of those with reason to hate her, too. But this woman had... how shall I say it? A bad reputation. She was not liked by some us here, in Berlin.'

'Why was that?'

Hettie Blumenfeldt took a moment before replying. 'Perhaps you are aware, Herr Rowlands, that we have a new government?' All laughter had gone from her voice, now. 'Some of us think that this is a bad thing. We do not wish to be ruled by such people. Others... Sybille Schönig was one of them... are less critical of the present administration. They are friendly— some might say *too* friendly—with such types.'

'Are you saying Sybille Schönig was involved with the NSDAP?'

'As to that,' said the girl. 'I do not know for certain. All I know is that she had some very strange friends. Dangerous friends. That is why I am not surprised that she is dead... Ah, here is Clara with the coffee! I will drink one cup, and then I must go.

It was good to meet you, Herr Rowlands.'

'You, too,' he replied, not a little perplexed by what she had just told him.

On the train to Babelsberg next morning, Metzner was silent and preoccupied, replying to Rowlands's remarks about the weather (still bitingly cold) with monosyllabic gruffness. More than this, he seemed half-asleep. Having gone out after dinner with some mumbled excuse, he'd returned very late; Rowlands had heard him come in around two. Now he yawned and fidgeted on the hard wooden seat of the third-class carriage, as if he were already worn out by the events of a day barely seven hours old. Suddenly, Rowlands wanted to shake him out of his apathy. 'Why didn't you say you'd taken Walter to the studio?'

'I didn't think it was important,' was the sullen reply. 'You must have realised it was important when Clara and I turned up there yesterday,' Rowlands persisted. 'Surely that would have been the time to speak up?' They were by now walking along the woodland path—a short-cut—which led from the station to the grounds of Babelsberg studios. The air was fresh and cold and there was a smell of pine. Apart from the steady crunch of their footsteps on the icy ground, there was no sound, except the chatter of a startled bird in the treetops, and the sudden thud of snow falling from a bough.

'I didn't realise, O.K.?' In his agitation, Metzner sounded much younger than his twenty-two years. 'By the time I thought of telling you, it was too late. The reason I didn't was that he wasn't supposed to be there at all—Walter, I mean. It's strictly forbidden to bring members of the public onto the set. I was afraid I'd lose my job if I admitted what I'd done.'

'It seems to me,' said Rowlands severely, 'that you've been worrying rather too much about the possibility of losing your job and not enough about finding your brother.' It was a cruel thing to say, and he regretted it instantly. The young man was silent a moment. 'You are right,' he said at last. 'Although you do not know what it is like here. If I were to lose this job, I might not find another. And my family relies on me...'

'I know.'

'But of course I want to find Walter—and little Billy. You think, then, that they may still be alive?'

'We have to hope so.'

'You are right. That is what we must hope. So what can I do?'

They had reached the gates of the studio.

Rowlands smiled. 'You can start by telling me all I need to know about the process of making a film,' he said. 'And I'm going to need a list of all the people who were in the studio with Fräulein Schönig that Friday night.'

'All right,' said Joachim. 'I will see what I can do.' He touched Rowlands's arm. 'You are to go to Studio 3,' he said. 'I will take you. First we must go left...'

'Then right,' said Rowlands. 'Then straight past the colonnade—it's about fifty paces—to the first building you come to. It's a one-storey brick building with large metal doors. Those are for the stage-hands and camera crew. The door to the left of it has a glass panel, and is for the actors.'

'You have a good memory'

'I've had need of it,' said Rowlands wryly.

The double doors to the studio stood open. Even though it was not yet eight, there were more people about than Rowlands remembered from before. In front of the doors, men were unloading scenery flats from a truck. There was a good deal of shouting of the 'up a bit... left a bit' kind. 'Props,' said Joachim, as the edged their way past. 'I suppose you will want to know if any of *these* people were working on Friday night?'

'Oh yes. And cameramen, lighting people and the rest,' said Rowlands. 'That's a lot of people,' was the glum reply. 'So I imagine. Do we go in here?' This was an inner set of doors, which led to the sound stage itself, and the rooms beyond it. '*Ja*. I will leave you with Fräulein Dunst,' said Joachim, as they reached the domain presided over by that formidable lady. 'She will tell you what you must wear...'

This turned out to be a suit of fine wool, smooth to the touch. 'English cloth,' said the wardrobe mistress. 'From your Savile Row. It is a suit for Spring,' she added, brushing her fingers lovingly across the lapels. And a damn good fit, too, thought Rowlands. He doubted that he'd ever get the chance to wear such a suit again. 'You will take this, please.' It was a Spring coat, in a lightweight tweed. '*Ja*. Like so. You will carry it over your arm.' The final touch was a soft felt hat. 'Now you look...'

'Very elegant,' said her assistant, Fräulein Müller.

Outside it was bitter weather, with the mixture of cold and damp that is the worst of February, but here, in this world of illusion, Rowlands was dressed as if for a mild day in April.

Once the clothes had been chosen—he supposed he should think of it as a 'costume'—it was time to go to make-up. Here, another young woman sat him down in a swivel-chair and, after covering his shirt-front with a cloth, proceeded to smear greasepaint on his face. When he opened his mouth to protest, she said, in English, but with a curiously American twang, 'I'd keep your trap shut, if were you, if you don't want a mouthful of this stuff.' He did so, meekly submitting to having powder dabbed on his nose and cheeks with a large brush, and his eyebrows touched up with cosmetic on the end of an orange-stick. 'There!' she said when she had finished. 'You look quite handsome. *Gutaussehend*, we would say in German.'

Uncertain how to respond to this flattery, Rowlands merely smiled. Then an awful thought occurred to him. 'I say,' he said. 'You haven't put *rouge* on my face, have you?' The make-up girl, whose name was Lena Pfeiffer, laughed. 'No, just Pan-Stick Number 14. A light bronze. See for yourself...' She swung the chair around so that he faced the mirror. Now it was Rowlands's turn to smile. 'But I *can't* see,' he said. 'Didn't they tell you?'

She didn't seem in the least abashed at her *faux-pas*. 'Nobody tells me anything in this damn joint,' she said. She must have taken a closer look at him then, for she added, 'Yes, I can see it now. Your eyes don't focus the way other people's do. Can you see anything at all?'

'I can distinguish very bright lights.'

'Well, you'll get plenty of *those* shining in your face when they start filming,' she said. 'And don't worry,' she added, whisking the cloth away from around his neck. 'The make-up won't show up under the lights. It's just to make you look brown and healthy, instead of as pale as a corpse.'

'That's reassuring,' said Rowlands.

When shown the poster of the missing children, the girl denied having seen them. 'Poor little scraps,' she said. 'I've a brother about their age. Tell you what,' she added, as Rowlands got up to leave, 'if you've a spare copy of that poster, I'll stick it up on the mirror. Then if anyone says anything about it, I'll let you know.'

In Studio 3, all was bustle and confusion, with orders being shouted—*'Hierher! Nein bisschen nach links'*—and equipment being shifted. Rowlands was heartily glad that he'd had the sense to ask for a guide (Fräulein Pfeiffer had duly summoned a runner), with whose assistance he'd several times narrowly avoided a collision—once with a low-hanging boom, and another time with the edge of a piece of scenery. Film studios could be dangerous places, he'd discovered. Once settled in one of the canvas folding-chairs to the side of the studio, he amused himself by trying to get a picture of what was going on around, using three of the four senses available to him, as well as his vague and now-distant memories of films seen in his youth.

Films with titles such as *A Fool There Was*, *The Devil's Daughter* and *Her Double Life* (he'd had rather a penchant for the sultry Theda Bara at the time). Adventure films, in which the heroine—usually played by Mary Pickford—would end up suspended over a crevasse, or tied to the railway tracks, while the hero (Mr Fairbanks) rushed to save her from impending doom. Comedies, starring Buster Keaton or Charlie Chaplin, in which the Little Man suffered various indignities, but always came out on top... These were all silent films, of course; the talkies hadn't been invented then. The only clues to what was happening were provided by the titles which came up on the screen from time to time, saying, 'All is lost!' or 'You Swine! Unhand me!' and by the cinema's organist, who could simulate a thunderstorm or a shipwreck with a few crashing chords, and a chase by a rapid scurrying up and down the keyboard.

These days, sounds were as important as pictures... which was as well, Rowlands thought wryly, if only because sounds had become all-important to him. And it was the sounds as much as the sense of what was being said around him to which he now made himself pay attention. And there was no mistaking the heated nature of the conversation that was taking place a few paces away from where he was sitting. 'I can't believe you've asked me to do this!' It was Helmut Hartmann who was speaking—or shouting, rather. 'My dear Helmut! All this fuss about nothing...' This was Klein, his tone emollient. *'Nothing!* You call it *nothing*? With Sybille not yet cold in her grave... I tell you, I won't do it...' Hartmann's voice had risen, or perhaps it was that the hubbub around them had diminished.

'What's all the excitement?' This was a voice Rowlands hadn't heard before. A woman's voice: low and husky, but with a surprisingly deep resonance; the voice of a woman used to being paid attention. 'Darling, I could hear you half-way across the lot. You shouldn't shout so. It's made you go quite red in the face.'

'Hallo, Magda.' Hartmann sounded distinctly apprehensive, Rowlands thought. 'Is anything the matter?'

'Matter? What should be the matter? Everything's perfectly fine.' There was a steeliness to her tone that suggested otherwise.

'Magda! But how delightful!' This was Bruno Klein. 'I am honoured that you should have decided to join us.'

The woman thus addressed gave a throaty laugh. 'You're such a liar, Bruno darling! As a matter of fact, I hadn't the least intention of coming into the studio at all. What would have been the point, when I don't even have a *cameo* in this *beautiful* picture of yours?' Her voice dripped sarcasm. 'No, it was simply that, having dropped my dear husband off at the gate, I realised that he'd walked off with my cigarettes...'

'Did I?' said Hartmann. He must have fumbled in his pockets then. 'So I did. Here. Catch.' He threw the cigarettes at her. She caught them. 'Thanks.' Magda Hartmann's voice was cold. 'Since I'm here,' she went on. 'I might as well stay. That is,' she added sweetly, 'if you don't mind?'

'Well...' began Klein. 'Oh, I promise not to intrude,' murmured the interloper. 'I'll just sit myself down here, out of the way, and... Hallo! Who's this?'

Rowlands had already got to his feet. 'How do you do?'

'But you are English! That is too delightful!' She took his hand—hers was expensively gloved, he noticed—and drew

101

closer, so that he could smell her musky scent, mingled, he thought, with another smell—could it be whisky, so early in the day? 'I adore the English. Such a civilised country—and such a civilised language, compared with our barbaric, German tongue...'

'Kind of you to say so...'

'Bruno! Introduce us, please.'

'This is Herr Rowlands,' was the reply. 'He is to appear in the last scene of the picture. That is,' said Bruno Klein, whose patience was evidently wearing thin, 'if we are ever able to begin shooting...'

'Oh, you may begin,' replied Magda Hartmann coolly. 'Don't mind me. I am going to sit here, next to your charming Englishman, and watch you make your beautiful film.' She sat herself down on the canvas folding-chair next to Rowlands's. Exquisitely soft furs brushed against him as she did so, and he received another gust of her perfume—rather too heavy for the time of day, thought Rowlands. 'Very good.' Klein made a valiant effort to regain control. 'But there must be no further interruptions...'

'Indeed not,' replied Magda Hartmann. 'Only you must talk to my husband about that. It was he who was making all the fuss—was it not, *Liebchen*?'

'I was merely expressing a point of view,' said Hartmann stiffly. 'I do not see how we can continue making this film under the circumstances. I mean, now that Sybille...' He faltered, and seemed unable to go on. 'Ah, yes, the lovely Sybille,' drawled the woman next to Rowlands. 'Such a terrible, terrible thing. She had quite a talent, I believe...'

As if she had not spoken, Klein went on: 'All I am asking you to do is a simple re-take of one scene.'

'A scene in which Sybille was to appear...'

'Yes, but only in silhouette. She had no lines at all. Fräulein Stöbel has agreed...'

'I refuse to act with a ghost!'

'Come, my dear Helmut,' said Klein. His tone was affable, but there was an edge of ice to his voice. 'You know that makes no sense. We are actors, after all—engaged in a game of

make-believe. We spend our lives conjuring up ghosts. We ourselves are but ghosts—here for such a little time...'

'Bruno was always something of a philosopher,' murmured
Magda Hartmann in Rowlands's ear. He caught a gust of her
whisky breath. Yes, definitely a drinker, he thought. '...so why
should this be any different?' Klein was saying. 'Fräulein Stöbel
will be seen in silhouette, you will say your lines, we will cap-
ture it all with our magical film-cameras and recording instru-
ments, and then we can all go home.'

'It just seems all wrong, somehow,' say Helmut Hartmann stubbornly, but he allowed himself to be fussed over by the make-
up girl. 'Good,' said Klein, once his star was ready. 'Let us now
begin. Fräulein Stöbel...' This was the understudy, Rowlands
guessed. 'Will you take up your position, please?' There was a
sudden flurry of activity from the camera crew, who had been
standing idle until this moment. *'Ruhe!'* called the studio manager. Quiet accordingly descended. 'Ready, Helmut?' This was
Klein again. 'Camera rolling... Action!'

Then came the mellifluous voice Rowlands had first heard
two days before, its tones still as heartfelt, and affecting. *'Ich
liebe dich,'* it said to the silent 'ghost'. I love you. *'Warum wend-
est du dein Gesicht von mir ab?'* Why do you turn away? To
Rowlands, listening from the shadows outside the circle of
brilliant light that played upon the actors, there seemed a real
emotion in the words. There was a moment, in fact, when he
wondered if Hartmann might not break down. But, consum-
mate actor that he was, he managed to get to the end without
faltering. It was done in one take.

'Cut,' came the command. Then: 'Print that. Thank you,
Helmut. Fräulein Stöbel, you did very well.'

'He knows how to get a good performance out of his actors,'
said Magda Hartmann to Rowlands. 'It's why—in spite of all his
shouting and screaming—my husband will never leave him.'

'I take it,' said Rowlands, 'that you've been in films yourself?'
He smiled apologetically. 'I'm afraid I don't get to the pictures
much, these days, and so...'

'Oh, yes,' she said, with the faintest note of irony. 'I was, as
you say, "in films" for a number of years. Perhaps you have

103

heard of me? I am—or rather was—Magdalena Brandt.' Had Rowlands not already been doing so, he would have had to sit down. '*You're* Magdalena Brandt?' he echoed foolishly. 'But I've been in love with you for years...' He broke off, aware of how ridiculous he was making himself. 'I... I mean,' he stammered, 'with the characters you played in your films...'

'Oh, don't spoil it!' she laughed. 'You were getting along so nicely.' She seemed quite unperturbed by his star-struck behaviour—seemed, in fact, quite to have expected it. 'You were in love with me, you say? Or at least with the parts I played. And there *were* some good parts,' she murmured as if to herself. 'Cleopatra. Héloïse. Marie Antoinette...' He had seen them all, and a great many others besides. She had specialised in tragic rôles, which displayed her ravishing, dark-eyed beauty to best effect. It struck him then, with the force of a blow, that he actually knew what she looked like. Or what she *had* looked like; this was fifteen... no, *sixteen* years ago.

As if she guessed his thought, she said: 'Of course, I haven't made a picture for a long time. Which of my films,' she went on artlessly, 'did you like best?'

Several came to mind (*The Temptress*, in which she played a cabaret singer, who falls in love with a young artist, but gives him up when appealed to by his virginal fiancée; or *Fools Rush In*, about an adulterous love affair), but he was saved from having to answer by the arrival of Hartmann, who said brusquely, 'Bruno doesn't need me anymore. So there is no need for you to stay, my dear.'

'Oh, but I want to stay,' said his wife. 'I'd forgotten how much fun being in the studio can be. One meets such interesting people—like Mr Rowlands here. Mr Rowlands is an admirer of mine, Helmut. He has seen all my pictures, he says...'

'Yes, I...'

'Hallo, Rowlands.' Hartmann's voice was scarcely warmer than it had been when he was speaking to his wife. 'I suppose you are waiting to be called?'

'That's right.'

'But I did not realise!' cried Magda Hartmann. 'You are an actor also?'

Rowlands smiled. 'Hardly that. Herr Klein has asked me to play a very small non-speaking part, that's all.'

'That is a great deal,' was the reply. 'Bruno is very particular about whom he has in his films—isn't he, my sweet?' This was to her husband—the animosity thinly veiled. Hartmann said nothing to this, and after a moment, he walked off, muttering something about needing some air, and leaving Rowlands alone with the star.

8

THE THOUGHT THAT HIS tyro efforts in acting were to be witnessed by so celebrated a practitioner of the art did nothing for Rowlands's confidence. As he sat down at the café table under the arc-lights, he felt far more nervous than he had done at the initial screen-test. His hands, as he reached for the newspaper, which had been laid ready for the purpose, were trembling, and he had to fight down an impulse to bolt. 'Cut!' There was the faintest edge of irritation in Bruno Klein's voice. 'Please do not look so worried, Herr Rowlands. You have only to do what we rehearsed yesterday.' He walked over from where he had been standing, behind the bank of cameras and lights, to where Rowlands was sitting. 'You pick up the newspaper— so.' He suited the action to the word. 'You unfold it—so. You look at the headline—or rather, the camera does that for you, so that the audience can see what it is that you are seeing. You hold the pose of looking at the newspaper headline until I say "Cut"… It is very simple, no?'

'I'm sorry,' said Rowlands. 'Perhaps I could try it again?'

'Oh, we will try and try, until we are satisfied,' was the reply. Even so, it took another three or four takes before this end was achieved. 'All right. Print that. Thank you, Herr Rowlands. I have finished with you now,' said Klein. 'Twenty minutes, everybody.'

A perceptible relaxation of the atmosphere ensued, as the director walked off set, and there was a murmur of conversation, as some people drifted away, while others stood around in groups, discussing the morning's shooting. Rowlands, who had got to his feet when Klein addressed him, now stood, irresolute, at the centre of this renewed activity. Even though he now had a clearer idea of the layout of such a place than he had had before, he was still reluctant to risk crossing the studio floor unaccompanied, for fear of tripping over a trailing wire, or walking slap-bang into some projecting object.

But at that moment, someone came up to him. A waft of musky scent told him who it was, even before she spoke. 'You were very good,' said Magda Hartmann, in her beautiful, whisky-soaked voice. 'Full of emotion.'

Rowlands smiled. 'You're very kind.'

'No, I am not kind. You have a sensitive face. I can see why Bruno wanted to use you. I did not realise,' she went on, in the same matter-of-fact tone of voice, 'that you were blind.'

'I haven't always been blind.'

'I rather supposed not, since you said you had seen my pictures,' she replied. She gave a little, self-deprecating, laugh. 'It is nice to meet someone who remembers them with such pleasure.'

Rowlands felt himself colour at the recollection of his callow outburst. 'I can't imagine anyone remembering them otherwise,' he said. 'Oh, you'd be surprised, Herr Rowlands! This is a very unpleasant industry. Very... how do you say? *Competitive*. One's efforts... such as they are... are all too easily dismissed...' He felt her sway unsteadily on her high heels, and wondered what had happened to the beautiful, self-assured, woman he recalled from her screen appearances, to turn her into this pitiful creature. 'Perhaps, he said gently, 'you would allow me to escort you to your car?'

'But that is *so* kind! You Englishmen are such gentlemen.' She took his arm, and they set off across the wide expanse of studio floor. Halfway across, something seemed to strike her as funny. 'I suppose,' she giggled, 'it is *I* who should be escorting *you*...'

'It was rather ridiculous of me to have put it that way,'

'You misunderstand me, Herr Rowlands.' Suddenly, she didn't sound tipsy at all. 'I only meant that I am all the more grateful for your courtesy. My *husband*'—her tone was scathing—'did not see fit to escort me. But then, he is not a gentleman.'

They had by now emerged onto the windswept *Platz* that lay between the Sound Stage and the administration block. Magda Hartmann gave a little shudder, and huddled closer to her companion. Even an ermine coat was not proof against the biting cold; a summer-weight suit offered almost no protection at all. Try as he might, Rowlands could not suppress a shiver. 'But you have no coat!' cried the actress. 'You will be frozen to death. Come, I have a flask of *Schnapps* in the car. That will warm you up...'

'No, that's quite all right...'

'I must insist!' She clutched his arm all the tighter. Suddenly, he was struck by the absurdity of it all. That *this* was Magdalena Brandt... A vision of the way she had once looked—a dark-eyed *houri*, draped in pearls and satin, gazing down from the cinema screen—flickered across his mind. 'My car's just over there. The dark blue Benz cabriolet.' She seemed momentarily to have forgotten his disability—or maybe, he thought, this was just another example of the notorious solipsism of the famous.

'Perhaps,' he said drily, 'you could lead the way?'

But before they could go a step further, there came the sound of a powerful engine—another Mercedes-Benz, thought Rowlands—as a vehicle drove rather too fast beneath the arch of the studio's entrance, and drew up in the forecourt. It was followed, moments later, by another. Car doors slammed, and men got out, their boots crunching on the icy crystals of compacted snow. 'Well, well,' said Magda Hartmann softly. 'Just look who's here...' Whoever it was appeared to be of some importance, to judge from the way the porter, who had rushed out of his gatehouse at this arrival, was bowing and scraping. Rowlands couldn't make out all that was being said, but the deference on one side—'*Jawohl, mein Herr... Nein, mein Herr...*' was unmistakable, as was the peremptory note of command on the other.

Orders were shouted and people ran to fulfil them. There came the tramp of boots; then: 'Halt!' said a voice, and the party came to a standstill. 'Fräulein Brandt?' the voice went on—an extraordinary voice, thought Rowlands, at once harsh and silkily insinuating. 'Is it really you?'

'Yes, it is I, Reichsminister. I did not expect to see you here...'

'Did you not?' A bark of laughter. 'You are behind the times, my dear. This has become my business, now... Yes,

109

Obersturmführer, what is it?'

Beside him, Rowlands felt Magda Hartmann stiffen. Her hand in its elegant glove clutched his arm. 'Herr Director Klein has been informed of our arrival, Reichsminister,' said von Fritsch. 'Good,' was the curt reply. 'Yes, indeed,' went on the Reichsminster, once more addressing Magda Hartmann. 'I intend to take a very close interest in all that is going on at UFA from now on. You will see some changes... but then,' he laughed—a curious sound, between a croak and a cough—'you have already seen a good many changes since you began in films, have you not?'

'Oh, yes,' she said. 'Many changes.'

At that moment, they were joined by someone else. Bruno Klein, as it turned out. 'Reichsminister,' he said, and it seemed to Rowlands that he was forcing an enthusiasm he did not feel. 'This *is* an honour...'

The Reichsminister ignored him. 'Enchanted,' he said, 'to see the incomparable Magdalena Brandt, who has done so much for the German film industry, looking so blooming... But where is your husband, dear lady? He, too, is an ornament of our German culture. I trust he is well?'

'Very well.'

'That is good. We would not wish it otherwise.' His gaze must have shifted to Rowlands, at that moment, for he said: 'I do not know your friend.'

'This is Herr Rowlands, from England.'

'Indeed?' said the Reichsminister coldly. 'Our Führer has many friends in England.' Abruptly, he turned towards Klein. 'Good day Herr Director. I believe you have a film to show me?'

'Yes. That is...'

'Good. Then let us see it. We must not keep this beautiful lady standing in the cold.' With a smart click of the heels, he bent and kissed Magda Hartmann's hand. *'Auf Wiedersehen,'* he said. She murmured a reply; then, as the Reichsminister's party moved off towards the studio buildings, she put her lips close to Rowlands's ear. 'He always was a little shit,' she said. She was trembling, Rowlands noticed, although she had seemed un-affected by the cold until that moment. They reached her car

110

without further incident. When she was seated at the wheel, she leant across, as he was about to close the door. 'You have been very kind, Herr Rowlands. I hope you will allow me to repay your kindness...'

'There's really no need.'

'Oh, but I should like to! I am having a small party—just a few, intimate friends. I hope you will join us?'

'Thank you. But...'

'Six o'clock. We are in Grünewald. The studio will arrange a car. Until tonight, Herr Rowlands.'

'Until tonight,' he said, stepping away from the vehicle as she put it in gear and drove off. Because after all, he thought, it'll give me a chance to ask some more questions about last Friday... knowing, as he had the thought, that there was another, less altruistic, reason why he wanted to be there. The spell that Magdalena Brandt had cast over him, all those years ago, as he sat in the darkened cinemas of his youth, had yet to be broken, it seemed.

Before six o'clock came, there was still much for him to do— talking to as many people as possible, to see if any of them remembered seeing Billy and Walter, the night they'd turned up here. First, though, he needed to get out of these clothes, and get this stuff off his face... He hailed the next person he passed—who turned out to be one of the runners—and enquired the way to the make-up department. Here, he found Fräulein Pfeiffer. 'Well, hallo, stranger,' she said, in that curious American drawl. 'What can I do for you?'

'If you could let me have a bit of cold cream,' he said. 'I'd appreciate it.' The girl laughed. 'What! And get it all over that fancy suit of yours? I don't think so! Keep still, Lili, or I'll poke your eye out...' This was to the starlet on whom she was currently working, Rowlands supposed. 'Sit down over there, why don't you?' she went on, addressing Rowlands. 'I'll be finished in a minute.'

Awaiting his turn, Rowlands let his thoughts drift. It occurred to him that, in all the excitement, he'd neglected to ask Magda Hartmann if she'd been at the studios on Friday night...

Well, he'd have his chance later that evening, he thought. Then if young Metzner was as good as his word, and provided him with the list of people he'd asked for, he could spend the time between now and six o'clock asking a few questions... 'O.K., you're all set,' said Fräulein Pfeiffer to the actress whose face she'd been making up. 'Tell Uta I said that shade of lipstick wasn't right for you. The light red's much better. And no more of the boo-hoo stuff. It ruins the mascara.'

When the girl had gone, with a tapping of high-heeled shoes, the make-up artist turned to Rowlands. 'Let's get you cleaned up,' she said. Having whisked a towel around his shoulders, she got to work, erasing the healthy tan she'd give him, and restoring his natural pallor, with copious amounts of Ponds' cold cream and cotton wool. As she performed this task, she threw out occasional remarks. 'It's been a crazy week,' she said. 'All the girls are in a terrible state. First Sybille getting stiffed, and now this business with poor Fritzi...'

'What's that?' said Rowlands sharply.

'Haven't you heard? Fritzi—that's our handyman—fell down some stairs and killed himself... Say, keep still, won't you! I haven't finished.'

But Rowlands was already out of his chair. He snatched the towel from around his neck and swiped his face with it. 'When did this happen?' he demanded. 'I couldn't say. First I heard of it was ten minutes ago, when Lili came in, crying her eyes out...'

'Where was he found?'

'In one of the Sound Stages. Studio 4 or 5, I think. Everybody's very upset. He was a good sort, was Fritzi...'

'Yes.' Rowlands found he was breathing hard. He knew now that he hadn't been imagining things. The boys had seen something, and Fritzi Henkel had seen the boys. It was for that reason he had died. 'Where are you going?' said the girl, as Rowlands reached the door. He realised he had no idea how to get where he wanted to go. 'If you wait a second, I'll come with you,' she said.

There was a little knot of people outside the Sound Stage—a large, hangar-like edifice, made of corrugated iron, Rowlands discovered, by the simple expedient of walking into one of the doors. Fortunately, Fräulein Pfeiffer caught hold of him, before he'd done himself too much damage. Doors left ajar were a perennial hazard for a blind man. 'What's going on?' he heard the make-up artist say to one of the film-crew, and then the man's reply: 'Nothing, at present. Doctor's still with him. Not that there's much he can do for him, poor devil... I wouldn't go in there,' added their informant, as Rowlands and the girl made as if to enter the building. 'It's not a very pretty sight. Broke his neck, did old Fritzi. Must've slipped and tumbled headfirst down the stairs. Stinking of Schnapps, too, he was. Must have been drunk as a lord...'

'Has anyone sent for the police?' said Rowlands. 'No idea,' was the reply. 'Although I can't think why they'd need to be involved. Accident, wasn't it?'

'I call it a damned nuisance,' said a gruffer voice. 'How we're going to get things set up for them to start shooting is anybody's guess. We've already lost nearly an hour...'

'That's a rotten thing to say, Franz Vogel!' interrupted another man. 'A man's dead, after all...'

'And not the first to die, either,' muttered the first man. 'If you ask me, there are altogether too many bloody corpses around here...'

This interesting discussion was brought to an end by the arrival of the police. 'All right,' said a voice Rowlands recognised as that of Sergeant Schultz. 'Stand away, there. Let the Inspector through...' Then Gentz himself appeared, sounding even more disgruntled than usual: 'What are all these people doing here?' he demanded; then: 'Get rid of them, will you? Unless any of them are witnesses, of course.' His eye must have fallen on Rowlands, for he gave a little grunt of amusement. 'Well, well!' he said in English. 'We meet again, Herr Rowlands! Why does this not seem surprising to me, I wonder?'

'Hello Inspector. Yes, it *is* a coincidence.'

'That is one word for it. Did you know this man?'

'I take it you mean the dead man, Fritzi Henkel? We had met, yes.'

'I knew it!' chuckled the policeman. 'Yes, Sergeant?'—this in

German. Schultz replied to the effect that the doctor had now completed his examination of the body. 'Tell him I'll be there directly... I suppose,' Gentz went on, addressing the Englishman once more, 'you would like to accompany me?'

'If that's all right,' said Rowlands meekly. 'And perhaps FräuleinPfeiffer...'

'Oh, let her come too. Why not? The more the merrier, as you English say. Now,' Suddenly the Inspector's *bonhomie* gave way to a more acerbic manner. 'Where's the man who found him?'

'That's me,' piped up this individual.

'Name?'

'Herman Gross. I was just going to set up, when I stumbled over him. Gave me a nasty turn...'

'Yes, yes. Save it for your statement. Well, Herr Gross, you'd better lead the way. I don't mind telling you,' said Gentz, reverting once more to English, as the little party entered the building, 'that I'm a bit worried about the way things are going, here in Babelsberg. This isn't Berlin, where we're rather more used to sudden death. But this—two people killed within a week. It "takes the biscuit", as you say in England.'

The body lay at the bottom of an iron staircase that led to a gantry. This ran around all four sides of the enormous space—or so Rowlands learned from his young informant. 'It's so that the crew can reach the lighting rigs,' she explained.

'I see.'

'Poor Fritzi must have missed his footing and pitched forward onto his head,' she said in a voice that trembled slightly. 'It's fifteen feet from the top of the stairs to the bottom, and the floor's made of concrete, so...' She broke off, in order to blow her nose. 'You're lucky you can't see it, that's all.'

'There's no need for you to stay,' said Rowlands gently. 'No, I want to stay,' she said stoutly. 'I feel I owe it to the poor fellow. Although what he was doing in this building, I can't imagine,' added the make-up girl. 'It's his job to keep the studios and corridors clean in the main block. He doesn't usually come in here.'

Rowlands, who had a pretty good idea how it was that the dead man had ended up where he had, said nothing. From where he was standing, a few feet away from where the corpse

114

of the unfortunate handyman was lying, he could make out only snatches of the conversation Gentz was having with his officers. As far as he could gather, the Inspector wanted to know where the deceased had last been seen alive. Nobody seemed to have a clear idea about that. There followed an exchange between Gentz and the doctor who had examined the body. This concerned the presumed time of death. 'He says he won't know until he's made a full examination,' whispered Fräulein Pfeiffer. 'I expect that means he'll have to open him up…'

'Yes,' said Rowlands, for whom this awakened distasteful memories. Suddenly, he found himself addressed: 'Herr Rowlands! I believe you said you knew the deceased?' Inspector Gentz was once more speaking in English—a useful way of excluding those of his colleagues who did not, Rowlands guessed. 'Well, yes,' he replied guardedly. 'That is, I'd met him once…'

'When was this, please?'

'Yesterday. In Sybille Schönig's dressing-room.'

'Indeed? And what were you doing there, may I ask?'

Rowlands started to explain. 'You were showing photographs,' said the policeman, cutting short this account. 'And when you showed these photographs to Henkel, what was his reaction?'

'He seemed agitated.'

'Did he? In what way?'

'He vehemently denied ever having set eyes on the boys—my nephew and his cousin, that is. But I think he was lying.'

'And now he turns up dead. Did did it not occur to you, Herr Rowlands, that this information might have been of some value to the police?'

'But I *did* mention it to the police,' said Rowlands. 'Inspector Schneider said he would look into it."

'I see.' Only someone as attuned to the nuances of voices as Rowlands was could have detected the anger in Gentz's voice. 'I knew nothing of this…'

Before Rowlands could reply, someone else spoke. 'There's not much more I can do here. As soon as your men have finished with him, I'll have him taken to the mortuary…'

'Of course, Doctor. I just need a few photographs, and then

we are done.' Gentz gave an order to that effect. 'I think,' he said, reverting once more to English, 'you had better come with me, Herr Rowlands. I should like to hear more of your conversation with the late Fritz Henkel—and indeed, if you have had any *other* conversations relating to these events…'

'I'll do my best.' The two of them, with Lena Pfeiffer in tow, began to walk towards the open doorway. 'Although I'm not sure that any of it means very much. There is one thing that puzzles me…' he started to say, but just then they were waylaid by Gentz's Sergeant, with an urgent query, as to whether the crew were to be allowed into the building to set up, or whether the area should be kept clear…'

'Tell them to wait until the photographer has finished,' said Gentz. Then, to Lena: 'You will want to get back to your work, Fräulein…'

'O.K.,' said the girl, not sounding entirely pleased at the prospect. 'Look in later, won't you?' she said to Rowlands, before strolling away. 'I would say you had made quite an impression on that young lady,' said the detective thoughtfully. 'Nice-looking girl she is, too, with that red hair—although I don't, as a rule, admire women in trousers. Call me old-fashioned…'

It was so much an echo of what Gentz's colleague, Schneider, had said, in his sneering tone, that Rowlands could not suppress an exclamation—turning this, rather unconvincingly, into a cough. 'You were about to say something?' said the Inspector. 'No… That is, yes. I wondered who it was who telephoned you… about Henkel's death, I mean. Only nobody I spoke to admitted to having called the police—and the body was discovered less than an hour ago…'

'That's easy,' said Gentz. 'It was his mother who telephoned.'

'His *mother*?'

'He lives with her. Or rather,' the policeman corrected himself. 'He did. Last night he did not return home. She—Frau Henkel—telephoned the police this morning at six. Of course, we get many such calls,' he added blandly. 'Most of those who are reported missing turn up, within a day or two. Some, however…' He let the sentence tail off. 'We will go in here,' he went on. 'There is a door to your right. They have given me an office.

116

It saves carrying a lot of paperwork between here and the Alex.'

'But I still don't understand how it was you turned up here,' said Rowlands, as they entered the low, brick building that was the studio's administration block. The Inspector laughed. 'I see that my friend Chief Inspector Douglas was right, when he said that you have the detective's mind,' he said. 'Third door on your left—that's right. We turned up at Babelsberg because we had another call, to say that Fritzi Henkel hadn't shown up for work...'

'Was it a woman who telephoned?'

'It was. You *do* have the detective mind.'

'There must have been something else,' persisted Rowlands, 'to make you think there'd been foul play...'

Again, the Inspector laughed. 'Now, who said anything about foul play? Henkel's death was an accident.'

'It was certainly meant to look like one. Did the woman who rang give a name?'

'She did not. Although I am sure,' said Gentz slyly, 'that you can supply one! All she said was that "poor Fritzi" had failed to appear, and that she was sure "something bad had happened to him".'

'What *did* happen to him?' asked Rowlands. 'Other than falling downstairs, of course...'

'We will have to wait for the doctor's report to know for certain,' was the reply. 'But I can tell you that his hands were tied before he was thrown downstairs. There were rope-burns on his wrists. Now. I believe you were going to tell me your theory as to why somebody might have wanted him dead?'

When Rowlands had finished speaking, the Inspector, who had sat himself down behind one of the desks with which the office was furnished, took a pencil from the tray in front of him and absentmindedly tapped his teeth with it. 'So you think,' he said, 'that these children were present in the dressing-room when Sybille Schönig was murdered?'

'Either that, or they got there soon afterwards,' said Rowlands. Tap, tap, went the pencil, as the Inspector thought this over. 'It does not augur well for their survival,' he said at last. 'The fact that Henkel saw them—or so you believe—and was himself

117

killed, suggests that whoever killed him, had killed Fräulein Schönig, too, or knew who had done so, and wished very much to conceal this...'

'Yes,' said Rowlands. 'I'm rather afraid you're right.'

'These are very dangerous people, Herr Rowlands. They will stop at nothing—not even the killing of children.'

'I know.'

'And so you are taking a great risk—blind as you are—if you continue to look for these two boys...'

'It's my nephew, Billy, and his cousin, we're taking about,' said Rowlands. 'I don't have any choice in the matter.'

'I see that you do not,' replied the policeman. 'And so what I am proposing is this: that we unite our forces. That is to say, you will continue to search for your nephew, but you will inform me of any further leads. In return,' he went on, as Rowlands made as if to speak, 'I will keep you informed of developments in the police investigation, in as much as they concern your family. Does that seem fair to you?'

'Very fair. But what about...' Rowlands broke off. 'You were going to say "what about Inspector Schneider?" were you not? I think,' said Gentz, with a grim little laugh, 'we will leave Inspector Schneider out of this. Needless, to say,' he went on, getting to his feet by way of signalling that their interview was over, 'you and I have had no such conversation and there is no such agreement between us. Do I make myself clear?'

'Perfectly.'

'Good. Then I will bid you good-day, Herr Rowlands.' The two men shook hands. 'Oh,' said Inspector Gentz, as the other turned towards the door. 'You had better have this...' A card was put into Rowlands's hand. 'It is my private line,' said the policeman. 'Any call, day or night, will find me there...'

'Thank you,' said Rowlands. 'But it might be better if you simply tell me the number. I'd have to ask someone else to read it to me, otherwise.'

'Very well.' Gentz did so. After repeating it to himself a couple of times, Rowlands knew he would remember it in future. Seven years of doing just that, in his days as a switchboard operator, had trained his memory for numbers, and a great deal else.

He handed back the card. 'Since we have not had this conversation,' he said, 'it might be better if there were no evidence of it.'

9

LEAVING THE ADMINISTRATION BLOCK, he almost ran into Joachim Metzner. 'I have been looking for you everywhere, Herr Rowlands. Somebody said you were over at the Sound Stage, but when I got there, some know-it-all turned me away. I must not come in, he says, because the police have not yet finished...'

'You'll have heard what happened, I suppose?' said Rowlands, as the two of them fell into step. 'That Fritzi Henkel is dead, you mean? Oh yes, I'd heard. If you want my opinion, there's something very suspicious about it, too.'

'Oh?' said Rowlands. 'You think so, do you?'

'I do. I mean, what was he *doing* over there, at all? He had no call to go to that part of the lot.' It was what Lena Pfeiffer had said, too, thought Rowlands. 'It's my belief that someone lured him over there, and then shoved him downstairs...'

'But why?'

'I couldn't say,' said Metzner. 'I've started making that list,' he went on. 'It's only a few names so far, but...'

'It'll do to be getting on with,' said Rowlands. 'Can you tell me what you've found out now—or do you have to get back to work?'

'It's my lunch break.'

'Good show. Then if we can find somewhere out of this infernal wind, you can put me in the picture,' said Rowlands. Over cups of just-about-drinkable coffee, in the staff canteen, they got down to business. 'I thought I'd start with those who were in Studio 3 that night,' said Metzner. 'Are you sure you won't have a bit of this cheese roll?' It had been difficult enough to get that, he said. Old Ernst, who ran the canteen, had been grumbling about some food that had gone missing. Although why

121

anyone would want to steal such horrible grub he—Joachim—couldn't imagine...

'No, thanks. So who *was* in the studio last Friday?'

'Well, excluding Herr Klein...'

'I'm not sure we should be excluding anybody at this stage. But carry on.'

'There were the actors. Herr Hartmann—whom you know. Herr Ziegler. He plays the ageing roué...'

'Oh yes, I remember him. A very cultured voice.'

'Fräulein Kuhn—who plays the wife...'

'Would that be Gudrun Kuhn? I think I remember seeing her in a couple of films before the War. She must be getting on a bit now, though...'

'She is one of our greatest character actresses,' replied Metzner, with some *hauteur*. 'Of course,' said Rowlands. 'Carry on.'

'The understudy, Fräulein Stöbel, was also there.'

'She was the one performing the scene with Herr Hartmann this morning, I take it?'

'Yes. She was in the studio all afternoon. We all were,' said Metzner. 'We started at two o'clock, and were there until around six...'

'Who else was there apart from the actors?'

'The film crew. Klaus Jung—he's Camera One—and Martin Winter—Camera Two. Neither of them left the studio between two and six, except Jung, who went outside for a cigarette—I'm not sure exactly at what time. There was also Gunther Herz, the lighting director...'

'Yes, I met Herr Herz yesterday.'

'... and Heinrich Wolff, the sound recordist. Oh, and Herr Brunning, the script editor—but he only looked in for a few minutes, to discuss a line change in the ballroom scene with Herr Klein. I didn't notice what time he left,' said Metzner. 'But it must have been well before six, because he had gone by the time Fräulein Schönig left the studio...'

'And what time was that?

'Just before six. Perhaps a quarter to.' The young man hesitated a moment. 'There was a row,' he said. Something about the way he said it made Rowlands think that here was more than met the eye.

'What was the row about?'

'Well...' In the silence, two girls at the next table could be heard laughing about something that had happened at rehearsals. 'So embarrasing... I thought I'd die.'

'Go on,' said Rowlands softly.

'All right. She... Fräulein Schönig... was not happy with something that Herr Klein said. It was to do with the penultimate scene. They were to have wrapped that night, but Herr Klein said he wasn't satisfied. He wanted to shoot that part of the scene again.' Metzner's voice tailed off. It seemed to Rowlands that there was more he could have said. 'And so Miss Schönig and Herr Klein quarrelled about that, did they?'

'Yes. She... she lost her temper. I do not think she meant to say what she said.'

'What *did* she say?'

'Why, that she was finished with the picture. That she was sick of being pushed around... and that...'

'Yes?'

'That he would regret it,' said Metzner in a low voice.

'She said that, did she?'

'She was upset,' said the young man. 'You did not know her. She was... how do you say this? *Empfindlich...*'

'Sensitive,' said Rowlands. 'Or perhaps highly strung. So what happened then?'

'She walked out. I... I believe she went to her dressing-room.'

'It seems likely, since that was where she was killed,' said Rowlands, aware that he was being rather brutal with Sybille Schönig's admirer. 'And the rest of you stayed behind in the studio, did you?'

'Yes. That is, for a few minutes. But there was not much more we could do. Herr Klein said that as his leading lady had decided to call a halt to proceedings the rest of us could go.'

'But you stayed behind?'

'I... I had a few things to see to and...'

'Can you tell me in what order people left?'

Metzner hesitated. 'Herr Ziegler was the first. Yes, I think it was he. And Fräulein Kuhn. They went out together...'

123

'What about Hartmann?'

'He had left earlier. They had finished shooting his scene about half-past four... Why do you ask me all this?' demanded Metzner. 'The police will have this information already.'

'That's true enough,' said Rowlands. 'But you see, I'd like to get a picture of what happened for myself. And what time did *you* leave?' he added.

'I?' Metzner seemed astonished at the question. 'I have told you—I stayed behind in the studio, after the others had gone. Perhaps half an hour. Jung and Winter will bear me out. They left just before I did...'

'So you were the last to leave?'

'Yes. No. I don't know!' cried the young man. 'What is the point of all these questions?'

'I've told you—it helps me to get a picture. So you left the studio at around half-past six. Now,' said Rowlands. 'I'd just like to know whether you left the studio for any reason, *before* that— say between five forty-five and six-thirty.' There was a long silence. Then Metzner said, 'I remember now—I *did* leave the studio for a few minutes. There... there was a canister of film I had forgotten to return...'

'I see. When was this?'

'I can't say exactly. It might have been six o'clock.'

Rowlands took another sip of his coffee. It had gone cold. 'How long were you away?' he said. Another pause. 'Maybe ten minutes,' said Metzner reluctantly.

'Ten minutes. That would give you time, would it not, to go from Studio 3 to Sybille Schönig's dressing-room? Ample time, in fact...'

There came another, charged, pause. 'So,' said the young man bitterly. 'This was all a trick. You are trying to pin this on me.' He got to his feet, almost knocking over the chair in his haste.

'Don't be an ass,' said Rowlands. 'I'm not trying to do anything of the sort. Don't you see? If you know anything—anything at all—which could help determine what happened that evening, and who killed Sybille Schönig, then we'll be that much closer to finding out what happened to your brother and Billy, and perhaps saving them from the same fate... If it's not already too late,' he added.

There was another moment of silence; then: 'I am sorry,' said Metzner. 'I have behaved like a fool. You are only trying to help, I know, and...'

'Sit down,' said Rowlands, 'and tell me exactly what you saw.'

'It wasn't anything I saw,' was the reply. 'Only what I heard.'

From the moment Sybille Schönig had rushed out of Studio 3, screaming that she was finished with them all, and that she'd go somewhere where her gifts would be appreciated, Metzner had made up his mind to follow her, he said. 'I wanted to beg her to reconsider what she'd said about leaving... because of what it would mean for the studio.' For weeks, UFA had been awash with rumours of this one and that one who'd managed to get a job in Hollywood, or Elstree. 'I could not let her leave,' said Metzner. 'That would mean the end for all of us...' He'd gone to remonstrate with her, he said. But when he'd got to the dressing-room, somebody else was already there.

'Who was it?'

'Hartmann,' said Metzner sullenly.

'Are you sure?'

'I know his voice, don't I? You couldn't mistake it. Especially not with him shouting at her, and her shouting back...'

'So they were quarrelling, were they? Did you hear what it was about?'

'I didn't hear much. He said something about wanting to talk to her, and she said it was too late for that. She'd made up her mind, she said. It was then he started shouting...'

'What did he say?'

'Oh, the usual things,' said the youth, with the casualness of a man twice his age and experience. 'She was a heartless bitch, who cared only for herself, and he was a fool for having cared for her.'

'I see,' said Rowlands. 'So they were lovers...'

'It looks like it, doesn't it?' said the young man dully. 'Although from what you say, the affair was over, or had already ended,' persisted Rowlands, conscious that he was twisting the knife.

'I suppose so. Does it matter?'

'It might matter a great deal. Was there anything more?'

125

'I suppose you think I'm a cad for eavesdropping...'

'I don't think anything of the kind. What else did Hartmann say?'

'I... I don't remember exactly. It was something about her running a risk... That's right. He said she might think that she was being very clever, but that she'd better be careful. One of these days, she'd go too far... I didn't stick around to hear any more.'

'And so you went back to the studio, I suppose?'

'That's right. Nobody'd missed me. They were all still talking about the row between Sybille and Herr Klein. Lili Stöbel said that if Fräulein Schönig was fed-up with working at UFA, she, for one, *wasn't*, and that she'd be only too happy to carry on working on *Fallen Angel*, if she had to work all night... Little cat,' he added. 'I can think of one person who's absolutely delighted that Sybille's dead...'

'Even if she didn't actually kill her,' said Rowlands. 'Which by your account, she couldn't have...'

'I suppose not,' said Metzner. He pushed back his chair 'I'd better be getting back...'

'One other thing,' said Rowlands. 'Did you notice if anyone *else* was missing from Studio 3? I mean of those people you just mentioned.'

'I'm not sure...'

'Think!'

'Now you mention it, I don't think Gunther Herz was there when I got back. No, that's right, because he came in just after I did. I've no idea what took him out of the studio. Perhaps he needed a breath of air...'

'Yes,' said Rowlands. 'It must have been that.'

One thing was certain, Sybille Schönig had been up to something, he thought, as he made his way slowly back towards the main studio building. He was glad of the chance to think things out. What the young man had told him had been illuminating—or at least up to a point. It cast light on certain aspects of this puzzling case, while casting others still deeper into shadow... He felt a touch on his arm.'Herr Rowlands.' There was no mistaking that gravelly, smoker's voice. 'What can I do for you, Fräulein Pabst?'

'I must speak with you,' she said. 'It's about my Sybille.' She hesitated. 'I was not quite honest with you when we spoke last. I have been worried, Herr Rowlands...' She broke off, as a noisy crowd of cameramen and lighting people went past on their way to the canteen. 'But we cannot talk here. Can you meet me in the dressing-room in five minutes?'

'All right.' Wondering a little at these elaborate precautions, he idled for a few minutes in the courtyard, smoking a cigarette, and amusing himself by trying to guess the identity of the passers-by, from the snatches of conversation that came his way. The cameraman, with their talk of focus-pulls and long-shots, were followed—it being the lunch-hour—by a group of secretaries from the administration block. An engagement ring was being admired. Then came a gaggle of extras (he recognised the type, from his brief spell as Man in Crowd), complaining loudly about the hours they'd been kept hanging about: '... thought my feet were going to drop off with cold... When he said "Take 12", I thought I'd scream...'

He finished his cigarette. Now for Fräulein Pabst...

'You look a bit lost, Herr Rowlands,' said a voice he knew. It was the Lighting Director, Gunther Herz. 'May I be of assistance?'

Rowlands smiled. 'No, that's all right, Herr Herz,' he said. 'I can find my own way. I've got to know the layout of the studio quite well, during the past few days... '

'You must have a good memory,' said Herz, falling into step with Rowlands. 'It is easy to get lost in so large a place, with so many buildings that resemble one another. Like a barracks, is it not? But as it happens, I am going the same way as you are. There are some things I have to see to in Studio 2. And you?' The question seemed a casual one, and yet Rowlands was not sure. There seemed something a bit suspicious about the way Herz had tagged onto him. Perhaps Greta Pabst's obsession with secrecy was affecting him, too, he thought. 'I left my hat in the make-up room,' he said. 'In all the excitement this morning I must have forgotten it...'

'Ah, yes,' said the Lighting Director. 'You are referring to the accident, this morning, are you not? So unfortunate for the studio, when such things happen...' Pretty unfortunate for Fritzi Henkel, too, thought Rowlands. They had reached the doors of Studio 2. 'I go in here,' said Herz. 'Goodbye, Herr Rowlands. I hope you find your hat.'

'Thanks.' Rowlands waited until the doors had closed behind the other man, before setting off in the opposite direction from the one in which the two of them had been walking—the late Sybille Schönig's dressing-room being located on the far side of the building. He found Fräulein Pabst in a strangely excited mood. 'Did anybody see you come here?' she demanded. 'Not as far as I know. That is...' But she cut him off impatiently. 'There is something very bad going on at Babelsberg,' she said. 'First Sybille, and now...' She was unable to go on. 'I was very sorry to hear about Fritzi,' he said gently. 'You know that it was murder, don't you?' said the dresser fiercely. 'They are saying it was an accident, but it was not an accident—any more than Sybille's death was suicide.'

'I'm afraid you may be right.'

'Of course I am right! First they put a gun in my girl's right hand—when she was left-handed. Then they try to make it look as if Fritzi fell down the stairs because he was drunk. But he did not drink, Herr Rowlands. He had a weak head for this.' Greta Pabst drew a rasping breath. 'There is something very bad going on. And Sybille was involved. I am not sure how—but I know that, in the days before she died, she was afraid...' It struck Rowlands, that she, too, was afraid. 'Did she say what it was that had frightened her?'

'No. But...' She broke off. 'Have you a cigarette?'

'Yes, of course.' He lit it for her. 'Thank you.' She took it from him, with fingers that trembled a little. When she had taken a drag, she grew calmer. 'There was a list,' she said. 'A list?'

'*Ja, ja*, a list!' She seemed exasperated by his failure to grasp her meaning at once. 'A list of names...'

'Whose names?'

'I... I do not know, exactly. Some of them were people at UFA, I think. She...' Again, Fräulein Pabst broke off. 'She was asking me a lot of questions. What did I know of this one and that one?

128

I did not think there was any harm in this, but now...'

'You think she might have been supplying information to someone else?'

'I cannot say. She... She was not a bad girl, my Sybille, but...' Greta Pabst sighed. 'She was ambitious. "One day you're going to see my name up in lights" was what she liked to say. She liked attention... from men, you understand...'

'And you think one of these men might have got her involved in something...'

'Perhaps. She did not confide in me. But in those last few days, I am sure she had something on her mind,' said the dresser.

'And the list? What became of that?

'I do not know any more than this. Only that'—she took another deep drag on the gasper—'Sybille said my name was not on it. She would see to that, she said.' Then, as Rowlands seemed about to pursue the matter. 'I have told you all I know. One thing more I will say to you, Herr Rowlands—be careful. You have been asking a lot of questions. That is not wise, in these times.'

The car dropped him off in the broad gravel drive leading to the Hartmanns' house in Grünewald. It was impossible to get closer than that, because of the number of cars already drawn up in front, Rowlands's driver explained. He seemed anxious that his client should not think him remiss for not having driven up to the door. Rowlands reassured him. 'If you'll just direct me...' The man did so. 'Twenty paces to the front door,' said Rowlands, repeating these instructions. 'Past the Daimler, the Mercedes cabriolet, and the Rolls-Royce...' He tipped the chauffeur, and got out, as another car drew up behind, honking its horn impatiently.

As he got within a few paces of the house, a group of people got out of one of the other cars, and ran ahead of him up the flight of steps that led to the front door. One of their number said something he couldn't catch, and somebody else laughed. Then another member of the party rang the bell, and the door opened, Rowlands entering on the heels of this boisterous group. He gave his hat and coat to the maid, and followed the sounds of talk and laughter to the room where the party was being held. He could tell it was a large room, from the echo which bounced off its walls and high ceiling; also that it was full of people—thirty or so, at a guess. That these were fashionable, well-to-do people was evident from their loud, self-assured conversation, and from the mixture of smells—expensive scent, American cigarettes, and hot-house flowers—with which he was greeted.

Feeling himself at a disadvantage, as always on such occasions, Rowlands took a step or two into the room, hoping that someone would come to his rescue before too long. But no one paid him any attention. From somewhere on the far side of the room, he could hear the unmistakable tones of his hostess, holding forth. Cautiously, he began to edge his way through the crowd which had congregated just inside the door, murmuring apologies as he inadvertently jostled this person and that. 'I say, haven't we met?' An Englishwoman. He turned towards the speaker, with a smile. 'I'm afraid I don't...'

'Iris Barnes,' said the young woman who'd hailed him. 'We met... Oh, it must be three or four years ago. At Celia West's... Well, she's Celia Swift, now...'

'Miss Barnes. Of course,' he said quickly, to head off any development of this theme. 'I remember now.' That party in Cadogan Square. They'd chatted for a few minutes—about films, he seemed to recall. In itself, the memory wasn't especially painful; it was what had come afterwards that made it so. 'You're the journalist.'

'That's me. How *are* you, Mr Rowlands? But you haven't got a drink. What'll you have? A cocktail?'

'I'd rather have a whisky.'

'Me, too. Cocktails are pretty filthy, aren't they? Waiter! Two whiskies. No ice.' While they waited for this commission to be fulfilled, his companion went on, with the irrepressible curiosity that was her stock-in-trade: 'So what brings you to Berlin?'

'Family business,' he said. 'You?'

Their drinks arrived. 'Oh, I'm here to work—although you mightn't think it, to see me now. Bung-ho!'

'Cheers,' he said, taking a swig of what turned out to be a

130

rather good malt whisky. 'Work? Oh, I see. You write about films, don't you?'

'For my sins,' she said. 'Yes, I'm here to do a piece—on rising stars in the German cinema—for *Sight & Sound*. At least,' she corrected herself. 'I was *supposed* to be doing a piece. I've not the faintest idea what I'll write about *now*...'

'Oh?' said Rowlands, with the feeling he knew what was coming. 'Why's that?'

Iris Barnes gave a brittle laugh. 'Well, it's all rather awkward,' she said. 'I turn up at the studio, all set to interview my Rising Star—only to find that the poor girl's been bumped off. I call it most unsporting...'

'I take it you're referring to Sybille Schönig?'

'Yes. Did you know the lady?' But before Rowlands could reply, they were joined by someone else. 'I see that you two English people have found one another,' said Helmut Hartmann, with what seemed a rather forced attempt at joviality. The man seemed distracted, thought Rowlands. After Metzner's revelations, it was not hard to guess why... 'Oh, we're old friends, aren't we, Mr Rowlands?' said Iris Barnes. 'That is good,' came the reply. 'My wife will be so pleased. She always likes her parties to be a success...'

'I'd say it's a tremendous success! One meets such interesting people in Berlin. Although,' said the girl, 'I'm not sure I care for *all* of them...' Because a brief, but discernible, lull in the conversational buzz that filled the room told Rowlands that someone else had arrived—a guest of someone importance, it would seem. 'Forgive me,' said Hartmann, confirming this impression. 'But there's someone I must...' A moment later, he could be heard greeting the newcomer: 'Obersturmführer von Fritsch! This is an honour... But I do not see the Reichsminister...'

'He sends his apologies,' was the brusque reply. 'Government business, you know.'

'Of course. Allow me to introduce you to some people...' Escorted by the famous actor, von Fritsch and his entourage began to move across the room, pausing from time to time, as Hartmann performed the introductions to this person and that. 'Do you know Herr Ziegler? Paul is one of our most distinguished actors...'

'I have heard of you, of course,' said the SS officer coldly.

'I must say, I call that rather rude,' said Miss Barnes in Rowlands's ear. 'Walking off like that, without so much as a handshake. But then Ziegler's a Jew...'

'And this is Fräulein Stöbel, one of our most promising young actresses...'

'I suppose, in the absence of the Schönig, I'll have to interview *her*,' muttered Rowland's companion. 'Can't say I relish the prospect. She looks a conceited little thing. Look how she's making eyes at the Stormtrooper! Quite revolting...'

'Herr Engelmann you know, I believe?'

'They say *he's* one of the Führer's favourites. Must be his Aryan good looks,' said Miss Barnes scornfully. 'Now they're going over to talk to the lovely Magdalena. Good. I was afraid they might have been heading in our direction. I can't abide Nazis, can you?'

'Not in the least,' said Rowlands.

'Tell you what, let's get ourselves another drink, and then you can tell me what brings *you* to this little gathering. I'd no idea you were a film enthusiast...'

'I'm not,' said Rowlands. 'Or not any more.'

'I suppose it must limit one's appreciation, being blind,' said the girl cheerfully. 'Waiter!' She took the empty glass from Rowlands's hand, and replaced it with a full one. 'Here's how,' she said.

'Here's how.'

'Funny to think of our meeting here, after all this time,' she said; then, with characteristic directness: 'Do you ever see her?'

There was no point in pretending he didn't know to whom she was referring. 'No. At least, not lately.'

'Yes, I suppose she's rather taken herself out of circulation, since she married... living in a castle in Scotland, or wherever it is...'

'Ireland,' said Rowlands.

'I knew it was somewhere at the back-of-beyond. Yes, I wouldn't have thought it was *at all* Celia's thing,' said this forthright young woman. 'Crumbling castles, and blood feuds, and all those dreadful, horsey people....' Perhaps divining, from Rowlands's silence, that this was unfruitful territory, she changed the subject. 'So if it isn't an interest in film that brings you here,' she went on, 'then what *is* it you're after?'

Rowlands laughed. 'Don't people ever tell you to mind your own business?' Iris Barnes seemed not in the least put out by the rebuke. 'Oh, I make a living out of asking impertinent questions. But if you'd rather not say...'

'There's no mystery about it. I'm here on family business, as I said.' Briefly, he put her in the picture about his search for the missing boys, leaving out any mention of his arrangement with Inspector Gentz. 'But how awful!' said the girl, with what sounded like real concern. 'Your poor sister must be desperately worried.' Then, reverting to professional inquisitiveness: 'So you think there may be a connection with the Schönig affair?'

'Only in as much as the night the boys disappeared was also the night she was killed,' said Rowlands guardedly. 'Perhaps,' he added, struck by a thought, 'you'd let me know if you hear of anything? I mean, while you're putting your questions to people...'

'I'll do what I can,' she replied. 'Although I'm not sure whether the magazine will stump up expenses for more than a day or two—given that Sybille Schönig is out of the picture, so to speak...'

'Alas, poor Sybille!' said a voice Rowlands knew. 'Such a loss to the profession! How we'll manage without her, I can't imagine... But I am sure we shall.'

'Good evening, Herr Herz,' said Rowlands. 'Oh, Gunther, *please*! It's what everybody calls me.' The Lighting Director gave a whinnying laugh. 'Yes, it's "Call for Gunther" when anything goes wrong with the lighting, you know... But I don't believe I've had the pleasure...'

'My apologies,' said Rowlands. 'Allow me to introduce Fräulein Barnes. Fräulein Barnes, Herr Herz.'

'Awfully glad to meet you.'

'Delighted. And what brings you to our beloved—or should I say *benighted*—city?'

'I'm a journalist.'

133

'Better and better! You are here to report on the exciting prospects we are to enjoy under our new administration, perhaps?' It occurred to Rowlands that 'Gunther' had had rather more than was good for him in the way of drink. 'I'm not a reporter,' said Miss Barnes, ignoring this provocative remark. 'My interest is in film.'

'Of course. Otherwise you would not be here. So,' went on the young man, in the same over-dramatic tone he had adopted throughout this exchange, 'you are here to discover our secrets...' He gave another high-pitched giggle. 'There are quite a lot of those, you may be sure... isn't that so, Klaus?' he said to the man who had just joined them. 'What's that?' was the grumpy rejoinder. 'I was just saying to this young lady—a journalist, you understand—that this is a place full of secrets...'

'I don't know about that,' said the man Herz had addressed. 'I know it is full of lies. Klaus König,' he said abruptly, addressing Rowlands. 'Frederick Rowlands.' Rowlands held out his hand. The other shook it. 'You're English,' he said. 'That's right. This is Fräulein Barnes, by the way.'

'The journalist, yes. Who is it that you write for?' asked König, his brusqueness perhaps no more than a cover for shyness, thought Rowlands; but then again, perhaps it was just his manner. 'Me? Oh, I do bits and pieces for everybody,' said Iris Barnes airily. 'At the moment, it's *Sight & Sound*—the new film magazine, you know...'

'I'm a writer myself,' muttered König, as if half-ashamed of the fact. 'Oh?' said Miss Barnes. 'What have you written? I'm afraid I'm not very up on German literature...'

'I write scripts,' he said. '*Fallen Angel* is one of mine, and a couple of other things you won't have heard of...'

'Klaus writes the words for the actors to say, and I light them when they are speaking,' put in Gunter Herz. 'In my opinion, it is my job which is the more necessary—since without light, the cinema would not exist... Nor indeed would our beautiful world—or not in the way we perceive it. Sight being the most important of the senses...'

'I don't know about that,' said Rowlands drily. 'Some of us get by quite well without it.'

134

'Yes, I was forgetting that you are blind. But I still maintain...'

'Have you been blind always?' asked the writer. 'No, I lost my sight during the War,' said Rowlands. 'A shrapnel injury.'

'Ah, that wretched War!' was the reply. 'We must hope that...' König broke off, as someone else joined them. 'Please,' said a gravelly voice Rowlands recognised as that of the character actor, Paul Ziegler. 'Do not let me interrupt. I could not help but hear that you were speaking English...'

'Oh, we are quite international here,' quipped Herz. 'Herr Rowlands, this is Herr Ziegler, one of our most distinguished actors...'

'I know who you are,' said Rowlands, as they shook hands. 'I had the pleasure of being present during the filming of the nightclub scene.'

The actor gave a self-deprecating laugh. 'Hardly my finest hour. But we jobbing actors must take what parts we are offered in these... shall we say... *uncertain* times.'

'You are not complaining about your lines, I hope?' interjected König. 'Not at all, my dear fellow,' was the reply. 'The lines themselves do very well. I only wish there were more of them... But one must be grateful for what one receives. I have a daughter in England,' he confided to Rowlands. 'She lives in Manchester. A pleasant town, I have always found it.'

Rowlands murmured his agreement. 'My daughter would like very much that I join her in England. She is married, you understand, with children. Two girls,' said the old man proudly. 'But I say to her, "Leah, *mein Liebchen*, what would I do in Manchester? Berlin is my home. It is here that I will stay, for as long as I am able to work"...' Across the room, Obersturmführer von Fritsch said something to Magda Hartmann which made her laugh: a deep, throaty chuckle. 'Of course,' said Ziegler wryly. 'it may be that the decision is taken out of my hands.'

It struck Rowlands that this would be as good an opportunity as any to quiz Ziegler as to what he remembered of that fatal Friday night. 'We were talking just now about Sybille Schönig,' he said. 'Miss Barnes here was to have interviewed her, but now...'

'That poor child,' said Paul Ziegler softly. 'Such a terrible thing. She had some talent, little Sybille. But she was was—how do you say this? *Eigenwillig.*'

'Headstrong,' said König.

'Thank you. Yes, she was headstrong. Not always pleasant to others. But, as I said, she was not without talent…'

'You were there the night she died, weren't you?' said Rowlands. 'In the studio, I mean…'

'Yes, I was there. We all were,' said Paul Ziegler. 'I understand that Fräulein Schönig was upset about something?' persisted Rowlands. 'I suppose you are referring to that silly quarrel she had with Bruno. To tell you the truth, I didn't pay much attention,' said the actor. 'In our profession, people are always losing their tempers about trivial matters—and then the next day it is all forgotten.'

'Except that by the next day she was dead,' said Klaus König. 'And we are all asking ourselves, "Who has done this?"'

'It is a great mystery,' said Herz, swallowing a yawn. 'Not because we cannot imagine who could have done this, but because we can all think of any number of people who could quite happily have killed Sybille Schönig. I include myself, of course,' he added, with a smile.

Around them, the room had filled up, and was now loud with the sound of people taking at the tops of their voices. Glasses clinked, and the smoke from Turkish cigarettes rose in a perfumed cloud. Here, in this elegant room, were gathered some of the cinema's greatest ornaments—the women in the backless satin or *crêpe de Chine* gowns that were being worn that season, Rowlands had been reliably informed by his new friend, Lena Pfeiffer; the men in evening dress. He himself had been thus kitted out by the obliging Fräulein Müller, at the insistence of her colleague. 'You can't turn up at one of Ma Hartmann's swanky parties in a lounge suit,' Fräulein Pfeiffer had said. 'Not that you wouldn't be the handsomest man there, regardless of what you wore…'

They were interrupted at that moment by a waiter bearing *canapés.* In the momentary distraction brought about by this, Ziegler started taking to König about a new script he was writing, in which, he said, he hoped there would be a part for him.

136

'This will be a charming story, about the early life of our great emperor, Friedrich,' he said to Rowlands. 'There is a vogue just now for films about our imperial past,' he added slyly.

'How interesting. But about that night...'

'I say!' said Iris Barnes. 'Isn't that Sabine Makowska?'

'I couldn't tell you.'

'I'm sure it *is* her. She's marvellous, isn't she? I adored her in *The Soldier's Return*. I wonder if *she'd* agree to do an interview?'

A moment later, she could be heard addressing the actress, in suitably awestruck tones. 'Excuse me,' said Ziegler. 'But I think I see my agent over there. It has been a pleasure, Herr...'

'Rowlands,' he said. 'Indeed,' replied the other politely. 'I remember now. That business with the newspaper. You were very good—for a beginner.'

'Thank you.'

'Well, goodbye, Herr Rowlands. My agent, you understand...'

'Of course.' It was proving impossible to get a straight answer to a question, thought Rowlands. All the people he'd spoken to so far had proved evasive—or had lied outright about what they'd seen and heard that night. And yet... His intuition—blind man's sixth sense—call it what you will, told him there was something he was missing... Something just out of the range of vision (metaphorically speaking), but which, once it came into shot, would bring the whole affair into focus...

CLOSE-UP

10

MAGDA HARTMANN WAS HOLDING court on a *chaise longue* in the centre of the room, surrounded by a group of admirers, of which Obersturmführer von Fritsch was apparently one. Hearing the clipped tones of that voice, Rowlands's first instinct was to back away. But at that moment, their hostess must have caught sight of him, for she cried: 'Herr Rowlands! I am so glad you are here! Do come and sit by me.' She patted the space beside her. There was an awkward moment as Rowlands, attempting to obey this command, half-collided with the Nazi officer, who had just that minute risen from the place of honour. 'Awfully sorry,' he said, realising to his satisfaction that he had trodden hard on von Fritsch's foot. 'It is of no consequence,' said the other coldly; then, turning back towards their hostess: 'You will not forgetwhat I have said, *gnädige Frau?*'

'You know that I will not.' It was said in an undertone. A moment later, the actress resumed her vivacious manner: 'But you cannot be leaving us already, Obersturmführer?'

'I am afraid that I must.' There followed a clicking of heels, as he bent to kiss Frau Hartmann's hand.

'A pity. Do give my regards to the dear Reichsminster...'

'Of course. *Auf Wiedersehen.*'

Von Fritsch barked an order to his subordinates, and the party of Stormtroopers left the room. A brief silence followed their departure. 'How I detest that man!' said Magda Hartmann, with a vehemence that surprised Rowlands. He realised that she was trembling all over. 'Now then,' she went on, with one of the shifts of mood he was coming to see as characteristic, 'I want to hear *all* the news from London. How *is* the dear place? It must be six or seven years since I was there. I was a guest of your charming Herr Hitchcock. Such a clever man! He wanted to make a film with me, but it came to nothing.' To a passing waiter she said: 'Bring two whiskies. It *is* whisky you're drinking, isn't it, Herr Rowlands?'

'Yes.'

'Such a very *English* drink...'

'I don't think the Scots would agree with you,' he said. 'What? Oh I see!' His hostess emitted a peal of laughter. 'What I meant was, it is one of the things we Germans regard as quintessentially English. Your tweeds and your Burberry raincoats. Your love of horses and dogs and...'

'Cricket,' suggested Rowlands.

'Exactly. Cricket. That's what you say, isn't it, when something is not right? "It isn't cricket"...'

'Sometimes,' he agreed. Their drinks arrived. 'Chin-chin,' she said, leaning closer, so that he felt himself enveloped once more in the musky fragrance of *Tabu*. 'I hope,' she went on, 'that you have been enjoying yourself? I am afraid it must be very boring for you, with nobody but a lot of actors to talk to...'

'I've met some interesting people,' he said. 'Yes, I saw you talking to Klaus. He is at least intelligent...' Given that she had been drinking since that morning, she was remarkably lucid, he thought. 'Also, his scripts are less stupid that most. It may surprise you, Herr Rowlands, but it matters very much to me that my films are not trash.'

'It doesn't surprise me at all.'

'Thank you. Of course, in the early days of my career, everything was done with looks and gestures. As an actor, one had to work harder to convey what needed to be expressed. Now it is all done with words...'

'I must confess I'm grateful for that.'

'Yes, I suppose looks and gestures are nothing to you. But you will perhaps remember what a difference they make. For example,' said the actress, lowering her voice, 'I can tell just by looking at him that my husband is not happy. He is smiling, yes, but the smile does not reach his eyes. That may be because he is talking to that idiot Stöbel girl, or it may be for another reason entirely. Then there is your friend, the English girl...'

142

'Iris Barnes.'

'That is the one. She is smiling, too—everybody in this room is smiling!—but there is something about her that I do not trust. She is talking to Sabine Makowska—what a vain creature that woman is, with her ridiculous dyed hair! But her eyes—the eyes of your Fräulein Barnes—are going all around the room...'

'I expect she's planning a story,' said Rowlands. 'She's a journalist, you know.'

'Undoubtedly she is planning something,' said Magda Hartmann. 'But I am not sure what. I would keep my eye on that young lady, if I were you. In these times,' she breathed, so softly that only Rowlands could hear, 'you can trust nobody.'

'Now, I call that unfair, Herr Rowlands!' said a voice. Gunther Herz. 'First you monopolise the delightful Fräulein Barnes, and now you have captured our charming hostess. Tell me, what is your secret?'

'Perhaps I've got a sympathetic face,' said Rowlands. He was beginning to find the Lighting Director's manner irritating. So, it seemed was his companion: 'Oh, do go away, Gunther,' she said crossly. 'Can't you see that Herr Rowlands and I are talking?'

'My apologies. I did not mean to disturb your *tête à tête*. Only there is a young man who very much wants to meet you.' He gave a simpering laugh. 'A *protégé* of mine. Quite an infant, really. But he has talent. He tells me that he has been an admirer of yours since he was a little, little child...'

Magda Hartmann sighed. 'And what is this prodigy's name?'

'Andreas Eisner. That blond boy, over by the window. He is a cinematographer, by the way. He will be working with me on *Young Friedrich*.'

'Tell him I'll be there in a moment.'

'He will be honoured. Already, he is trembling with nerves at the thought of meeting his idol...'

'What an imbecile that man is,' said the actress, when Gunther Herz had gone to join his friend. 'But he is good at his job, which is why I tolerate him. When I began my career in films, all those years ago, he was just starting out...' So Herz must be older than Rowlands had thought. 'I made his name, as much as he made mine,' she added, with what seemed a note of real affection. 'But I must leave you, Herr Rowlands, for the present. Unless you would care to meet a lovestruck cinematographer...'

Rowlands smiled. 'I'd rather not,' he said. Magda Hartmann began to get to her feet—with some difficulty, for the chaise longue on which they had been sitting was low. He got up first, and gave her his hand. It struck him that there was no time like the present to ask what he wanted to ask. 'There was one thing...' He took the photographs from his breast-pocket, and held them out to her. 'I wondered if you recall seeing either of these boys?'

She took them from him; glanced at them swiftly, then handed them back. 'No,' she said, 'I have not seen them. Who are they?'

Rowlands explained.

'So that it why you are here. For a moment I thought...' She broke off. 'You thought what?' he said. Magda Hartmann laughed. 'Why, that you had come for me,' she said. 'What else should I think?'

'So you think Hartmann killed her?' said Inspector Gentz, puffing thoughtfully at one of the evil-smelling, cheap cigars he favoured, as the two of them sat over a *Schnapps* in a bar not far from the Alex. 'I didn't say that,' said Rowlands. 'All I'm saying is that I've reason to believe he was in Sybille Schönig's dressing-room at around the time of the murder...'

'And what reason might that be?' said the policeman, sardonically. 'Not your famous intuition, I hope?'

'A witness,' said Rowlands.

'Ah! Now we're getting somewhere. The name of this witness, if you please?'

'I'm afraid I can't tell you that.'

'Then what are you suggesting? That I should haul Helmut Hartmann out of bed and interrogate him? He has an alibi for Friday evening, by the way. He was at home with his wife. She confirms it."

'I'm sure she does.'

'Besides which, your witness did not actually *see* him, you tell me. All he—or she—heard was a voice.'

144

'A very distinctive voice.'

'Perhaps,' said Gentz gloomily. He gave an order to the waiter to bring another round of drinks. 'No more for me,' said Rowlands. 'I'll have a thick head tomorrow, as it is...'

'Then you are becoming one of us,' said the Inspector. 'But seriously, Herr Rowlands, you want me to arrest one of Germany's most well-loved actors on suspicion of murdering his mistress? Oh, we know all about that,' he added, when Rowlands opened his mouth to protest. 'There were plenty of people eager to tell us about the affair that their esteemed colleague Helmut Hartmann was having with the girl. But that does not make him a murderer...'

'No, indeed,' said Rowlands.

Gentz drew a notebook from his pocket and flipped it open. 'All right,' he said. 'Let's see what we *do* have. You say the boys—your Billy and Walter—were last seen at their school around four-fifteen?'

'Yes.'

'They couldn't have got to the studio much before half-past five. It takes thirty-five minutes on the train, and then there's the walk at either end...'

'They must have arrived by five forty-five,' said Rowlands, 'because they were in Sybille's dressing-room when she got there soon after.'

'So you say. And this was when, exactly?'

'My witness thought it was around ten minutes to six. She'd left the studio after the quarrel with Bruno Klein...'

'Ah, yes. The famous quarrel.'

'There were a number of witnesses to the fact that they had words. Paul Ziegler, for one...'

'Strange that he didn't mention it during his interrogation.'

'Perhaps,' said Rowlands, 'nobody thought to ask him.'

'Hmph!' The Inspector took a swig of his *Schnapps*, and banged the glass down on the table. 'All right. So she quarrelled with Klein about something, and left the studio about five forty-five, reaching her dressing-room—when?'

'About three minutes later, my informant thinks. The dressing-room is only a short distance from Studio 3...'

'Yes, I gathered that you had already familiarised yourself with the layout of the place,' said the policeman, with scarcely veiled irony. 'So she gets to the dressing-room at around five forty-eight, and finds these boys...'

'Not the boys,' said Rowlands. 'Helmut Hartmann.'

'But you said...'

'The boys were hidden behind the screen. I think they took refuge there, when they heard Hartmann coming. I found Billy's pencil, you will recall...'

'Yes, yes. The pencil. So she walks in, and finds Hartmann there... always assuming it *was* Hartmann, and not some other man...'

'My informant is sure it was Hartmann.'

'Yes, yes. His voice. All right. Then *they* quarrel—or so you tell me. Does your informant have any idea what the quarrel was about?'

'No. Only that Hartmann said something to Fräulein Schönig about the risks she was running, and told her she'd better be careful or it would end badly for her...'

'That sounds like a threat.'

'Or a warning.'

'Indeed. Did your informant hear anything more?'

'Unfortunately not. I was hoping you'd be able to fill in the rest,' said Rowlands meekly. 'Seeing as it's more your department than mine.'

'Murder, you mean?' Inspector gave a dry chuckle. 'It is indeed my department, as you call it. Very well.' He lowered his voice a notch or two, although to the best of Rowlands's knowledge, they were alone in the place, apart from the barman, who was busying himself polishing glasses, or whatever it was that barmen did. When Rowlands had earlier remarked on how quiet it was, Gentz had said drily, 'Perhaps you had not heard? Our Leader is addressing the nation tonight. Everyone will be at home, listening to their radio sets...'

Now he said into the unaccustomed quiet: 'Sybille Schönig was killed with a .22 calibre bullet to the head, fired from a pearl-handled Colt pistol. Another bullet had been fired, but this went wide of the mark, and was retrieved from the wall

146

opposite. Curious,' he said. 'One would have thought the first shot would have put her on the alert, but it seems she stood there and allowed herself to be shot at point-blank range...'

'Perhaps she was frozen with fear,' said Rowlands.

'Perhaps. At any rate all this took place at some time between five-forty-five, when she left the studio, and eleven minutes past seven, when her body was found by her dresser, Fräulein Pabst... I know what you are going to say,' he went on, as Rowlands made as if to speak. 'According to your evidence, or that of your informant, she was still alive at, shall we say, five minutes past six?' Gentz allowed a pause to elapse. 'Or even later, if, as you suggest, there was someone else with her in the dressing-room after Hartmann left. Someone who might very well have been her murderer.'

The car dropped him off in front of the Metzners' building in Marienburgerstrasse. He had a latchkey, supplied by Sara Metzner, and so was able to let himself in without the necessity of rousing the whole household. So he was surprised—and not a little startled—to find his sister waiting for him, just inside the door of the flat. 'Where have you been?'

'I told you I might be late...'

'Well, come on!' she said. 'There's no time to lose. No, don't take your coat off. We'll be going out again soon.' Mystified, he allowed her draw him towards the living-room, where he found a committee of women—Frau Metzner, Clara, and someone he did not know—awaiting him. He wondered, briefly, what had become of Joachim. 'They've been seen,' said Dorothy, without further preamble. 'This lady—Frau Hüber—recognised them from our poster...'

'Oh?' Rowlands's heart gave a leap. 'Where was this?'

'There is a house for orphans a few streets from here,' said Clara Metzner. 'This woman works there, in the kitchens...'

'She says Walter has been staying there, for the past two or three nights,' put in Dorothy. 'She isn't sure about Billy...'

'The children come in off the street.' This was Sara Metzner. 'It is always so in cold weather. But why my Walter did not come home, I do not know...'

147

'I'm sure we'll find out soon enough—if it *is* Walter she's seen. When did she—Frau Hüber—get here?'

'She has been here an hour. Perhaps an hour and a half,' said Clara. 'She will take us to the place. There is a way in, at the back, she says. The boys' dormitory is not locked at night. But we are to wait, she says, until everyone in the house is asleep. She would not want to get into trouble...'

'Of course not.'

'She does not speak English,' said the girl. 'But...'

'*Ich will mein Geld*,' said the woman, Frau Hüber, suddenly.

'She says...'

'I know what she said.'

'I've said she can have half now,' said Dorothy. 'The rest when we find the boys.'

'All right.' he took what change he had from his pocket—about fifty marks—and counted it into the woman's outstretched palm. 'I've got a hundred-mark note in my purse,' said Dorothy. 'Good. But I thought we said...'

'She says it isn't enough. It was risky for her to come here, to a Jewish family, and...'

'Pay her whatever she wants,' said Rowlands. 'But surely we should get going? It's after ten.' A thought struck him. 'Have the police been informed?'

'Of course. It was they who gave her this address.'

'Then we'd better lose no time,' said Rowlands grimly.

After a brief altercation between mother and daughter as to who should be the one to go, and who should remain behind, they left Clara in charge of her young cousin and set off, into the Berlin night. It was icy underfoot, and Rowlands was glad of the support of his sister's arm, as, with Frau Metzner walking ahead of them, and the woman from the orphanage leading the way, they plunged into the network of little streets which lay between Greifswalderstrasse and Prenzlauer Allee. All the while that they were walking, in a silence broken only by their guide's brusque instructions: '*Links*,' or '*Rechts*', Rowlands was thinking, 'Perhaps it'll be all right...' Hoping against hope that the forces which had silenced Fritzi Henkel had not caught up with them yet.

148

But as they turned the corner into Danzigerstrasse, they could smell the smoke. A low cry of horror came from the women, and then Dorothy let go of Rowlands's arm, and broke into a run. By the time Rowlandshad caught up with her, the fire, which had ravaged the building, had been put out, but the terrible stench of burnt wood and scorched masonry hung in the air. 'When did it happen?' said Rowlands to a man who was standing by—to which the answer was, he didn't know exactly, but he'd heard the fire-truck go by about forty minutes ago. It had woken him up, he said. He and the wife had come out to see what all the fuss was about. A terrible thing. The building had gone up like matchwood. Deathtraps, these old houses. And this was the result. Six dead. Five of them children...

Rowlands thanked him with a nod, and turned away, sick at heart. If he'd only come home earlier! If he'd thought to warn Dorothy... If, if, if. But it was no use tormenting himself with such thoughts now. Frustration at his own uselessness in such an emergency exacerbated his mood of self-reproach. He cursed himself for a fool. Hadn't Gentz warned him at the start? 'These are dangerous people... They will stop at nothing—not even the killing of children.' Over the shouts of those engaged in the rescue operation, he could hear his sister's voice. 'Billy!' she was shouting. 'Where are you? Billy!'

Just then, a groan arose from the watching crowd. Rowlands guessed that another body had been brought out. 'I must see,' cried Sara Metzner. 'It may be that it is my Walter...' Rowlands held her back. He'd seen enough of what fire can do to a human being to know that this was a sight she should be spared. In the same moment, he felt a tug on his sleeve. It was Frau Hüber, the woman who had led them here. 'Give me my money!' She sounded terrified. He was about to reply that she could whistle for her money—because what had she done to earn it? Only brought them to this place of death and destruction. But then it struck him that she'd put herself at risk too. 'All right. I'll get your money.'

He pushed his way through the crowd, until he found Dorothy. She was weeping now, her sobs interspersed with soft cries: 'Oh, Billy, where are you? Billy!' Rowlands put his arm around her. 'Come on, old thing,' he said. 'There's nothing for us here.'

'How can you say that?' she cried. 'He might be here. I'm not leaving until I find him...' The grim thought that her son might be among the dead had not yet occurred to her, it seemed. 'Look,' he said gently. 'How would it be if I stayed? You and Sara should go home. Then if there's any news, I...' But just then he felt her freeze. 'My God,' she said. 'I don't believe it... That boy. Over there. The one with the glasses. Oh, I do wish he'd look this way, so that I can be sure...' But the boy himself must have seen her, or perhaps she'd managed to attract his attention, for a moment later, someone came running over to where they were standing, and a voice said, 'Please, Aunt Dorothea, I would like to go home now...'

'I cannot be sure, because the light was bad, but I think they were Brownshirts,' said the boy. In spite of the hot soup with which he had been fed, and the blankets in which he had been wrapped, he could not stop shivering. 'There was a noise—of breaking glass—and then a noise like...' He faltered, as if the effort of describing this were too much for him. 'It is time you were in bed,' said his mother. '...like the sound the boiler in the bathroom makes when it catches light,' the boy went on, sounding pleased to have found this analogy. 'An explosion,' said Rowlands. 'Yes. But a quiet sound, not a loud bang, you know...'

'I think I do.' A petrol bomb, thought Rowlands. It didn't need a charge, just the application of a match to a gasoline-soaked rag, thrust into a bottle. Cheap, and untraceable. 'What happened then?'

'Fred, the boy's exhausted,' put in Rowlands's sister. 'Can't this wait until morning?' Because after it had been established that Billy wasn't at the orphanage—had never been there, in fact—she'd lost the sense of urgency which had informed all her movements that evening, and reverted to her earlier mood of listless fatalism. 'I think he'll tell us when he's had enough,' said Rowlands. 'Won't you, Walter, old chap?'

'Yes.'

'Good lad. So you saw some Brownshirts throw something, and then there was the sound of breaking glass, and right after that the building caught fire—that right?'

'Yes.'

'Where were you at that moment?'

'I was on the top floor—where the boys' dormitory is... The girls are on the floor below,' said Walter. 'I... I couldn't sleep, and so I was at the window, looking down into the street, when I saw the men...'

'A good thing you were,' said Rowlands. 'So you gave the alarm, did you?'

'I... I tried to.' Walter's voice trembled slightly. 'But... but it was hard to wake some of the boys. They were so tired, you know, and the smoke was very thick...' He broke off. 'Fred, *really...*' protested Dorothy, but the boy said fiercely, 'No, I want to tell.'

'Go on.'

'Then some of us got out onto the fire-escape. It goes up to the top floor, you see, so there was a way out. But you had to climb out of the window to get onto it and... and not all the boys could manage it. Some of the little ones...' Again, his voice faltered. 'I *will* tell it,' he said, as if to himself. 'Some of them couldn't make it,' he went on, in a flat voice. 'The girls, too. We tried to wake them, by banging on the window, but...'

'All right,' said Rowlands, reaching out to pat the boy's shoulder. 'We know you did your best.'

'It wasn't good enough,' said Walter, still in the same monotonous tone. 'I could have saved more of them, if I had tried harder...'

'Don't think about that,' said Rowlands gently. 'Think about the ones you *did* save. Now I think you'd better head off to bed, old chap—or your mother will want to know why.' Dorothy was right, he thought. After all the child had been through that night—to say nothing of what had happened before, about which he remembered little—it would have been cruel to have questioned him further. He could recall leaving Babelsberg, and catching the train to Anhalter Bahnhof, he said. He'd been meaning to come straight home, but the next thing he remembered was waking up in the orphanage. How many days had passed since he got there, he couldn't say. He thought perhaps he'd had an accident, because he had an awful pain in his ribs, and his knees and hands were grazed. He'd only remembered who he was and what had happened when he saw Aunt Dorothea... Even though Rowlands was impatient to know the answers to a whole raft of questions, he knew it'd have to wait until Walter was better able to face such a grilling. All he'd said, when Dorothy had asked him where Billy was, was that he didn't know. They'd split up, he said, because Billy had forgotten his satchel and insisted on going back for it... 'Back to the school, do you mean?' said Rowlands. 'No.' Walter hesitated. 'We'd left school by then.'

'So this was at Babelsberg?'

'Yes.'

'Was this before or after you went to Sybille Schönig's dressing-room?'

'After.'

'All right. Go on...'

But there hadn't been that much more to say. Walter had waited in vain for Billy to come back—they'd previously arranged a meeting-place, in a deserted part of the Back Lot: 'It was a house, you know... only not a real house. Just the front part, with steps going up to a door, and windows, and part of a roof. It looked as if it were made out of stone, but it was only painted wood...'

'Like a theatre flat,' said Rowlands. 'Yes,' said the boy. 'There is a whole street of houses like this. Another one of shops. From the front, you cannot see that there is nothing behind, but steel struts and girders... We chose the third house in the street. If anything went wrong—that is, if anybody saw us—we were to separate and meet up later. Whoever got to the meeting-place first, was to leave a sign that he had been there...'

'What kind of sign?'

'Oh, you know...' Walter seemed embarrassed to admit that he'd ever taken such childish stratagems seriously. 'A mark of some kind, that only the other would recognise. A message. I left my handkerchief,' he said. 'It has my initials on it and so I knew he would know I had been there...'

'Where did you leave it?'

'I tied it to the door-knocker,' said Walter. 'So that Wilhelm would see it.'

'Perhaps he did,' said Rowlands. 'Now, off you go...' They'd go into things in the morning, he thought. In the meantime, he'd consider the vexed question of what was to happen to Walter. One thing was certain, it wasn't safe for him here—or it wouldn't be for long... But he said none of this to the others, as Walter, having wished them all a sleepy Goodnight, was bundled off to bed by his mother.

'You can be certain of one thing,' said Joachim Metzner. 'They'll blame the Communists for this. After what happened on Monday...' He meant the shooting of a Stormtrooper, during the torchlight parade, Rowlands supposed—'...they're determined to get their revenge. This won't be the last outrage of its kind, you'll see!'

The youth, who had been back at the flat in Marienburgerstrasse by the time Rowlands and the women had returned with Walter, had refused to be drawn as to his whereabouts that evening. 'It's better if you don't know,' he said, when taxed by his mother as to what he'd been up to. Now he said to Rowlands: 'So you think they were out to kill Walter and Billy, all along?'

'Don't say such things!' This was Clara. 'Even if they *were* out to get them, for some reason—and who exactly are we talking about, please?—they couldn't have known Walter would be at the orphanage tonight...'

Rowlands, who suspected that 'they' could have known it all too easily, was silent. There was no sense in frightening the girl more that she already was.

153

11

IN THE MORNING, THERE was a letter for Rowlands from his wife. It was the usual family news. Edith's mother had recovered from her cold. There had been another fall of snow, but it didn't look as if it would lie. Edith hoped he was wearing his warm coat. She didn't ask when he would be coming home, but a noncommittal sentence—*I imagine that you'll be staying on awhile*—showed that his wife was well aware of his intention to see the thing through. There followed a series of postscripts: 'Dear Daddy, I hope you are well, and that you are having a nice time in Berlin,' wrote his eldest daughter, Margaret. 'I came top in Algebra and am quite enjoying Latin...' The few lines from his eleven year-old made him smile: 'Daddy, I hope you come home soon. It is very dull without you. I have been trying to teach Joanie to play *Beggar My Neighbour*, but she doesn't like giving up any of her cards. When you see Billy, tell him he can borrow my bicycle if he likes. I miss you. Love from Anne...'

'*Walter, Schatz, du musst...*'

'Don't fuss, *Mutti!* I've told you, I'm quite all right...'

'Ah, here's the man I want to see,' said Rowlands, as Walter, followed by his anxious parent, came into the kitchen, and sat down at the table. 'I hope you slept well?'

'Yes, thank you,' said the boy, attacking with some enthusiasm the bowl of porridge which his mother set down in front of him. 'Then when you've finished getting outside that,' said Rowlands, 'perhaps you'd like to tell me about the last time you saw Billy.'

'I told you,' said Walter. 'It was when he and I left the dressing-room... Fräulein Schönig's dressing-room,' he amended. 'I went to the meeting-place—the third house, as I said—and waited there more than an hour. It was very cold...'

'I'm sure it was. Even so, when Billy failed to turn up, wouldn't the simplest thing have been to go in search of him?

'I did,' said the boy. 'After he didn't show up, I tried to go back to the dressing-room. But when I reached the corridor outside it, there was no sign of Billy. Only...' His voice faltered. 'There were lots of police about. I was afraid they must have arrested him,' he said. 'Because we were trespassing, you know. Either that, or he'd gone back to Berlin without me...'

'And you thought there was little point in hanging around. You decided to make your own way back. So you didn't see Billy again after he went back for his satchel?'

'That is so. I told him it was stupid, but he insisted. When he makes up his mind, there is nothing you can do to change it...'

'I'm sure his mother would agree, wouldn't you?' Rowlands said to Dorothy. 'Billy knows his own mind,' she said.

'Now, Walter, I want you to go back a bit—to when you and Billy first arrived at the studio. You got past the gatekeeper—I don't need to know how—and went to Fräulein Schönig's dressing-room...'

'Yes. I knew she would be at the studio that day, and so...'

'You had no business going there without permission!' snapped Joachim, coming in at that moment. 'You could have got me into a lot of trouble...'

'Let's leave that for now,' said Rowlands. 'You were in the dressing-room, when Fräulein Schönig came back from the studio, weren't you? She must have been surprised to see you...'

'She didn't know we were there at first. We... we hid behind the screen when we heard someone coming. We didn't know if it was her or not, and so...'

'Why didn't you come out, when you realised it *was* her?'

'Because someone else came in just then.'

'Do you know who it was?'

Walter hesitated a moment before replying. 'Yes. It was Helmut Hartmann.'

'I see. And what happened then?'

'Fräulein Schönig said, "What are *you* doing here?" And then *he* said, "I want to talk to you..." Herr Hartmann was angry with Fräulein Schönig. He called her a bad name. I do not wish

156

to say this word in front of my mother...'

'Quite right,' said Rowlands. 'They were quarrelling, in fact?'

'Yes. He—Herr Hartmann—said something about Fräulein Schönig's being in danger. He said she'd better take care, because one of these days, she'd go too far...'

This much Rowlands had already heard from Joachim Metzner.

'Then Fräulein Schönig got angry, too. She... she said if he hadn't been such a coward, they could have got away before now, and then none of this would have happened...'

'What do you think she meant by that?

'I don't know.'

'And what did *he* say?'

Walter took a moment to reflect. 'He said that even if he *was* a coward, it would never have worked. She was too ambitious for that. Why, just look at the way she'd dropped him, as soon as a better opportunity came along... and she said: "That's a horrible thing to say." Then Herr Hartmann said: "But it's true, isn't it?"'

There was silence for a moment. 'Go on,' said Rowlands.

'There's not much more to tell. Wilhelm sneezed, because the dust had got in his nose... and Fräulein Schönig found us,' said Walter. 'She was angry with us at first...'

'And Herr Hartmann?'

'He was angry, too. He said: "If this is one of your stupid tricks, Sybille, I've had just about enough of them. I'm not staying here to be made a fool of anymore..." Then he went out...'

'What happened after Herr Hartmann left the dressing-room?'

'She... Fräulein Schönig... was nice to us. She said she wasn't angry with us anymore, because she knew we hadn't meant any harm...'

'All right,' said Rowlands. 'Now, I want you to think very carefully before you answer my next question, Walter. You say that you and Billy left the dressing-room, after your conversation with Fräulein Schönig? And then Billy went back.'

'Yes. I've already said...'

'I just want to get it absolutely clear. So when you left her, Sybille Schönig was alive and well?'

'Fred...' There was a warning note in Dorothy's voice. 'He'll have to know sometime,' said Rowlands. 'It might as well be now.'

'Know what?' This was Walter, sounding suddenly very young and scared. 'Has something happened to Fräulein Schönig?'

'I'm afraid so.'

'Oh.'

'No need to cry about it, you great baby,' said Joachim roughly. 'She's dead. And it looks as if Helmut Hartmann killed her.'

'I don't think,' said Rowlands, 'that we ought to jump to conclusions. 'From what Walter says, Herr Hartmann had already left...'

'Yes. But he could have gone back,' said the young man, in a voice that trembled with barely suppressed emotion. 'He threatened her, didn't he?'

'It sounded like a warning rather than a threat,' said Rowlands.

On the journey to Babelsberg, Metzner was silent and abstracted, speaking only in monosyllables, and giving the impression to Rowlands, who paid attention to such things, of having more on his mind than he had so far admitted. 'Where do you want to go?' said Joachim, as they reached the gate. 'Only I must be at work very soon.' He muttered a *'Guten Morgen'* to the porter, and the man grunted and waved them through. 'Oh, I won't keep you long,' said Rowlands. 'I'd just like you to take me to this famous Back Lot—with the street of houses your brother mentioned...'

'Why do you want to go there?' interrupted the youth. 'There is nothing to see.'

'That's for me to judge, since I'm the one doing the "seeing",' said Rowlands mildly.

A few minutes' walk brought them to the site, which lay to the right of the studio complex. It was as Walter had described it, like a small town—only a town without cars, trams, buses or people; a town without noise or bustle—without any sign of life, in fact. Here, Metzner said, was a street consisting of shops—a chemist's, a tobacconist's, a dress-shop—all of them closed-up and deserted now, in the depths of winter. 'They

158

don't shoot here, at this time of year,' he added. 'The weather's too uncertain.'

'What happens if you need to film a street scene?'

'We mock it up in the studio.'

'So you do,' said Rowlands, remembering his turn as an extra. 'Describe the rest of it, please.'

'All right. Beyond the commercial district set, is a set made up of houses. These are city houses, from a poor area, so they are old and broken-down. Like our street in Prenzlauerberg, in fact,' he added. 'Over there is another street, with much bigger houses, like the ones in Grünewald...'

'And which street was it that your brother arranged to meet Billy, I wonder? Let's find out, shall we?'

'But...'

'Come on,' said Rowlands. 'It won't take a minute.'

'What are we looking for?' Joachim sounded far from pleased at this disruption of his morning's schedule.

'A handkerchief.'

'*What?*'

'You heard me. Now let's get on with it.' But although they walked up and down both sides of the false street, they didn't find what Rowlands was looking for. 'He said the third house along, with steps up to the front door, and a door-knocker,' he murmured, half to himself. 'Do any of these have steps?'

'No. They are workers' houses, as I told you. Their doors open straight onto the street.'

'Then let's try the next lot.' This was a row of much finer houses, according to Joachim. 'It is meant to be Paris, in the last century. We were filming *La Dame Aux Camélias*, with Sabine Makowska as Marguerite...'

'It sounds delightful. Do these houses have steps?'

'No.'

'Then let's forget about Paris. What about the next street? The one you said was like Grünewald?' Grumbling a little under his breath, Joachim led the way. 'Now, that sounds more like it!' said Rowlands, when the former had put him in the picture as to the layout of these edifices. Because not only did they have steps leading up to the front door, and two rows of windows on

159

either side, as Walter had said, but each was furnished with a brass letterbox and door-knocker. 'It was the third house along, he said...'

Rowlands's elation was short-lived, however. For there wasn't a handkerchief to be seen, on this, or any of the other doors. At his insistence, they searched the area round about in case the thing had blown away, but found nothing. 'This is a waste of time,' said Joachim.

'Hang on a minute.'

They were by this time standing behind the structure—you couldn't call it a building, although he supposed it must resemble one. He sniffed the air, then stooped and ran his fingers over a patch of ground. 'Someone's been having a fire here. Quite recently, too...' This in itself wasn't much—just a ring of stones, surrounding a few charred twigs. 'It hasn't snowed heavily since the night I arrived,' said Rowlands. 'Otherwise it would have been covered up. And look here...'

Because now that he knew where to search, it wasn't hard to find signs of habitation, in this rough shelter. A couple of cushions, now heavy with damp, and an old velvet curtain. A scrap of paper, torn from an exercise-book, which had wrapped a crust of bread and some crumbs of cheese... 'This is where your stolen food ended up, I'll warrant,' said Rowlands. 'And this, unless I'm much mistaken is where young Billy was hiding out.'

'You don't know that for certain.'

'I don't. But it stands to reason. This is where they arranged to meet.'

'But...'

'The fact that we didn't find Walter's handkerchief proves it,' said Rowlands. '*We* didn't find it. But Billy did. It shows he must have been here.'

'So where is he now?'

'That,' said Rowlands, 'is what I'm going to find out. First of all, I'm going to to check whether anything has been missed from the Props Room. Such as this curtain and these cushions. My guess is that's where he got them from.'

In the corridor on the way to carry out this bit of investigation, he met Lena Pfeiffer. 'Herr Rowlands! But how good to see you...'

'It's good to see you too,' he said.

'And what of the little boys? Have you found them yet?'

'I'm still looking.'

There was no reason not to confide in the girl, and yet... What was it that Magda Hartmann had said? *You can trust nobody.* 'That must be difficult, when you cannot see,' said the make-up artist, linking her arm with his, as they walked along. 'What you need is a sidekick. A Girl Friday...'

'That's what my wife says, too.'

'Oh, oh! Married are you? I might have guessed. So, that's me put in my place!'

'I didn't mean...'

'They never do,' said Lena Pfeiffer. 'Well, this is where I get off...' They'd reached the Make-Up Department. 'Unless you want to meet for a cup of coffee later?'

'I'm afraid I...'

'Thought not. It's always the same,' went on the girl airily. 'The good ones are all spoken for, and the bad ones... well, let's just say I've had more than my share of the bad ones... *Auf Wiedersehen, mein Herr,*' she said suddenly. He laughed, thinking this reversion to a more formal mode of address was all part of the joke, but then he heard who it was that was coming towards them, and knew it wasn't a joke at all. Because the first voice—sharp, peremptory—was von Fritsch's, the second—placatory—was Bruno Klein's.

'Ah, Herr Rowlands!' said Klein, as they drew near. 'I am glad to see you. There is some money due to you, for your performance in my film.'

'Thank you,' said Rowlands, turning towards him with a smile. 'But I wasn't expecting to be paid...'

'What nonsense!' Klein's laugh had a forced ring to it. 'You shouldn't have to work for nothing—should he, Obersturmführer?'

'I could not say,' was the cold reply. Then, reverting to German, and addressing Klein: 'You will let me know tomorrow at the latest?'

'Of course.'

'Good. The Reichsminister does not like to be kept waiting.' The SS man stalked away.

'Herr Rowlands, you have, as they say, saved my life,' said Klein, when the Nazi was out of earshot. 'And there *is* some money to give you, if you would care to call at the Accounts Department... What are you staring at, Fräulein?'

'Oh, nothing,' said Lena Pfeiffer. 'It's just that I think there must be something wrong with my hearing. You're actually offering to pay him before his payment's due?'

'Haven't you got work to do?' said Klein severely. 'Oh yes. I have forty-two peasant girls to give rosy, peasant faces to. Such a delightfully *wholesome* picture this will be!' she said to Rowlands. 'It is called *Love Among the Haystacks*...'

'Like the story by D.H. Lawrence?'

'Is that the man who wrote that dirty book? Oh no, I do not think this is that kind of story! It is about love, and peasant girls, and noble, virtuous young men. That is the kind of thing people like in the New Germany...'

'You watch your tongue,' said Klein. 'Really, that girl forgets herself sometimes,' he said, as he and Rowlands began walking back towards the studio block. 'But she is good at her job, and so I put up with her... Tell me, Herr Rowlands, how much longer are you planning to stay in Berlin?'

'That rather depends,' said Rowlands guardedly. 'on how soon I achieve what I set out to do...'

'Ah, yes. You were looking for your nephew, were you not? I take it you have not found him?'

'No.'

'A pity,' said Klein. They had reached the doors of Studio 3. From inside, came the cheerful hubbub of people moving to and fro, as the set for *Fallen Angel* was struck, and a new one—presumably, the one for *Love Among the Haystacks*—was erected. Shouts of *'Ein bisschen nach oben...'*, *'Links ein bisschen...'* and *'Nein, du Idiot, ich habe links gesagt!'* could be heard above the banging of hammers and the sawing of wood. 'One thing I will say to you, Herr Rowlands—do not stay a moment longer than you have to. Things are changing very fast in our country, and it is not safe for anyone. If you take my advice,' said Bruno Klein, 'you will leave as soon as possible.'

A body had been found. That was all the police had said. The message had come not ten minutes before Rowlands had walked in; the young policeman who had brought it was even now waiting outside—a car having been sent to conduct them to the mortuary at the Alex. All this Rowlands got from Frau Metzner; Dorothy being in far too agitated a state to make much sense. 'Oh God, Oh God,' she kept saying. 'What if it's him? What if it's my Billy?' As Rowlands did his best to calm his sister—'Now then, old thing! It might *not* be him, you know...'—the other woman spoke up: 'I will come, too,' she said. 'Oh, that's all right,' said Rowlands. 'No need for us both to go.' But she was insistent: 'She will need a woman with her.'

'All right.' He lowered his voice. 'I take it,' he said, 'that you haven't said anything to the police about Walter's being found?'

'I have said nothing. Walter knows that he is to stay out of sight.' This had been decided earlier. 'I am afraid that we can trust nobody—not even our neighbours,' said Frau Metzner. 'As for the police...' She let the sentence tail away—the aural equivalent of a shrug. 'Did you hear that, Dottie?' It would be a disaster if his sister, in her present distressed state, were to blurt out the truth. But she said: 'I'm not a complete fool, Fred. Of course I won't say anything...' As if, her tone implied, she, of all people, would be likely to trust the police.

As they entered the echoing foyer of the vast building, she clutched his arm. 'Oh, Fred, I'm not sure I can go through with this...'

'I'm sorry you have to,' he said. 'If it weren't for my blessed eyes...'

'It's not your fault. And I'd still want to see him. But...' She was weeping now. 'What if it's Billy? My poor, precious boy...'

'There now,' he murmured, patting her arm—an ineffectual gesture of consolation. With a policeman leading the way, they walked down what seemed like miles of corridors, their footsteps striking sharply on the tiled floor. Again, it seemed to

Rowlands, caught up as he was in the dreamlike atmosphere of the place, as if the very walls resounded with the shrieks and groans of those incarcerated there. A door slammed with a hollow sound. A shout of anger—or pain—was instantly quelled. A sick feeling of dread was never far away. Not in these times. He thought, 'This is a prison,' and was not sure whether it was the building itself he meant, the city in which that building was contained, or the country which held them both.

They descended some stairs, and found themselves in some kind of basement, for the ceiling was lower and there was an airlessness to the place, which had not been so before. Another corridor brought them to a heavy door, with, beyond it, a kind of ante-room. Here, the reek of disinfectant was strong, and Rowlands braced himself for what he knew was to follow. It had been four years since he had last set foot in such a place, and the memory of that horror was with him still. Now, as then, he was grateful to be spared the worst of it—although imagining what there was to be seen was, in some ways, as bad as having to see it... Then the policeman who had led them there opened a door, and the four of them went in, to where an orderly was waiting, beside a metal table.

The smell of disinfectant grew stronger still—and there was another smell... he had smelt that smell, too, often enough. It was the smell of the butcher's shop. The smell of the dressing-station. A smell of blood and viscera. He reached for Dorothy's hand, and squeezed it. Soon, they would know the worst, he thought. He was glad, now, that Sara Metzner had accompanied them. She would know what to do, if the thing they feared had come to pass... The policeman gave an order, which sounded strangely loud in that chill room. The orderly lifted the sheet. Beside him, Rowlands felt his sister stiffen. A long moment passed. Then she said, in a curiously flat voice, 'It's not him. But... Oh, Fred... It's so very like him. Poor little boy! I wonder who he is?'

As they crossed the courtyard in front of the police station, a car drew up in front of the gate, and someone got out—Inspector Gentz, as it transpired a moment later. 'Good day, Herr

Rowlands,' he said, with what seemed to Rowlands a certain irony. 'We seem always to be meeting, do we not?' But when Rowlands had explained the reason for their presence there, the policeman was grave for a moment. 'So you still have not found the boy—or his cousin?' The lie came easily. 'Not yet.'

'I am sorry to hear it. Sorry, too for your sister and her family,'—Rowlands having introduced the two women—'but I cannot help feeling that they—or your sister, at least—should not have to endure this. Can you not persuade her to return to England? There is nothing that she can do here...' It was the second time in as many hours that Rowlands had received such advice. He shook his head. 'I can try,' he said. 'But until the boy is found...' He had almost slipped up. 'I mean, until they are both found...'

Gentz sighed: the gusty sigh of a large, heavy man, much beset by troubles. 'It would be far better if people left such matters to the proper authorities,' he said, raising his voice a little. 'We have the means and manpower, while you you do not... Isn't that so, Schneider?' For it appeared that his colleague had joined them. 'I was just saying to Herr Rowlands that it would be better for him if he were to leave this investigation to us...'

'Much better,' was the brusque reply. 'We have not found your nephew yet—but be assured, we *will* find him.' It seemed to Rowlands that he gave a sinister emphasis to the words. 'Herr Gentz, a word with you, if you can spare the time...'

'One minute,' replied the Inspector; then, as Schneider strode away, his boot-heels clicking on the cobblestones, he muttered, 'What a stuffed-shirt that man is!' Rowlands, who thought that that was far from being the worst thing one could say about Inspector Schneider, maintained a diplomatic silence. 'But I have something to tell you, Herr Rowlands,' Gentz went on. 'Something that will interest you, I am sure. We have made a breakthrough. The Schönig case. I see from your face that you are surprised! We are bringing him in for questioning now. If you wait another few minutes you will see him...'

'Who?'

The Inspector laughed. 'Why, you were the one who put me onto him!' he said. 'Because you were right, as it turned out. He *doesn't* have an alibi for the crucial period. He did indeed leave the studio at half past four—but he was not home until at least a quarter past six. We have the maid's evidence. As for the wife...'

'Are we talking about Herr Hartmann?'

'Of course. He is the only one who fits the bill. He had the motive and—as it now appears—the opportunity. Ah, here is the car now,' said . 'They have been quicker than I expected.' As he spoke, a car drew up and three men got out. 'Well,' said the Inspector, 'I must leave you now. But we will see one another before too long, of that I am sure. Remember: you have only to call me, on my special number...'

The informer's prerogative, thought Rowlands sourly. 'Of course,' he said. Just then another voice broke into his thoughts. 'Herr Rowlands?' It was Hartmann. 'What are you doing here?' Then, before Rowlands could reply, the actor gave a bitter laugh. 'Although why would you *not* be here? There is no one in this blighted country who is not at the beck and call of these people...'

'Be careful what you say,' said Gentz. 'Herr Rowlands is here on a private matter, concerning his family...'

'My apologies,' said Hartmann, addressing Rowlands. 'I should have known you would not be mixed up in our sordid affair. They are trying to make me say I killed her, you know...'

'That's enough,' said Gentz. 'Come along now, Herr Hartmann. We can talk about this inside...'

'But I did not kill her,' went on Hartmann, his beautiful voice growing ever more impassioned. 'I loved her, my Sybille. Why would I kill the woman I loved?' This question was flung over his shoulder, as he was marched unceremoniously away, and the words hung in the air, after he had gone...

'What was all that about?' said Dorothy. Rowlands told her. 'So *that's* the great Helmut Hartmann! I must say, he's very good...'

'He is one of our finest actors.' said Sara Metzner, as the three of them went out through the great arched gateway onto Alexanderplatz. 'I myself saw him once in the theatre, many years ago, when Jakob—my husband—was alive. It was a theatre run by one of our workers' collectives. He was just a young man, then—Herr Hartmann—but already a great talent.'

'I could see that,' said Dorothy. 'It was as if he were playing a scene... You wouldn't have been able to appreciate the full effect, Fred, but from where Sara and I were standing, it looked very dramatic—didn't it, Sara? Those policemen in their black coats, and Helmut Hartmann in the middle of it all, with the wind whipping his coat, and his head flung back... Just like a scene from a film.'

Leaving the fortress-like edifice behind, they crossed the wide expanse of the busy square, whose eternal roar of traffic seemed oddly comforting, after the oppressive silence of the place they had just been. 'God, I'm glad to be out of there,' said Dorothy with a shudder. 'I hope I never have to set foot in that building again. But I can't help thinking about that poor little boy,' she went on. 'He looked so forlorn lying there. What must his parents be going through at this moment? To think that...'

'Don't think,' said Rowlands. 'It's probably best not to.'

12

SINCE THERE WAS NOTHING to be done in the way of furthering the investigation that day—it being a Sunday—Rowlands and his sister decided to go for a walk. "Because with all that's been going on, you've hardly seen anything of Berlin,' she said. 'Unless you count the inside of the police station...' Despite the unrest of the night before—there had been gunshots in the street, and shop windows smashed—the city was quiet by the time their little party ventured forth. At the last moment, Dorothy had decided that little Victor should accompany them. 'He's been cooped up in that flat all week. It'll be good for him to have a walk.' And so the three of them caught the tram to Alexanderplatz, and leaving that busy intersection behind, began making their way towards Unter den Linden. Their goal was the Tiergarten: its tree-lined gravel walks offering a pleasant excursion, even on a raw February day.

But, as it transpired, they were destined to get no further than a quarter of the way. Because the violence which had infected the streets of this, and many another German city, in the preceding days, was here given a different kind of expression. The first indication of this, for Rowlands, was the sound of a drum beating: a steady pulse, echoed and amplified by the rhythmic tread of marching feet. Thousands of them. 'Oh, no!' murmured Dorothy. 'I should have realised...' But it was too late to turn back. Before they knew it, Rowlands and his companions were caught up in the crowd that was flowing along Kaiser Wilhelmstrasse towards the Cathedral. Outside the great baroque building, the crowds were massed even more thickly, so that to get across the bridge that lay on the far side of the Lustgarten would have been impossible.

And so they were forced to remain, trapped on the narrow

island that lay between the two forks of the river, until the crowds of brown-shirted men had ceased pouring into the square in front of the Dom, and the watching crowd, amongst which they found themselves, had also come to a standstill.

'What's it all in aid of?' asked Rowlands. His answer came a moment later, with the emergence from the Cathedral of a funeral *cortège*, followed by another. There came the sound of horses' hooves, loud on the cobblestones, as two hearses drew up in front. 'It's the funeral of those two Nazis who were shot on Monday night,' whispered Dorothy. 'I should have remembered it was today...'

'It sounds like a big crowd.'

'Tens of thousands, I'd say.' Dorothy gave a bitter little laugh. 'They believe in doing these things properly, you know.'

With the departure of the hearses, the crowd surged forward, so that Rowlands and his sister, with the child between them, were able to worm their way towards the front, and the eventual possibility of escape. Before they could go any further, however, they had to wait for the square to empty, which—since there must have been close on a hundred thousand men assembled there, Dorothy said—was certain to take a considerable time. The detachments of foot and mounted police, which had accompanied the black-plumed and caparisoned hearses, were followed by detachments of Brownshirts, each with a senior Nazi official in front. 'That's Göring,' she said, nudging her brother, as the newly-appointed Minister for Aviation strode past. 'What an ass he looks in that big brown cloak of his! Can you believe it's actually lined with pink satin?'

'Pipe down,' muttered Rowlands. In a crowd this size, he thought, there might be people not only capable of understanding her remark, but of taking violent exception to it. But then something happened which drove this and everything else, out of his mind. Because just at that moment (he was only to piece this together afterwards) a troop of Hitler Jugend—the youth division of the Nazi party—marched past, with drums beating.

It was then that five year-old Victor piped up: 'There's Billy!' Dorothy, who had been holding Rowlands's arm, suddenly let go of it. 'It *is* him!' she cried. 'It's Billy! Oh, my Billy!' Before

170

Rowlands could stop her, she had lunged forward, and having wriggled her way through the crowd, began running after the procession, shouting her son's name at the top of her voice. For a moment, Rowlands stood there, rooted to the spot. From all around him, came the hoarse shouts and guttural murmuring of the vast crowd. He made a decision. 'We'd better go after her. Come on, Vicky, we're going to find Mummy...' Scooping up the child, to protect him from the worst of it, he proceeded to shoulder his way through the ranks of close-packed bodies—*'Bitte... Bitte... Danke schön...'*—until he, too, found himself on the street, caught up in the inexorable momentum of the parade. 'Can you see her?' he said to Victor, hoisting the little boy up onto his shoulders. 'Over there!' cried the child.

Which didn't help him much, apart from letting him know that Dorothy was still in sight. The steady marching of the crowd prevented any deviation from the route. But it wasn't until he heard his sister's voice, that he knew he'd found her. She, it soon became apparent, was not alone: a policeman held her by the arm. *'Lass mich in Ruhe!'* she shouted; to no avail. 'Fred!' she cried, as he and Victor came up. 'This idiot won't let me go...'

'Just calm down, will you?' he said; then, to the official, in German: 'What has she done?'

'And who are *you*?' was the sneering reply.

'I'm her brother. Where are you taking her?'

'To the Alex, since you ask. She'll be charged with creating a public disturbance.'

'It was hardly that,' said Rowlands. 'She's a little upset, that's all. It's an emotional occasion...'

'We'll see what my Sergeant has to say about *that*,' said the man. 'And what will Inspector Gentz say?' said Rowlands. 'He is a good friend of mine. Ask him whether he knows Herr Rowlands. The Englishman.'

'What's that?' said the policeman. But he loosened his hold on his prisoner's arm. 'Just ask him, if you don't believe me,' said Rowlands. 'Come along, Dottie...'

But she refused to move. 'Fred, I saw him,' she said again. 'It *was* him... My poor Billy... wearing that horrible uniform...'

'Come *on*,' he said, conscious that, at any moment, the policeman might change his mind about letting them go. 'You can tell me about it later...'

'But you don't understand,' said Dorothy, as she allowed herself, reluctantly, to be led away. 'I *spoke* to him, Fred. I called his name and he... he looked round when he heard me...'

'But I thought you said he was wearing the H.J. uniform? Are you sure it *was* Billy, and not just some boy who looked like him?'

'I know my own son,' she said. 'Vicky saw him, too—didn't you, Vicky?'

'Yes.'

'But I haven't told you the worst of it,' Dorothy went on. 'He looked at me with such... *hatred* in his eyes. As if he wished I were dead. "Leave me alone!" he shouted. "I don't know you. Get away from me!" Oh, Fred, it was awful!' Her voice trembled. 'I think he really meant it,' she said.

The Embassy official listened in silence to what Rowlands had to say. Then he sighed. 'I'm afraid there's not a lot I can do,' he said. 'Given the way things are. It's all rather awkward...' He must have made some gesture indicative of helplessness, for Dorothy said, with some asperity: 'Then that's all? You're saying you wash your hands of us?'

'Dear lady!' protested the civil servant. 'It isn't as simple as you seem to think to... to *demand* the return of the boy. Our relations with our friends at the Chancellery'—the Embassy building in which they stood was across the way from this—'are not so good that we can afford to jeopardise them, willy-nilly. Why, only the other day, there was that absurd row about some film-show the Führer had attended. It was a war-film, you know—with a rather anti-British tone—and some fool of a reviewer in the *Times* picked up the story.' He chuckled reminiscently. 'You've no idea of the fuss it caused! Letters flying back and forth between our people and the Chancellery, deprecating the tone of the review, and asserting our mutual friendship, and the need to let bygones be bygones...'

'I don't give a damn about all that,' said Dorothy. 'I want to know what you're going to do to get my son back.'

'As I've said, it isn't as straightforward as you seem to think...' began the official. 'But surely,' put in Rowlands, 'as he's a British subject...'

'His father was a German national,' replied the man. 'Or have I got that wrong?' There was a silence, then: 'No, that's true,' said Dorothy in a low voice. 'So you see it makes it rather tricky,' went on the official, whose name Rowlands hadn't managed to catch. 'Are you saying there's nothing we can do?' he said. 'Well...' Again there was a pause, as if the man were considering the question from all its angles. 'If we had a little more to go on—an address where the boy was to be found, for example— we might be able to pull a few strings. You've spoken to the police, you say?'

'Yes,' said Rowlands. 'An Inspector Schneider's in charge of the case. But...'

'Ah, Schneider,' said the official. 'A very able man, I believe. One of the "new brooms" they've brought in, to raise a bit of dust, you know...' He chuckled at his own joke. 'I've also been put in touch with Inspector Gentz,' added Rowlands. 'Hmm. Due for retirement, isn't he?' murmured the civil servant. 'But able enough, in his own way, I'm sure. The fact is, Mr Rowlands... Mrs Ashenhurst... this is very much a matter for the police.' He laughed. 'We don't want to tread on any toes, you know!'

'Even though *they're* doing rather more than treading on toes,' said Rowlands. He was having difficulty keeping his temper. 'Beating up people in the street, and intimidating Jewish shop-keepers seems more in their line...'

'I know, I know. It's deplorable, the way this new crowd have been carrying on. Quite deplorable,' said the Embassy official, getting to his feet. His tone and manner indicated that they had reached the end of their interview. 'We're hoping that things will quieten down, once the elections are over, and the government's got its majority. They'll feel more secure, you see, and so won't have to resort to such extreme tactics...'

'I very much hope you're right,' said Rowlands, feeling, for the first time in his life, a little ashamed of his county. It was the day after the State funeral—the day after Billy had been sighted—and their little delegation had arrived at the Embassy with high hopes. Or at least, Dorothy had; her brother having cautioned her against placing too much faith in the authorities. Now, as they left the grand neo-classical building on Wilhelmstrasse in which the British Embassy was housed, and began to walk towards the tram-stop on Leipzigerstrasse, she seemed more cast-down than ever. 'I keep telling myself that he was *there*—in front of me—and now I've lost him,' she said. 'It's as if he's been spirited away, by some evil force, and now...'

She could not go on.

'Chin up, old girl,' said Rowlands gently. 'We mustn't give up when we're so close. Since the Embassy can't or won't help, we need to follow up this H.J. link ourselves...'

'I don't know what you're talking about,' said Kurt Bauer. It was the lunch break at Heinrich Heine Oberschule, and Rowlands was once more face to face with Walter Metzner's two classmates, in an empty classroom thoughtfully provided by Bauer's teacher, Herr Hinck. Clara Metzner was with them—Rowlands having once more enlisted her assistance as guide. He'd persuaded Dorothy to stay at home; the events of the past few hours had exhausted her, and she seemed close to breaking-point. 'You were at the Cathedral yesterday, weren't you?' he said patiently. 'What if I was?' replied the boy in a sullen tone. 'Show a bit of respect!' snapped Clara. 'You, too, young Geisler! You might start by sitting up straight, instead of slouching... Now. Were you at the Cathedral yesterday, or weren't you?'

'Yes. I mean... we were,' was the muttered reply. 'I assume you were there with the Hitler Jugend?' asked Rowlands. 'No,' said Bauer; then, with a certain condescension: 'We're D. J.— Deutsches Jungvolk. You have to be fourteen, to be in the H.J.'

'All right,' said Rowlands. 'So you were with this D. J. lot, marching in the funeral procession. I suppose there were quite a number of you there?'

The boy must have nodded, for Clara Metzner said: 'Speak up, when you're asked a question!'

'Yes,' said the boy. 'And how many of you H.J. and D. J. lads would you say there were? Fifty? A hundred?'

'At least a hundred, I'd say.'

'Jolly good. And all from different groups, I suppose?'

The two boys agreed that this was so. 'I imagine you must get to recognise some of the other boys—from groups apart from your own, I mean? Seeing them, as you do, at rallies and... summer camps, is it? You must get pretty friendly...'

'We don't have much to do with the other groups,' said Kurt Bauer disdainfully. 'Those stiffs from Wedding and Moabit aren't a patch on the Prenzlauerberg boys...'

'But you're recognise the ones from your district—and perhaps from some of the other districts—wouldn't you?' said Rowlands slyly. ''Spose so,' was the reply. 'Seeing the same faces, week in, week out,' went on his interrogator. 'Must be obvious when there's a new face, I suppose...'

Suddenly, Bauer seemed to understand what was being asked of him. His boastful manner gave way to one of wariness. 'Y-es,' he said. 'Depends.'

'You didn't, by any chance, seem someone you knew in the crowd of D. J. boys on Sunday?' said Rowlands softly. 'Someone you didn't expect to see...'

'I...' The boy seemed momentarily dumbfounded. 'You'd better tell him, Bauer,' said his friend suddenly.

'Shut up, Geisler!'

'We saw him,' said Dieter Geisler, ignoring this. 'Wilhelm, that is. He was with the Neukölln group... Ouch!' Evidently his friend had kicked him. 'The Neukölln group,' said Rowlands. 'That's very helpful. Thank you. Did either of you speak to him, by any chance?'

'I told you,' said Kurt Bauer savagely. 'We don't have anything to do with the other groups. That Neukölln crowd are a shabby lot. They're useless at drill, too...'

Receiving this news of her son's probable whereabouts, Dorothy was all for dashing down to Neukölln at once, and knocking on doors until somebody answered who would admit to harbouring the child; Rowlands managed to dissuade her from this impractical plan. 'We need to find out who's running the show,' he said. 'He'll be the one to give us the information we need.'

175

It occurred to him that this was where Inspector Gentz might prove useful; surely *he* would know something of how so large and evidently ubiquitous an organisation was run, and perhaps be able to supply the names of its leaders? He decided to try the telephone number Gentz had given him, rather than to risk telephoning the police station. After the fate that had so nearly overtaken Walter, he no longer trusted Inspector Schneider. 'A new broom,' the Permanent Secretary had said. A broom that was sweeping away all that stood in the path of the new administration and its dubious objectives, thought Rowlands.

But when he tried the number—telephoning from the cabin outside the building superintendent's office—there was only the monotonous jangle of the ringing tone. 'So much for being able to get hold of you at any time of the day or night,' he muttered. He was about to hang up when the receiver was lifted and a woman's voice said, '*Ja?*' Rowlands asked to speak to Inspector Gentz. 'He is not here,' was the reply. 'Who is this?'

Conscious of the presence of the building superintendent, ostentatiously shuffling papers in the room beyond, Rowlands merely supplied his name. 'He will know what it is about,' he said. 'I will tell him,' said the woman—a wife? A daughter? Gentz had made no mention of either; but then, what did he know of Gentz? Precious little, beyond his name and rank, and the fact that he smoked those foul cheroots. He was due for retirement, hadn't the Embassy official said? Too 'old-fashioned', no doubt, for the liking of the Nazi government. So there must be *something* good about him, thought Rowlands, hooking the earpiece back onto its wall-mounted bracket.

A trip to Neukölln seemed unavoidable. Although what they were to do when they got there, he hadn't the least idea. But Dorothy, he knew, would want to *do* something. Patience had never been her strong suit. 'Don't you see?' she'd cried. 'He's here, in the city—perhaps in danger... I can't believe,' she kept saying, 'that he'd have spoken to me so... so *cruelly*... if he hadn't been forced to...' Which made a kind of sense, thought Rowlands, as he climbed the stairs that led to the third floor. Because if the people who'd tried to kill Walter knew that Billy was still at large... well, it didn't bear thinking about, that was all.

It all came back to the night of the twenty-seventh, and what had happened in Sybille Schönig's dressing-room. Whoever had killed her was making very sure that no witnesses to the crime remained. He'd have to go very carefully, thought Rowlands. Very carefully indeed. Because in instituting a hunt for the missing child, he might inadvertently lead the killers to him. These grim thoughts were interrupted a moment later, as the door of the flat flew open. 'Well?' said his sister. 'What did he say?'

'He wasn't there. I left a message.'

'Oh.' She sounded utterly cast down. It seemed to Rowlands that his sister couldn't stand much more of this strain. She had turned away, and was walking towards the sitting-room, when she remembered something. 'This came for you.' It was a letter: the envelope so small and thin it barely had any weight at all. There was a faint scent of... *Chypre*, was it?

'Lilac note-paper,' said his sister. 'I didn't know you had a secret admirer, Fred.'

I don't,' he said. 'Well, open it then.' She did so. '"I hope you can take tea with me at 4 o'clock today. There is something I wish to discuss. Yours, Magdalena Brandt." Isn't that the film-star? What elevated circles you move in these days!'

'She's one of the Babelsberg crowd, that's all.' He checked his watch. 'It's half-past three now. I'd better see if I can pick up a cab...'

'I shouldn't bother,' said Dorothy. 'There's a great big car waiting for you outside. A Mercedes Benz, I think. Midnight blue. You'll get yourself talked about,' she said, with the ghost of her old sense of humour.

Magda Hartmann was waiting for him in the small sitting-room opposite the room in which the cocktail party had been held. There was a pleasant smell of hothouse flowers—lilies, he thought—and of pine-cones; a fire, no doubt augmented with these aromatic seed-pods, was giving out a delicious heat. 'So good of you to come, Mr Rowlands,' she said, when the maid had announced him. 'Please. Come and sit by me. There is a chair in front of you, a little to your left. Be careful to avoid the small table to the right of it.' He did as she said, and was

177

soon comfortably ensconced. 'I hope that chair suits you? Men always seem to prefer a straight-backed chair...'

Tea was rung for, and appeared within a matter of moments. The maid was then dismissed, with a sharp injunction that they were not to be disturbed. Her mistress poured the tea—it was freshly made, and piping hot, Rowlands discovered gratefully, as she handed him the delicate bone-china cup and saucer. 'Will you have something to eat? There is bread-and-butter. Cake. You see, we have all the English customs here...'

'Nothing for me, thanks. There was something you wanted to talk to me about?'

'Yes. You are aware, are you not, Herr Rowlands, that my husband has been arrested?'

He hesitated. 'I saw him... that is to say, we met... at the police-station,' he admitted. 'There is not much you miss—even though you are blind,' said Magda Hartmann, with a soft laugh. Listening to that husky, seductive voice, as deep as a man's, it was hard not to picture the *femme fatale*—all pale skin, dark tresses, and smoky eyes—she had portrayed in so many of her pictures. Although of course, he reminded himself, her voice had played no part in the illusion.

'...and so I have decided to tell you the truth...'

With a start, Rowlands returned to the here-and-now.

'My husband could not have killed that girl. He does not have it in him to do such a thing.' Was it his imagination, stimulated by memories of the woman in front of him as Salome or Lucretia Borgia, that made him discern a tinge of regret in her voice? 'He was in love with her, yes... or thought he was.' This time, he did not imagine the note of scorn. 'But he did not... *could* not... have killed her. I know, Mr Rowlands. I have been his wife for eight years. Helmut is not a violent man. And to choose such a method!' She had the actress's trick of pausing, to give a line its full effect. 'To blow a hole in that pretty face...' She shuddered. 'Oh yes, I know what was done! It is not the action of a lover.'

'Men do such things in anger.'

'They commit murder—that is true. But even murder should be in character. Have you ever been in love, Mr Rowlands? With anyone apart from myself, of course...'

178

'Well, that is... I...'

'I see from your face that you have. And have you, in your blackest moments, ever contemplated killing the one you love?'She laughed: a throaty chuckle. 'You need not answer that! But I suggest to you that, were you to be driven to such an act, you would not coldly dispatch your lover with a gun. That is the way of the executioner, is it not? You might strike a girl, in hot blood, or strangle her—but shoot her? No.'

'You seem to know a lot about it,' said Rowlands drily. 'I know a lot about men,' was the cool reply. 'And I am an actress, you will recall. I think a great deal about character—about whether something works, or does not.'

'Since you're so convinced that your husband did not kill Sybille Schönig,' he said, 'perhaps you've some idea who did?'

'I am afraid I cannot help you.' Something about the way she said this—some faint tremor in the voice, which had up to now been so assured— made him think that she was lying. As if she was aware of having given herself away, she changed the subject. 'Would you care for a cigarette?' She reached for the engraved silver box upon the low table, took a cigarette from it and offered the box to Rowlands. 'These are American. I hope they are to your taste.'

'Thanks.' He waited until she had lit first her own cigarette, then his. 'If you know anything about what happened that night—anything at all -' he persisted, 'you would be well advised not to keep it to yourself. Whoever killed Sybille Schönig has already killed again...'

'Are you trying to scare me, Herr Rowlands?'

'I'm trying to warn you. You could be in danger...'

'Do you think I don't know that?' she cried. The sultry temptress had vanished. Now she sounded like a frightened girl.

'Frau Hartmann, if you know something, you must tell me...'

'What? And get myself killed, too? You don't know what these people are like...'

'I'm beginning to find out,' he said grimly. 'Well, if you change your mind, you know where to find me.'

'Indeed,' said Magda Hartmann. 'And do not think I am ungrateful. I know you want to help me. But there is nothing

179

to be done,' she said sadly. With which he had to be content. That she knew something—and something potentially damning—he was no longer in any doubt. 'How did you find out?' he asked. 'I mean about the affair between your husband and Fräulein Schönig?'

'I found a letter. It was quite apparent from the tone of it that...' She let the sentence tail off. 'It referred to a plan they had made—or that *she* had made—to run away together. They were to go to California.' She allowed a brief pause to elapse. 'This of course I could not allow.' It seemed to Rowlands that there was something she was not saying. 'Do the police know about this?' he said.

Magda Hartmann laughed. 'My dear man, do you take me for a fool? I have no wish to put a noose around my neck! The fact that I had such a good reason to want the girl dead makes me a suspect, does it not? Or perhaps you do not read detective stories?' Her bantering tone disguised more serious emotions, he thought. Anger and fear—of which fear was uppermost. 'I couldn't say,' he replied, ignoring her last remark. 'No doubt the police will have their ideas about all this...'

'Oh, the *police*!' Her laughter had a scornful ring. 'They will think what they are told to think. You do not imagine,' she said, 'that they care what really happened?'

'And what did happen?'

'As to that, I do not know. All I can tell you is that Sybille Schönig was playing a dangerous game. She thought she was clever, that girl, but it turned out she was too clever for her own good...' Bruno Klein had hinted at something similar. 'A very *ambitious* young woman,' he had said. Then there was that remark of Hettie Blumenfeldt's: 'She had some very strange friends, our Sybille...'

'What exactly do you mean?' he said. But his hostess would not be drawn. 'I mean that she was careless of other people's feelings,' she said; although he got the impression that she'd meant something else. 'She didn't care whom she hurt, to get what she wanted. Nor whose husband she stole,' added Magda Hartmann.

Refusing her offer of a drink 'a *proper* drink: whisky and

180

soda is so much more enlivening than tea, I find'—he took his leave, feeling that he had learned little more about those crucial hours on the night of the murder than he knew already. Magda Hartmann had merely confirmed what he had guessed—that she'd known of her husband's affair. More than that—if indeed, there *was* more—she wasn't saying.

REVERSE ANGLE

13

A S HE EMERGED FROM the overheated atmosphere of the house into the crisp, pine-scented air of the quiet Grünewald street, he heard a car engine start up. Magda Hartmann had insisted on lending him her car and driver, even though he'd said a lift to the railway station would suit him just as well. 'Nonsense. Prenzlauerberg is on the other side of the city. It is too far, even for someone who is not...'

'Blind, you were going to say?'

'I was going to say a stranger,' she said, with a laugh. 'But of course you are also blind... I have enjoyed our talk, Herr Rowlands. I hope you will visit me again, one day.'

Now he turned towards the sound of the engine, surprised that the chauffeur had not got out to open the door of the vehicle for him. But then the window of the car was rolled down and a voice he knew said, 'Get in, Herr Rowlands. I am on my way back to the Alex. It is no distance from there to Marienburgerstrasse...'

'Inspector Gentz.' Somehow it didn't seem surprising that the man had turned up here. 'Thanks for the offer. But Frau Hartmann's driver is going to take me home...'

'Don't worry about him,' said the other brusquely. 'I've told him to make himself scarce. What I'd like to know,' he went on, as Rowlands, resigned to this change of plan, got into the car, 'is what you and the charming Frau Hartmann have been saying to one another...'

'How did you know I was here?'

Gentz laughed. 'I could say "I have my methods," like your estimable Sherlock Holmes—or what is in fact the truth, which is that your sister told me where you had gone.'

'I'd prefer the truth,' said Rowlands. 'Of course,' said the policeman. 'It is a scarce commodity, these days. But it would seem, Herr Rowlands, that you have not been entirely truthful with me...' He gave an instruction to their driver, slid the glass panel which lay between them closed, and settled back against the comfortable leather seat of the Benz. 'We agreed, I think, that you were to inform me of any developments in what we might call the Babelsberg Affair, and that I was to do the same. But now I find you have kept some information to yourself...'

'I telephoned you.'

'Indeed. That is why I am here. But you did not tell me when we last met that you had found the missing boys...'

'Only one of them so far,' said Rowlands. 'I know. It was he—young Walter—who answered the door to me. We had quite an interesting chat, he and I...'

'Inspector ,' said Rowlands in a low voice, 'I must ask you not to mention that you have seen Walter to any of your colleagues...'

'You are referring to Inspector Schneider, are you not? Rest assured that I will say nothing of this to *him*.'

'The boy's life may depend on it.'

'So your sister was at pains to tell me,' was the reply. 'I gather, then, that you too believe that the fire at the orphanage was not an accident?'

'It seemed awfully convenient, that's all. If one assumes that the objective was to remove an *inconvenient* witness...'

'And yet young Walter was unable to tell me who it was that murdered Sybille Schönig.' Gentz lit one of his pungent-smelling cigars. 'He said that when he and his cousin Billy left the dressing-room at ten minutes past six, the lady was still very much alive...'

'Yes, but Billy went back to the dressing-room,' said Rowlands. 'So Walter said,' replied the other. 'He did not see him again after that. But your sister *has* seen him, I understand?'

'That's right,' said Rowlands. 'I suppose she told you *where* she saw him?'

'She did. It seems to me,' said Gentz, meditatively exhaling a cloud of smoke, 'that your nephew must be a resourceful young man. To hide himself in full view of the enemy, so to speak...'

'If indeed he *is* hiding, and hasn't gone over to the enemy,' said Rowlands. 'There is that possibility, of course,' was the reply. 'You know your nephew better than I do. His father was German, I believe?'

'He was.' Although the truth was a good deal more complicated than that.

'The boy speaks good German, your sister informs me. That,' added the Inspector, 'is lucky for him. I need not tell you,' he went on, 'that organisations such as the one of which we are talking are not welcoming to outsiders. The father was a Jew, was he not?'

'Yes.'

'Then it is to be hoped, for your nephew's sake, that no-one in the Hitler Jugend finds out...'

'It was about that I wanted to talk to you.' Rowlands outlined the plan he has in mind for tracking down the missing child. Gentz listened in silence, puffing at his cigar. 'I don't think you realise, Herr Rowlands, quite what these people are like...'

'On the contrary,' was the reply. 'I had a very good introduction to their particular brand of manners the night I arrived in Berlin...' He described the encounter he and Joachim Metzner had had with the H.J. gang. *'Ja,* that is like them,' said the policeman grimly. 'They were excited that night. It was a great triumph for them. Like many young men, they like to celebrate by breaking heads. Now the whole country is at it. Why, only two nights ago, the Mayor of Strassfurt was shot in the back and killed by a red-capped schoolboy—another of your H.J. crowd... So,' he went on, suddenly changing tack. 'Since I have failed to discourage you from this plan of yours, how can I be of help?'

'I need a name,' said Rowlands. 'That I can provide, easily enough,' said the Inspector. 'But I must urge you to be careful. And now, Herr Rowlands, since I have agreed to help *you,* it is your turn to help *me.* That is only fair, is it not?' Rowlands agreed that was. 'I want to know,' said Gentz, 'what you talked about with Magda Hartmann. You did not go there to discuss her films, I take it?'

'There isn't much to tell. She is convinced that her husband did not kill Sybille Schönig.'

'Her reasons?'

'She... she didn't give any particular reason. Other than to say that it was out of character for him to have done so.'

'I see. And this was *all* you spoke of? Come, Herr Rowlands, you will have to do better than that!'

'It was a private conversation.'

'As is this one,' was the reply. A pause ensued. Inspector Gentz sighed. 'I see that, in spite of all you have said, you do not trust me,' he said. 'If you are afraid that anything you say will put Frau Hartmann in danger, I can assure you it will not. Why, we have even let her husband go. He is back at the film studios at this very minute...' Gentz laughed. 'I see from your face that you are surprised. But we had not enough evidence to hold him. Oh yes, he lied about where he was that night—saying he went straight home at four thirty, when he finished at the studios. But when I told him we had a witness who had overheard his conversation with Fräulein Schönig at ten minutes to six, and another who could place him in the dressing-room until a few minutes after six, he collapsed like a pricked balloon. Says after the quarrel with Sybille, he left Babelsberg in a terrible state. Went straight to a bar and spent the rest of the evening there, drowning his sorrows. We're checking his story, but I think he's probably in the clear. Now his *wife's* a different matter...'

'There's no evidence that she was at the studio that evening.'

'No, but there's nothing to say she wasn't. And she had every reason to pull that trigger...'

'It seems... I don't know. Out of character,' said Rowlands.

'Murder *is* out of character for most people,' said the Inspector. 'Then there is the circumstantial evidence. The gun, for example. That type of pearl-handled pistol is a woman's gun. Just the sort of thing an actressy type might carry around in her purse. Then there's that first shot—the one that went wide. It suggests she was nerving herself for the kill...'

'And what about Fritzi Henkel's death? Are you saying she murdered him, too?'

'I am not saying anything of the kind,' said Gentz, as the car drew up in the forecourt of the Alex. 'That can wait until after I have interrogated the lady. All I will say to *you*, Herr Rowlands, is that you will have to be extremely cautious when it comes to asking questions about the whereabouts of your nephew. Because *someone* is very anxious that the truth of what happened that night should not be told. And the child is the only surviving witness, is he not?'

'This looks like the right place,' said Joachim Metzner. 'I mean—you can hardly miss it, with all those *Hakenkreuz* flags, and posters of the Leader's ugly mug plastered all over the walls. Seems like we've arrived at the right time, too...' Because as he spoke, the doors of the building opened, and a laughing, chattering mob rushed out. If Metzner hadn't pulled him out of the way, Rowlands would have been knocked off his feet. 'Unruly bunch, aren't they?' he murmured, to which the young man's only reply was a scornful laugh. Both men withdrew to the other side of the street—a better vantage point for their purpose. 'Can you see him?' said Rowlands. 'Not yet. These are the older ones... Ah, this lot looks more like it!' And indeed the adolescent growl of the boys' voices now gave way to a higher, more feminine, pitch. 'Just like break-time at school,' muttered Metzner contemptuously. 'Only instead of rushing off to play football, they'll be picketing shops and handing out leaflets saying "Don't buy from Jews"... Still no sign of Billy. It *was* the Neukölln group young Geisler saw him with?'

'So he said.'

'He must have been lying,' said Metzner. 'Billy isn't with this crowd, that's for sure. Just wait till I see that Geisler. I'll make him sorry for spinning you such a yarn...'

'Perhaps it wasn't a yarn,' said Rowlands. 'The boy might have made a genuine mistake. But I'd still like to check that Billy isn't inside the building...'

'O.K.'

Entering through a set of heavy oak doors, they found themselves in what had been, in happier days, the meeting-room of a bicycling club. Now it was stripped of all but the most utilitarian furniture. Nor was it empty: a trio of young men was engaged in stacking chairs, while an older man directed them. '*Gut, gut... Weiter so, Jungs!*'

'Herr Gruber...' Having spotted the newcomers, one of the

189

youths was trying to attract his attention. Another took a more direct approach: *'Ja? Was wollen Sie?'* he said aggressively, placing himself directly in their path. A ripe odour of adolescent sweat came from him. *'Jude,'* he added, with a sneer, thrusting his face towards Metzner. The electric silence which followed was broken by Rowlands. 'I am sure Herr von Schirach will be glad to know of the welcome his friends receive,' he said, in an amused tone.

He was taking a chance, he knew—but Baldur von Schirach, H.J. leader and friend of the Führer, was renowned for his aristocratic eccentricities. Having English friends might be counted as one of these. Certainly, Rowlands's ruse seemed to do the trick—at least temporarily. 'What's that?' said the man who'd been addressed as Gruber. A local butcher, Inspector Gentz had said. He'd been running the group for a couple of years—'No doubt in the hope of advancing his career in the Party,' Gentz had remarked scathingly. 'You are a friend of Herr von Schirach, you say?'

'Oh, yes,' said Rowlands. 'We're great chums. But it isn't about that I've come. I'm looking for a boy called William Ashenhurst. Joined your outfit about a week ago, I gather. Tall for his age— he's eleven. Dark hair, green eyes...'

'I do not think...' began Gruber doubtfully. 'He means Aschenbach,' put in one of the chair-stackers. 'Quiet kid. Tagged along with the Braun twins. Didn't know he was *English*,' he added, in a jeering tone. 'Aschenbach, of course,' said the butcher. 'I remember now. But you tell me this is not his real name? He is English, you say?'

'Half-English. His father was German.'

'I see. And you thought to find him here? I am surprised,' said the H.J. leader suspiciously, 'that your *friend* Herr von Schirach did not give you better information. The boy is not here. He was taken away—by, ah, another of our leaders. I do not recall the name...'

Rowlands's heart sank. 'When was this?'

'Yesterday, after the march.'

'Of course. A fine turn-out,' said Rowlands, keeping his voice level. It would not do to let these thugs know how much this

190

news had shaken him. 'I don't suppose,' he went on, 'you know where he was taken?' Gruber laughed: a fat, complacent sound. 'Ah, that I cannot tell you,' he said. 'You will have to ask Herr von Schirach about *that*...'

A letter had arrived from England. Rowlands only became aware of this fact when he heard his sister give a choking cry. 'What is it?' he said at once, but she seemed unable to reply. 'It's Jack,' she said at last. 'He's had an accident...' Her hands were shaking so much that it was a moment before she could hold the letter steady enough to read it. 'He's broken his leg...'

'What rotten luck! How did it happen?'

'I'll read you what he says... It's Cecily's writing. "Dear Dottie, I'm dictating this to dear old Ciss, as I'm a bit too shaken up to use the typewriter just at present, having taken a tumble down the cliff steps—they were rather icy, with all the snow we've had..." Oh, the idiot!' cried Dorothy. 'Those steps are terribly steep. He should never have risked it, in this weather...' She drew a breath, then resumed: '"The result, I'm sorry to say, is a nasty fracture in my left leg, which has never really recovered after having a chunk of shrapnel embedded in it, circa 1916... And so I'm afraid I'm a bit 'crocked', to say the least. Dear old Ciss is holding the fort, although looking after her invalid brother makes a lot of extra work for her, poor girl. Luckily, we don't have anybody booked into the hotel until Easter. But it's still a bit of a blow, as I won't be able to get the painting done before we open again. But never mind about that. Is there any news of young Bill? I'd hoped when my brother-in-law the detective got his teeth into the case, that I'd soon be hearing that the little shaver had been found. If I thought I'd be the slightest use as regards tracking him down, I'd be over there like a shot. However, as things stand, I think I'd be more of a hindrance than a help—being not only blind, but one-legged..."'

It was like Jack to make light of his own troubles in the face of their greater trouble, thought his friend wryly. But the light-hearted tone of the letter did not entirely disguise the gravity of the situation. Ashenhurst's had been a blind man's accident—stairs being more than usually hazardous to one who couldn't see where he was placing his feet, nor tell from looking if there was ice or any other obstacle of which to beware. That it had not been a fatal accident, was simply a matter of luck. 'What will you do?' said Rowlands.

'I don't know.' Suddenly, Dorothy burst into tears. 'Oh, poor Jack! Poor Jack! I should be there to look after him...'

Rowlands got up, and went to comfort her. 'You should go,' he said, when he judged she was calmer again. He felt her shake her head. 'How can I leave, without Billy?' He waited until she had collected herself. 'The fact is,' he said gently, 'there's nothing much to be gained by your staying here. Inspector Gentz and I are doing all we can to find out who's taken Billy—and I think we're getting close... No, let me speak,' he went on, as she seemed about to protest. 'You're eating your heart out worrying about him—and now there's this worry about Jack. You can't be in two places at once, and you can do more good there...'

'But... Billy...'

'You leave Billy to me,' he said. 'We mustn't give up hope now, when we're so close. We know that Billy's alive, and somewhere in Berlin. I promise you, I won't leave without him,' he added, fervently wishing he could be sure of fulfilling this promise.

Looking back on these events, months later, it seemed to Rowlands that this—the day before his sister returned to England—was the worst day of all, perhaps because, notwithstanding his brave words to Dorothy about not giving up hope, that was in fact what both of them had done. In the week since Rowlands's arrival in the city, there hadn't been a day when he hadn't had some lead to follow—some clue which might prove the vital one, that would lead him to the truth. Now the clues seemed to have run out. All they led to was a dead-end, and the depressing realisation that all their efforts had been in vain. It was a melancholy thought; although, for his sister's sake, not one to which he could admit.

Dorothy herself seemed strangely calm, once the decision to return had been taken—busying herself with mundane tasks of sorting and packing clothes, perhaps by way of avoiding more distressing topics. That Walter was to accompany her and Victor on their journey home had given her something else to think about—a welcome distraction from her prevailing anxiety. It had been Sara Metzner who, late that night, had suggested it. 'He cannot stay here,' she said. 'It is too dangerous for him—and for all of us. In England he will be safe.'

Now both women managed to keep up a front of cheerfulness which neither of them must be feeling. 'Only think, my son, how happy you will be to see England, and to meet your cousin's family!' Frau Metzner had exclaimed, with only the slightest tremor in her voice. And: 'You'll like Cornwall,' Dorothy said to the child. 'It's ever so jolly. Heaps of things to do. All the boys love it...' The fact that her own boy would not be returning with them was something she didn't have to mention. All she'd said when the idea of Walter's taking his place had first been put forward, was: 'He can travel on my passport. A good thing that he's about the same age...' The same age as Billy, she meant.

Rowlands himself wasn't sure how long he'd be able to stay on—at least until the middle of the month, he thought. By then, if there'd been no news... Well, he'd just have to come home, that's all. On the telephone to Edith the night before, he'd said what was in his mind. 'I can't let her down now—especially as she's going back, to look after Jack. I want to be sure we've tried every possible avenue...'

Edith was thankfully of his opinion: he could always rely on her to do the right thing, he thought. 'Of course you should stay. As long as there's a chance of finding the child,' she said. 'That's right. As long as there's a chance,' echoed Rowlands. And there *was* still a chance, he told himself. It was a slim one, admittedly, but... At the H.J. headquarters in Neukölln the night before, there'd been a name mentioned: Braun. It had been the Braun twins who'd brought Billy Ashenhurst—or Aschenbach, as he'd been calling himself—along to the meetings. If he could get a line on these people... A trawl through the telephone directory might prove useful.

When he'd suggested as much to Clara Metzner, she'd sounded dubious. 'There are many people with this surname in Berlin,' she said. He pointed out that not all of them lived in the Neukölln district. 'It is a poor area. Not many people have telephones.' Even so, she agreed to ask the Building Supervisor if he would lend her his copy of the local directory.

But it turned out to be an unproductive effort. Most of the telephones in the area were registered—as the one in their building was—to communal use, rather than to individual families. Of the private numbers listed, most were to be found in 'good' streets, such as those fronting the river, or were registered to businesses. Tracking down the Braun family, about whom nothing was known, except that they had twin boys enrolled in the Neukölln branch of the Hitler Jugend, proved no less difficult.

There were five Brauns on Clara's list: of these, one was a dentist, with daughters; another an elderly spinster. A third demanded to know who the caller thought she was fooling, and threatened to report her to the police. Braun, T. and Braun W. were more promising, since both admitted to sons. But Thomas Braun's sons were both married, with children of their own, and Wilhelm Braun's sons had gone to America.

And after all, thought Rowlands, even if they'd succeeded in their quest, it wouldn't have helped them much. They'd still have no way of knowing where Billy was now. 'Taken away,' old Gruber had said, his manner reflecting the mingled admiration and fear of a bully for a bigger bully. But taken *where*, exactly? And who was it who had taken him? 'Another of our leaders,' the butcher had said. That meant someone higher up in the H.J. hierarchy, one must assume. But what could they want with Billy? Unless someone had recognised him as the boy Schneider and his men were seeking...

Even so, would they (whoever they were) risk an international incident by killing him? Rowlands found it hard to believe. Ruthless these people might be, but the summary execution of a child—and a foreign national at that—would surely cause more trouble than it was worth? Hadn't the Leader gone on record, only a few days before, to say that, with regard to their former enemy—Britain—it was time to 'let bygones be bygones'? This seemed a poor way of showing it.

On Wednesday morning, Rowlands, accompanied by Sara Metzner, was at Zoo Station to see the Ashenhursts off on their homeward journey. The fact that she might not see her younger son for a very long time was clearly uppermost in Frau Metzner's mind, although she did not allude to this directly. 'You will write, won't you?' was all she said to the boy, as their little group stood on the windswept platform, awaiting the arrival of the Paris train. '*Ja, Mutti.*'

'You must speak English,' she said. 'Remember: you are an English boy now.'

Dorothy, who seemed to have thrown off her depressed mood for one of nervous agitation, walked rapidly up and down the platform, as if she couldn't wait to be gone. 'I should never have come here,' she muttered. 'If only I hadn't come here, I might still have Billy...' So she went on, round and round in a hellish circle of self-recrimination, that led back always to the same point: her decision to bring her son to Berlin. 'I wanted him to see where Viktor lived,' she went on, relentlessly. 'And now I've lost him forever...'

The train pulled in, and the usual commotion ensued—of porters heaving baggage into racks, and people shouting to be heard above the noise of the engine. Rowlands kissed his sister and younger nephew, and shook hands with Walter. 'Look after these two, won't you?' he said. 'I'm relying on you, as the man of the party, you know. Send me a wire when you reach Paris,' he added to Dorothy. 'Give my regards to Jack, won't you? And try not to worry. It'll all be all right, you'll see...'

'I hope so,' she said, sounding utterly forlorn.

Last farewells were exchanged. Those departing got on board. Then with a tremendous shrieking of whistles, and grinding of wheels, the engine began to move. As it did so, two men came running up the steps and leapt onto the moving train. 'Police,' said Frau Metzner, in Rowlands's ear. 'I wonder what they want,' he said. 'I do not know. But I know one thing...' She shivered, although the day was mild. 'It will be nothing good.'

14

WHEN THEY GOT BACK to the flat in Marienburgerstrasse, there was a message waiting for Rowlands. 'From a man calling himself Gentz,' said the Building Supervisor, Dollfuss, suspiciously. The number he recited was neither the one for the main switchboard at the Alex, nor the private one Gentz had given him. Nevertheless—and to Rowlands's relief—it was the Inspector who answered. 'Thought you'd like to know,' he said without preamble. 'There's been another death. A suicide—or so we must assume.'

'Do you mean...?'

'At Babelsberg, *Ja*. It is the dresser. Margarete Pabst.' Then, when Rowlands remained silent: 'I thought, as you'd talked to the woman, you might be able to cast some light on the matter.'

'Perhaps.' Rowlands was aware of the stertorous breathing of Dollfuss, who was hovering within earshot. Any further discussion would have to wait. 'I'll pick you up in ten minutes,' said Gentz, and hung up. In the car on the way out of the city, the Inspector filled Rowlands in on the details of what had happened. 'She was found this morning, by the cleaner. Poisoned, apparently.'

Rowlands shuddered. 'Horrible way to choose.'

'Indeed. If she *did* choose it...'

'I thought you said it was suicide?'

'I did say that, didn't I? It seems to me,' said Gentz, 'that I've had nothing but suicides, since I started on this case.' Then he said nothing more until they arrived at the studio. 'I imagine, Herr Rowlands, that you must know your way around here quite well?' he said, as the car drew up in the courtyard, just inside the great concrete arch of the studio gates. 'Well enough,' said Rowlands. 'Then perhaps you will lead the way? It is the Schönig's dressing-room we want. An unlucky room,' said Gentz. 'Would you not agree?'

Rowlands wondered if this were some kind of test; if so, he was confident of passing it. Now. Straight ahead for twenty paces... then sharp left. Another ten paces... then right... five paces... right again... and the first door you came to. 'In here,' he said. Then straight along the corridor, a distance of ten or twelve paces, until you came to another corridor, running at right angles to it. One, two, three, *four* doors along and... 'This is it,' he said. But in any case, this last direction was superfluous, because even from twenty yards away, an excited buzz of voices could be heard. Drawn by the news of what had happened, a small crowd had gathered outside the door of the dressing-room. As Rowlands and the Inspector drew near, a voice said: 'It looks bad for the studio, all this. Think they'll close us down?'

'No idea. Did you know her?'

'Old Greta, you mean? Yes—very decent sort. Never have put her down as the type to do herself in, but then you never know, do you?' The other man agreed that you did not. 'All right,' said Gentz, addressing the officer stationed outside the door, who appeared to be having little success at keeping the crowd at bay. 'Let's get this lot cleared away, shall we?' He raised his voice a fraction. 'Now then, gentlemen—and ladies,' he added, as a couple of woman shoved their way to the front. 'I'd like you to leave now. You'll only get in my officers' way, if you hang about here...' Grumbling, the onlookers began to disperse. 'Right,' said Gentz. 'Let's see what's what, shall we?'

The cramped space of the dressing-room was made still more so by the presence of several large men: these, it transpired, were the Medical Officer and his assistants. ''Morning, Hubert.'

'Ah, Werner! Just finishing up here...'

'Hmm. So I see. Nasty.'

'Yes. No doubt about the *cause* of death, even without the lab-boys' say-so. Arsenic, in the form of rat-poison. There's a tin of it in the caretaker's cupboard, apparently...'

'How did she take it?'

'In a glass of *Schnapps*, by the look of it. See, there's the remnants of it here...'

198

'I take it this has been dusted for fingerprints?' said the Inspector to his subordinate. 'Yes, sir.'

'Good.' Gentz picked up the empty glass and sniffed at it. 'Yes, this must be the culprit. Stinks of the stuff… Pah!' He replaced it on the dressing-table with slightly more force than necessary. 'The things people think of!'

'It keeps us busy, anyway,' said the doctor. 'Hmm. S'pose it does. So it was a dash of rat-poison in the drink, then a quick lie-down on the what-d'you-call-it…'

'*Chaise-longue.*'

'That's the one,' said Gentz. 'Death followed pretty swiftly, I imagine?'

'Not as swiftly as all that. As you can see from the way she thrashed around… Knocked over the screen, for one thing.'

'And the other?'

'Well…' The doctor hesitated. 'It's just a small thing, but… There's a bit of bruising around the throat. As if…'

'As if somebody might have helped her on her way?' supplied the Inspector. 'I'm not saying that,' said the Medical Officer hastily. 'Indeed you are not,' said the Inspector. 'Any idea as to time of death?'

'Difficult to say. Some time last night, I reckon. Rigour had gone off when I examined her, and …'

'Yes, yes. Just give me some times I can work with.'

'Well, these are very approximate times, but…' While the two men were thus engaged, Rowlands, who had remained standing just inside the door, made what observations he could. For while his blindness meant he was mercifully oblivious to certain aspects of the scene, there were other ways of perceiving it. Smell, for instance. Because in addition to those he recalled from before—smells of theatrical make-up and powder, and discarded garments still retaining the faint odour of their wearer—was the sour reek of spilt alcohol, mingled with that of vomit.

And there was another smell—sweetish, floral—he recognised from the last time he had stood here. He'd smelt it somewhere else, too… the question was—where? While he was puzzling over this, the doctor got to his feet, peeling off his rubber gloves with a snap. 'All right. I'm done here.'

Gentz gave a grunt, by way of reply, and turned to his Sergeant. 'Get the photographer in here, will you?' Then, as the latter duly appeared: 'I want a couple of shots of the room—and the body, of course. One of the face—no beauty, was she, even before all this? When he's finished, *you*'—this was to the Sergeant again—'can get the lads to take her away. Come, Herr Rowlands. We have seen enough here, wouldn't you agree? You may be wondering,' the policeman went on, as the two of them made their way back along the corridor towards the exit, 'why I asked you here?'

'It had crossed my mind.'

'You spoke to the woman—Pabst—a few days ago, did you not? Did she seem to you to be in a frame of mind to make away with herself?'

Rowlands thought about it. 'She was certainly worried about something.' he said. 'Distinctly uneasy, I'd have said. But suicidal… No, I wouldn't have said that…'

'That was what I thought, too,' said Gentz. 'Hey!' This was to a couple of men who were now approaching. 'Where do you think *you're* going?'

'Hello, Chief,' said the first one of these. 'Just doing my duty to my readers, you know. I don't suppose, he added cheerfully, 'you'd give us a nice quote?'

'You know me better than that, Herr Winkler,' said Gentz. 'Now, if you'll let me pass…'

'Oh, go on, Chief! What would it cost you? I take it there's a connection between this latest stiff and the previous one—the Schönig kid?'

'No comment,' growled the policeman. 'No need to be like that, Chief! Say, who's the red-head?' Because at that moment, someone else came around the corner. 'Herr Rowlands!' said a familiar voice. 'Is it true what they're saying—that Greta's dead?'

'I'm afraid so, Fräulein Pfeiffer,' he replied. 'Oh! That's too bad. Poor Greta! She was a nice old thing…'

'Perhaps *you'd* like to give us a quote, Miss?' said the reporter, Winkler. 'Oh, go and boil your head!' snapped the girl. 'Come on, Karl, we're wasting our time here,' said the other man. 'Let's go and talk to some of those actresses…' When the two journalists had sloped off, the Inspector turned to Lena Pfeiffer. 'So you knew the deceased, did you, Fräulein?'

'We all knew her,' was the curt reply. 'She'd worked here a long time. I can see you're busy, Herr Rowlands,' the girl added pointedly. 'So long...'

'Just a minute,' said Gentz. 'I'd like to ask you a few questions...'

'Ask away.'

'Not here,' he said. 'We'll go to my office. You, too, Herr Rowlands.'

'It comes to something,' said Lena Pfeiffer, 'when the police become a permanent fixture in our studio... Although I don't know why I should be surprised,' she went on airily. 'From what I hear, we will soon become no more than just another branch of the Ministry of Propaganda...'

'You'd better watch what you say,' said Gentz, as they left the studio building and crossed the courtyard towards the administration block where his office was to be found. 'You could get yourself into a lot of trouble with that tongue of yours...'

'Like Greta did, you mean?'

'Now, what makes you say that?' The Inspector opened a door. 'In here. 'In here,' he said. 'No, that's all right, Drucker,' he said to the uniformed policeman who was found therein—typing up a report, to judge from the busy clattering of keys. 'You can take five minutes...'

'So this isn't an interrogation?' said Fräulein Pfeiffer, when the man had gone. 'I've told you,' was the reply. 'I just want to ask you a couple of questions. Sit down, won't you?' All three did so. 'Now,' went on the Inspector, 'I'd like to know what you meant just now, when you said that Greta Pabst had been speaking out of turn...'

'Did I say that?'

'Answer the question.'

'All right. But it's nothing any of the others couldn't have told you. She... she wasn't the most discreet, old Greta...' The Inspector must have raised an eyebrow at this, for the girl laughed. 'Yes, yes. I know I tend to shoot my mouth off a bit. But this was more than that.' She hesitated a moment. 'The fact is, she liked a drink, poor old girl. It had got a bit worse, recently. Since Fritzi died...'

'Ah!' said in a meaning tone. 'It's no secret she loved that man,' said Lena Pfeiffer. 'Oh, not in the usual way, of course, but...'

'He was like a child,' said Rowlands. 'That's right. She protected him. When he died... well, she went off her head, I think...'

'And said what?' asked Gentz patiently. 'Oh, lots of things she shouldn't. That his death wasn't an accident. That he'd been murdered by Brownshirt thugs. That he'd been there when Sybille Schönig died, and that *her* death wasn't suicide, either...'

'She said that, did she?'

'Oh yes, and a lot more. That she'd got *proof* that Sybille was murdered, and that she knew who had done it, too...'

'My God,' muttered Gentz. 'Why didn't she come to me?'

'None of us trust the police,' said the girl. 'No offence, but that's just the way it is.'

'Hmm,' grunted the policeman. 'And you, Herr Rowlands— did Fräulein Pabst say any of this to you?'

'She did suggest she knew more than she was letting on,' said Rowlands. 'And she hinted that Sybille—Fräulein Schönig—had been up to something, in the weeks before she died. It was something about a list,' he said. 'But I can't tell you much more than that.' Briefly, he related all that the dresser had told him. When he had finished, Lena Pfeiffer gave a scornful laugh. 'A list of names. That sounds as if our Sybille was an informer. She was just the type, if you ask me...'

'If so that might have been the reason she was killed,' said Rowlands. 'I mean, if she was threatening to give the game away...'

'It's a possibility.' Gentz didn't sound convinced. 'But one wonders why they would have gone to so much trouble.' He was careful not to specify who it was he meant. 'These days, there is no shame in being an informer. One is merely doing one's duty as a citizen.'

'Unless it was the other side who killed her?' said the girl. 'I'd have put a bullet between her eyes myself, if I'd known what she was up to...'

'And you would have ended up on the scaffold,' said Gentz

sharply. 'What would have been the use of that, Fräulein?'

'There is such a thing as principle...'

The Inspector laughed. 'I thought like that, too, when I was your age,' he said.

As they left the Inspector's office, the girl said suddenly, 'You know, Herr Rowlands, I am very disappointed in you...'

'Oh?' he said. 'And why's that?'

'Why, because you have not been to see me once, since the first time we met. Yet you have been to Babelsberg several times in the past few days. Perhaps,' she said, with a shade of petulance, 'you would rather spend your time with famous actresses?' He supposed it was Magda Hartmann she meant. 'Not at all,' he said. 'It's just that I've been so busy...'

'Ah, yes,' she sighed. 'I have heard that story before. "I am busy, too busy to see you..." It is not very original, Herr Rowlands.'

'Fräulein Pfeiffer...'

'You are going to mention your wife. I would prefer that you did not do this.'

'All right.'

'Good. We understand one another, I think?' At the door of the make-up room she came to a stop. 'Tonight,' she said.

'I don't quite see...'

Again she sighed. 'It is my birthday. I am twenty-six years old. This may not seem like a reason to celebrate, but we must make the best of it. Tonight, some friends and I will be having some drinks in a little piano-bar in the Kurfurstendamm. It is called the Blue Salamander. You are welcome to join us—if you are not too busy,' she added sarcastically.

'I'd be honoured.'

'Then I will see you there. Eight o'clock,' she said.

The cab dropped him off halfway along the broad street, down which traffic roared at breakneck speed. Rowlands was glad he hadn't had to navigate it on foot; being in an unfamiliar city was bad enough, but having to deal with scores of vehicles apparently intent on running one down, would have proved too much even for one of his determination. For a blind man, crossing a street was always hazardous. On the whole, cars weren't

203

so bad, because they made such a racket; it was the noiseless and unforeseen—the bicycle, whizzing out of nowhere, or the woman with the little dog on a long lead—which could spell disaster.

In London, Rowlands had a visual memory of streets and landmarks to rely on; by comparison, Berlin was a blank: a stony labyrinth. In the past week, it was true, he'd built up a map of the place in his mind—one that was formed of street names, smells, sounds, and fleeting encounters, and in which each district had its distinctive quality. Quiet Grünewald, with its pine-scented air; noisy Prenzlauerberg, smelling of coal fires, lung soup, and bad drains. Just now, as he paid off the cabbie, he was conscious of a new atmosphere—something unsettling and invigorating. Perhaps it was the sound of high-heels clicking past on the pavement, or the music that was coming from somewhere close by… Syncopated. Arrhythmic. Or the smell of beer and cheap cigars emanating from a local *Kneipe*… Whatever it was, it was different from anything he'd come across in the city before. A mood, if he had to describe it, of *freedom*.

The entrance to The Blue Salamander was down a flight of greasy steps. It didn't seem like much of a place, he thought. He knocked and waited. After an interval, a panel in the door slid open. 'Yes?'

'This *is* the Blue Salamander, isn't it?'

'Maybe it is. What do you want?'

'I'm with Fräulein Pfeiffer's party.'

'Why didn't you say so in the first place?' The door opened, and he went in. 'Two marks,' said the person who'd admitted him—although whether it was a man or a woman was hard to tell. 'They're in the back room. Other side of the bar and through the arch.' Then, in a slightly warmer tone: 'Shall I send you over a bottle of *Sekt*?'

Rowlands made his way gingerly across the bar, skirting a number of small tables and rickety chairs, until he came to a doorway, over which hung a heavy chenille curtain. He pushed this aside, and found himself in a hot little den, full of smoke and the murmur of voices. One of these was familiar. '…not if you paid me five hundred marks,' it said with a gurgle of laughter. 'A thousand, then?' said another voice: a man's. 'Not even a thousand. Oh! Herr Rowlands!' cried Lena Pfeiffer, as he made his way over to the table where she was sitting. 'You've arrived just in time. Tell this crazy loon that I'm not to be bought, at any price...'

'I'm sure you're not,' said Rowlands, with a smile. It struck him that, even though it was still relatively early, his hostess was already somewhat 'lit'. She gave a crow of triumph. 'You see! My Englishman thinks I'm incorruptible. And he should know. The English are a very moral people—are they not, Herr Rowlands?'

'Well...'

But she was in full flight. 'Max! A chair for Herr Rowlands.' Then, when this had been brought: 'Come, you must sit by me...' Rowlands did so, then took the small, tissue-wrapped parcel from his pocket and handed it to her. 'I hope these are the right size,' he said. 'A gift? But that's swell!' Excitedly, she ripped the paper off. 'Gloves! And such nice ones!' She kissed him soundly on both cheeks. 'I'm glad you like them,' he said. They were the best that Tietz's department store could provide. It had given him great pleasure to march past the braying picket of H.J., exhorting shoppers like himself not to 'buy Jewish'.

'Well, this put you fellows to shame,' said Lena. 'Except for you, Ute... The perfume is just dandy. You know Fräulein Müller, don't you, Herr Rowlands?' she added. 'She's the one you can thank for that fancy suit you're wearing...'

'Good to see you again, Fräulein Müller.' He was uncomfortably aware that he'd kept the borrowed suit for rather longer than he should have. But if the wardrobe mistress was put out by this, she gave no sign of it. 'Hello,' she said. 'I remember you, now. You were the one Herr Direktor was so taken with...'

'Can you blame him?' said the make-up girl. 'I mean, *what* a profile! This is Max Ullmann,' she went on. This was the man who'd gone to fetch the chair. 'Delighted,' said Rowlands, as the two men shook hands. 'Max is a composer,' said Lena. 'He's writing an opera—aren't you, Max?'

'Well...' said the other; but before he could elaborate, the girl rushed on: 'And this reprobate is Simon Meyer. He calls himself

205

an artist...'

'I *am* an artist. A painter, actually,' said the young man. 'I knew a painter, once,' said Rowlands. 'He painted my portrait, as a matter of fact.'

'Yes, I can see you'd be an interesting subject,' said Meyer, having considered the other for a moment. 'Was the painting any good?'

'I believe so. It's not something I was able to verify for myself,' smiled Rowlands. 'No, I suppose not.' There was the moment's silence that often followed a mention of his blindness. 'Still, it's a pity,' drawled the artist at last. 'One always likes to know what one's rivals are up to...'

A glass was put into Rowlands's hand. 'Time for a toast,' said Lena. 'Since it's my birthday, I get to propose it. Now what'll it be? "Confusion to our enemies"?' Max Ullmann laughed. 'Now *that's* a crowded field...'

'*L'chaim,*' said Simon Meyer gravely. The five of them clinked glasses. Rowland's took a sip. Champagne, he thought—or the German version of it. The taste reminded him of the last time he had drunk the stuff, and of the women in whose company he had been. He wondered where she was at the moment, and if she was happy... 'You're looking sad, Herr Rowlands,' said Lena. 'You know you are not allowed to be sad on my birthday.'

'I should hope not.' He raised his glass to her. 'Many happy returns,' he said. As he spoke, the band, which had been tuning up in the far corner of the room, began to play: a jaunty, faintly mocking tune, which was unfamiliar to Rowlands. His companions seemed to know it, however, for they clapped appreciatively. Then the singer—perhaps the deep-voiced woman who had taken Rowlands's money, or perhaps another, no less androgynous-sounding—began to sing. 'Oh,' breathed Lena. 'I love this song.'

Ich war jung, Gott, erst sechzehn Jahre
Du kamst von Birma herauf
Du sagtest, ich solle mit dir gehen
Du kämest für alles auf...

As the singer's powerful voice filled the room, people started to drift in from the bar. Before long, every table in the cramped little dive was occupied. Bottles of the house champagne were called for, and conversation grew increasingly animated. This was a Bohemian crowd. The air, of which there was not a great deal, grew thick with cigarette smoke and the scent of patchouli, and each verse of the bitter-sweet love-song was accompanied by whistling and clapping, making Rowlands wish he could share the joke they all seemed to be in on...

Du sagtest viel, Johnny,
Kein Wort war wahr, Johnny,
Du hast mich betrogen, Johnny,
zur ersten Stund...

'I've met this Johnny!' shouted a woman at the next table. 'We all have, darling,' shouted someone else, to general laughter. The music grew louder. Rowland's head was ringing; the effect, no doubt, of several glasses of champagne on an empty stomach. He felt Lena take his hand. 'Who is she?' she murmured in his ear, over the raucous rhythms of piano and saxophone. 'The woman you're in love with?'

'I've told you—I'm married.'

'That's not what I asked.' Then, perhaps tiring of the game: 'Let's dance. You won't refuse me *that*, at least...' So, to the irresistible strains of *Tonight or Never*, they began to circle the floor, already crowded with dancers, so that it was a wonder either of them could move at all. Nor was it always plain sailing for a new partner to have to lead... But after a few false steps, Lena got the hang of it, and they were soon gliding around the floor as if they had been partnering one another for years.

Heute Nacht oder nie
sollst du mir sagen nur das Eine:
Ob du mich liebst...

Unlike the strident jazz numbers which had been playing before, this song was one with which Rowlands was familiar.

Hadn't there been an English version released only a year ago? It had been all over the airwaves, he was sure of it...

Tonight or never
You will say to me only one thing:
That you love me...

He found he was humming the tune under his breath, as he and his partner dipped and twirled, matching their steps to one another's with perfect synchronicity, as if there were nothing else but this graceful, fluid motion of bodies in time, and no world outside this stifling, smoke-filled cellar. For an instant he was transported back to another moment. The lithe young body he held against his was, briefly, that of the woman with whom he'd been dancing that night—was it three... no, four... years ago? He remembered the scent of her hair. The way she'd felt in his arms. 'You dance well,' said Lena Pfeiffer. 'I like a man who knows how to dance...'

15

THE SONG HAD COME to an end, and they were making their way back towards their table, when the sound of raised voices came from the outer bar. A moment later, the plush curtain was pushed aside, and some people came in: two men and a woman, apparently. A brief silence fell; then conversation started up again, at an even more feverish pitch than before, it seemed to Rowlands. 'I don't care for the company,' muttered Lena in his ear. 'It's too "brown" for my liking…' From which he gathered that the men were in SS uniform. The loud confidence with which they conducted themselves supported this assumption. At once, the band struck up again, as if to drown out this unwelcome addition to the audience.

Meine Herren, heute sehen Sie mich Gläser abwaschen
Und ich mache das Bett für jeden…

The hoarse, whisky-soaked voice of the singer seemed to fill the room, as the sanguinary tale of Pirate Jenny began to unfold. This time there was no clapping and cheering, as verse followed verse, but only a strained silence, as if those assembled there were all-too aware of how precarious the continued existence of such entertainments might be. This overheated little room, reeking of sweat, spilled beer, and cheap perfume, had seemed a refuge from the harsher realities of the world outside. 'They closed down the Montmartre last week,' said Simon Meyer morosely, as the song drew to its close. 'And the Russian Bar the week before that. Soon there won't be a drinking den in Berlin that hasn't been raided by the "Storms"…'

'Time we were going, anyway,' said Max Ullmann. 'Before some more of their friends show up…' But as their little party got up to leave, taking advantage of the lull in the music to do so, there came another interruption. 'I say, is that you, Mr Rowlands?' The voice was that of Iris Barnes, and it came from a table near the door—the table at which the SS officers were sitting. Reluctantly, Rowlands turned his face in that direction. 'How awfully funny that you should turn up here,' Miss Barnes went on. 'I might say the same to you,' he replied, in an even tone. 'Yes. *Quite* a coincidence!' Was it Rowlands's imagination, or did her gaiety sound rather forced? 'So *authentic*, these places, aren't they? Full of local colour. I *insisted* that Lieutenant von Fritsch should take me to at least *one* real Berlin nightclub, didn't I, Rudi?'

'You did,' was the dry response.

'But how *terrible* of me! I haven't introduced you. Mr Rowlands, this is Lieutenant von Fritsch...'

'Oh, we already know one another, do we not, Herr Rowlands?' said the other. 'Yes,' said Rowlands. 'I believe we do.' A few more desultory exchanges followed, during which Rowlands found himself acutely conscious of the awkwardness of the moment: that cold, clipped voice, with its disconcerting 'Oxford' accent, counterpointed by Irene Barnes's gushing tones... He was glad to make his escape at last. Outside, in the street, Lena and her companions were waiting for him. 'Well,' said Ute Müller, in her rasping voice. 'You never said you were a friend of dear Rudi's...' He supposed it was von Fritsch she meant. 'I'm not,' he said. 'A useful friend to have, surely?' said the composer, Ullmann. 'Oh, why don't you take a running jump?' said Lena furiously. 'Can't you see he's no more a friend of that creep than I am?'

'O.K., O.K.,' muttered Ullmann. 'You just can't be too careful, that's all.'

'In point of fact,' said Rowlands mildly. 'It's Miss Barnes who's my friend... Not that I know her all that well,' he added. 'The English woman? She's been hanging around the studios all week,' said the make-up girl with some scorn. 'She's a film critic,' said Rowlands. 'It's her job to interview people...'

'Then I suppose she must be interviewing von Fritsch about his new film,' was the reply. Suddenly Rowlands was tired of the sarcasm. 'I don't know about that,' he said. 'But in any case, I'd better be on my way. If one of you could hail me a taxi, I'd be grateful. Goodnight, Fräulein Pfeiffer. It was an enjoyable evening...'

'But you mustn't go yet! The night's still young—and it's still my birthday.' Before he could walk away, she linked her arm through his. 'Come on,' she said. 'Let's find a bar where they don't serve Stormtroopers.'

Rowlands woke in a strange bed. That it was a bed, and not the put-you-up on which he'd been sleeping, in the Metzners' flat, alerted him to this interesting fact at once. He was still wearing his clothes—minus his jacket and shoes. He levered himself upright—and immediately wished he hadn't. His head ached like poison. What *had* he been drinking last night? Scattered memories of the previous evening's events passed through his mind. They'd gone to a bar. The Blue Salamander... no, that was before. The Marrakesh... wasn't that what it was called? There'd been a band, and dancing, and someone had fallen over, and smashed a lot of glasses... He'd thought this very funny at the time... At some point, they'd all gone back to Lena's flat— himself, that painter chap, and several others. He remembered dancing to the gramophone. The *St Louis Blues* and *All of Me*...

All of me
Why not take
All of me?
Can't you see
I'm no good without you?

Cautiously, he slid from under the blankets and sat up, feeling around for his shoes. They must be somewhere... The movement must have disturbed the other occupant of the bed, for a muffled voice said something incoherent. As Rowlands found his shoes, and began to put them on, his brain still whirring unpleasantly, the girl—it was Lena Pfeiffer—sat up. 'What time is is?' she said. He touched his watch-face (his watch was still attached to his wrist, thank God). 'Twenty past eight.'

'*Verdammt!* I'm going to be late.' She made as if to get up, then fell back against the pillows, with a groan. 'I feel lousy.'

'I don't feel too good myself.'

'Get me a glass of water, will you?'

'Of course,' he said. 'If you point me in the direction of the kitchen.'

'There isn't a kitchen. Just a gas-ring. But there's a basin just behind you... Yes, there. You'll find a tooth-mug on the shelf.'

He did so, and ran some water into the glass. 'Here you are.'

'You angel,' she said, as she took it from him. Then, perhaps seeing the expression on his face: 'You needn't look like that! Nothing happened last night, if you want to know...'

'I... I...' he stammered. Lena laughed. 'It comes to something,' she said, 'when a girl has to swear a man *hasn't* made love to her...'

To have said he was sorry would have been to add insult to injury, and so he said nothing. 'Don't look so miserable,' she said. 'I don't hate you. I wish I did, but I don't. I guess that's always been my trouble—too damn nice for my own good.' Gingerly, she began to ease herself out of bed. 'Now if you'll just be a gentleman, and turn your back,' she said. 'Although, under the circumstances, I suppose it doesn't make much difference...'

'I should go.'

'You've time for a cup of coffee. Throw me my robe, will you? It's on the end of the bed.' He found the robe, a silky bit of stuff, and handed it to her. 'Thanks. God, what a mess this room looks!' she said. 'That's something else you won't be able to see...' She began absentmindedly putting things to rights. 'Did we really get through a whole bottle of Schnapps? And all these empty beer-bottles! God, these ashtrays smell disgusting... Who does this jacket belong to, I wonder?'

'It's probably mine.'

'Oh yes.' She handed it to him. 'Your tie's hanging on the lampshade. Here. I'll put it on for you...' He stood still while she did so. 'Now where's that coffee?' She bustled about, filling a saucepan at the basin and banging it down on the gas-ring with rather too much force, it seemed to him. 'I'll just make myself respectable,' she said. 'Won't be a moment...' Sounds of water running and teeth being brushed followed. 'I've no time for a bath, worst luck.'

He'd have left her to it, but in truth he badly needed a cup of coffee. When it was made, they sat either side of a small deal table that served (he guessed) as dining-table, desk, and ironing-board combined. 'Good coffee,' he said. 'Oh. Thanks. One of my grateful clients gave it to me, in lieu of payment.' Then, when he looked puzzled: 'It's how I supplement my income from UFA. Doing make-up for weddings. I've turned out quite a few blushing brides, I can tell you. Including some who had plenty to blush about, if you get my meaning!'

Rowlands smiled, although he wasn't sure if it had been meant as joke, or not. She had such a droll way of putting things that it wasn't always easy to tell. He finished his coffee, and pushed back his chair. 'If you'll just direct me to the nearest tram-stop,' he began, but she caught him by the sleeve and made him sit down again. 'Don't be ridiculous,' she said. 'You'll never find your way out of here unaided—it's a warren. They built these flats for workers five years ago, and they're already full to bursting—mainly with artists and journalists and that sort of riffraff...' The 'artists' colony' of Friedenau consisted of three tenement blocks, she explained, putting on her hat and coat. 'There's a kind of village mentality about the place. Everybody knows everybody else, and we all look out for each other...'

He said it sounded very civilised.

'Oh it is,' said the girl. 'At Friedenau we're all what you might call like-minded...' She frowned at herself in the mirror: 'God, I look like Death...'

A tram was approaching, as they reached the stop. They jumped on it. 'This'll take us to Ausstellung,' said Fräulein Pfeiffer to Rowlands, as they took their seats in the rattling, swaying, car. 'I'll be getting the S-Bahn to Babelsberg from there. You'll be going in the other direction, towards Alexanderplatz. Do you think you can find your way?'

He reassured her.

'If I'm lucky, I might still catch the 9.14. I just hope,' she said gloomily, 'that there isn't a huge crowd waiting for me in Make-Up. They've started filming a new project. It's been something of a rush job. Orders from on high,' she said cryptically. 'Mm.' Rowlands wasn't really paying attention; his late night was catching up with him. 'Since I'll be passing the Alex, I'd better drop in on Inspector Gentz,' he thought. 'Not that there's much he'll be able to tell me...'

'...all part of the new regime,' the make-up girl was saying. 'Nothing but lousy propaganda, if you ask me.'

'Of course,' he murmured distractedly.

'Still, it's work,' Lena Pfeiffer was saying. 'So I can't be too choosy... I suppose,' she went on, suddenly changing tack, 'I won't be seeing you at the studio again?'

'Not unless Herr Klein offers me another starring role,' he smiled. 'Although, come to think of it, I *do* have to return this suit. Your friend Fräulein Müller will be thinking I've made off with it.'

'Oh, Ute won't mind! But I don't want her getting into trouble with that old dragon, Ilse Dunst... I could take it back for you, if you like. That is, if you'd care to meet me one evening after work, to hand it over...'

'Thank you,' he said. 'I'd appreciate that.'

'I wouldn't want you to think it was just a way of getting to see you you again.'

'I wouldn't think that for a minute.'

'Good. So you'll be going back to England soon?'

'Well, not very soon. I still have to find my nephew,' he said.

'I thought it was two boys you were looking for?'

Rowlands hesitated, not quite sure how far he could trust her. 'One of them has been found.'

'But that's good news!' she said. 'Your nephew, you say, is still missing?'

'Yes.'

'Very sad for your poor sister.' He agreed that it was. 'You know it was strange,' she said. 'The way that photograph disappeared—the one I'd put up on the mirror. I thought it must have been the janitor who'd removed it, but when I asked him, Herr Braun said he didn't know anything about it... Oh, here's our stop. Come on, or you'll miss your train...'

But Rowlands no longer cared about catching his train. 'Say what you just said again,' he said. 'Starting with the bit about the photograph.'

When questioned, the janitor was surly. 'I don't know what you're talking about,' he said. 'A boy? I don't know anything about a boy. My job's to make sure everything's as it should be, on UFA premises. There's not a lightbulb goes, or a toilet that gets blocked, that I don't hear about,' he said, with gloomy satisfaction. They were in the cramped little office—really more of cupboard—in which the janitor cooled his heels when he wasn't doing his rounds. It was here that Lena had conducted Rowlands, on their arrival at the studios, with a warning to 'Watch out for Herr Braun. He's a nasty piece of work. NSDAP member, of course...'

He was beginning to see what she meant. 'It sounds like quite a responsibility,' he said. 'You can say that again! Especially now I'm short-handed...'

'You mean after what happened to Fritzi Henkel?'

'I do. Not that he was ever much use,' said Braun, contemptuously. 'He had a screw or two loose, had poor old Fritzi. But ever since he chucked himself down the stairs, I've had to manage on my own. It's not easy, in a place this size...'

'Difficult for you,' said Rowlands. 'But let's return to my original question. I mean about whether or not you remember seeing the boy... You've two sons of your own, I gather? Twins, aren't they?'

'How do you know that?' demanded the other. Rowlands shrugged. 'It doesn't matter how I know. They're members of the junior branch of the Hitler Jugend, too, aren't they?'

'What if they are?'

'Just answer the question, Herr Braun. After all,' said Rowlands coldly. 'It surely can't reflect anything but credit on your family to have your sons pledged to the Nazi cause?'

'No! Certainly not!' blustered the janitor. 'Proud of my lads, I am. But what's it got to do with you?'

'A week ago,' said Rowlands, 'your boys took another boy—a

boy calling himself Wilhelm Aschenbach—along with them to the H.J. meeting in Neukölln. I've witnesses to this, so you needn't deny it. Just tell me how it was you found the boy.'

'I... I don't see that it matters.' Braun seemed decidedly rattled by this challenge. 'I mean... it's not a crime to help somebody...'

'One would hope not. So you *did* help him?'

'He was hungry,' said the janitor. 'He'd been camping out in the Back Lot, he said. Perishing cold, it was, that week. I caught him stealing food from the canteen. Stuff had been going missing for several nights, and I lay in wait for him. Gave him a taste of the back of my hand he won't forget...' He chuckled reminiscently. 'But then I thought, "Poor little devil." So I took him home with me...'

'To Neukölln,' put in Rowlands. 'It's where I live, isn't it? was the reply. 'The Missus wasn't best pleased to have another mouth to feed, but I soon shut *her* up. Told her I could do what I liked in my own house. Women,' said Braun heavily, 'should know their place. And my Helga soon came around. Took quite a shine to the kid, as a matter of fact...'

'So he—young Aschenbach—went with your boys to the H.J. meetings?'

'Didn't seem no harm in it,' said the man, resuming the surly tone he'd adopted at first. 'He *wanted* to go, as a matter of fact. We had a spare Deutsches Jungvolk uniform, that had belonged to my eldest—*he's* fully-fledged H.J. now,' he added proudly. 'So yes, we sent him along. Another recruit for the Führer's cause, we thought...'

'Indeed,' said Rowlands. 'And where is the boy now?'

Braun laughed. It wasn't a pleasant laugh. 'There's no sense in asking me *that*. I haven't laid eyes on the kid since last Sunday...'

'The day of the funeral parade.'

'Yes. Last I saw of him, he was marching along beside my two boys. Looked very smart, they did, in their uniforms. All I know is, when they came home—Heinz and Horst—the other lad wasn't with them. They said he'd gone off with one of the Leaders. Didn't say which one.'

More than this he could not, or would not, say. Which meant, thought Rowlands, that they were no further forward than they had been before—except that what had previously been mere supposition, had now been confirmed as fact. Billy had last been seen at the parade on Sunday—by his mother, by Grüber, the H.J. leader, and now, it appeared, by the Braun siblings. After that, his whereabouts were unknown...

Leaving the janitor skulking in his cubby-hole, Rowlands made his way back along the corridor towards the exit, and pushed open the heavy metal door that led out into the yard. He had a bad feeling about all this, he thought. 'Herr Rowlands! A moment, if you please...'

It was Klein who had called Rowland's name. Now he drew level with him. 'I had not realised that you were still in Berlin,' he said. 'But we must not stand here. Come to my office, where we can talk privately. I have been so busy, these past few days, or I should have been in touch...'

With Klein leading the way, they entered the building on the far side of the cobbled yard—it housed Studios 1 and 2, Rowlands recalled—and walked along a corridor. 'There will be a party to celebrate the wrap—that is, finishing the shooting—of *Fallen Angel*,' said Klein. 'The studio's last, great project,' he added softly, as if to himself. He opened a door. 'Please. After you,' he said, ushering Rowlands into the room. 'I should like you to be there, since you were a small, but important part of it. The party will be at the Adlon Hotel. Do sit down, Herr Rowlands. There is a chair just in front of you... Yes. That one. All the important people at UFA will be there,' he went on. 'That is to say, those who are now running the show, and those, like myself, who must answer to them... Cigarette?'

'Thanks.' He took one from the case Klein offered him, and the director lit it for him. 'Turkish,' said Klein. 'They're not too bad. Although I prefer American.'

'Is the film finished then?' asked Rowlands. He'd an idea it all took rather longer than this, but what did he know? Klein laughed. 'As finished as it will ever be,' he said. 'There is still the editing to do. That will take some time. It can make all the difference, in fact, between a film that is merely good, and one that is great. But the Minister says we must not delay. He wishes us to complete the project with all speed, so that we can get on

217

with making films that The People actually want to see...'

Rowlands was startled at the bitter sarcasm with which this was said. 'Oh yes!' went on Klein, 'you would be surprised at how important a role "The People" are to play in German film-making from now on. It is they whose tastes must be consulted, and whose prejudices must be indulged... Why, even as we speak, I have three films in production which have fulfilled these exacting criteria. One is a charming fable of peasant life—a real picture of the New Germany—with a fresh-faced maiden sacrificing her all for the love of a brown-shirted Hero...'

'Ah,' said Rowlands. 'That must be *Love Among the Haystacks*.'

'We have given it a new title. *Love and Honour*. That is more suitable for our pure-minded audience, you know. Then there is our historical picture...'

'The one about Frederick the Great?'

'The same. Our writers have been working day and night to finish the script. They have just written a scene in which the young Frederick lays aside his books and music, and picks up a sword... It is a very beautiful scene.'

'I'm sure it is.'

'Then there is *The Triumph of Youth*. That will be a wonderful picture, starring Rolf Norkus, one of our brightest new talents... so new, in fact, that he has never made a film before. He will play the Youth, struggling with the forces of evil (the Reds, you know) in order to establish the New Order. This involves dressing up in a very smart brown uniform, and parading up and down, waving a very large Hakenkreuz flag. Fortunately he does not have many lines to say. All he must do is expose his handsome blond face to the cameras as much as possible. I am glad to say that there are several more experienced actors in the cast. Frau Hartmann, for one. She will play the Mother.' Klein laughed. 'She was not best pleased at being cast in this role at first. But it was explained to her that The People would want nothing less...'

'That must have made a difference,' said Rowlands, thinking that he could well imagine the reaction of the former *femme fatale* to being offered such a part. 'So you see, Herr Rowlands, why it is that I attach such importance to my last film—*Fallen*

Angel, I mean. It represents… but I cannot say exactly what it represents. My lost honour, perhaps.'

'I should imagine,' said Rowlands, 'that it must make all the difference, being able to work without interference from… outside elements.'

'You are right! It makes all the difference in the world. One is free to… to say whatever one wishes to say. To invent.' Klein gave a self-deprecating laugh. 'Even if what one invents may seem no more than a foolish fantasy…'

'I'm sure it was more than that,' said Rowlands.

'You are very kind, Herr Rowlands. One might argue that a little fantasy does no harm. And my *Angel* was a very beautiful fantasy… with a very beautiful star as its centrepiece…' It seemed to Rowlands that the director was speaking as much for his own benefit as for that of his listener. 'My poor Sybille,' he murmured. 'Such a promising talent. It was her first big picture, you know. She would have gone on to do greater things.' He sighed. 'But it was not to be…'

'At least she was able to finish the picture.'

'Yes, yes. There is that,' said Klein. 'It will be her monument, I think. Perhaps it is for the best. To go out in a flash—like that! When one is at the height of one's powers, and before one has done anything of which to be ashamed…' He broke off, as if thinking better of what he had been about to say. 'And had she?' said Rowlands. 'Done anything to be ashamed of, I mean?' But the director would not be drawn. 'It was just a figure of speech, Herr Rowlands. Enough of such topics. You have not told me what you have been up to, since we last met.'

'I've been looking for my nephew. I have reason to believe he is still in Berlin.'

'Ah, yes. The boy in the photograph,' said Klein. 'But surely there was another child with him?'

'That's right,' said Rowlands quickly. 'The boy's cousin. I… I'm hoping he'll turn up, too, of course.' He explained about the previous Sunday's sighting. 'So he was with a group of H.J. boys, your nephew?' said the director thoughtfully. 'Rather a coincidence, that…' Before he could expand on this, there came a sharp rap at the door. A moment later, someone put his head in.

'Ah ha!' said a voice Rowlands knew. 'I am glad to find you, Herr Klein. And Herr Rowlands, too—you have been lying low, have you not?' Inspector Gentz gave a bark of laughter. 'I cannot say that I blame you,' he said. 'It is much the best policy, in our New Germany, would you not agree, Herr Klein?'

'If you say so,' replied the other stiffly. 'You wanted to see me, Inspector?'

'That is so. I have to tell you that we will be standing down the police investigation, as of today. Headquarters is of the opinion that our resources can be better deployed elsewhere. A string of suicides—however deplorable—does not constitute a threat to the public, and so...'

'You have concluded that all three deaths are suicides?' interrupted Klein. 'What else could they be?' replied the Inspector, his tone one of wooden officialdom. 'A young woman—an actress—has shot herself. A sad waste, but hardly surprising, given the instability of her temperament. A drunken cleaner brains himself, falling downstairs. An accidental death, you might say, rather than suicide—although he, too, was unstable. An elderly woman poisons herself, out of grief, or remorse—we do not know. Yes, it is clear to the authorities that these deaths, though regrettable, are in no way connected.'

'But I thought...' began Rowlands; then broke off. 'You were saying?' said the Inspector pleasantly. 'Wasn't there evidence suggesting foul play?' said Rowlands. 'Nothing that could not be explained away,'was the reply. 'The police have to consider every eventuality. But in the end, we have satisfied ourselves that no third party was involved, in any of these cases. My men and I will be returning to Berlin this afternoon,' he said to Klein.

'Thank you, Inspector.'

'Well, that is all I came to say,' said the policeman. 'If you have nothing to do for the next few minutes, Herr Rowlands, I should appreciate your company—that is, if you have finished your business with Herr Klein?'

'Oh, we have said all we wished to say, have we not, Herr Rowlands?' said Klein. 'I must return to the studio. We are shooting the scene in which our young Hero faces down a gang of cowardly Reds. They outnumber him ten to one, but he makes

220

short work of them all, using only his bare fists... Goodbye, Herr Rowlands. Remember: the Hotel Adlon—Saturday, eight o'clock.' The two shook hands; then Klein and did the same. 'Goodbye, Inspector,' said Klein. 'I must confess, it will be a relief not to have policemen swarming all over the studio. I was starting to think we had a crime wave here at Babelsberg—but you have told me that is not so. It has merely been a series of unfortunate coincidences. Well, we must live with that, must we not?'

JUMP CUT

16

THE INSPECTOR OPENED A door, and the by-now familiar smell of perfume and face-powder tickled Rowlands's nose. Overlaying this sweeter fragrance was the sourer smell of vomit—a reminder that not one, but two, women had died in this room, one of them poisoned. 'The scene of the crime,' said Gentz, echoing this thought. 'All right, Kluge, you can go,' he added to the uniformed man stationed outside the door. 'Officer Schultz can use a bit of help shifting those files from my office into the staff car...'

'I suppose, legally speaking, it *was* a crime,' said Rowlands, as the sound of the young policeman's footsteps died away along the corridor. 'Even if it wasn't murder.' Gentz, who had been poking disconsolately through the rubble of bottles and jars on the dressing-table, seemed unaccountably outraged by this. 'Of course it was murder!'

'Then...'

'...this is what is referred to in all the American gangster films as a whitewash. Yes, Herr Rowlands, I am afraid that it is so. It does not suit my masters for these murders to be investigated further. That is the fact of it.'

'I see.'

'I believe you do.' Gentz's tone was sombre. 'I am afraid, Herr Rowlands, that you will not think very highly of our German police force, which can allow itself to be coerced in such a way...'

'I'm not in a position to judge the German police force as a whole,' said Rowlands. 'But what I've seen of the behaviour of one member of it has given me no reason to think badly of its methods.'

'That is generous of you, Herr Rowlands—and I accept the

compliment for what it is worth. Because—had I been permitted to do so—I like to think that my methods, as you call them, would have led me at last to the murderer of Fräulein Schönig. And indeed to the killer of Fritz Henkel and Frau Pabst—for I believe the same person or persons were responsible for all three crimes.' Gentz sat himself down on one of the flimsy gilt chairs with which the dressing-room was provided. It creaked alarmingly under his weight. 'Perhaps,' he said, 'you would indulge me, Herr Rowlands, since I feel that I can trust you not to betray me? I should like, with your permission, to go over once more the events of Friday 27th January. For my own satisfaction, you understand—since I am prohibited from taking the case any further...'

'By all means,' said Rowlands. He was about to sit down on the *chaise longue* that occupied the far wall of the room, when he remembered that it was here that Greta Pabst had died. He chose another of the gilt chairs instead. 'Go on,' he said.

'Very well. We begin at around a quarter past five, with the arrival of your nephew, Billy, and his cousin, at the UFA studios. They get past the doorman, and go to Sybille Schönig's dressing-room. We know that at this time, Fräulein Schönig is in Studio 3, filming a scene with another of the actors, Herr Ziegler. Herr Hartmann, we have since learned, had already left the studio, since he had no part in the scene. Also in Studio 3 at around a quarter past five are Herr Klein, who is directing the scene, Fräulein Stöbel, the understudy, and Herr Herz, the Lighting Director. Others present apart from these six include Herr Jung, operating Camera One, Herr Winter, on Camera Two, and Herr Hands, the Sound Recordist. Is that clear so far?'

'Very clear.'

'Good. At around five thirty-five, according to the statements of those present, a quarrel breaks out between Herr Klein and Fräulein Schönig. It appears that he is unhappy with the way the scene has been played—and is critical of Fräulein Schönig's performance in particular. He announces his decision to reshoot the scene in the morning. This makes his leading lady unhappy. Her response is to say that, if he is going to pick holes in everything she does, she wants no more to do with his stupid

226

film…'

'I take it everyone you mentioned just now overheard this?'

Gentz laughed. 'They couldn't very well have missed it. She was screaming at the top of her voice. Klein gave back as good as he got, mind. Told her she could take her wares elsewhere, but she'd never amount to anything, without him to direct her. Then she storms out…'

'Was she the only one who left the studio?'

'You don't miss much, do you? As a matter of fact she wasn't. Herr Herz went out, just after she did—that was at around five forty-five. Had to answer a call of nature, he said. He returned about five minutes later, according to the others. Herr Hartmann was already in Schönig's dressing-room. He says he was not present for the quarrel with Klein, but that he had some private business to discuss with the girl. He was at first reluctant to tell us what this business might be, but we got it out of him eventually,' said Gentz, with some satisfaction.

'He knew she'd been seeing someone else,' said Rowlands.

'Precisely. He wasn't happy about that, at all. He'd been planning to leave his wife for her, and then… She'd made him look a fool,' said Gentz.

'So that was what they were quarrelling about, when Joachim Metzner overheard them?'

'So it would seem.'

'The boys must have overheard it, too,' said Rowlands.

'I was coming to them. According to young Walter, they were hiding behind *this*.' Gentz rattled a row of hangers on the clothes-rail. 'Then young Billy got a bit of dust up his nose and sneezed, and they were discovered. No wonder Hartmann was angry! It comes to something when you can't even break up with your mistress without an audience of grubby schoolboys…'

'At least Walter was able to corroborate Hartmann's story. I mean, that he'd left the dressing-room well before the girl was killed…'

'His brother's story, too,' said the Inspector drily. 'Otherwise we might have had our suspicions about *him*. I mean, what exactly was young Metzner doing in the corridor at that time? By rights, he should have been in the studio, with the others…'

'He says he went to remonstrate with her. To persuade her not to leave…'

'Oh, I know what he *says*.' Gentz's tone was sceptical. 'But we'll leave it for now. Then *he* leaves—young Metzner, that is—because he thinks it isn't quite nice to eavesdrop on a lovers' quarrel. A few moments after *that*, Herr Hartmann storms out of the dressing-room. Temperamental types, these actors, to be sure! The boys are then given a not-too-serious dressing-down by the lovely Sybille, at the end of which they leave, passing Fritzi Henkel in the corridor…'

'But Billy came back…'

'Yes, in the excitement of meeting his idol, he'd forgotten his satchel, silly kid. So he returns to fetch it, having arranged to meet his friend at the agreed place…'

'The Back Lot.'

'As you say. But let us stay in the dressing-room, for the moment. Because this is where things become less certain. We know that Billy *said* he would return, but did he do so?'

'Yes,' said Rowlands. 'Because the satchel…'

'… was not found. That is true. Only the pencil which had fallen out of it was found. Which would suggest that he was at some point behind this screen…' Gentz gave the object in question a shove. 'Yes,' said Rowlands. 'I think we can assume that.'

'Which begs the question—Why? If he only come back to collect his satchel, and perhaps to catch another glimpse of his adored Sybille, then why was he behind the screen?'

'You know why,' said Rowlands. 'It was because he heard someone coming—someone by whom it was important he should not be seen…'

'Agreed,' said the police inspector. 'The question is, who? My money's still on Hartmann…'

'If you're saying he killed her, what reason did he have? He was in love with her…'

'Ah, *love!*' said the Inspector disgustedly. 'That's always a fine excuse. But I take your point. Well, if he didn't do it, then his wife did. You can't deny that *she* had a motive. Her husband was planning to run away with a younger woman.'

'True. But we don't know that she was ever in the dressing-room.'

'She has no alibi for the time between a quarter to five and half-past six,' said Gentz. 'She claims she went for a drive—she cannot say where it was she went...'

'Can't the chauffeur corroborate her story?'

'She was driving herself. She likes driving, apparently. But when I asked her to say what direction she took, she can only say it was towards the city...'

'So you're saying she might have gone to the studio?'

'Grünewald is an hour and a half's drive from Babelsberg studios,' said the policeman. 'She could have done it comfortably.' He sighed, But this is all speculation. If we had a witness who could place her in the dressing-room, I would not hesitate to arrest her. As it is...' He let the sentence tail away. 'It's those crucial thirty-five minutes between ten minutes past six and the time the body was discovered by Frau Pabst at a quarter to seven we don't know enough about,' he went on. 'Somebody came to this dressing-room during that time, but we don't know who. Somebody shot Sybille Schönig through the head at close range, and then wrapped her fingers around the gun to make it look like suicide. Except that they got it wrong, by putting the gun into the girl's *right* hand, when she was left-handed, according to the late Frau Pabst... An elementary mistake.'

'Or perhaps whoever did it was in a hurry,' said Rowlands.

'No doubt,' said the policeman drily. 'Murder is seldom a leisurely business. This person or persons unknown then went away unseen...'

'Not unseen,' interrupted Rowlands. 'There was a witness.'

'Of course. Your young nephew was hiding behind the screen the whole time, according to you...'

'Well, can you think of any other reason why someone should want to kill him?' said Rowlands quietly.

'No.' The Inspector gave an awkward cough. 'But I was assuming that, since he hasn't been found, that... well, that the worst had happened.'

'He's been seen,' said Rowlands. 'Fairly recently, too.' He told Gentz all that he'd learned since the previous Sunday. The other listened in silence. 'Do you mean to say,' he said, when

Rowlands had finished speaking, 'that he's been taken up by one of the von Schirach crowd?'

'It rather looks like it.'

Gentz let out a low whistle. 'Talk about going into the lions' den! So you've no idea where the kid might be at this moment?'

'I'm afraid not. He could be anywhere in the city. Trouble is,' said Rowlands, with a wry grimace, 'I'm not the best person to go looking for him...'

'That is so.' Gentz was silent a moment; then: 'Do you still have that photograph of the boy with you?'

'Yes.' Rowlands took it from his breast-pocket and handed it over 'Speaking of which, something rather odd's happened...' He explained about the disappearing poster. 'Fräulein Pfeiffer's convinced it was in the Make-Up Room until yesterday. Braun knew nothing about it, he says, and so...'

'Somebody else must have taken it down,' said the Inspector thoughtfully. 'If Braun is telling the truth, that is...'

'Why should he lie?'

'Hmph! That type lies for the sake of lying. But you're right—there's no reason why he should. Have you asked around to see if anyone else can throw some light on the matter?'

'I was just going to,' said Rowlands. 'I thought of starting in the staff canteen. It must be nearly time for the film crews to break for lunch...'

'Good idea.' Gentz handed him back the photograph. 'Here. You'll need this. It was good talking to you, Herr Rowlands' he added. 'It has relieved my mind a little, to know that at least one other person knows the truth.'

Outside, the courtyard between the buildings was thronged with people, in complete contrast to its deserted state half an hour before. A crowd jostled around the door of the canteen, from which appetising smells of coffee, spice buns, and hot soup emanated. Rowlands took his place in the queue. The room was full, and at first it was hard to distinguish individual voices from the buzz of conversation. He paid for his coffee and stood for a moment, deciding where to sit. Then a voice he knew detached itself from the rest, and he directed his steps towards the mellow tones of Paul Ziegler. 'Hallo, Herr Rowlands!' the actor hailed him, as he approached. 'You are becoming quite a regular at UFA, are you not?'

'I suppose so,' he smiled. 'May I join you?'

'But of course. Magda and I were just gossiping about this and that, were we not, *Liebchen*?'

'Like the two old women we are,' said that lady acidly, as Rowlands sat down at the table—one reserved for the stars, he guessed, since it was a little removed from the others. 'Oh, oh,' laughed Ziegler. 'Let us have less talk of being old, if you please!'

'Well, it's the truth. I mean—look at me! Not yet forty, and already I am playing the Mother! I would not mind so much,' she said bitterly, 'if I had not been made up to look like such a frump, with this hideous grey wig...'

'Don't worry,' said Ziegler in a soothing tone. 'No one will know it's you underneath all that make-up.'

'It certainly won't change the image *I* have of you,' said Rowlands. 'That's fixed forever, in...'

'You need not say the year.'

'I don't recall it,' he said tactfully. 'But Cleopatra was the last role I saw you play. And very beautifully, too.'

'You are gallant, Herr Rowlands,' she said sounding a little mollified. 'But it is no good. I will never play a leading lady again. It is old women—mothers, ageing duchesses, ancient hags—which will be my lot from now on...' She seemed so sunk in gloom that it was almost risible. How these actors loved to dramatise things! Perhaps it was this fondness for histrionics that made it hard for him to envisage her as the murderess of Sybille Schönig. She might have killed out of passion, he thought, but to carry out such a cold, calm *execution*... It didn't fit with what he knew—or thought he knew—of Magda Hartmann's character.

'I am afraid that we must be getting back,' said Ziegler, interrupting this train of thought. 'Herr Direktor is a stickler for punctuality...'

'All right, all right! I'm coming,' grumbled his co-star. She was getting to her feet when Rowlands remembered the task he had set himself. 'I don't suppose,' he said, taking out the

photograph once more, 'you could take another look at this?'
She must have given it a cursory glance, for she said in a bored
tone: 'Ah, yes. Those boys. I am afraid I have not seen them.
Come, Paul, we will be late...'

But Ziegler took his time examining the image. 'Do you know,
it's funny,' he said thoughtfully. 'I believe I have seen *this* one...'
He tapped the photograph. 'The boy without the glasses,' he
added, seeing Rowlands's look of enquiry. 'The good-looking
one.'

'That's my nephew, Billy.'

'Yes, I am sure that I have seen him... but where? Of that I am
not sure. We are so besieged with boys, at present. They all look
the same in uniform, do they not?'

'I'm not sure I understand,' said Rowlands. But before the veteran actor could explain, there came a commotion at the door
of the canteen. Shrill, adolescent voices, and a trampling of feet.
Then a gruffer voice, shouting orders: 'Fall in, there! Keep in
line! No shoving!'

Silence followed these hoarse injunctions. Rowlands was
conscious of a quality to that silence—a feeling of unease.
Around him, people were getting up to leave. 'You see,' murmured Ziegler, handing back the photograph. 'Babelsberg is
swarming with boys, at present. You might almost say—and
Magda will forgive me for saying so—that *they* are the real stars
of our picture. There are any number of them lurking about the
studios just now...'

'Little beasts,' said Magda Hartmann, with venom. 'Always
smirking and pulling faces when one's trying to remember
one's lines. Fortunately, I don't actually have to share any scenes
with them...'

For Rowlands, the penny had dropped. 'You're talking about
this propaganda film,' he said. 'Triumph of something...'

'That's the one,' said Ziegler. 'Only we don't call it propaganda. "A beautiful work about Truth and Justice,"' he intoned,
as if reading from a script. They had by this time reached the
exit. Rowlands made as if to turn back, but the older man put a
hand on his arm. 'I shouldn't go back in there, if I were you, my
dear fellow. You'll only make yourself conspicuous—and that's

something best avoided, wouldn't you say?

'But my nephew...'

'He isn't among them. I took the opportunity of taking a good look, as we went past. And I'm as sure as I can be that the boy in the photograph isn't with this particular group.'

'But you said...'

'Oh, I've seen him all right,' said the veteran actor. 'I've a good memory for faces. It may be that he is with another H.J. group.' At the entrance to Studio 3, he stepped aside to allow Rowlands to go ahead of him. 'If the boy is on set, Bruno will know about it. I should ask *him* to keep an eye out for your nephew.'

But Bruno Klein wasn't sure if he'd seen Billy, or not. 'All these kids look the same to me,' he said, having studied the photograph for a moment. 'I won't say that I *haven't* seen him, but if I have, it will have been as part of a larger group. There's one scene—the parade, at the end—where I've fifty of the little blighters marching up an down, with their flags and drums. I couldn't pick any one of them out of the crowd, and say for certain I'd seen him.'

'Perhaps you could let me know if and when you *do* see him?' Rowlands was unable to keep the disappointment out of his voice. It was hard to have his hopes raised, then dashed once more. 'Of course,' said Klein. Then, adopting a brisk, official tone: 'Places, everybody. We will do another take of Rolf's scene with Magda. And this time, Rolf, my dear chap, it would be nice if you could *look* at her, while you are speaking. You are addressing your mother—not a public meeting...'

As the actors took up their stations, Klein said sotto voce: 'Why don't you stay a while, Herr Rowlands? The scene after this one might be of interest to you. It is the one in which Rolf—that is, young Hans—addresses his H.J. comrades about his burning desire to dedicate his life to the Führer. A most affecting scene—and one in which your nephew might very well be playing a minor, but important, role, as part of a crowd of eager young recruits to a noble cause.' The director's voice was heavy with irony. 'I will let you know if I spot him.'

'Thank you.' It was the best Rowlands could hope for. Because even if the boy *were* at Babelsberg, it was not going to be easy for a blind man to discover the fact. His only hope was if someone—Klein, or Ziegler—were to alert him to Billy's presence. Even then it wasn't going to be easy to separate the lad from his H.J. companions. To draw attention him, and risk revealing his true identity, would be dangerous for both of them, he thought.

As it turned out, however no such opportunity—risky or otherwise—presented itself. Because, whether he'd been seen at Babelsberg or not, Billy Ashenhurst wasn't among the crowd of thirty-odd boys taking part in the 'Führer speech' scene of *Triumph of Youth*. Klein was certain of that, he said. he'd made absolutely sure, by getting each one of them to say a line, on the pretext of trying him out for a speaking role—a device by which Rowlands, too, would have been able to identify the speaker. But no such recognition came. Either Billy had made himself scarce, or he'd never been part of this crowd at all. There seemed little point in sticking around any longer.

His spirits depressed as much by the failure of his mission, as by the effects of too much alcohol the night before, Rowlands decided to call it a day. He was making his way towards the gate, on his way to catch the train back to Berlin, when he heard his name called. 'I've been looking for you everywhere,' said Lena Pfeiffer. She sounded out-of-breath, as if she had been running. 'You're a hard man to find.' Rowlands forced a smile. He wasn't in the mood for any more of her flirtatious games. 'I'm sorry,' he said. 'But I've really got to...'

'Only I think I've seen him,' she interrupted. 'That boy. Your nephew.'

'Yes,' he said wearily. 'You're not the only one. But he's not with the H.J. crowd, if that's what you mean...'

'Maybe he isn't now,' she said, falling into step with him. 'But he was yesterday. There was a group of five or six of them, in the Make-Up Room. We didn't do much with them... just a lick of Vaseline on the eyebrows and a dab of powder on the nose to take away the shine, but...'

· Rowlands stopped dead. 'You saw him *yesterday*? Then why on earth didn't you say something?'

'I didn't recognise him at first,' she said. 'The boy in the photograph had dark hair, remember? This boy was blond. But it was the same one, I'd swear to it...'

'I wish you'd told me this before.'

'Wouldn't have made much difference, would it?' she said, tucking her arm through Rowlands's. 'You're here now, aren't you?'

'For all the good it'll do,' said Rowlands glumly. 'If he's here, he's lying low. His hair's dyed blond, you say?'

'Yes. They're all blonds, in this film. So they all resemble each other. It's rather sinister.'

'I can see that it might be.' A thought struck him. He turned to face her. 'I think he's here,' he said. 'But I'll need your help to find him.'

The Back Lot was as deserted as it had been a week ago, when Rowlands had first set foot there; the snow, which had melted in Babelsberg's more populous areas, remained thick on the ground. It crunched under their feet—the only sound in that eerie silence. 'I can't think why you wanted to come here,' said Lena crossly. 'There's no one about. And my feet are frozen...'

'It's just a feeling I had.'

'You and your feelings!' But she said nothing more until they had reached the spot where Rowlands had found traces of the boy's presence on that earlier occasion. 'Here we are,' she said. 'Grünewald—or Dahlem, or wherever it's supposed to be. We filmed Trudi Reinhardt's last comedy here. *The Girl from the Wrong Side of the Tracks*. She plays the pretty maid, who falls in love with the son of the house...'

'Shh.' He held up a hand. 'Did you hear that?'

'What?'

'I'm not sure.' The cracking of a twig underfoot, perhaps. He had a strong sensation that somebody was there. He listened again, but there was nothing. 'Billy,' he called. 'If you're there, you can come out, now. It's quite safe.' His words echoed in that hollow space, resounding off the walls of the house that was not a house. 'Billy!' he called again; then, to his companion: 'Can you see him?'

'No, but...' Suddenly, she gave an exclamation, and leaving

235

him standing in the middle of the mocked-up street, dived off along the side of the first building in the row. 'What is it?' he cried. 'What have you found?' Stumbling a little in his eagerness, he followed her across the snow-covered lawn that lay in front of the false house, and round to the back of the structure. 'What is it?'

'Footprints, leading from the street. I think they're fresh ones. And...'

'Yes?'

'A child could have made them,' she said.

So his instinct had been the right one. The boy *had* been there—and recently, too. The question was: where was he now? Something had evidently frightened him very badly, to make him choose to remain hidden at all costs. It wasn't hard to imagine what... 'If you're listening, Billy,' Rowlands cried, with a feeling of increasing desperation, 'there's a train to Paris on Sunday night. If you can get to Zoo Station by ten, I'll be waiting for you. I won't leave without you, I promise...'

17

'THERE IT IS,' SAID Joachim Metzner, as they reached the intersection between Prenzlauer Allee and Lothringerstrasse, and stood facing the building in question. 'Not that you can miss it, with that enormous Hakenkreuz banner hanging down in front. Apart from that, it looks like what it used to be—a fancy department store—instead of what it is. A barracks. I won't come any closer, if you don't mind. I wasn't too popular that time at the local H.Q. in Neukölln—and this is a much bigger affair. Probably holds a thousand of the swine. 'He shuddered. 'Hate to think what a crowd like that could do to one poor Jew...'

'That's all right,' said his sister, who was holding Rowlands's arm. 'We don't want you. Herr Rowlands and I can manage very well on our own...'

'Then again,' said the young man, 'I don't much like the idea of leaving my sister to fend for herself, with no one to protect her but a...' He broke off. 'A blind man, you were going to say?' said Rowlands. 'You're quite right, of course. But I can assure you, I'm prepared to do this on my own... that is, if one of you will keep a look-out.' Although in truth he was starting to feel more than a little apprehensive about the whole enterprise. What was it Gentz had said? *Talk about going into the lions' den...*

He wondered why it was he felt so nervous—then decided it was because of the disguise. 'Do I look all right?' he said in a low voice to Clara, as, leaving young Metzner skulking in the doorway of a building opposite, they crossed the street to the former department store, now the headquarters of the Hitler Jugend. 'What a distinction for our neighbourhood!' the young man had remarked sarcastically.

'You look fine.' It had been Sara Metzner who'd suggested that

237

Rowlands should wear her late husband's field-grey uniform. 'His medals, too,' she'd added proudly. 'He got this one during the Spring Offensive, in 1918... and this one at Amiens...' She'd touched each medal in turn, as she'd pinned them to Rowlands's chest. 'Amiens was where he was wounded,' she said. 'A bullet through the lung. He was lucky to survive...' She did not need to add that Jakob Metzner had not survived very long. Three years, in worsening health, before succumbing to a bout of pneumonia. The blue glasses had been a final touch— that, and the tray of matches. 'You look every inch the down-at-heel War Veteran,' was Joachim's verdict. 'Good thing father's uniform fits.'

It wasn't, in fact, a perfect fit—Herr Metzner having evidently been somewhat shorter and narrower in the chest than Rowlands himself—but the illusion was what mattered. 'This will be a good spot, I think,' said Clara. When Rowlands had first come up with this plan, she'd been the only one who'd thought it a good idea. Joachim had been sceptical, and Frau Metzner had—not unnaturally—been afraid for their safety. 'You do not know what these people are like, Herr Rowlands,' she said. 'They have no respect for anyone... not even the heroes of the War...'

She'd tried to dissuade her daughter from being part of the expedition, but Clara had overridden her objections: 'Don't be silly, *Mutti!* Of course I must go. Herr Rowlands won't be able to find the place on his own. And besides—who will look out for Billy, if I do not?'

This was unanswerable, and so she had her way. At the last minute, Joachim had said he, too, would come along. He hadn't been called for work that day, as it happened. 'They're working flat-out on that Nazi picture,' he'd said scornfully. 'Funny that they don't seem to want *my* kind on set just now...' He it was who'd suggested delaying the visit until early evening. 'If you think Billy's with the lot that are being used as extras for this film, then there's no point in going until after six. That'll give them time to get back from Babelsberg. As they're minors, they won't be kept late. I should think they'll have them back at H.Q. by suppertime...'

'It's very good of you, to give up your evening,' he said to Clara, as they installed themselves in a corner of the building's monumental facade, out of the bitter wind. 'Oh, I wasn't going to be left out of the fun!' she said. 'I've always wanted to play at detectives. Like Emil, you know...' He didn't, but he smiled. A moment later, he felt her clutch his arm, as a man came out of the building, and addressed them in the rough Berlin dialect. 'What do you think you're up to?' was the gist of this; then, presumably catching sight of Rowlands's medals: 'We don't allow beggars here, as a rule. But seeing as you're an old soldier...'

'That's kind of you,' said Clara sweetly. 'You'll buy a box of matches, won't you, *mein Herr*?' When the man had done so, and returned to the warmth of the porters' lodge, she whispered, 'Passed with flying colours—isn't that what you say?'

'Yes,' he replied. 'But that was only the first test.'

An hour went by, during which nothing very much happened, except that Rowlands's feet got colder, and his confidence in the usefulness of what he was doing dwindled sharply. Although it had seemed a good idea, at the time. Because if Billy—as now seemed likely—had been taken up by a member of the elite of this organisation, in order to play a part in a film glorifying the same, then it made sense to run him to earth at the organisation's headquarters. At least... it *had* made sense, though Rowlands, who was starting to doubt his own.

Beside him, Clara kept up a stream of bright chatter, as the indifferent crowds flowed past, on their way home to the comfort of the family circle, and the pleasures of a hot dinner. 'We're doing really well, today, Papa! Ten boxes sold already! If we sell ten more, we'll have enough for a nice beefsteak for your supper...' He was nodding and smiling inanely, and thinking what he'd give for a nice beefsteak right here and now, when there came the tramp of marching feet. A division of H.J. was approaching from the Alexanderplatz direction—quite a large one, from the sound of it. Perhaps they were in luck at last, thought Rowlands...

'Left. Left. Left,' commanded their leader, and then: 'Halt!' as the mob of thirty or so young men reached the doors of the H.Q. building. A certain amount of excited chatter ensued, as the troop fell into line, from which it became apparent that his guess had been the right one: '...made us stand so long during that final "take" I thought my leg was going to sleep...' '...d'you think he'll want us for the deathbed scene?' '...what about the actress that's playing the village maiden, eh? See the size of those knockers?'

Rowlands saw his chance. It was now or never, he thought. Stepping forward a pace, he held out his hand towards the group leader and said, in as good an imitation of the beggar's whine as he could: 'Please, young sir. Buy a box of matches...'

'What's that, Pops?' was the reply. Then, having inspected the contents of the tray the blind man was carrying: 'It's no good asking me to buy your matches—I don't smoke!' He obviously thought this was a good joke, for he gave a loud guffaw. 'Yeah!' shouted another youth. 'It's a filthy habit, smoking. We don't want this old geezer cluttering up the front of H.Q. with his dirty old matches, do we boys?' Then a hand shot out of nowhere—or so it seemed to Rowlands—and tipped up the tray containing the matchboxes, so that they fell on the ground. 'Oops,' said a voice. 'Silly me.'

'You beasts,' said Clara. 'You did that on purpose...'

'Listen to the lady! "Beasts" are we?' A chorus of grunts and squeals confirmed the truth of this. A moment later, Joachim Metzner flung himself into the *mêlée*. 'Don't speak to my sister like that,' he said, 'or I'll...'

'You'll *what*?' jeered the other. Almost before the words were out of his mouth, there came the juicy smack of hand on cheek. 'Oh, oh,' muttered Clara. 'That's torn it.' And indeed it did seem as if her brother's hot-headedness had landed them in more trouble than they were going to be able to get out of lightly. 'You bastard,' said the youth who'd been hit, in a voice that trembled between surprise and anger. 'Now you're for it...'

'Run,' said Rowlands in Clara's ear. 'I'll stay and deal with this.' But before she could follow his suggestion—not that she'd been *going* to follow it, she said afterwards—there came the sound of a powerful engine, and a Mercedes Benz drew up in front of the building. Doors opened and men got out, slamming the doors behind them. At once the shouting subsided, and

240

the rabble transformed itself back into the orderly troop it had been, minutes before. 'What's going on?' The voice was evidently that of someone in authority—at least to judge from the response. In the silence that followed, you could have heard a pin drop. 'Well?' said the voice, when no reply was immediately forthcoming. 'Who's in charge here?'

'I... I... That is... I...' stammered the youth who had first addressed Rowlands. One of his comrades came to the rescue. 'We were just helping this poor gentlemen, Reichsjugendführer,' he said glibly. 'He dropped his tray of matches. We were picking them up for him...'

'Then don't let me stop you,' said the man who'd asked the question. He turned his attention to Rowlands. 'I trust you are all right, sir?'

'Yes, thank you.'

'Good. Our War Veterans must be treated with respect—do you not agree, Obersturmführer?'

'Indeed,' said a voice Rowlands knew. The speaker came closer, so that he was no more than an arm's length away. 'It is they—our Veterans—who have given up their youth and strength so that younger generations can forge the New Germany.' His tone was dry, and it seemed to Rowlands, faintly amused. It was as if the hackneyed words concealed another meaning altogether—one that was colder and more menacing.

'Well said, my dear von Fritsch! That is indeed the spirit I wish to impart to these fine young men of ours. That's it! That's it!' he said encouragingly to the fine young men now squatting to retrieve the spilled matches. 'Pick them all up!'

He turned once more to his colleague. 'Come, we must not keep our friends waiting,' he murmured. Then, with a laconic 'Heil Hitler,' he turned on his heel, and went into the building, followed by the rest of his *entourage* and, after a moment, by von Fritsch. 'Well, *he'll* certainly know you again,' said Clara, when—the H.J. troop having taken itself off, with many muttered imprecations in the direction of Joachim Metzner—the three of them were alone once more. 'He *does* know me,' said Rowlands. 'I think he recognised me at the start.'

'Then why he didn't say anything?'

241

'I don't know.' Whatever von Fritsch's reasons for keeping silent, thought Rowlands, they could mean no good. 'That's the kind of man he is.'

'Well I think it's a great joke!' said Metzner, who had seemed in high spirits since the encounter with the Nazi gang. 'To think of it...' He spluttered with laughter. 'Baldur von Schirach in person...'

'What's that you're blathering about?' said Clara. With the mission having proved itself a failure—for there had been no sign of Billy amongst the H.J. group, she had assured Rowlands—they were making their way back along Prenzlauer Allee.

'Oh, nothing,' chuckled her brother. 'Only that it's quite something to think of the Reichsjungendführer himself coming to our rescue! Kind of him to get his thugs to pick up the matches they'd spilled, wasn't it? I knew him straight away,' he went on. 'You can't mistake that patrician swagger—or those chiselled looks. He probably thinks he should be in films himself. I guess he must have been out to the studio to see how his boy Norkus is getting on...' Metzner gave a scornful laugh. '*He'll* never make an actor, that's for sure! He's so stupid, Herr Klein's given up trying to direct him. He just says, "Rolf, turn your handsome profile this way, will you?" or "Rolf, dear boy, do you think you could manage to say the next couple of lines without looking utterly bored?"'

'Just a minute,' said Rowlands, stopping to divest himself of the cumbersome tray, with its remaining matchboxes. He hadn't relished playing the part of a blind beggar, and saw no reason to continue in the role, now that it had outlived its usefulness. Assisted by Joachim, he lifted the strap over his head. 'It's a relief to get rid of *that*,' he said. He began to stuff the matchboxes into the pocket of his greatcoat. As he did so, he encountered the crumpled pack of cigarettes he'd put there, and forgotten. Just what he needed. He extracted a cigarette, and put it between his lips. There was a half-full box of matches in the other pocket, he recalled. But when he went to withdraw this, he found it was strangely light. He slid it open. 'Well, I'll be damned,' he said. 'It looks as if our little foray into the enemy camp wasn't such a waste of time, after all...'

'What is it?' said Joachim. 'Have you found something?'

'This,' said Rowlands, holding out the torn-off scrap of paper which had been folded inside the empty box. One side of it was shiny. 'It's part of a photograph, isn't it?'

Clara took it from him. 'Yes. It's the photograph of Billy. The one that was on the poster. So he *was* here, just now...'

'He must have been. Although I didn't see him—did you, Clar?'

'No. He was too quick for us,' she said. 'He must have dashed up when we were being set upon by those louts... Hallo! There's something else. A message of some kind...' Scrawled in faint pencil on the back of the photograph were the letters 'H' and 'A'. 'I wonder what it means? 'H, A...'

'Ha, ha! Perhaps he's laughing at us,' said Metzner. Rowlands shook his head. 'I don't think so,' he said.

Outside the Hotel Adlon, the queue of limousines stretched all the way around Pariserplatz. Arriving a little before eight, Frederick Rowlands paid off his taxi in Unter den Linden, to avoid getting caught up in this. A strip of carpet had been laid from the kerb to the entrance of the hotel; along this, a crowd of guests was slowly shuffling, watched by another crowd of onlookers, whose comments on the arrivals could be heard at intervals. 'Who's that, then?' said one, as Rowlands joined the queue. 'No idea. He might be an actor... Ooh! There's Sabine Makowska! I saw her in *Loves of an Empress*. She was ever so good. And look at her lovely furs...'

In the opulent, marble-floored entrance hall, people were milling around, talking in loud voices. 'Isn't that Bunny over there? He *has* put on weight...'

'Such a crush! Half of Berlin must be here...'

'Brr! Filthy weather...'

A footman relieved Rowlands of his coat, and directed him upstairs—which was where everybody else seemed to be heading. Guests thronged the broad staircase, with its ornate, ormolu bannisters. 'Hello, old man! Haven't seen you since Monte Carlo,' said a voice close to Rowlands's ear; then: 'Sorry! I took you for someone else...' Behind him, two women were discussing a third. '...seen her latest? My *dear!* Far too old for the part, if you want my opinion...' At length, Rowlands reached the mezzanine, where another functionary enquired after his name, then announced it in stentorian tones, as he entered the room where the reception was being held. Whether anyone heard it or not was debatable, since the noise was terrific. He guessed there must be upwards of a hundred people there already, with no apparent let-up in the number of those still arriving.

A waiter appeared at Rowlands's elbow. 'Champagne, sir?' He took a glass from the proffered tray. He must make it last, he thought; this wasn't a night for losing control of one's wits.

He began to make his way into the room, edging past groups of men clad like himself in evening dress, and women (he supposed) attired in the latest evening gowns. A smell of expensive scent rose from their naked backs and shoulders. Actresses, he thought—although perhaps some of these were the wives and daughters of local dignitaries. He had no way of knowing for certain. Fragments of talk came towards him, out of the general murmur of voices. '...totally miscast, I thought. The part's written for a much older man...'

'Yes, but audiences will always pay to see a name, more's the pity...' Rowlands moved towards the last speaker, whose voice he recognised as that of Herr König, the writer. But as he was about to make himself known, he felt a hand on his arm. 'Why, it's Mr Rowlands! We *do* seem to keep running into one another, don't we?'

'Good evening, Miss Barnes. I suppose we do, rather. Are you here with your friend, Lieutenant von Fritsch?' he couldn't resist adding. 'Yes, I think Rudolf's about somewhere.' She gave his hand a playful tap. 'I have a feeling you disapprove...'

'It's none of my business who your friends are,' he said coldly. 'Although I rather thought...' He broke off. 'Yes?' Her tone was amused. 'Weren't you supposed to be interviewing actresses for that magazine of yours?' He knew his behaviour was verging on rudeness, but something about the girl's flippant manner annoyed him. What did she think she was playing at, consorting with a man like von Fritsch? Iris Barnes gave a tinkling laugh. 'Oh but I *have* been doing just that! Interviewing all sorts of other interesting people, too. I find Berlin a very fascinating place...

and Rudolf has proved an excellent guide...'

Again, came that light tap on Rowlands's hand, as somebody joined them. 'We were just talking about you,' she said. 'Indeed? Then I hope you were saying only good things?' said Rudolf von Fritsch.

'Of course. I believe you know Mr Rowlands?'

'Yes, indeed. We know one another quite well. You are looking a little better than when I last saw you,' added the Nazi, with a smile. 'More prosperous, shall we say? But you must excuse me. I see someone to whom I must speak.' Then, to Iris: 'Later, *Liebling*...'

'What exactly did he mean by that?' said Miss Barnes, when her 'friend' had removed himself. 'I mean about your looking prosperous?'

'I think he was just letting me know that he's keeping an eye on me.'

'Then I should take care.' There was no laughter in her voice now. Before she could say any more, they were joined by Bruno Klein and some of the Babelsberg crowd. 'So glad you could make it this evening,' said the director, shaking Rowlands's hand. 'It will be a Gala occasion, I think. The launch of my last, great film...'

'You're too modest, Herr Klein,' said Miss Barnes. 'Why, I'm sure you will make others just as good. My paper depends on it!'

'Perhaps,' said Klein. 'But I fear this is the end of an era. Ah, Helmut! Good to see you. It would not have been the same if you had not been here...'

'I would not have missed it for the world,' said the actor, his beautiful, warm tones effortlessly making themselves heard above the general murmur of conversation. 'To have this opportunity of paying homage to the greatest of directors...'

'You are too kind, my dear fellow...'

'...and to see my wife in her element. Quite the toast of Society, once more! No, I would not have missed it,' said Hartmann, with a laugh. In one of the momentary lulls that sometimes occur in a noisy room, Magda Hartmann's voice could be heard from across the room: '...really, my dear Reichsminister, you flatter me...'

'We are all glad that her star is once more in the ascendant,' said Klein. 'And I feel sure that there will be many interesting parts for you to play, also...'

'That is what I am afraid of,' said Hartmann, and now the bitterness which had underlain his earlier remarks was obvious. 'They will harness me to their machine, just as they have harnessed her...' He tossed back the last of his champagne, and signalled to a passing waiter. 'Another,' he said curtly. 'I should be careful what you say,' murmured Klein.

'Oh, it's all right for you!' The actor's voice, trained to carry effortlessly across the footlights, seemed to fill the room. '*You* will be departing for America, as soon as you can...'

'Nothing is certain,' said the director, with an uneasy laugh. 'You are right,' was the reply. 'As for you, my English friend,' went on Hartmann, suddenly switching his attention to Rowlands, 'I wonder what you make of all this? Our brave new world...' He was, Rowlands realised, quite drunk, and becoming more so, with every glass he downed. 'I think, like many such Utopian visions, it leaves much to be desired,' he said quietly. 'Ha, ha! That is true. There is still much work to be done, to build our New Jerusalem... Jerusalem without the Jews. Now *there's* a fine thought...'

Someone appeared at that moment out of the crowd. 'Come along, my dear old fellow,' said a voice. It was Paul Ziegler. 'Time you had a breath of air...'

'Hello, Paul. You always did know how to interrupt a man's big scene...'

'And *you've* always known how to deliver an exit line,' murmured Klein, as the two men, with Hartmann still talking rather wildly, made their way to the far side of the ballroom, where tall windows gave onto a balcony. 'I'm a little worried about Helmut,' said the director in an undertone. 'He is so very indiscreet. Of course,' he added, 'he is a famous man, and such people can get away with a great deal. But not, I think, forever...'

In the brief silence which followed Klein's remarks, Rowlands became aware of other sounds. The clinking of glasses: 'Your health, *Liebstes Fräulein*...' The polite murmur of conversation—which broke, here and there, into something louder and more primitive-sounding: a hoarse shout of laughter, or a tiny scream, as a women cried that something or someone was 'too, too, shocking'. A cluster of starlets near the door were discussing new arrivals. '…there's Lili Stöbel. She didn't get those baubles she's wearing round her neck for nothing, *I* can tell you!' A group of men closer at hand were discussing the political situation: '…suppose you heard his speech yesterday?'

'Couldn't have missed it, old chap. It was on all the stations.'

'I'll say this for him—he knows how to work up a crowd.' Which was certainly true, thought Rowlands, who had caught the end of the speech in question, on his way to Gentz's office, the previous night. The corridors and ante-rooms of the police station had been strangely deserted, as people clustered round radio sets in offices and interview rooms. As he'd walked along the now-familiar corridor, he could hear that harsh, guttural voice booming out from all sides. The speech was being broadcast from Berlin's Sportspalast, and relayed by loudspeaker to ten of the city's main squares. No, you couldn't very well have missed it. To do so would have been tantamount to treason, he supposed.

Although Joachim Metzner had been adamant that *he* wasn't going to listen. 'I'll be tuning into the BBC as usual,' he said. 'There's a Chopin concert I particularly want to hear.' Rowlands couldn't suppress a smile at the young man's sheer bloodymindedness. 'Something amusing you, Herr Rowlands?' said Bruno Klein. 'Not really. I was just thinking what an interesting city this is…'

'Berlin, you mean? Oh yes, it has a great heart. Will you excuse me, Herr Rowlands? There is someone I must…'

'Of course.' Rowlands was conscious of a growing nervousness. He noticed in the same moment that the glass in his hand was empty. 'Careful,' he told himself. It wouldn't do to lose his grip on things, just when he most needed to be in control. But just then the glass was whisked from his hand.

18

'This will not do!' said a voice. It was Gunther Herz. 'You cannot celebrate our great new venture without a full glass of champagne. I will get you another...' He clicked his fingers to summon the waiter, but Rowlands shook his head. 'No, I don't want any more, thanks.'

'Oh, but I insist!' The smell of the man's pomade was overpowering. It stuck Rowlands there and then that he had never liked Gunter Herz. In the same moment, he remembered something that had been puzzling him. 'You were in the studio that night,' he said. 'The night Sybille Schönig died.' For a moment, Herz seemed taken aback. 'What if I was?' he said.

'Only you weren't in the studio the whole time, were you? You left, just after Fräulein Schönig had walked out...'

'What of it?' The other's voice was cold.

'I was just wondering where you went. Oh, I know what you told the police. But I'd like to know the real reason. Had you gone to telephone to your masters, perhaps?'

It seemed for a moment that the other man had not heard him. But then Herz said: 'I do not know what you are talking about, Herr Rowlands.'

'Don't you? You surprise me...'

'But I will say one thing.' All trace of affectation was gone from Herz's voice now. 'Be careful what you say in this company...'

'People keep telling me to be careful,' said Rowlands. 'To tell you the truth, I'm getting a little tired of it.'

Herz laughed his whinnying laugh. 'That is what I like about you Englishmen,' he said. 'You are so forthright. Always it is straight from the shoulder, is it not? But I will only repeat what I have said. Be careful what you say, and who you talk to.' Suddenly he wasn't laughing anymore. 'It's very easy to make yourself enemies...'

Before Rowlands could think of an answer to this, he felt a touch on his arm. 'Won't you dance with me, Mr Rowlands?' said Iris Barnes. 'I seem to recall that you're rather a good dancer.' Because just then, a string quartet began to play a waltz tune. 'I'd be delighted,' said Rowlands. He gave her his arm, and with a nod at Herz, allowed her to lead him onto the floor. 'I thought you looked as if you needed rescuing,' she said. Rowlands smiled. 'You were right.'

'I'd be careful what you say to Herr Herz,' she said, her mouth very close to his ear. 'Oh, I'll be careful,' said Rowlands. Then neither of them said anything for a few minutes, surrendering themselves to the flow of the music. It was a song Rowlands had heard before, he realised. *Tonight or Never*, that was the one. Rather apposite, he thought grimly. 'I wonder,' he said to his dance partner, as they moved slowly around the floor, surrounded by other couples similarly revolving, 'whether you'd do me the favour of describing the room for me?'

'With pleasure,' she said. 'Well, it's a great big grand affair, in keeping with the rest of the place. Lots of marble and gilt, and tall mirrors all round the walls, in between the windows. A Versailles effect, you might say...'

'I was thinking more of the people.'

'I was coming to that. It's pretty full, as you can probably tell. Half the crowd's what you might expect at this sort of function. Film people. A few visiting celebrities. Then there's what you might call the 'political wing'. *They're* very much in evidence. The Reichsführer himself hasn't appeared—although it's rumoured he might turn up later—but the Minister for Air is here, with his latest conquest. An actress, of course. Mitzi or Milli Something... And there's the Minister for Propaganda, with his charming wife. *She's* talking to Magda Hartmann. What a pretty picture they make! The two Magdalenes. One so dark and the other so fair. The little weasel doesn't know which way to turn. Look at him! Shifting his gaze from one to the other, and grinning that rictus grin...'

'Are you saying that he and Frau Hartmann...?'

'Oh, that's old news,' she said. 'If there was ever anything

250

between them, it was over long ago. Not that there haven't been others since, if one believes the rumours…' The music came to an end. As the two of them began threading their way through the crowd towards the edge of the dance floor, the journalist said: 'I say, do you fancy a breath of air? I know *I* do…' Still keeping up a stream of inconsequential chat, she drew him after her through one of the pairs of tall windows that opened onto balconies overlooking the street. As he was still wondering what she was up to—for that she was up to *something* he was perfectly sure—she said: 'I've a message for you.'

Rowlands's heart gave a jump. 'A message?'

'Yes. It was as I arrived at the Adlon, about an hour ago. I'd just walked in and was about to hand over my cloak, when one of those H.J. kids they'd got forming a guard of honour on either side of the door came sidling up to me. Asked was I the "English Fräulein"? When I asked *him* why he wanted to know, he said he'd got a message for "the blind Englishman". Well, you're the only one I know who answers to that description, and so…'

'What was the message?'

'"Be ready at ten o'clock."'

'Is that all?'

'Yes. Sounds a bit cloak-and-dagger, doesn't it? But you know what boys of that age are…'

'What age was he?'

'Hard to say.' Iris Barnes gave a little laugh, that turned into a shiver. The night wind was cold, and her thin silk frock offered little in the way of protection. 'They all look much the same in uniform. About eleven or twelve years old, I suppose…'

'Can you describe him?'

'He was just a boy. Fair-haired. I didn't really get a good look at him.'

'It doesn't matter. You've been very helpful,' he said. It struck him that he had perhaps misjudged Miss Barnes. 'That's quite all right. I think,' she said, 'I'd better go in, or my escort will be wondering where I've got to. Give me a few minutes' start, will you? I don't want him to ask any awkward questions…'

Then she was gone. Rowlands did as she'd asked, and remained where he was, for the time it took to smoke a cigarette.

251

Be ready at ten. But ready for what? And where was he to wait, until the moment came? He checked his watch: there was an hour still to go before the rendezvous—if that was what it was. Something was to happen at ten, that much seemed clear. As for the rest, he was as much in the dark as ever...

Nor had the Inspector been of much help, when the two of them had talked it over, the night before, in Gentz's office. With the words of the demagogue booming around them as they spoke, they had discussed the possibilities raised by the matchbox message. 'It's the young 'un, right enough,' Gentz had said, fingering the torn scrap of photograph. 'And you think 'H.A.' must be the Hotel Adlon?'

'Well it fits, doesn't it? And there's likely to be contingent of H.J. there tomorrow night—because of the film...'

'Yes, yes. You have explained all that,' said the Inspector. 'The question is, what do you want me to do about it?'

'I wanted you to know,' said Rowlands. 'In case... well, let's just say if things don't go according to plan.'

'And what is this plan?'

'I haven't the least idea,' said the other, with a shrug. 'But you think the boy will be there?' Gentz lit one of his cheroots.

'I have to hope so.'

'Then it is also to be hoped,' said the policeman softly, 'that others do not become aware of this fact.'

Rowlands finished his cigarette, and ground the stub beneath the toe of his patent-leather shoe. This elegant but impractical footwear had been found for him by the helpful Lena Pfeiffer, in the UFA wardrobe from which the rest of his evening clothes had come. 'It is a pity I won't be there to see how devastatingly handsome you look,' she had said, handing him the parcel earlier that day. 'But I am not invited. It is too grand an affair for the likes of Ute and me...' He went back into the room, whose stifling heat contrasted sharply with the chill from which he had come. Now he hovered at the edge of the crowd, uncertain what his next move ought to be. A group near him was discussing the merits or otherwise of a new restaurant that had opened on Jägerstrasse: 'You can't get a table there for love nor money...' A couple behind him were quarrelling in low tones:

'But you *promised*!'

It was then that there came an announcement: 'Ladies and Gentlemen, please make your way to the Screening Room...' At once, the crowd began to move slowly towards the ante-room which had been set up for the purpose. On the threshold of this, he heard himself once more addressed: 'Herr Rowlands! But how delightful! You have not yet deserted us, I see...'

'Good evening, Frau Hartmann. No, I'm still here,' he said. 'But that is charming! Herr Rowlands is an old admirer of mine,' said the actress to her companions, with a little, self-deprecating laugh.

'Then he is one of many,' came the reply. Even if Iris Barnes had not told him of the man's presence, Rowlands would have recognised that strangely seductive voice. 'I believe you already know the Reichsminister?' said Magda Hartmann. 'Indeed.' Rowlands composed his features into the bland mask he assumed when his feelings were at war with the circumstances. 'Good evening, Minister.'

'I know your face,' said the other, in a musing tone. 'Ah, yes. You are the man who was at the studio that day... You are an actor?'

'Not exactly. I...'

But before Rowlands could explain, another voice cut across him. A woman's voice—cold and clipped. Rowlands guessed this was Magda Goebbels, although no one had troubled to introduce them. 'We should take our seats. They are about to begin.'

'You are right, my dear,' said the Reichsminister. 'Come, Frau Hartmann, we will go in together. Von Fritsch, you will escort my wife...'

'It will be an honour, Minister.'

'I hope you enjoy the film, Herr Rowlands,' said the actress, as she turned to go. 'It is not, to my mind, Bruno's finest work, but it has its better moments. My husband's performance being one of them.' Then she was gone, in a cloud of perfume and a rustle of silk-chiffon. Rowlands waited a moment or two before following; he had no desire to find himself caught up with the Minister's party. Anxiously, he checked his watch once more. It was a quarter past nine. Never had his blindness seemed more of a barrier to understanding what was expected of him.

He took his place at the back of the crowd, as the lights went down, and the title sequence began to play. 'You'd have thought they'd have waited,' murmured a man standing next to him to another man. "Oh, he's always late,' was the reply. 'If he turns up at all...'

Onscreen, the first appearance of Helmut Hartmann was greeted with a smattering of polite applause. Once more, Rowlands found himself enjoying the cadences of that beautiful voice. He—Hartmann—was playing a version of himself: the urbane, married man. Sophisticated, charming and susceptible to women. '*Wer ist sie?*' he was enquiring of his companion, the ageing *roué* (played by Paul Ziegler). 'Who is she?' As Hartmann delivered the line, there was collective intake of breath from the audience, as they saw what he was seeing: the Girl in the Case; the soon-to-be Fallen Angel, Sybille Schönig. Was the gasp because of her beauty, or simply a response to the terrible fate that had befallen her? Rowlands had no way of knowing. 'Let me introduce you,' said the *roué*, with a knowing laugh. Introductions were duly performed. 'I hope,' said Hartmann's character, following an exchange of supreme fatuousness, 'we will meet again...'

'Perhaps. Who can say?' The line was delivered with just the right mixture of archness and sincerity; the slight catch in the crystalline voice given the words a poignancy they would not have had in the script. The story unfolded along all-too familiar lines: the casual encounter followed by the clandestine meeting; the cynical seduction followed by the stunned realisation on the part of the seducer that he had fallen in love...

Rowlands was only dimly aware of the vagaries of the plot, his mind distracted by more pressing concerns. It was almost ten. Another couple of minutes, and the hands of his watch would signal the fateful hour. Yet he still had no idea what was to happen. On the glaring screen, whose images were only perceptible to him as a series of flickering shadows, the Married Man was pleading with his lover not to leave him for another man. 'You knew what I was when you met me,' said the Fallen

254

Angel, with a brittle laugh. 'Did you think I would change my nature just for you?'

As the voice of the dead girl echoed in the silence of that gilded chamber, Rowlands felt a hand slip itself into his. It was a child's hand; a young boy's rather. His nephew, Billy, beside him in the darkness. Because of course, thought Rowlands, he must have been in the room all the time, watching and waiting for his moment. And that moment was now—now that the attention of all those in the room was fixed on what was happening onscreen: a quarrel scene, during which the rejected lover was threatening to shoot himself and his faithless mistress, but only succeeded in putting a bullet through the mirror in which her laughing face was reflected, splintering both mirror and reflection into a thousand pieces... The shot duly rang out, to a gasp from the watching crowd. 'Come on,' whispered Billy. 'Now's our chance.'

Quick as a flash, he pulled Rowlands towards the door which led to the ballroom. Another moment, and the two of them were through it, before anyone had time to notice they were gone. Together, they hurried across the now-deserted room towards the stairs, that would take them to the exit and to freedom. Rowlands had time to marvel at the coolness with which it was done; it had been the perfect moment, with everybody's eyes upon the screen. They began to descend the stairs, slowing their pace to a more leisurely one; there would be doubtless be an SS guard stationed at the door, and it would not do to seem in too much of a hurry.

But the attention of the guards was, in any case, focused on something else. The sound of a car, drawing up outside the hotel. Doors slamming, and barked commands. The tramp of feet. Moments later, a party of late arrivals entered the foyer. Beside him, Rowlands felt his nephew freeze. A faint exclamation escaped him. The boy stood to attention, as the group of men—there were three of them, Rowlands guessed—divested themselves of coats, and advanced towards the stairs. With them was the hotel's manager, earnestly professing his gratitude for the unexpected honour.

Then it was that Rowlands heard that gruff, curiously

uncouth, voice he had heard only the day before, denouncing its several enemies, over the wireless. 'We are late,' said the voice; then, ignoring the manager's protestations that it did not matter at all, the hotel was proud to serve him at any time, he said to his companions: 'Nevertheless, we will look in for half an hour. I promised Josef...'

'Yes, and his wife will be disappointed if you do not appear...'

The three of them had reached the stairs. As they began to ascend, the Leader paused, just where Rowlands and the boy were standing, and close enough for Rowlands to catch a powerful whiff of halitosis. 'One of yours, Baldur?' he said, resting his hand for a moment on the boy's head. Of Rowlands he took no notice, perhaps assuming that, dressed as he was, he must be one of the hotel's staff.

His friend gave a sycophantic laugh. 'Oh no! One of *yours*, my Führer,' said Baldur von Schirach. He, too, paid no attention to Rowlands—nor, to the latter's immense relief, did he recognise him as the blind man selling matches of the previous day's encounter. The other gave a grunt of approbation at these sentiments, before proceeding on his way, with his companions swaggering after. Only when they were out of earshot did the boy relax his posture of frozen obedience. 'Quick!' he said, tugging Rowlands's sleeve. 'Let's get out of here...'

Rowlands didn't need telling twice. Every passing second increased their danger. Abandoning thoughts of retrieving his coat, he allowed the boy to lead him through the hotel's double doors, and into the bitter cold night. 'This way,' said his young companion, pulling Rowlands after him, in the direction of the Brandenburg Gate. Rowlands made no demur—although it occurred to him afterwards that it might have made more sense to have tried to lose themselves in the more populous side-streets off Unter den Linden. But at that moment, all he could think was how to get away from the Hotel Adlon as quickly as possible. With luck, the remaining guests at the gala performance of *Fallen Angel* would be too distracted by the arrival of the Guest of Honour to bother themselves overmuch about a missing Englishman and a boy in the uniform of the Deutsches Jungvolk.

He had reckoned without the adversary's celebrated efficiency. Before they had gone fifty paces along Pariserplatz, a voice behind them shouted: 'Halt!'

'Run,' said Billy. The sound of a gunshot made this injunction all the more imperative.

Slipping and sliding on the icy street, the fugitives ran at full tilt towards the only shelter available, which was that of the famous Gate. Another bullet struck the pavement behind them, ricocheting off the cobblestones, but by this time they were under that noble portal, whose bronze goddess in her chariot rode high above their heads. What protection she could offer them could only be temporary, however. As the two of them took cover behind one of the pillars, Billy whispered, 'I know a way through the park. Come on!' With that, he dashed across the broad street that divided the government quarter from the great wooded space that lay beyond it, with Rowlands stumbling after. A taxicab hooted at them, but they made it across unscathed.

Another shot rang out behind them. They had by this time reached one of the broad gravel paths that led into the park. At the sound of the shot, Billy dived off into the snowy wastes that lay beyond. Rowlands followed suit, both of them dodging between the trunks of trees and snow-covered bushes, as they ran headlong over the uneven ground. Billy had let go of Rowlands's hand, but the blind man was able to follow the sound of the child's frightened breathing, and the snapping of twigs underfoot as he crashed through the undergrowth. No doubt the gunman could also hear these sounds... It darted across Rowlands's mind that, fit as he was, he could not hope to outrun their pursuer indefinitely. His blindness would ensure that. Whereas Billy...

'Listen,' he whispered urgently to the child, as they stopped to catch their breath. 'You must go on without me.'

But Billy had ideas of his own, apparently. 'In here—quick, Uncle Fred!' he hissed, half-dragging his companion up the shallow flight of steps that led into what was evidently some kind of ornamental building: a miniature temple, or folly. Hearts pounding, they flattened themselves against the curved

257

stone wall of the building. It was only when standing still that Rowlands realised how cold he was—his evening clothes and thin-soled shoes offering little protection against the elements. And if he was cold, Billy must be colder still, in his shorts and long-sleeved shirt...

But such considerations, pressing as they were, were put out of his mind a moment later. 'Well, well, Herr Rowlands,' said a voice. It belonged to Rudolf von Fritsch. 'It seems we are destined to meet yet again.' The Nazi officer laughed: a surprisingly warm and full-throated sound. 'What a pity only one of us will go away from this meeting!'

'It's him,' whispered Billy in Rowlands's ear. 'The one who killed Fräulein Schönig...'

'Are you sure?'

'I recognise his voice.'

So it had been the SS man who had been in the dressing-room that night, thought Rowlands. Which meant that Hartmann was in the clear... 'Listen, von Fritsch,' he said. 'I won't deny you've got me in a corner. But let the boy go. He can't do you any harm, on his own—and, as you've just pointed out, I won't be around much longer to corroborate his story...'

Again, came that amused laugh. 'You are a brave fellow, Herr Rowlands, I give you that. But you must see that what you ask is out of the question. First of all, because it is not you but the boy who knows too much. Although I must assume that you know some of what he knows already...'

'I know you killed Sybille Schönig.'

'Of course I killed her,' was the amused reply. 'She had become... what is it you English say? A confounded nuisance.'

'You tried to make it look like suicide. A pity you didn't make a better job of it.'

'It would have convinced most people. It was just unfortunate that the Pabst woman noticed that the gun was in the wrong hand...'

'A careless mistake,' said Rowlands. 'I suppose that was why you used her gun—to make it seem more authentic...'

'That is where you are wrong, my dear Rowlands. I used that gun because it had already been fired. By the lovely Frau

258

Hartmann, as it happens…'

So Magda Hartmann had been in the dressing-room too! 'Go on,' said Rowlands.

'There is not much to tell. I was coming along the corridor when I heard a shot. It was fired by the Hartmann woman. She had thoughtfully brought along her gun—a silly little pearl-handled object—and had been waving it about, in her rather excited state. She was quite drunk, of course. These women!' said von Fritsch, with cool contempt. 'They pull out a gun and then are surprised when it goes off. Which it did, of course. It was then that the Schönig girl screamed. She wasn't hurt—but you know how these actresses love a scene… Fortunately I had arrived by this time,' said the SS officer drily, 'and so I intervened.'

'You shot her in cold blood, you mean?'

'That is a rather dramatic way of putting it. But yes—that was what I had come to do. Whether it was with my own gun or another's made not the slightest difference…'

'Yet you left Magda Hartmann under suspicion…' It seemed important to keep von Fritsch talking—not only as a way of buying time, but also, Rowlands thought, so that he could judge from the sound of the man's voice how far away he was standing. Had he come closer? Rowlands thought he had. 'On the contrary, said von Fritsch. 'I did my best to conceal the fact that she was there. If the Pabst woman had not made a fuss about the gun's being in the girl's right hand instead of her left, it would all have passed off without comment. Naturally,' von Fritsch was saying. 'Frau Hartmann cannot expect to get off "scot free". You see I know your expressions! Her husband, too is implicated in this affair…'

'Go,' whispered Rowlands to the boy, under cover of this. 'When I give you the signal, run as fast as you can, and don't look back…'

'Yes, the Hartmanns are a great asset to our German film industry. We would not want to lose them to America. Nor will we, as long as they remain useful to us… Oh, yes, Frau Hartmann will do as she is told—or it will be the worse for her,' said von Fritsch, no laughter in his voice, now. 'I have only to say that she was in that room on the night in question. And the gun was hers, you know...'

'What I don't understand is *why*,' said Rowlands. 'I mean, I know about the list, but...'

'How do you know about this?' said the other sharply.

'Greta Pabst said something about it. So it's true, then? Sybille Schönig was working for you as an informer...'

'She was an informer, yes. But it was not I, but Reichsminister Goebbels, who ordered her to make the list. A test of her loyalty, one must assume. It was of no particular importance, apart from that. The fact is, we can get the information we need on suspicious persons very easily. Oh yes,' laughed the SS man. 'All the Jews and the Reds that think themselves safe at UFA will have a nasty surprise, when the Reichsminister takes control, as Minister of Propaganda...'

'But...' Rowlands's ears were cocked for small sounds—a twig snapping, a footfall in the snow—that would indicate his opponent was edging closer. 'I still don't see why the loyalty of one film actress was so important...'

'No? Then you do not know the full story. I suppose,' drawled the other, 'it would not hurt for you to know—since you will not be alive very much longer to tell the tale. Our Fräulein Schönig was a very beautiful, but also a very stupid, young woman. She thought that she could make use of her position to gain advantage in her career. Not content with the devotion of a man who could give her everything she wanted, she thought she could do better...'

Hartmann had said much the same thing, thought Rowlands. But it wasn't Hartmann that von Fritsch had meant. 'She was your mistress, wasn't she?' he said. Again, the SS officer laughed. 'You are very astute, Herr Rowlands! And you are right, of course. Sybille Schönig allowed me to share her bed for a time—until she decided that she would rather share it with Hartmann...'

'Then...'

'You will be thinking that it was out of jealousy that I killed her,' von Fritsch went on. 'But I can tell you that it was not so. I was not so enamoured of that little bitch that I would have risked my career by killing her. The Reichsminister had already expressed an interest in her. It was not in my interests to thwart his desires. In fact, it was I who introduced them. Our revered Minister for Propaganda has always had an eye for the looser kind of woman.'

'But I still don't see…'

'I killed her for another reason,' said von Fritsch. 'That confounded list, you see. It was my misfortune—and hers—that my name was on it. She was foolish enough to try to blackmail me.'

'*Your* name was on the list?' Rowlands's incredulity must have been apparent from his tone, for the Nazi officer laughed. 'Absurd, is it not? But my grandmother was a Jewess. That is not a pedigree one would want to be widely known, in my position…'

'I can see that.'

'Yes, it all makes sense, does it not?'

'I wouldn't say that exactly.'

He was quite close now, Rowlands judged—no more than three or four feet away. He must have been circling closer and closer to the little building, narrowing his line of fire down to point-blank range. 'So it was in order to cover your tracks that you had Fritzi Henkel and Greta Pabst killed?' said Rowlands. 'Yes of course,' said von Fritsch. 'Henkel saw Frau Hartmann go into the dressing-room. He heard the shot. And he had seen that nephew of yours arrive some minutes earlier. If I had known you were there, young man, he added, in a jocular tone that made Rowlands's blood run cold, 'you would never have left that room!'

'And what of Fräulein Pabst? Why was *she* killed?' It seemed important to keep von Fritsch talking—not only as a way of buying time, but also, Rowlands thought, so that he could judge from the sound of the man's voice how far away he was standing. Had he come closer? Rowlands thought he had. 'She saw me in the corridor with Frau Hartmann, just after we had left the dressing-room.' Von Fritsch sounded almost bored by this revelation. 'I knew she would guess the truth, eventually, and I could not trust her to keep her mouth shut. She was devoted to the Schönig girl…'

'And to Fritzi Henkel.'

'Indeed. But enough of this,' said the SS officer. 'I have enjoyed

261

our little talk, Herr Rowlands, but all good things come to an end, do they not?' The temple was open on three sides; as the killer drew near, Rowlands gave Billy a hard shove towards the side that was furthest away from the enemy. In the same moment, he rushed out from behind the pillar where he had been hiding towards where he knew von Fritsch must be. 'Run, Billy!' he shouted, as he launched himself at the man. All he knew after that was the deafening sound of a gunshot—that, and the sensation of falling.

Time, which had seemed to stand still, now regained its momentum. A voice from somewhere above where Rowlands was lying, spreadeagled on the ground, said: 'I hope you are not hurt, Herr Rowlands?'

'Is he dead?' said Rowlands, his ears still ringing with the sound of the shot. 'Oh yes. He is dead.' Still winded from his fall, Rowlands struggled to his feet. 'So it was you,' he gasped. 'I thought I heard somebody...'

'I was trying to make as little noise as possible,' said Inspector Gentz. 'But of course your hearing is better than average, is it not?' Rowlands paid no attention to this. 'Where's Billy?' he demanded. 'I imagine the boy must be keeping out of sight,' was the reply. 'A wise precaution, under the circumstances...'

'Billy!' shouted Rowlands. 'It's all right. You can come out, now.' A moment later, the child came running out from wherever it was he had concealed himself. 'Uncle Fred!' he cried; then stopped short, seeing the policeman. 'It's all right,' said Rowlands. 'Inspector Gentz is a friend. He saved my life.' And yours, he thought, but did not say. The boy, however, was more interested in the fate of their pursuer, the Nazi officer. 'He's dead, isn't he?' he said in a flat voice. 'It was either you or he,' said Gentz, in a reproving tone, as Rowlands bent to check the body for vital signs. He found none. 'I know,' said Billy. 'I don't care a bit that he's dead. In fact, I'm jolly glad,' he added fiercely.

'Be that as it may, it might be a good idea to conceal the fact of his death for as long as possible,' said the policeman. 'Herr Rowlands, you will assist me, please.'

'Of course.' Rowlands found that his teeth were chattering.

Cold, or the shock of what had so nearly happened, suddenly overcame him. It may be that Gentz noticed this, for he said: 'Perhaps you should start by removing your jacket...'

'What?'

'The boy. He has no coat. I do not wish to find myself with another corpse on my hands,' said the Inspector, with a grim little laugh. 'Good point. Billy, you'd better put this on,' said Rowlands, stripping off the by-now somewhat bedraggled jacket, and handing it to the boy. 'I'm all right,' insisted the other stubbornly, but he did as he was told. 'Now you, Herr Rowlands,' said Gentz, who had been carrying out a similar operation, it seemed, because a moment later, he put a thick bundle of cloth into Rowlands's arms. Von Fritsch's greatcoat. 'Put it on,' he said. Rowlands did so, with a faint shiver of distaste. The coat was still warm. 'Now,' said the Inspector. 'Let us make haste. Herr Rowlands, you will take one arm, and I will take the other...'

Both stooped to this unlovely task, hauling the body of the late Rudolf von Fritsch upright between them, as if he were a drunken comrade, being helped home after a night on the tiles. 'We cannot leave him here. It is too public,' said Gentz. 'They will start to search for him soon, and we must delay their finding him as long as possible.'

'Is there much blood?' said Rowlands. 'Some,' grunted the other. '*Mein Gott*, but he is heavy! Billy—I may call you that, may I not? As a good member of the Deutsches Jungvolk, you will know the importance of leaving no traces for your enemy to find...'

Billy didn't need telling twice. As the two men began to move off, lugging their grisly burden with them, the boy kicked snow over the blood which had stained the snowy ground; then, snapping off a branch from a nearby shrub, began dragging it behind him, to cover his own tracks and theirs. 'Where exactly are we taking him?' panted Rowlands, after they had gone a little way further into the woods that lay beyond the little temple. 'The river,' was the curt reply. 'It is not too far from here, I think.' And indeed another fifty yards brought them to one of the tributaries that ran off the Spree. 'It is not, unfortunately, the main channel,' said the Inspector, pausing to catch his breath. 'But with the snow we've had, it should be deep enough to hide what we have to hide...'

Here, the bank sloped steeply down towards the water, from which a smell of mud and rotting leaves arose. 'We'll roll him in,' said Gentz. 'If we had time, we would weigh him down with stones... but we do not have time. Come. One, two...' With an effort that made both men break out in a sweat, they heaved the dead weight of the body down the bank and into the water, into which it fell with a surprisingly loud splash. 'Damn, he's not sinking,' muttered the policeman. 'Well, there's no help for it. We'd better get out of here—and quickly. Let us hope nobody decides to walk his dog in these woods too early tomorrow.'

LONG SHOT

19

ENTZ HAD LEFT HIS car in Behrenstrasse, and so they doubled back through the Tiergarten to get to it. Even though it was unlikely that anyone had yet missed von Fritsch, said the policeman, it might be prudent to avoid going back past the Adlon Hotel. 'You came alone, then?' said Rowlands, as having left the fatal woods behind them, they found themselves once more in the bustling reaches of Friedrich Ebertstrasse. 'Oh yes,' was the reply. 'I was acting, you might say, in an unofficial capacity.'

'I'm very glad you did.' said Rowlands warmly. 'I still haven't thanked you for saving my life—and Billy's...'

'No thanks is necessary. That man killed three people—or had them killed. As you have just said, he was on the point of killing two more. It was the only way to stop him, since one no longer has recourse to the Law, in such cases... Still, I could have wished not to have shot him in the back,' said Gentz, with a mirthless little laugh. 'That is not the code by which I was brought up. But in these murderous times, even the guardians of the law must resort to the tactics of murderers.' He said nothing more until they were in the car, heading East along Unter den Linden. 'I hope very much, Herr Rowlands,' he said, 'that you and young Billy here will be leaving Berlin very soon?'

'Tomorrow evening,' said Rowlands. 'Not that it hasn't been a pleasure to work with you,' said Gentz. 'For me, too,' said the blind man. 'That is kind of you to say. You will, I hope, pass on my good wishes to my old friend, Alasdair Douglas?' said the policeman. 'Of course.' The Inspector sighed. 'He and I had some good times together, also. But that was many years ago. Now my career is at an end. It has been good, nevertheless, to have had this last case to deal with. Even though it has not concluded in precisely the way I could have wished.'

It was almost midnight when they got to Marienburgerstrasse, and the street was silent and deserted. The street-door to the apartment had been locked; they had to rouse the building superintendent to let them in, which he did with a good deal of muttering at the lateness of the hour, and the inconvenience to himself. They climbed the stairs. The door to the flat was answered, after an interval of hammering, by an indignant Joachim Metzner: 'What the hell... Oh, it's you, Herr Rowlands. But why on earth...?'

'Just let us in, old chap,' said Rowlands. Frightened whispers from inside the flat suggested that Metzner's mother and sister had also been woken by the disturbance. 'Who is it, Joe?' called the latter; then, taking in the whole situation at once: 'Oh, *Mutti, Mutti*—come quickly! They've found Wilhelm...'

Only then did her brother grasp the truth: 'Is it really you, young Billy? I didn't recognise you with your hair that colour.'

'The poor child!' This was Frau Metzner's response. 'Are you all right? They didn't hurt you?' It was clear from her tone that she meant the child's abductors, and not present company. 'I'm all right,' muttered Billy. Gentz brought this reunion to an abrupt end. 'There's no time for this. Wilhelm... Billy—whatever your name is—I need to ask you some questions. We haven't a lot of time before we leave...'

'You are leaving?' cried Sara Metzner. But you have only just arrived. The boy is exhausted. He needs rest...'

'It isn't safe for him here,' was the curt rejoinder. Gentz had moved to the window. 'There's somebody out there, now.'

'What!' said Rowlands. 'You mean we've been followed?'

'I think that's unlikely,' said the policeman. 'But the building is certainly being watched. My colleague, Inspector Schneider, is a very thorough man. Like me, he does not like to let go of an investigation until it is concluded to his satisfaction.'

'But that means...' Clara Metzner broke off with a shiver. 'None of us is safe.'

'Certainly not while the boy is here,' agreed Gentz. 'And we do not have much time, as I said. Your building superintendent will no doubt have telephoned to his paymasters at the Alex, to inform them of our arrival.'

'The bastard!' said Metzner. 'Didn't I say he was one of them?'

'Perhaps,' said Rowlands gently to the now-distraught Frau Metzner, 'you could pack up Billy's things? He'll need to get out of that uniform...'

'My God, yes!' said Metzner disgustedly. 'What do we do with the foul thing? Put it in the furnace?'

'I've a better idea,' said Rowlands. 'If you'll just wrap it up for me, I'll take the uniform with me. I know someone who will know how to get rid of it, without drawing attention to the fact...' He, too, needed to divest himself of his evening clothes, pack his few possessions, and retrieve his passport. There was a train which left Zoo Station at eleven the following night. He and Billy must be on it. But they would have to hide themselves until then. An idea had just occurred to him as to where they might do just that.

'All right, Billy,' said Gentz, when the boy, now dressed in his own clothes, was seated at the kitchen table, around which the rest of the family was assembled. 'I'd like you to give me as detailed an account of the events of Friday 27th January as you can manage... Good coffee, this, Frau Metzner,' he remarked, as that lady seemed about to protest; then to the boy: 'Very well. Let's hear it. You can start with your arrival at the studio. Some of it I've already heard from Walter...'

'Where *is* Walter?' interrupted the boy. 'He's quite safe. I'll explain later,' said Rowlands. 'Just do as the Inspector says, there's a good boy.'

They listened in silence as Billy told his story—parts of which were already familiar, as the Inspector had said. Rowlands guessed that, following correct procedure, he wanted to have his theories as to what had taken place corroborated by a second eye-witness. To Gentz's orderly police mind, the fact that the case would go no further made no difference. And so they heard once more of the boys' arrival at the UFA studios; of their visit to the dressing-room of the beautiful young star; of their confusion when they heard her return: 'We had to take cover. There was a rail, with clothes. We hid behind that.'

'Go on.' Because the boy had fallen silent. 'Somebody else

269

came in, didn't they?' prompted Rowlands. 'Yes.'

'Who was it? Herr Hartmann?'

The boy must have nodded, for Gentz said, with an edge of impatience, 'Get on with it. Hartmann came in and... what?'

'They were talking,' said the boy miserably. 'Herr Hartmann and... and Fräulein Schönig...' It struck Rowlands that, young as he was, Billy too had succumbed to the the beautiful starlet's allure. 'Herr Hartmann was angry. He said she'd made a fool of him...'

'He said that, did he?' Gentz sounded almost pleased. 'Yes. He... he said that she didn't care about him at all. That... that she'd been using him to advance her career. Now that she'd got what she wanted from him, she was moving onto bigger game, he said. But she was making a bad mistake, because the people she'd got herself mixed up with were dangerous...'

'Interesting,' said the police inspector thoughtfully.'And what did *she* say?'

'She told him to mind his own business. She knew what she was doing, she said, and she'd thank him to keep his nose out of it...' The boy broke off. 'Then what?' said Gentz. 'Then I sneezed. It was dusty behind there, with all those clothes, and...'

'Yes, yes,' said the Inspector. 'So you came tumbling out from behind the rail. What happened then?'

'Herr Hartmann was angry. He said something about this being another of her stupid tricks, and that he wasn't going to put up with it any longer...'

'So he left then, did he?'

'Yes.'

'And what was Fräulein Schönig's response when she saw you?'

'She was awfully cross at first,' said the boy. 'But when she saw it was only us, she laughed. We weren't the first naughty boys she'd had in her dressing-room, she said, but we were certainly the youngest...' For an instant, as he repeated the words, the ghost of the young woman who had spoken them was conjured up. 'She said she remembered queuing up outside the theatre to catch a glimpse of *her* favourite star, when she was about the same age as us,' Billy went on. 'Now she was starring in a movie opposite him... It was Herr Hartmann she meant,' said the boy. 'She said we weren't to take it seriously, the disagreement they'd had—because that was just the way stars behaved. If we were good boys, and kept what we'd seen to ourselves, she'd autograph her picture, so that we could show it to our friends. But we must let her get on with her packing, because she was going away for a while, and so...'

'Hold on,' said Gentz. 'She said that, did she? About going away...'

'Yes.'

'But I thought she'd quarrelled with Hartmann?' The policeman sounded perplexed. 'Then who was she going away *with*, I wonder? I don't suppose she mentioned a name?'

'No.'

'I think perhaps Joachim could tell us, couldn't you?' said Rowlands. 'All right,' said Metzner wearily. 'I don't suppose it matters now. Yes, she was supposed to be meeting me. You need not look so shocked, *Mutti!* There was no plan to run away together. I was merely to drive her to the airport that night, in one of the studio cars...'

'Is this true, Joachim?' cried his mother. 'Oh yes,' said the young man. 'It's true all right. I thought...' He broke off. 'What's the use?' he said. 'You thought she cared for you,' said Rowlands gently. 'Whereas in fact she was simply using you to effect her escape from UFA.'

'That's about the size of it,' agreed the youth bitterly. 'I was a fool, if you like. But I really thought that she... that she and I...' Again, he let the sentence tail away. 'What's the use? She's dead, isn't she? And I let her die...'

'How can you say that?' This was Clara. '*She* was the one who'd let *you* down. Stringing you along, and all the time she was having an affair with a married man...'

'That was why you didn't turn up, wasn't it?' said Rowlands. 'You'd overheard their conversation—hers and Hartmann's—and realised that they were lovers—although it was over by then, of course. So you decided not to keep the rendezvous you'd made with Fräulein Schönig, after all...'

'If I'd turned up, she might still be alive,' said Metzner. 'I can

271

never forgive myself for that...'

'As you said, it hardly matters now,' said the inspector. 'So what happened then?' he went on, addressing Billy. 'After she said she was going away...'

'Well, she—Fräulein Schönig—signed a copy of her picture, like she said, and then she told us we had to leave. She was expecting somebody, she said...'

'Yes, we've heard about that,' said the policeman. 'Did you see anybody in the corridor, as you were leaving?'

'Only the janitor. We were in a hurry, because Walter was afraid we might be seen. He didn't want his brother to know that we'd been there...'

'Little blighter,' muttered Joachim. 'I'd have given him what for...'

'Then I realised I'd forgotten my satchel. It... it had my collection of cigarette cards in it,' said the boy hastily. 'I said I'd go back. Walter wasn't keen, in case I got caught, but I insisted. So he said we'd meet at the place we'd agreed...'

'The house in the Back Lot,' said Rowlands. 'Yes. I suppose he told you... Anyway, I went back, and saw Fräulein Schönig, and explained why it was I'd come. I got my satchel, and I was just about to leave, when we heard someone coming. "This'll be my friend," said Fräulein Schönig. "Quick! He mustn't find you here..." Then she pushed me behind the screen, and... and someone came in. I don't think it was the person she was expecting, though.'

'Who was it?' said Gentz. The boy hesitated. 'You can tell, us, Billy,' said Rowlands. 'It was her,' said the boy. 'That actress. The one who plays Norkus's mother...'

'What's that?' The Inspector sounded baffled. 'He means Magda Hartmann, don't you?' prompted Rowlands. 'The one at the screening tonight.'

'Yes,' said Billy. 'That's her.'

'Well, what happened then?' Gentz was starting to lose patience. 'Come on, lad—we haven't got all night!'

'She... she was angry with Fräulein Schönig. She said that if she—Fräulein Schönig—didn't learn to leave other people's husbands alone, it would be the worse for her...' The boy was silent a moment. 'She said… Oh, a lot of other things I didn't understand. Something about Fräulein Schönig having stolen her life. It ought to be her, up on the screen, playing the part of the Fallen Angel—didn't she know the part was written for her? Only she—Fräulein Schönig—had stolen the part, just as she had tried to steal Frau Hartmann's husband…Then she—Fräulein Schönig—laughed. "My dear Magda,' she said. "You don't suppose for a moment that I could have 'stolen' your husband, as you put it, unless he had been willing? The fact is, my dear, that he had become tired of you, and your drinking, and your endless scenes…"'

For an uncanny moment, it was as if the dead actress spoke through the medium of the child. Rowlands felt the hairs on the back of his neck stand up on end. 'That's enough,' he said to Gentz. 'Can't you see how upsetting this is for him?'

'No, I want to tell it,' said the boy. 'Frau Hartmann was very angry. She… she had a gun. I didn't see it, but I guessed that was what it was, because Fräulein Schönig was frightened. She said, "What are you going to do with that?" and then Frau Hartmann said, "I'm going to make sure you never steal anyone else's husband ever again, that's what I'm going to do…" Then there was there was the sound of a shot and Fräulein Schönig screamed. I thought she was dead,' said Billy. 'But it turned out that she wasn't. She said, "That was a stupid thing to do. You might have killed me." And Frau Hartmann started crying and said, "You shouldn't have said what you said…" It was then that he came in.'

'Von Fritsch, you mean?'

'Yes. The SS officer.' The boy shuddered. 'I didn't know who he was until later… when I saw him at the studio, with Herr Klein.'

'Yes, yes,' said Gentz. 'We'll get to that later. Just tell us what you saw—or rather, what you heard…'

'He… he said: "What's going on, here?" and Fräulein Schönig laughed, and said, "Magda and I have been having a little chat—haven't we, Magda?" Then he said, "You should be more discreet, my dear. I could hear you halfway down the corridor. Then the other lady—Frau Hartmann—said something about leaving, and he said, "But you can't go yet. You haven't finished what you came to do..." And Frau Hartmann said, 'Let me pass, please..." But he wouldn't let her leave. And Fräulein Schönig said, "For God's sake, let her go, Rudi. She's made quite enough of a scene already..." The boy was silent a moment. 'She was laughing,' he said, as if he could not quite believe it. 'Go on.' There was an edge of impatience in the Inspector's tone. Once or twice, as the boy had been speaking, he had got up, and gone over to the window. 'He took the gun from her,' said Billy in a flat voice.

'You saw him do that, did you?'

'No. I was behind the screen, I've told you. But I heard him say, "A pretty little toy. What is it? A .22? American-made." And *she*—Frau Hartmann—said, "Give it back, please..." But he didn't give it back. He said, "A lady's gun, I'd say. Personally, I prefer a .38. But it's still quite an effective little thing, wouldn't you say?" And Fräulein Schönig said, "What are you playing at, Rudi? I don't have time for this..." Then he said, "I don't think you're in a position to make terms, my dear. You've been a very foolish young woman—thinking you could play games with me..."

"What do you mean?" she said. She wasn't laughing now. "You've got it all wrong. I never meant..." Then I heard the sound of a shot, and... a kind of groan... and Fräulein Schönig fell down.' The boy was fighting back tears, now. 'He'd shot her,' he said. There was silence in the room for a moment. Then Rowlands said, 'That was brave of you, Billy. But you see, we had to know the truth...'

'Yes,' said the child, in an uncertain tone.

But Gentz was no longer paying attention. He had gone over to the window, and there was a note of urgency in his voice. 'They're here,' he said. 'We need to get out. Now. Is there a back way out of here?'

'I'll show you,' said Joachim Metzner.

When he came to look back on it years later, it was this moment which come to Rowlands's mind: that hurried farewell to mother and daughter, as he and Billy prepared to follow the Inspector through the kitchen window and onto the fire-escape, where young Metzner was already waiting. 'Look after yourself, Wilhelm,' said Frau Metzner, bestowing a hasty kiss on the boy's cheek. 'Give Walter my love, won't you?' There was no time to say more. But in that last, sad plea was all that needed to be said. 'Goodbye, Herr Rowlands,' said Clara. 'Don't forget this.' She thrust the parcel containing Billy's uniform into his hands. 'Come on!' hissed Gentz, from the other side of the window.

Then all was haste and scurry. As Rowlands helped the child over the sill, and began to follow suit, heavy footsteps sounded on the stairs, and there came a hammering on the door. 'Open up! shouted a voice. 'It's all right, *Mutti*,' were the last words he heard Clara say, as he began to descend the iron staircase that led, he hoped, to safety. 'I'll go. You put the coffee cups in the sink...' Reaching the bottom of the fire-escape, Rowlands found himself in what appeared from the dank smell of it, to be a narrow courtyard or alley. 'Now you understand why I said we must hurry,' panted the Inspector, as the four of them, with Metzner leading the way, hurried along it, emerging onto a back-street. 'The car is this way,' he added. 'With luck, we will be away from here before they finish searching the flat.'

At this, Metzner stopped dead. 'But my mother and sister... I should be with them...'

'Better that you're not,' said Gentz, who appeared to have got the measure of this volatile young man. 'Two women on their own will offer less of a challenge to any over-zealous young officer, anxious to prove his worth to his superiors... I know,' he added. 'I was one, once. No, my advice to you, young man, is to lie low for an hour or two, until things quieten down. You have a girlfriend, I take it?'

'In a manner of speaking,' said the other sheepishly. 'But...'

'Then I should go there, if I were you.'

'What about Herr Dolfuss?' objected Metzner. 'He would have directed them to our flat...'

'Where they will find nothing,' said the policeman. 'Even building superintendents make mistakes. They will then search the other flats. By the time they realise that they have been sent on a futile errand, it will be too late.'

'I hope you're right, that's all,' said Metzner, echoing

Rowlands's thoughts. It would be the worst kind of luck if, in saving Billy, they had inadvertently brought disaster to the Metzner household... But there was no time to worry about that, now. They had reached the car. 'Get in,' said Gentz. 'We'll go the back way.'

The moment of parting—the second of that night—had come. 'Goodbye, Herr Rowlands,' said the young man. 'Goodbye.' They shook hands. 'I just want to say...'

'There's no need to say anything,' said Rowlands. 'I'll send word when we reach London.'

'I would appreciate that. So long, youngster,' said Metzner to Billy, as the child got into the car. 'Don't go getting yourself into any more scrapes, will you? Tell my brother when you see him that he can have my ivory chess-set,' he called after them, as the car pulled away from the kerb.

As for *where* they were going, that was something to which Rowlands had already given some thought. When he heard the destination, Gentz laughed. 'I might have known it would be there!'

'Is there something wrong with the place?'

'Friedenau? Not at all. Only that it has something of a reputation as a hotbed of Communist agitation and Bohemianism...'

'Then we should fit in very well,' said Rowlands. But the Inspector's remark had given him to think. Would he, by throwing himself on her mercy in this way, be bringing trouble to the door of an innocent party? Again, it was a bit late to think of that, now. And certainly, despite the lateness of the hour, Lena Pfeiffer displayed remarkable *sang froid* at the fugitives' arrival. 'This *is* a surprise!' was all she said. Then: 'I guess you'd better come inside.' Taking his cue from her, Rowlands waited until the door was firmly closed behind them before explaining why they had come. 'So you need a place to stay?'

'Yes. I know it's a lot to ask, but...'

'That's O.K., she said. 'I'm not in the habit of throwing people out when they come to me for help—even if one of them *is* wearing an SS officer's coat...'

'That's very good of you.'

'Oh, I try to be good,' said Fräulein Pfeiffer. 'Do I take it all

276

three of you are staying?'

'Not I,' said Gentz hastily. 'No, I don't suppose this is quite your sort of place, Inspector,' said the girl, with some amusement. 'And you, young man,' she went on, addressing Billy. 'I think we have met before, have we not?' The boy must have nodded. 'Yes, I recognise that face! It was stuck up on the mirror in the Make-Up Room for at least a week... until somebody stole the picture.'

'I had to take it down,' said Billy. 'Somebody might have recognised me.'

'Of course. Although with your hair no longer dark but fair, there was less of a risk. It certainly fooled me!' laughed the make-up artist. While they had been talking, she had been busy boiling water on the gas-ring; now she measured spoonfuls of coffee into a jug. 'You'll stay for a cup, Inspector?'

'Thank you, Fräulein. But I should be going. I hope,' he said to Rowlands, 'you will have a safe journey back to England.'

'Thank you.'

Gentz was silent a moment. Then he said, the gruffness of his tone not entirely concealing a softer emotion: 'It has been good to have had you at my side.'

'I feel just the same. Goodbye, Inspector—and thanks.'

The two men shook hands. Rowlands waited until the sound of Gentz's footsteps descending the stairs had died away.

Then he turned to Lena Pfeiffer. 'I appreciate this very much, you know...'

'You'd do the same for me,' said the girl simply. 'Now.' She took his arm, and drew him over to the flat's one easy-chair. 'Sit down there, and I'll bring you your coffee. You look all-in.'

'It's been a long night.' He took the cup from her and sipped the scalding liquid gratefully. 'It would perhaps be better if you did not tell me too much about it,' she said. Rowlands agreed. It was indeed better that she knew as little as possible of the events which had brought them here. He drank his coffee, and allowed himself to relax in the warmth of the little gas-fire, which was throwing out a surprising amount of heat. Time enough for thinking about what had happened, when they were safely away from Berlin.

'One thing I *can* do,' said Lena Pfeiffer, breaking into this pleasantly numb mood, 'is do something about that hair...' It was Billy she was addressing, now. 'I think it best if we restore you to your former appearance, don't you? Luckily, you've come to the right place. You can always count on a make-up artist to have a bottle of hair-dye handy. But we'll take care of that little problem tomorrow...'

'There is one other thing,' said Rowlands. He took the parcel from the chair where he had dropped it and pushed it across the table towards her. 'I wonder if you could get rid of this?' When she had unwrapped the parcel she let out a low whistle. 'I can see why you would not wish to keep it! But I think I can find a place for it in our costume department, amongst some others like it... I will take that coat, too,' she said. 'It would not do for you to wear it again in public...'

'I know. I'm sorry if I've exposed you to any risk on my behalf...'

'As to that,' said the girl. 'It does not matter. We are getting used to taking such risks in Berlin. I will give you another coat. Some fellow left it,' she added carelessly. 'Now I think we should all get some sleep. It is past one o'clock.' She began pulling out pillows and blankets from a cupboard, and swiftly made up a bed on the divan for Billy. 'It isn't the most comfortable of perches, but from the look of you, young man, it won't matter too much *where* you lay your head.'

She turned towards Rowlands. 'As for you...'

'I'll take the chair,' he said, perhaps a little too quickly, for Fräulein Pfeiffer laughed. 'I was about to suggest the same. Here!' She threw a blanket at him. 'I'll leave you gentlemen to your rest. The lavatory's on the landing. Take care not to be seen, won't you? I have what remains of my reputation to consider. More to the point, every building has its informer.'

20

AFTER THE STRAIN OF the past few hours, Rowlands had expected to fall asleep at once, but in fact it took him a while to drop off. Whirling around in his head were snatches of all that had taken place since that moment at the Hotel Adlon when he had felt Billy take his hand in the darkened screening room, at the very moment Helmut Hartmann had fired his gun at the reflected image of the woman with whom he was so madly in love... Then there had been the flight from the Hotel Adlon, and the desperate life-and-death struggle in the snowbound wastes of the Tiergarten which had followed. The horror of those moments would, he knew, haunt him for a long time to come.

Wrapped in his blanket in the uncomfortable chair, Rowlands shivered at the memory. Dragging the man's dead weight across the snowy ground, to what would surely prove to be an all-too temporary hiding-place... Suddenly, he shot bolt upright. The gun! What had happened to the gun? It was von Fritsch's weapon he meant. He wondered if Gentz had thought to retrieve it—or if, in all the haste of stripping the body of its greatcoat, the thing had been lost, perhaps trampled underfoot into the snow... Well, if that was what had happened, there was nothing to be done about it now. Still troubled in his mind, he drifted at last into uneasy sleep, waking, a few hours later, with a stiff neck and the beginnings of a headache.

He touched his watch-face: a quarter past six. He knew he wouldn't sleep again. Reaching his jacket from the back of the chair, he found the crumpled pack of cigarettes he'd stuffed into the pocket. As he did so, he became aware that someone else was in the room. 'Couldn't you sleep, either?' said Lena Pfeiffer softly. 'I slept a bit,' he said. He drew a cigarette from

279

the pack and felt around for his matches. 'Here,' she said. 'Let me do it.' She lit the cigarette for him. 'Thanks. The boy's still asleep, I suppose?' he murmured. 'Oh, yes, He's tired out, poor kid.' She lit a cigarette for herself, and the two of them sat for a while in companionable silence. 'Do you think,' he said, 'that you could manage to look after him for an hour or two? Only there's something I need to do before we leave Berlin...'

'I don't see why not,' said Lena. 'As long as you're back in good time to catch your train.'

'That's not for hours yet. But I'll leave my passport and the tickets with you, just in case...' He took them from his jacket and slid them across the table towards her. She caught hold of his hand before he could withdraw it. 'Do you really have to go?' He knew she wasn't referring only to the errand he had to run. 'I'm afraid so,' he said softly. Lena Pfeiffer sighed, and relinquished Rowlands's hand. 'I never expected anything else,' she said.

From just outside the flat, he could get a tram to Ausstellung station—a route he had followed once before, when he and Lena had travelled together to Babelsberg. Was it really only two days ago? It seemed as if a lifetime had passed. At the station, he enquired for his train and was told there was one leaving in fifteen minutes. He didn't mind the wait. It was still only nine o'clock, and he had an idea that the Grünewald household were not early risers. Besides which, the journey itself would take him over an hour. He'd be there by half-past ten, which seemed a reasonable time to call, even on a Sunday. He wondered idly what time they'd all got to bed, the night before. When he and Billy had made their precipitate departure from the Adlon Hotel, the party had been in full swing. Well, if they were still in bed, he was prepared to wait. What he had to say wouldn't take long, but he wanted to be sure that there was someone to hear it.

As he sat on the slowly moving train, he allowed his thoughts to drift. It had been a gruelling few days; he couldn't wait to be back at home, with Edith and the girls. He wondered what they'd be doing at this moment. Edith would be doing the vegetables for Sunday lunch, he guessed. In the light of all that had happened since his arrival in Berlin, his life with them seemed suddenly very precious. The murderous events of the past twenty-four hours seemed to belong to another world—one he fervently hoped he would soon be leaving behind...The train pulled out of Berlin-Nikolassee; Grünewald was the next station, he recalled. He'd have to ask directions when he got there. Fortunately, the stationmaster tuned out to be the helpful sort: it was a twenty minute walk from here to Bismarckallee, he said; or you could cut through the woods, which would shorten the journey by half.

Rowlands decided to go the shorter route: it meant he wouldn't have to worry about motor traffic. And with the stout stick with which he'd provided himself before setting out, he'd be able to find his way along even the most uneven path. Although, as it turned out, this proved to be a model of its kind—a smooth and level surface of bark chippings, from which the snow had been cleared, at some time earlier that day. He couldn't miss his way, his informant said. All he had to do was keep straight on, until he came to the road, then take the first right and then the left. 'They're big houses, mind,' he said, perhaps struck by the discrepancy between Rowlands's somewhat shabby appearance and the affluence of the district in question. 'Some of 'em more like palaces than dwellings for ordinary folk. We get film stars and all sorts out here, you know...'

Thanking him with a wave of the hand, Rowlands struck out along the path, and was soon swallowed up in the silence of the forest. Even though he could only guess at the height of the pine trees which rose on either side of the path, the muffled quiet of the place cast its own spell. This, he thought, was an older, more peaceful, world, far removed from the crude violence of the new regime. It was the world of Goethe, and Schiller, and Schubert's *Lieder*. Of Grimm's fairytales... although those could be dark enough, he supposed. *Nibble, nibble, little mouse...* He remembered how much that particular tale had frightened Anne, when he'd read it to them at bedtime.

Arriving at last at the villa in Bismarckallee, he mounted the steps, and rang the bell. He heard its sonorous note sound within the house, but it was several minutes before an answer came to his summons. 'Yes?' It wasn't the man he remembered from

281

his previous visit—the butler, presumably—but a woman. A girl, really. She sounded young, and rather timid. He stated his business.

'She's not in.'

'Do you know when she'll be back?'

'No.'

'Then maybe I could come in and wait?'

'Oh... I don't know about that. There's nobody here but me. Herr Voigt said I was to look after the house while he was away. They're all at church...' By which he supposed she meant the rest of the servants. But she allowed him to enter the lofty marble hall, whose very echo confirmed the absence of other occupants. 'Did your mistress say where she was going?' Rowlands enquired. To which she must have shaken her head, for she made no other reply. She would have left him then, to wait until such time as the lady of the house returned, but he forestalled her. 'Wait. I'd like to leave a message, if I may. Can you let me have pen and paper?'

She hesitated a moment, as if trying to decide whether she was likely to get into trouble for this. Then she said: 'All right. It's this way.' The room to which she led him was a small annexe to the right of the drawing-room; it had been closed off on the evening of the Hartmanns' party by double doors. These now stood open. 'She writes her letters in here,' said the girl, in a tone of indifference. 'There's some paper in the drawer. She doesn't keep it locked.'

'Thank you.' He sat down at the desk, and opened the drawer. As she'd said, there was paper there—a plentiful supply of it. He drew out one of the thick, watermarked sheets and laid it on the blotter in front of him. Still the girl lingered, as if unsure whether he was to be trusted alone in her mistress's domain. He reached for the inkstand, which stood convenient to his right hand. 'I'll manage now,' he said. 'What did you say your name was?' Although she hadn't said.

'Trudel.'

'Well, Trudel, you've been most helpful. As soon as I've finished this, I'll take my leave. No need to see me out.' He listened until he heard her footsteps going away, then took up one of the pens left ready for the purpose in the tray, dipped it into the cut-glass inkwell, and began to write.

Leaving the Hartmanns' house a few minutes later, Rowlands decided to return to the station by the way he had come. Even though he would have preferred to see Magda Hartmann in person, it hadn't been an entirely wasted journey. If it meant that she and Hartmann were released from the nightmare of mutual suspicion into which this affair had cast them, he would have achieved something, he thought. As he stood on the pavement in front of the house, getting his bearings, a church clock some distance away struck eleven. If there was a train within the next half-hour, he could be back at Friedenau by midday... But before he could take another step, a car pulled up alongside, with a screech of brakes, and two men got out. One grabbed Rowlands by the arm, while the other gave him a hard push towards the open door of the car. 'Get in.' It all happened so fast that Rowlands himself barely had time to object, before he found himself bundled into the back of the vehicle. Nor was there the slightest chance of escape, pinioned as he was between two burly men in leather coats—the second of these even now slamming the door shut, as the car accelerated away.

Rowlands drew a breath to steady his racing pulse. 'Who are you?' he said. 'What do you want with me?' But there was no reply from either of his captors, nor from the driver of the vehicle, although the man on his left guffawed briefly. It struck him that if they meant to kill him, they could hardly have chosen a better spot, surrounded as it was by the dense forest through which he had walked barely an hour before, and which had seemed to him then a haven from the city's terrors. Now he saw how wrong he had been. 'Where are you taking me?'

'You'll find out soon enough,' said the man who'd laughed.

'Shut up, Koch. And *you* pipe down, too,' said the man on Rowlands's right, giving him a sharp poke in the ribs. Then there was nothing but a heavy silence, broken only by the creaking of the leather coats, as the two men shifted their weight to adjust to the momentum of the speeding car. There was a smell inside the car, which became more oppressive as the journey wore on. It was the smell of leather, mixed with that of stale tobacco and body odour. There was another smell, too, thought Rowlands—one he recognised from somewhere. The smell of cheap hair-oil. 'It was *you* that day in the dressing-room, wasn't it?' he said, addressing the man to his left—the one named Koch. 'You killed Fräulein Pabst...'

'Don't know what you're talking about.'

'I thought I told you to shut up,' said the other man viciously. Before Rowlands knew what was happening, a fist slammed into his stomach. He felt the bile rise in his throat. If he'd been in any doubt as to the danger he was in, the way these two had reacted would have removed it. They'd been the ones to hold Greta Pabst down, and pour the poison down her throat. They had killed Fritzi Henkel, too. The sweetish stench of hair-oil had betrayed the one, just as much as his violent response had betrayed the other. The car, which had been moving at a reckless pace, now slowed down, as they entered the outskirts of the city. Because it was evident that, rather than travelling deeper into the Grünewald Forest, as Rowlands had feared, they had been heading back to the centre—a realisation that afforded him some relief. Whatever the fate these thugs had in store for him, at least it wouldn't be the one his imagination had conjured: a bullet in the head and a shallow grave in amongst the towering pines.

They had been travelling for about half an hour, by his watch, along what seemed to him a dead straight road. Now, as the car entered what he judged, from the noise of traffic, to be a more populous area, Rowlands considered what his next move should be. If, as he guessed, they were taking him to the Alex, then his best chance of getting away was to wait until he was actually out of the car. Could he make a break for the gate, in the few moments he'd have at his disposal? He dismissed the idea almost at once. Even if he managed to catch them off-guard, they'd bring him down before he'd gone twenty yards. Unlike their British counterparts, these men were armed. It would be an act of suicide.

And yes, he was right about its being the police station to which they were going: the rattle of trams and stink of motor-traffic in Alexanderplatz told him that. With a final lurch over the cobblestones of the courtyard, the vehicle came to a halt, and the door to his right swung open. The man who'd hit him got out. 'You, too,' said Koch, on his other side, giving the prisoner a shove. 'Am I under arrest?' said Rowlands. But the only reply to this was a burst of rude laughter. 'He doesn't give up, does he?' said Koch to his companion, as, with another shove, he directed Rowlands towards the entrance of the building. There was no mistaking this, either: its smell, a mixture of floor-polish and something less reassuring—a human, faecal smell, that was perhaps the smell of fear—was one he had come to know, this past couple of weeks.

Once inside, he found himself marched down a flight of steps, to what he deduced from the lowness of its ceiling, to be a subterranean floor. This, he recalled, was where the mortuary was to be found; in his present state of mind, it did not seem overly fanciful to think that he could feel its chill. But instead of turning in that direction, they took the opposite one, which led along a narrow tiled corridor. Towards the end of this, one of his gaolers opened a door. 'Put him in here,' he said, to the man who held him. After a brief, unpleasant interlude, during which Rowlands was stripped of his overcoat, watch, tie, shoelaces and cigarettes, the two men left him. The hollow tramp of their footsteps echoed along the corridor until it was swallowed up in the silence.

The room in which Rowlands found himself was furnished with a deal table and two chairs. It smelt of damp, and unwashed bodies. The walls were tiled to a distance of four feet from the floor, which was covered by linoleum, worn in several places. There was a single, barred, window, and the metal shutter in the door could only be opened from outside. All this he ascertained in the first few minutes—his investigations hampered by the looseness of his shoes, which made walking more difficult, and would have made running impossible. The inconvenience had been imposed for that reason, he surmised, and not because they thought he'd try and hang himself.

He wished they'd left him his cigarettes. Even more than this, he felt the want of his heavy coat. To keep warm, and because it stopped him brooding too much on what a pickle he was in, he walked up and down, stamping his feet in their too-loose shoes, to keep the circulation going. The room was not a large one—eight paces by five. As he walked, following the worn track left by previous occupants, he tried to get a sense of what time it was. He'd left the Hartmanns' place just on eleven. The journey back to Berlin had taken a little over half an hour. He'd been here—what? Three-quarters of an hour? He wondered if Lena was getting anxious... No, he hadn't said how long he'd be, when he'd set out that morning. It would be another hour or so before she would start to worry.

At last there came the sound of boots in the corridor outside, and the sound of a key in the lock. The door opened and someone came in, followed by another man. 'Ah, Herr Rowlands,' said a voice, in what seemed an affable tone.

'Inspector Schneider.'

'Indeed. I am sorry to have kept you waiting.'

'What is this all about?'

But the police inspector seemed in no hurry to explain. He pulled out a chair and sat himself upon it. The other man remained by the door. 'Please. Sit down.'

'I'd rather stand, thanks. And you haven't answered my question.'

The Inspector gave a dry little laugh. 'You ask what this is about? I think you have a very good idea!'

'I'm afraid not,' said Rowlands. It seemed important not to let this man know how frightened he was. 'I'm completely in the dark...'

'Ha ha! That is good, from a blind man! But there is no need to play games with me. I know you have been to see Frau Hartmann...'

'She wasn't in.'

'I know this also. She and her husband are at present attending a luncheon at the home of the Reichsminister, in Friedrich Ebertstrasse...'

'Then...'

'We both know that this is about the boy. You were seen arriving with him at the Metzner apartment building last night at

286

around midnight...'

'Was I?' interrupted Rowlands. 'That's news to me. Are you sure your informant has his facts straight?' For a moment Schneider sounded doubtful. 'You are saying you did *not* go to the apartment? But the fellow'—it was the building super-intendent he meant, guessed Rowlands—'said he was sure...' Rowlands shrugged. 'Be that as it may, I wasn't there. I had an engagement at the Hotel Adlon...'

'Yes, we already know about that,' snapped the policeman. 'But you were not there the whole night...'

'Indeed not.' Rowlands gave an embarrassed laugh. 'Are you a married man, Inspector?' For the first time since he had come in, Schneider seemed taken aback. 'I fail to see what relevance that has...'

'Only if you *are*—married, I mean—you will understand that I'd rather my whereabouts last weren't made public... both on account of the, er, young lady concerned, and because I'd real-ly rather my wife didn't get to hear of it...' His expression, he hoped, was suitably sheepish.

'You spent the night with a woman?' The distaste in the Inspector's voice was almost palpable. Rowlands wondered if he'd laid it on too thick. ''Fraid so,' he said. 'Pretty little thing, too. Wish I could remember her name...'

'Oh, you will have time to remember,' said Schneider coldly. 'So where was it you met this lady? At the Hotel Adlon?'

'Suppose it must have been. I'm afraid the whole evening's a bit of a blur...' Rowlands gave a foolish grin. 'Too much of your excellent German champagne. I'm afraid it went right to my head.'

'Yes,' said the other drily. 'It certainly seems to have affect-ed your memory! And where did she live, this nameless young woman?'

'Couldn't tell you, I'm afraid. One of the streets off the Kurfurstendamm, that's all I know. After we left the Adlon, we went to a nightclub, I think... yes, that's right. It's all start-ing to come back to me. The Green Carnation, or some such. Wonderful, your Berlin nightspots! One of those Negro jazz bands was playing, I seem to recall. Infernal racket. Anyway...

we met up with some of the lady's friends, and the evening rather went on from there... By the time we got back to her place—there was quite a crowd of us, you know—I wasn't paying much attention to where we were...'

'Evidently not.' Something seemed to strike the police officer, for he said coldly: 'You did not wear those clothes you are wearing to the reception at the Hotel Adlon, I think?'

'No, indeed. That was a white-tie affair. Very smart indeed—with some very important people. Why, the Leader himself put in an appearance...'

Schneider was silent a moment. 'The Führer was there?'

'Oh, yes. I had quite a pleasant chat with him, as a matter of fact...'

You *spoke* to him?'

Rowlands smiled. 'Why, yes. Only for a moment or two, you know. I gather he was anxious to see the film... Awfully good, I thought it...'

But if he had hoped that this tissue of lies would deflect the policeman from his inquisition, he was mistaken. 'You were about to tell me what happened to your evening clothes,' said Schneider. 'Was I? So I was.' Rowlands shook his head as if still befuddled by the night's excesses. 'To tell you the truth, Inspector, I haven't the faintest idea what became of them. I woke up this morning with the most frightful head, and found my clothes missing. One of the young lady's friends must have pinched them. They were rather a rough lot, you know... Artists. Writers. That sort of thing...'

'You say that one of these stole your clothes?' Schneider did not attempt to conceal his incredulity. 'Oh, don't worry! I've no intention of lodging a complaint,' said Rowlands. 'Been hard-up myself. The money you could get from pawning a nice set of evening clothes would set some poor chap up for a week, I shouldn't wonder. Must have been too much of a temptation for the fellow. Left me his togs in exchange.' He was counting on the fact of the borrowed overcoat to lend credence to his story. 'The thing is,' he went on. 'I'd really rather none of this got out. Terribly embarrassing for everyone concerned. And if my wife were to hear of it...'

'That would be most unfortunate.' Schneider seemed sudden-ly weary of the whole charade. It struck Rowlands in the same moment that the other had made no mention of Gentz, and that the omission was sinister. Had Gentz—perhaps under duress—betrayed him? If so, why hadn't Schneider confronted him with evidence which would—surely—give the lie to his tale of where he'd spent the night? An edge of impatience had crept into the police inspector's voice. 'In any case, where you spent the night or did not spend the night is of no interest to me. You say that you were not at Marienburgerstrasse. But I have reason to believe that you *were* there—and that the boy was there. Also that another person was present—a known agitator...'

'I don't know what you're talking about.'

'Don't you? Then let me tell you that Joachim Metzner was arrested last night at the home of one of his associates, a Communist. Both were found to be in possession of seditious material. I need not tell you what is the penalty for conspiring against the State...'

'But that's...' Rowlands began; then checked himself. 'When was this?'

'Ah, of course you do not know, since you were on the tiles last night,' said the police inspector, with a sarcastic laugh. 'We picked them up a little after midnight. And you say you knew nothing of young Metzner's activities?'

'Of course not. I don't believe for a moment he was involved in any such thing. It has to be a mistake,' said Rowlands. Even as he spoke, the memory of Joachim's late-night return to the flat in Marienburgerstrasse on more than one occasion, came back to him... Yes, he could believe that Metzner and his girlfriend had been up to something. God help them now—if Schneider was telling the truth, that is, and this wasn't merely a ploy to get his prisoner to confess... 'What will happen to them?' he asked.

'That is not for me to say,' replied the other indifferently. 'They will be lucky to keep their heads, in my opinion. Perhaps, as it is a first offence, a few years in a K.Z. will suffice... That rather depends on you.'

'On *me?*'

'On your co-operation, Herr Rowlands.'

'I fail to see...'

'You have the boy. No need to shake your head! You know where he is to be found. All I ask is that you tell me his whereabouts. Then you will be free to go...'

'I've told you, I've no idea where he is...'

'...and young Metzner and his girl will, perhaps, be spared a more severe penalty.'

Rowlands was silent a moment. 'What is it you want with the boy?' he said at last. 'He's only a child...'

'That makes no difference. A child can still commit a crime.'

'And what crime has he committed?' Rowlands controlled his temper with difficulty. 'He has taken something which does not belong to him,' said Schneider. 'I haven't the slightest idea what you mean.' He was taken aback at the fury with which the other reacted: 'You're lying!' Schneider was on his feet now, leaning towards the seated prisoner across the table—so close that Rowlands could smell the sour tang of his breath. 'You think it amusing to play games with me, Englishman, but I assure you that this is *not* a good idea!'

He must have made some sign to the man standing at the door, for a moment later, Rowlands felt his arm being seized and twisted up behind his back. A sharp blow to the face followed—all without a word being said by his invisible assailant. That it was Koch he knew, from the smell of that filthy hair-oil. 'All right,' snapped the Inspector, as the man made ready to deliver another blow. 'Leave him. Now then, Herr Rowlands, we will have no more lies. You will tell me where is the boy, and then you will be free to go...'

Rowlands drew a breath to quieten the ringing in his ears. He began to massage the feeling back into his twisted arm. 'You go to Hell,' he said.

A stifled exclamation from Schneider brought the thug back from his post at the door, but before he could fall to his work once more, Rowlands said: 'Tell your man that, if he touches me again, I will make sure the British newspapers know that policemen in Herr Hitler's Germany do not scruple to assault blind war veterans. Believe me, it is a story which will interest them very much, but which your Leader may be less pleased to read. He is sensitive about such matters, I understand...'

There was a charged silence. Then Schneider said to his henchman: 'Wait outside.' When the man had gone, the police inspector addressed Rowlands once more. This time his tone was conciliatory, almost pleading—as if his job depended on it; which perhaps it did, thought the other. 'Herr Rowlands, we are men of the world, you and I. We understand one another, do we not?' Rowlands nodded his assent. 'Good. Then you will believe me when I tell you that no harm will come to the boy, if he gives us what we want...'

'And what is that?'

There was another pause, as if Schneider were weighing up the risks of letting the Englishman in on the secret. 'There is a list,' he said at last. 'We believe that the woman—Schönig—had it, and that she gave it to the boy, on the night she died. It was not amongst her possessions when they were searched. And it seems that the boy was the last person to see her alive...'

'Not quite the last,' said Rowlands. Something which had been puzzling him now became clear. 'What was on this list?'

Again, a hesitation. 'Names,' said the policeman curtly. 'Those of undesirables.'

'Jews and Communists, I suppose that means?'

'Enemies of the State,' snapped the other. 'It is surely of no concern to you?'

'Oh, you'd be surprised,' said Rowlands. 'Where are they to be found, these enemies of the state? At UFA studios, perhaps?'

'You are very quick, Herr Rowlands! But you need not smile at this. Our German film industry has been infiltrated by these traitors. Our task is to root them out...'

'But surely,' said Rowlands, interrupting this splenetic dia-tribe, 'you don't need a list of names to do that? From what I've seen during my time in Berlin, you're managing very well without any such evidence. Unless,' he added, 'there's a name on the list that ought not to be there...'

'That, too, does not concern you,' said Schneider hastily. But Rowlands was not to be silenced so easily. 'So that's how it is,' he said. 'It isn't the *other* names you care about—those you can find out easily enough—but the fact that there's one name you'd rather didn't get out...' Perhaps, he thought, Sybille Schönig's blackmailing career hadn't ended with Rudolf von Fritsch? If so, she had signed her own death warrant. 'You try my patience with your speculations, Herr Rowlands,' said Schneider. 'I should remind you that if you do not co-operate, there are others who will suffer for it.'

'And what of those whose names are on the list?' said Rowlands quietly. 'Will they, too, suffer?'

'That would depend on whether they have deserved it. But we are wasting time. Tell me where to find the boy and you—and your friends—will be released without charge. Five minutes,' he added. 'That's all I ask. He will give us the list, and then...' A frantic knocking at the door of the interrogation room made him break off. 'I said no interruptions!' he shouted angrily. But the hammering continued. With an exclamation of disgust, the inspector pushed back his chair and went to the door. A rapid exchange ensued between officer and uniformed man, of which Rowlands caught certain significant words: '...the river... Tiergarten... an hour ago...Yes, quite dead...' They'd found von Fritsch's body, evidently.

When Schneider returned from this brief conference, he seemed agitated—as well he might, thought Rowlands. A dead SS officer turning up on his turf wasn't something any police inspector looking for promotion was likely to relish. 'You will wait here,' he said to Rowlands. 'It will do you no harm to have an hour or two to think about what I have said. When I return, you will give me the answer I wish for—or it will be the worse for you.' Then he was gone, locking the door behind him.

21

ALONE ONCE MORE IN the cold and airless room, Rowlands considered his situation. It was pretty dire, by anybody's reckoning, he thought. He could be stuck here for hours—days, even. Certainly until it was too late to catch his train... He wondered if Lena would remember the arrangement they had made, in the event of his being delayed. With any luck—and unless the police were watching the railway stations, Billy could still catch the eleven o'clock express. He was a resourceful child: if he could get as far as Paris on his own, then someone could be sent to meet him, and bring him the rest of the way home. The telegram Rowlands had asked Fräulein Pfeiffer to send, as soon as they were *en route*, was circumspect in its wording, but, he hoped, would be clear enough to Dorothy: ARRIVING GARE DU NORD 3AM STOP BOTH OF US SEND LOVE STOP FRED...

Now he shivered in his thin jacket, and wondered how the hell he was going to get out of the mess he was in. He guessed it must be around four o'clock. Seven hours until he had to be at the station. He thought: 'There has to be some way out of this...' But he couldn't for the life of him think what it could be. He realised that he was very hungry. Well, *that* he could do something about. He banged on the door. 'Hey! You there! Open up!' After about ten minutes of yelling and banging, he was rewarded by the sound of boots in the corridor. '*Was ist los?*' say a stern young voice. Then, in halting English: 'You must not this noise make.'

'I'll make all the noise I want until you open this door,' shouted Rowlands. He heard the metal shutter slide back. His fierce expression must have been convincing, for a moment later, he heard the key turn in the lock. The door opened. 'What is it you want?' said the guard. 'A cup of tea would be nice,' replied the prisoner. 'And something to eat. But first I need the lavatory. *Toilette,*' he added helpfully. Before the other could respond to this unlooked-for demand, there came the sound of someone else approaching. This was a more senior man, to judge by the curtness with which he addressed his colleague: 'What's going on here?'

'He… he wants the toilet,' stammered the youth. 'Well, take him along there, then,' was the gruff reply. 'And be quick about it.'

'Yes, Sergeant.'

'All right. Carry on. As for you,' said the police sergeant to the prisoner. 'A bit less noise, if you please. You'll be getting my lad here into trouble.'

'I've no wish to do that, said Rowlands, as, escorted by the two policemen, he began walking along the corridor towards where he supposed the 'usual offices' were located. 'But I'd like to know what's going on.'

'Wouldn't we all?' Something about the way in which this was said made Rowlands think he could take a chance. 'Wait,' he said, as they reached an intersection with another corridor. 'This is important. I'd like to speak to Inspector Gentz.' The sergeant stopped in his tracks. 'Inspector Gentz has been relieved of his duties,' he said in a flat tone. 'I would advise you to say no more about Inspector Gentz.'

'Why? What has happened to him?'

'That's enough!'

'On the contrary,' said Rowlands. 'It's just the beginning. You've no right to keep me here. I demand to have a lawyer present. And I want to speak to the British Consul…'

'You want too much,' said the man. Without another word, he walked off, leaving Rowlands in the charge of the first man. They reached a door. '*Toiletten,*' said the guard, giving him a not-unfriendly shove. Inside was a row of foul-smelling cubicles, and another of urinals, which smelt little better. Having relieved himself, Rowlands made a rapid search of the room, in the hope of finding some way out. But the only window was a tiny, barred slot high up in the far wall. He thought about making a run for it, once he was back in the corridor—but rejected the idea almost at once. Even if he managed to get away from the guard, who was probably two stone heavier and twenty years younger, he'd wouldn't get very far. Being blind meant one was effectively at the mercy of other people.

Back in the interrogation room, there was nothing to do but wait. They'd brought him some food—a bowl of watery soup, and a hunk of stale bread—which revived him a little. As he ate, he took stock of his situation: it didn't look good. For all his bluster about complaining to the British Consulate, he knew his chances of getting out of there any time soon were slim. He didn't think they'd kill him—or not yet. Not until they had the information they wanted about Billy. As to how they'd get it... well, he'd already had a taste of that.

Then there was the question of what had happened to Gentz. 'Relieved of duties'—that could mean what it said, of course. In which case, things still looked bad for his friend and former collaborator. In such a climate of fear and suspicion, the slightest deviation from the official course could mean instant dismissal. Or worse. He wondered how much they knew about Gentz's involvement in all of this. Did they know or suspect that he'd killed von Fritsch? He thought about the warning the bluff sergeant had given him. *I would advise you to say no more about Inspector Gentz...* That certainly had an ominous ring to it.

Suddenly the crust of bread on which Rowlands had been gnawing turned to ashes in his mouth. What a dirty business this had been.

His thoughts returned to Billy. The boy had to be got away from here as soon as possible—that much was obvious. Rowlands hoped that the instructions he'd left with Lena Pfeiffer had been clear enough. In the event of his—Rowlands's—non-appearance, she was to take the boy to Zoo Station, in time to catch the eleven o'clock train. She had the tickets, and Rowland's passport, on which Billy was listed... although that would be no good without Rowlands there to vouch for him. Perhaps she'd find a suitable adult who'd be willing to accompany the child as far as Paris...

Round and round went these thoughts, and still he could see

295

no way out of the conundrum. Nor did thinking about something else—what was going to happen to Joachim Metzner and his girl, for instance—offer any relief. In the weeks since his arrival in Berlin, Rowlands had grown fond of the hot-headed youth. Now he feel responsible for what had befallen him. *They'll be lucky to keep their heads...* There'd been a chilling matter-of-factness about Schneider's remark. From all that Rowlands had gathered, the new administration had no compunction about eliminating anyone that stood in its way. He thought about Sybille Schönig, and the dangerous game she'd been playing. She'd thought she was the one who held the cards, but she'd been wrong about that, as it turned out.

It must have been going on for six o'clock when he heard the tramp of footsteps in the corridor. Schneider and his cohorts returning. He turned to face the door, to be ready for what might come. Even though there was no way that Schneider could have connected him with von Fritsch's death, the discovery of the body would not have improved the former's mood—of that Rowlands was sure. And indeed the police inspector seemed barely to be containing his anger. Gone was the conciliatory tone of their earlier conversation. 'You will come with me,' was all he said, before turning on his heel and striding off in the direction from which he had come, leaving Rowlands, with a guard on each side, to follow. They came to the stairs. One of the guards prodded him the back, and said, 'Up.' When they reached the upper floor, he was directed to turn right. This, he recalled was the corridor leading to Gentz's office. Were they going to interrogate him there?

But it was outside another of the offices that their party came to a halt. Schneider turned to him. 'You are a lucky man, Herr Rowlands,' he said softly, putting his face so close that Rowlands could feel the sour breath against his cheek. 'You would not have got out of here so easily if it had been left to me.' He opened the door. To Rowland's surprise, he did not go in, but stood back, to let his prisoner enter, before closing the door behind him. Bewildered by this turn of events, Rowlands stood still a moment. There was someone else in the room, he was sure of it. Senses sharpened by long hours of waiting and listen-ing picked up tell-tale sounds. The shifting of a body's weight in a chair. The slither of one silk-clad leg over another... For that it was a woman, he was in no doubt: the smell of her perfume told him that. 'Well, don't just stand there, Herr Rowlands—or may I call you Frederick? Sit down, why don't you? There is a chair two paces in front of you...'

Suddenly Rowlands needed very badly to to sit down. 'Frau Hartmann. What are you doing here?' The actress laughed. It was the same, warm sound which had enchanted him the first time he had heard it, all those weeks ago. 'I am here for you, what do you think? I cannot let my devoted admirer languish in a police cell...'

'But...'

'There is a mark upon your face. Have they beaten you? No, do not tell me. It is better if I do not know...'

'Frau Hartmann...'

'Call me Magdalena, please! There is no time for questions. I have a car waiting outside.' She stood up, and came towards him. 'Come. Let us go. I have been here a quarter of an hour—and that is a quarter of an hour too long.'

He wasn't going to argue with that. She rapped on the door, and it was at once opened. Not Schneider, but another officer, stood there. 'We are leaving,' said Magda Hartmann. She took Rowland's arm, and he was enveloped as once before in the scent of her, and in the softness of her furs. 'You are cold,' was all she said. Wondering, in his lightheaded state, if it was all some bizarre dream, and if he would wake, half-frozen and alone, in the interrogation room, Rowlands allowed himself to be led back along the corridor to the entrance hall. Here, at his rescuer's prompting, he signed for and received his overcoat, watch and cigarettes. The tie was in his pocket.

'Wait,' commanded Frau Hartmann, as they were on the point of leaving. 'His shoelaces. He cannot go without shoelaces...' Only when these had been found, and restored to their prop-er function, did she relinquish the role she had been playing, which was that of the *grande dame*. It was one she had played so often that it had become second-nature to her. But that it *was* an act was apparent from the way she trembled, clutching his arm, as they went out through the great portal of the building and crossed the courtyard. In the car—her Benz—which was parked outside the main gate, she let out a sigh of relief. 'Home,' she said to the driver. 'As fast as you can. I can't bear another minute of that prison stink.'

'Frau Hartmann... Magdalena, I mean...'

'How cheerful all the flags look along Königstrasse!' Magda Hartmann exclaimed, apropos of nothing. 'It's as if Berlin were permanently *en fête*...'

'So I gather.' It occurred to him that perhaps she was being cautious about what she said in front of the chauffeur—an impression confined by her next remark: 'How many cars there are on the roads, these days!' When I was a girl, only the rich had cars. Now they're everywhere...'

Rowlands made a sound vaguely expressive of agreement, and Magda Hartman laughed. 'You are thinking I am a chatterbox... that is the word, is it not?'

'I wasn't thinking that.'

'Perhaps not—but there are other things you are thinking,' she replied, patting his hand. Hers wore an expensive kidskin glove. As she moved closer, the better to say what it was she had to say, he felt the silken brush of her fur collar against his cheek. 'You are thinking,' she murmured, so softly that it was barely above a whisper, 'that you would like to know what is going on...'

'Yes.'

'Do not be afraid.' This time she took his hand and held it for a few moments. 'I am your friend, Frederick.'

'I don't doubt it,' he said. 'Since it was you who got me out of that place. Although I'd like to know how you managed it.'

'Ah, that is easily explained. You are fortunate that you have made such an impression on a young girl. It is the maid, Trudel, to whom I refer...'

'She gave you my letter, then?'

'Yes. And we will talk of this later.' She gave his hand another pat—perhaps a warning. 'But she also saw what happened. She was watching from the window, when you left. "A big black

298

car, with three men in it," was what she saw. "They made the gentleman get into the car..." In Berlin, that can mean only one thing. So you see, Frederick, it is not I but Trudel you must thank for your release from the clutches of our police force.'

'Of course I am watched all the time,' she said, in an indifferent tone. 'There is someone out there even now...' She turned from the window, where she had been standing, and crossed the room to where Rowlands sat, nursing a glass of whisky. They had arrived back at the house in Grünewald half an hour before. Frau Hartmann had first sent for tea and sandwiches: 'You look as if you could do with something to eat, you poor man. Do you like caviar?' Tea and sandwiches had accordingly been brought, and consumed—at least by Rowlands; Magda Hartmann wasn't hungry. 'Only think of the enormous lunch I have eaten! The Reichsminister does not stint himself, you can be sure!' It wasn't until they were alone that the conversation, which had had remained general, while the maid was in and out of the room, became more specific.

'You could leave Berlin,' said Rowlands. The heat from the fire in front of which he was crouched, was delicious. He could feel it warming his chilled body, dispelling the nightmare of the past few hours. 'There's nothing to keep you here. I've told you: von Fritsch is dead. You don't have to worry about him anymore...'

'No.' She was silent a moment. He heard the rustle of her silk dress, as she got up and went to the door. He heard her open it, and, having checked that there was no one there, close it once more. 'That is true. And for that I am grateful.' She sat down beside him once more. 'How much do you know of what happened that night?' she said.

'I know some of it. You arrived at the studio a little after six...'

'Yes. I was looking for Helmut. I had an idea that he was still at the studio... He hadn't come home, and so..."

'You went to Sybille Schönig's dressing-room.'

'I thought I might find him there. I knew he was besotted with the girl.' She knocked back the rest of her drink. 'The affair had ended but... He was still... how do you say? Infatuated. He thought he could win her back, the fool! I decided to put a

299

stop to it.'

'So you expected to find your husband with her that night?' said Rowlands.

'Yes, I thought I'd find him there. But he wasn't—or if he had been, he'd gone by the time I got there.' She took a meditative swig of her whisky. 'What made me angry was how pleased she seemed with herself. If it hadn't been for that...' She let the sentence tail away. 'Of course,' she murmured. 'I would rather she had not died. You may find this hard to believe, but I only meant to frighten her...'

Von Fritsch said he arrived just after you fired the gun...'

'Yes. It was a stupid thing to do—pulling out that gun. I never intended to hit her. But I was angry. She should not have laughed at me the way she did...' Magda Hartmann took a cigarette from the box on the low glass table front of the sofa where they sat. She lit it, and passed it to Rowlands, with a hand that trembled a little. Then she lit one for herself, drew in a lungful of smoke, and let it out again. 'You must believe I had no intention of killing her. She was a stupid little bitch, who had stolen my husband, but I would not have risked my neck for her.'

'It was von Fritsch who killed her,' said Rowlands. 'He would have done so, even without your intervention.'

'Yes. But it was my gun,' she said. 'So I am at least partly to blame.'

He didn't disagree with her. 'The fact is,' he said, returning to the first thing he had said, 'with von Fritsch dead, you are free to go. There is no one who knows you were ever in that room... apart from myself. And I will be gone in a few hours.'

'Ah, yes. I will take you to Zoo Station...'

'Thank you.'

'But first, I want you to do something for me.' She got up once more, and crossed the room. There came the sound of a bureau being unlocked, then locked again, after something had been taken out of it. That something—a letter, rather bulky; a document of some sort, he guessed—was placed in Rowlands's hand. 'That is my Will,' said Magda Hartmann. 'I would be obliged if you would take it to the firm of solicitors in London who executed it for me: Scott, Waverley and Dunn. Fine English names, are they not? I have a daughter,' she went on. 'Thirteen years old. She is at school in England. In Sussex,' she added, and with maternal pride: 'It is a good school. One of the best for young girls, I understand.'

'I see,' said Rowlands. 'But surely...'

'She does not know who her mother is,' said the other, over-riding his protest. 'I thought it best at the time, and nothing that has happened since...' She gave a small, but perceptible, shudder. '...has changed my opinion. You will please deliver this letter—my Will—to Messrs Scott, Waverley and Dunn. Then if anything should happen to me...' Again, there was a momentary hesitation, as if she was considering exactly what that might mean. 'I will know that Ursula has been provided for.'

'All right,' said Rowlands. 'I'll do as you ask.'

'I was sure I could count on you. 'There was the sound of a stopper being removed from a decanter. 'Another whisky?'

'Thanks.'

She poured them both a measure, and handed him the glass. 'Yes, von Fritsch had orders to kill her,' said Magda Hartmann. 'She—Sybille—had become an embarrassment to certain people. I do not have to mention names...' Again, she allowed a silence to fall. It was an actress's trick, to let the line just spoken resonate. 'No,' said Rowlands. 'You don't have to mention names. But *someone* has been very thorough about covering all this up. He must have wanted that job very badly, that's all I can say.'

She laughed. 'There is not much that escapes, you, is there, my dear Englishman? Yes, he wanted the job very badly—Minister of Propaganda is a powerful position, you will agree? Having seen off his rivals for the post, and dealt with the sordid little affair which might have brought him down, his situation is now impregnable...' Her voice dropped, so that it was no more than a husky purr. 'But of course, he did not achieve this without help. Others have been active on his behalf. His wife being one.' Then, seeing his startled expression: 'You did not suppose that Obersturmführer von Fritsch was acting under orders from Josef? Oh no! He was always Magda Goebbels's man.' Again, she laughed. 'Poor Sybille! She stood no chance against

301

the two of us, did she? A pair of jealous wives...'

'One thing you should know,' she said. 'My husband was not involved. He loved her, poor fool. He wanted to run away with her, to America. Instead, he will stay here with me.' Another silence. 'That will be punishment enough for both of us,' she added, on a dying fall.

Zoo Station at twenty-five to eleven on a freezing February night was surprisingly busy—thronged with people intent on catching trains, those seeing them off, and porters carrying luggage. The Nord Express was already waiting on the platform, emitting clouds of steam into the icy air, like the breath of some great resting beast. 'Do you see them?' said Rowlands to his companion. He was unable to keep the anxiety from his voice. 'No. Who exactly are we looking for?' Her voice, coming out of the darkness, was a throaty murmur. 'A girl,' he said. 'With a child. A young boy.'

'The boy in your photograph...'

'Yes. He's eleven years old, with dark hair... At least, I hope it's dark,' he muttered under his breath. 'I do not see them. Come, let us walk to the end of the platform. It may be that they are there...' Once more, he felt the soft touch of of her furs, and breathed her musky scent, as she took his arm. He had tried to dissuade her from accompanying him, thinking it dangerous for both of them, but she'd brushed his objections aside: 'Nonsense. You cannot manage on your own. It will be crowded. And besides...' There was the ghost of a smile in her voice. 'It will do you no harm to be seen with me. I still have some influence, you know.'

That much Rowlands already knew. It was Magda Hartmann's influence which had got him released from the interrogation room at the Alex. Whether even that would be enough to save him, if Schneider got wind of the fact that he'd been there when Obersturmführer von Fritsch was killed, was another matter. Of course, he thought, unable to suppress a shiver, *that* would only come about if the man who had killed von Fritsch talked... 'Feeling the cold?' said his companion. 'I'm afraid your coat is not warm enough for our Berlin winter.'

'I'm quite all right.' But he was feeling very far from all right—his nerves strung taut, as he strained his ears to catch a familiar voice, in all that babble of voices. He touched the raised dots on his watch-face: it was a quarter-to. It struck him that if those for whom he was waiting did not arrive soon, he, too, would be forced to remain. Without his passport he would be effectively trapped in what for him, as for others, had become a dangerous city. He wondered grimly how much use the British Embassy would prove, in the event of his having to throw himself on their mercy. His last encounter with the Embassy's man had not inspired confidence. 'What does she look like, this girl of yours?' said Frau Hartmann; then realised what she had said. 'Stupid of me. I don't suppose you can have any idea...'

'I believe she's pretty, with red hair,' said Rowlands—at which the actress laughed. 'That does narrow the field somewhat! Let us walk back the way we have come, and I will look for your pretty redhead...' It was ten minutes to eleven. The porters were still busily loading trunks and suitcases into the baggage cars. Doors slammed, and windows were pushed down, so that those on board could exchange last-minute endearments with those seeing them off. The station master shouted to the late-comers to hurry along. A great cloud of smoke belched from the waiting engine: Rowlands could taste it at the back of this throat. It seemed obvious to him that Lena and the boy were not coming now. 'Look,' he began. He'd wait until the train had left—just to make sure, he thought. Then he'd make his way to the Embassy, in the hope they'd give him shelter until the next day. 'There's no sense in our both hanging around...'

But she paid no attention to this. 'A girl, did you say?'

'Yes.'

'I don't know whether she's got red hair or not, under that terrible felt hat, but there's a child with her—and a young man,' said Magda Hartmann. Before she could say any more, they were there—all three a little out of breath, as if they had been hurrying. 'Lena?' Rowlands turned his face towards her. 'Is that you?'

'Yes, it's me. And Billy. Simon's with us, too. He insisted.'

'I couldn't let her brave the streets on her own at this time

303

of night,' said Simon Meyer. 'Idiot,' said the girl, but she didn't sound too displeased. 'When you didn't come back, I knew something had happened,' she said to Rowlands. 'I'm sorry,' he said. 'There was no way of letting you know…'

'That's all right. I knew you wouldn't let us down.' There was a moment's pause. Rowlands guessed that she was looking at him. She must have realised by now that there was no comfort to be gained from that. 'Have you got my passport and the tickets?' he said gently. 'Of course. Here they are.' She took a step towards him and he felt her slip the documents into the breast-pocket of his coat. For a moment, she let her hand linger there, over his heart. 'I'm very grateful for all you've done,' he said. 'That's all right,' she said, in a flat little voice. 'I packed everything else in the suitcase—Billy's things, too.'

'Thank you.'

'Simon, give him the suitcase, will you?' The young man did so. 'You'll remember to send the telegram, won't you?' said Rowlands, still addressing Lena. 'I hope the money will cover it…'

'Don't worry about that,' she said. In the brief, awkward pause which followed, the station master could be heard shouting that the train was about to leave. Rowlands had the feeling that something more should have been said. 'Take care of yourself,' was the best he could do. 'Oh, don't worry, *I'll* take care of her!' said Simon Meyer cheerfully. 'Goodbye, sir.' Rowlands felt his hand being seized and vigorously wrung. ''Bye, young Billy.' The boy muttered a reply. 'We'd best be going,' said the young man in an undertone to Rowlands. 'There are rather too many cops about for my liking.'

Then they were gone, as if they had never been.

DISSOLVE

22

OWLANDS TURNED TOWARDS THE other member of the party, who had withdrawn a few paces, while these exchanges were going on. 'That young woman is in love with you,' she said, adding in a sardonic tone: 'But I expect you know that already. Goodbye, my dear Englishman. I hope, in spite of everything, that you can find it in your heart to forgive me...' Another scene, and one she was playing beautifully, he thought sardonically. As she drew near, he was enveloped in the heady scent of her skin and hair. Long ago, in the darkened cinemas of his youth, he'd fallen under this woman's spell. Now, knowing her for the flawed creature she was, he still found her irresistible. 'Goodbye,' he said. Then she, too, was gone, disappearing into the night, as the others had done—as indeed all others did, for him, always.

'Hurry along, ladies and gentlemen! The train is about to leave!'

'Come along, Billy,' he said. The door nearest to where they had been standing stood open. They got on—and not a moment too soon, for the guard had blown his whistle, and doors all along the platform were being slammed shut. 'Let's see if we can find our seats, shall we?' But as they edged their way along the narrow corridor—passing others who, like themselves had just got on—there came a hoarse shout from the platform, and the engine, whose great wheels had begun to grind slowly forward, seemed to freeze in the act of doing so. 'What's going on?' said Rowlands to the boy, who had paused, evidently transfixed by this commotion. 'Police!' said Billy. 'Lots of them. They're getting on the train...'

'Quick!' Rowlands was all too horribly aware of what this untoward intervention might mean. 'This way.' From behind him, came the sound of heavy boots and orders being shouted. People fumbled for passports and tickets. It would only be a matter of time before he, too, was challenged to produce his own. Not that there was anything suspicious about the actual documents he was carrying, but he had a nasty feeling that this peremptory checking of papers was just an excuse. What they were really in search of was a pair of fugitives, one of them a child...

Trying not to appear in too much of a hurry, he hustled Billy along the corridor in front of him, grimacing apologetically as he did so. 'Do excuse us,' he murmured, elbowing his way past a portly gentleman in tweeds, and a fur-clad matron. 'My son needs the W.C. rather urgently... Keep walking,' he muttered *sotto voce* to Billy; then, in a louder tone: 'I told you you should have gone before, you silly child! Be careful—you're treading on people's toes...' If they could just reach the end of the corridor they could take refuge in the lavatory until the policemen— or SS officers, or whatever they were—had gone past. It was a slim chance, but one they had no choice but to take.

But just then, there came an altercation from up ahead: someone indignantly protesting—'This is preposterous! You have no right...'—and someone else bluntly insisting: 'Your papers. I will not ask you again...' Evidently another group of policemen had got on, further down the train. They were trapped, Rowlands realised. 'Hell,' he muttered, under his breath. He contemplated alternatives—all of them unappealing. Jumping from the train was one, but they'd never make it. Even so, he had his hand on the door, ready to open it, when a voice close at hand said: 'I shouldn't risk it, if I were you.' A hand seized him by the lapel. 'In here,' said the voice. It was one he knew. 'Miss Barnes?' he gasped, unable to believe his ears. 'The very same.' She drew him inside the compartment, and the boy after him. 'Put your suitcase in the rack—that's it! Now sit down here with me. They'll be here in a minute. Let me do the talking.'

Too bemused to say another word, Rowlands did as he was told, pulling Billy down beside him. The glass door, which their rescuer had shut, now slid open, and a man put his head in. 'Papers,' he said curtly. Now they were for it! Rowlands was

308

about to retrieve his passport, when Iris Barnes put her hand on his, preventing him from doing so. 'This is most irregular,' she said in good German, as she handed a document to the SS man. 'The Embassy will want to know the reason for the delay.' A moment elapsed, during which the official had time to glance at the proffered papers. When he spoke again, he seemed abashed: 'My apologies, Fräulein. But we have orders to check the papers of everybody on this train.'

'Well, you can give me back *my* papers... and no, you needn't bother checking those of the rest of my party. They're with me—and under the same diplomatic protection.' For a long moment, the man seemed to consider this—perhaps weighing up the respective risks that might be incurred from displeasing either His Britannic Majesty's government, or that of his own masters. 'I was only saying to Reichsminister Goebbels last night how very good the relations between our two countries had remained,' said Miss Barnes, in a meditative tone. 'It would be a pity if some unfortunate incident were to damage that good relationship.'

Whether it was this, or some other consideration, that made up the other's mind for him, Rowlands couldn't afterwards be sure. What was certain was that he decided to take it no further. 'Your papers, Fräulein,' he said, handing them back, with a clicking of heels. He left the compartment, sliding the door behind him. 'Nothing there,' they heard him say to the man who was with him. Rowlands waited until he was sure they had gone, before he spoke. 'I hadn't realised,' he said, 'that journalists enjoyed quite such an exalted status with the agents of a foreign power...'

Iris Barnes laughed. 'Ah, well,' she said. 'I suppose the fact of the matter is that I'm not just a journalist... Although I *do* write for *Sight & Sound*. But sometimes I'm asked to do rather more than that... Such a *useful* job, journalism! It allows one to go to all sorts of interesting places, and to ask impertinent questions of all kinds of interesting people... I'm glad to see that you're still in one piece, Mr Rowlands. And you,' she went on, addressing Billy, 'I don't believe we've been introduced.'

'I'm William. William Ashenhurst. Although my friends call

me Billy.'

'Of course. You're the young man who's been leading us all such a dance... I'm very glad to meet you, Billy—I may call you Billy, mayn't I?' Billy must have nodded, for she said: 'That's good. I'm awfully glad to be going home, aren't you? I say, are we moving at last?' Because while they had been talking, there had come the sound of doors being slammed, as the policemen, having abandoned their search, left the train. Moments later, came the shriek of the guard's whistle, followed by the clank and grind of the engine's wheels, as the train began to move. Miss Barnes gave an audible sigh of relief. 'Well, that's that,' she said. 'I can tell you, I'll be jolly glad when we get over the border, won't you?'

Rowlands's mind was afire with questions, but he knew that most of them would have to wait. For the present, he turned his attention to his young charge, with whom he had exchanged no more than a dozen words since their meeting on the platform at Zoo Station a bare half-hour before. 'Are you all right, old chap?' he asked. 'You seem very quiet.'

'I'm fine, thanks.' Billy had never been a talkative child. 'I'm rather hungry, though...'

'Didn't you have anything to eat at Miss Pfeiffer's?'

'Yes,' the boy admitted. 'But that was a long time ago.'

'There's some chocolate in my suitcase, if you'd like to fetch it down from the rack,' said Miss Barnes. 'I know how hungry boys get between meals. I've nephews of my own.' As Rowlands got to his feet to reach for the case, she put a hand on his arm. 'No, let him do it. He's a strapping lad. And it's not heavy... Although,' she added, addressing the boy, 'you might put your satchel down first. No one's going to take it from you here.' It struck Rowlands as she said it, that Billy must have been carrying it all along—the satchel he had left in Sybille Schönig's dressing-room that fateful night, the retrieval of which had caused him to become a witness to her murder.

With some reluctance, it seemed to Rowlands, the boy put the satchel down on the seat between them, as he reached to take down Iris Barnes's suitcase. Rowlands picked it up by the strap. 'It's quite a weight,' he said. 'What on earth have you got

310

in there?'

'That's mine!' said Billy, unceremoniously dumping the suit-case down on the unoccupied seat opposite. He tried to wrest the strap from Rowland's hand. 'Steady on, old chap!' said the latter mildly. 'I only wondered what was in it. But I won't ask you to reveal your secrets, if you'd rather not...'

'Sorry, Uncle Fred,' muttered the boy. 'But now she's dead, it's all I've got...'

'You're talking about Fräulein Schönig, aren't you?' This was Miss Barnes; then, when Billy remained silent: 'She gave you something, didn't she? A keepsake of some kind?'

'It's a photograph,' he said.

'May I see it?'

'I... I don't know.' The boy's reluctance seemed out of propor-tion to the inoffensiveness of the request. 'It's private...'

Iris Barnes laughed. 'Go on, there's a good chap,' she said. Her tone brooked no refusal. The boy must have opened the satchel then, for a moment later, Iris Barnes said: 'You didn't mention it was a *framed* photograph. How very kind of Fräulein Schönig to give you such a handsome present!'

'She... she didn't exactly give it to me,' said Billy.

'No? Then it was very wrong of you to take it. But never mind that now...' While she had been talking, Miss Barnes must have been fiddling with the back of the frame, because just then she said: 'Ah! Here we are...'

'You've broken it!' said Billy furiously.

Rowlands decided to intervene. 'You'd better mind your man-ners, young man.'

But the journalist seemed unperturbed. 'It's not broken,' she said. 'See? It's just that the back lifts off. It can easily be put back, once we've removed what's inside...' She must have done so, for having replaced the photograph in its frame, she handed it back to Billy. 'There!' she said. 'Good as new.'

'What have you found?' said Rowlands, although he had a pretty good idea. 'It's a list,' said Iris Barnes. 'One that's of some importance to our people in London. We knew she had it, of course—just not where she'd hidden it. Quite a lengthy list, it is, too. I don't mind telling you,' she added, folding what seemed, from the stiff crackle of pages, to be several sheets of paper, and stowing them in her bag, 'that our organisation will be rather glad to have this...'

'That's good to hear.'

'Yes,' murmured the S.I.S. agent—or whatever she was, thought Rowlands—'I think I can safely say that if this had fallen into the wrong hands, we'd be looking at a very different story.'

Later, when they had crossed the border, and were hurtling across France, Rowlands ventured to ask the question which had been bothering him since the previous day: whose name *was* it on the list which was of such interest to the authorities on both sides of the Channel? Billy was by this time asleep on the seat beside him, his head resting, warm and heavy, on Rowlands's arm, his precious satchel still clutched to his chest.

The silence went on so long, when he had asked the question, that he wondered if Miss Barnes, too, might have fallen asleep. But then she said: 'I don't suppose it would matter if you knew. It's one of our people, you see. He's been sending us information for the past few months on what's been going on since this new lot got hold of the reins... In fact it was he who alerted the Service to the fact that we'd soon have to deal with a new Minister of Propaganda. Terribly useful to have him in place—and of course they trust him implicitly, given that he feeds them titbits of information from time to time, to keep them happy...'

Rowlands was beginning to understand. 'And Sybille Schönig discovered this?'

'Oh, no. She hadn't the least idea, thank Heaven!'

'But if his name was on the list...'

'It was because he was Jewish,' said Miss Barnes. 'His name was originally Herzog. But the family changed it to...'

'Herz,' said Rowlands. 'Gunther Herz.' The man he'd accused of being a spy—quite rightly so, as it turned out. Only he was spying for the right side, after all. 'I suppose it was *you* he telephoned the night Sybille Schönig was murdered?'

'That's right. He told me she was threatening to do a bunk.

We'd been keeping an eye on her—well, Gunther had—all the time she was at UFA. She was von Fritsch's mistress, of course, which made her a potential risk. And then when Reichsminister Goebbels took her into his bed, the stakes became even higher—especially when he recruited her as an informer.'

'Yes, I knew about that.'

'Did you?' Iris Barnes lit a cigarette, and exhaled a cloud of aromatic smoke. 'I wonder who told you? I suppose you knew about the list, too?'

Now it was his turn to remain silent.

'Well, I don't suppose it matters, now,' said Miss Barnes. 'But it meant Sybille had become even more of a liability. She'd been indiscreet, you see. Couldn't resist hinting that she had information worth paying for about some of the people at UFA. Gunther got to hear about it. Said he was afraid his own name might be on the list. That's when we knew we had to move quickly, to get to it before our Nazi friends did...'

'Would Herz have killed her, if von Fritsch hadn't got there first?'

Another silence fell, in which only the panting of the great engine, and the clacking of the wheels along the track could be heard. When she eventually spoke, it wasn't to answer his question. 'She brought it on herself, you know...' Iris Barnes's voice, emerging from the darkness that now prevailed both inside the carriage and out, seemed to belong to another person entirely from the cheerful young journalist of Rowland's recollection. *This* woman was altogether more ruthless. 'You see, Mr Rowlands, people choose which side they want to be on. It was Sybille Schönig's misfortune to choose the wrong side, that is all.'

With which Rowlands could not argue. 'At any rate,' he said. 'She did the right thing by the boy—in hiding him, I mean. If it hadn't been for that, your side—*our* side, I should say—would have come unstuck.'

'Indeed,' she said drily. 'Yes, we're grateful to him—and to you, Mr Rowlands, for keeping on his track so doggedly. Without that, it would have been much harder to find him, and to retrieve this incriminating list...'

'So you knew all along where he was?'

'We had a fair idea. The main thing, as I said, was to make sure that the other side didn't get to him before we did.' In which case, you doubtless had contingency plans, thought Rowlands bleakly. Protecting an agent in the field being of a higher priority than preserving the life of one small boy. Never had he been so glad to be on his way home—not even on that previous occasion, so many years before, when he'd been returning from France an invalid, with a world of darkness before him. Now, it felt as if he were leaving the darkness behind... He closed his eyes, feigning sleep, although he was conscious that his interlocutor remained alert. As he dozed, drifting in and out of nightmares, he could sense her restless presence, and smell the smoke from the cigarettes she smoked throughout the night, as if only by this ceaseless vigilance could the worst be kept from happening.

'"Three hundred policemen, sixty detectives and twenty plain clothes Nazi auxiliary police today descended on Friedenau, the Chelsea of Berlin, raiding several hundred flats, the occupants of which are described by the Nazi paper, *Der Angriff*, as "Jewish literati and drawing-room Bolshevists..." More of the same, I'm afraid,' said Edith, starting to fold up the newspaper.

'No—go on,' he said. Since his return from Berlin a month ago, the news had become an obsession for Frederick Rowlands.

'All right.' She cleared her throat, and found the place once more. '"The 'artists' colony' of Friedenau consists of three large blocks of small modern flats, where writers, artists, Socialist and Communist journalists and the like have settled. Many of them are persons of tolerant views..."'—here, the *Times's* Own Correspondent betrayed his own—"'...of liberal or Socialist opinions, and unconventional or original thought. Few people would have realised, until they read today's *Angriff*, that a 'Communist murder headquarters' and a 'Bolshevist plague centre' were concealed in these pleasant tenements." That's all,' said Edith. 'Do you want me to look and see if there's anything else about Germany?'

'No, that's all right.'

'Then I'll make the tea,' she said, folding up the paper once more, and getting to her feet. 'Would you like the wireless?'

'No, thanks.'

When she had gone out, he fell into a brown study. So they had destroyed Friedenau! It was only the latest of their acts of destruction. Two weeks before, there had been the burning of the Reichstag—undoubtedly an act of sabotage; the question was, by which side? The official line was that the Communists had done it—a convenient fiction, as it turned out, enabling a state of emergency to be imposed by the regime, in the interests of rooting out Communist 'enemies of the people'. Then there had been the elections, earlier this month—the result of which had been a foregone conclusion. Yes, it wasn't surprising that they'd closed in on places like Friedenau, thought Rowlands. What was surprising was that it had taken them so long to do it.

'Shall we have a fire?' said Edith, returning with the tea-tray. 'It's really awfully chilly—although it *is* only March...'

'I'll do it.' He set a match to the balled-up newspaper and kindling which had been laid ready. Once it had caught, he took a sheet of newspaper from the pile beside the fireplace and held it across the grate, to help quicken the blaze. When the fire was well alight, he sat back in his chair again. 'Your tea's on the table beside you,' said his wife.

'Thanks.'

'You mustn't brood about things,' she said, after a moment. 'You did what you could.'

'Which wasn't much.'

'You got Billy safely home, which was the main thing.'

'Yes.'

'And it sounds as if Sara's boy got out all right...' They'd received a letter from Viktor's sister a week ago. Its guarded phrases conveyed the news Rowlands had been desperate to hear. Joachim was visiting relatives in Amsterdam, the letter said. It was likely to be an extended visit... That—Joachim's release from prison and subsequent escape—had been Magda Hartmann's doing, Rowlands knew, the price he had extracted for agreeing to deliver her letter to the lawyers. Whatever else she had done, she had not let him down in this. He wondered

315

about the girl, Hettie Blumenfeldt. He hoped she, too, had made the journey to Amsterdam... 'Fred, you're not listening...'

'Sorry.' He gave himself a mental shake. Edith was right. There was little point in dwelling on what could not be helped... 'What was it you were saying?'

'I asked what Jack had to say, when you telephoned him earlier,' said his wife patiently. 'They're all well, I take it?'

'Oh yes. They're all well,' he echoed.

'Jack's on the mend, I hope?'

'Seems to be.'

'That's good. And the little German boy's settled down all right?'

'I think so.'

'Dorothy will be glad to have *her* boy back...'

'Very glad,' he said. Although it had been Jack's comment on the affair of which he had been thinking. 'He's a rum character, that stepson of mine,' his old friend had said. 'I still don't know what to make of him. He seems to have come out of his Berlin adventure all right—but then he says or does something odd, and I find myself wondering... Take yesterday,' Ashenhurst went on. 'Extraordinary thing. We had quite a row about it, I can tell you...'

'What happened yesterday?'

'Oh, didn't I say? I found a gun...'

'*What!*'

'My reaction, too. Yes. A Luger .38 pistol. Nasty-looking thing. He had it hidden in his satchel, under his bed. Dangerous thing to have around the house. What if young Vicky had stumbled across it? You can be sure I gave him a piece of my mind.'

'I expect you did,' said Rowlands, for whom one mystery, at least, had been cleared up.

'He'd had the sense to take the bullets out of it,' said Ashenhurst. 'But even so... I told him that if he wanted to learn to shoot, I'd teach him. But not with a weapon like that. Why, he might have blown his head off...'

'What did you do with it?'

'What do you think? I chucked it in the sea. I say—I don't suppose *you* know how Billy got hold of such a thing, do you?'

'Oh yes,' said Rowlands. 'I know exactly how he got hold of it—and where and when he did so. You could say it was evidence—although it's a crime that will never be solved. At least, I very much hope not,' he added, with what was not quite a sigh of relief.